THE IRON CASTLE

ANGUS DONALD

SPHERE

First published in Great Britain in 2014 by Sphere
This paperback edition published in 2015 by Sphere

1 3 5 7 9 10 8 6 4 2

Maps drawn by John Gilkes

A CIP catalogue record for this book
is available from the British Library.

ISBN 978-0-7515-5196-9

Typeset in Goudy by Palimpsest Book Production Limited,
Falkirk, Stirlingshire
Printed and bound in Great Britain by Clays Ltd, St Ives plc

Papers used by Sphere are from well-managed forests
and other responsible sources.

MIX
Paper from
responsible sources
FSC® C104740

Sphere
An imprint of
Little, Brown Book Group
100 Victoria Embankment
London EC4Y 0DY

An Hachette UK Company
www.hachette.co.uk

www.littlebrown.co.uk

For Mary, Emma and Robin with all my love

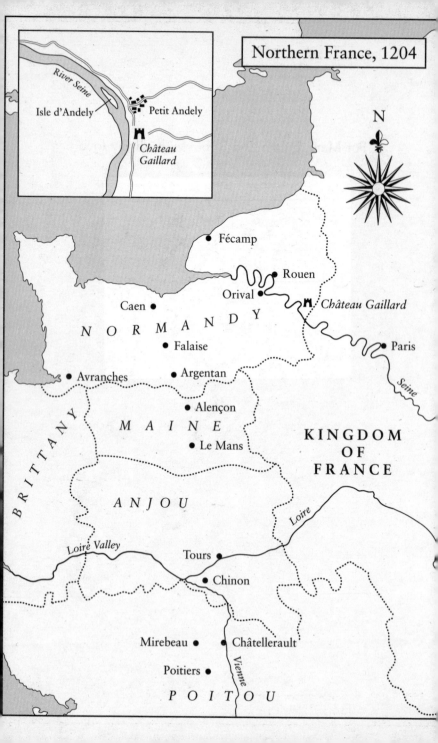

Northern France, 1204

River Seine

Isle d'Andely

Petit Andely

Château Gaillard

N

Fécamp

Rouen

Orival

Château Gaillard

Caen

NORMANDY

Paris

Falaise

Avranches

Argentan

Seine

BRITTANY

MAINE

Alençon

Le Mans

KINGDOM
OF
FRANCE

ANJOU

Loire

Loire Valley

Tours

Chinon

Mirebeau

Châtellerault

Poitiers

Vienne

POITOU

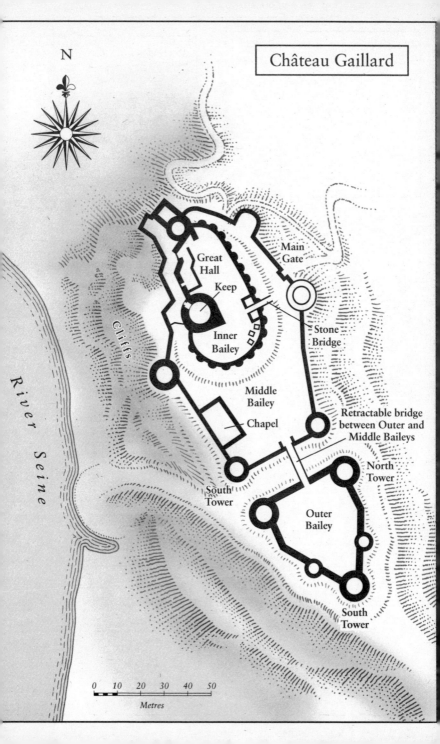

Château Gaillard

N

Great Hall

Keep

Inner Bailey

Main Gate

Stone Bridge

Cliffs

Middle Bailey

Chapel

Retractable bridge between Outer and Middle Baileys

North Tower

South Tower

Outer Bailey

River Seine

South Tower

0 10 20 30 40 50

Metres

Part One

Chapter One

This is a tale of blood. This is a tale of slaughter and sacrifice, of betrayal and loyalty, of the magnificent deeds of noble warriors and the miserable deaths of those decried as traitors. This is the tale of a rich homeland beyond the shores of England, a cradle for so many of our greatest knights, and how, through bad faith, bad leadership and the schemes of bad men, it was lost. It is not an easy tale to write, no joyous task to recall the futile deaths of so many good comrades, but I feel honour-bound to set it down on this parchment so that future generations will learn of these fighting men, the good and the bad – what they struggled for, what they died for and what they achieved in their short time here on this sweet, green earth.

My own time in this world is, I fear, drawing to a close. I

3

have lived nearly three score years and ten – far longer than most men – and I have seen much of battle and hard living, both of which exact a heavy tax from a man's soul. My whole body hurts in these end days of my life: my legs swell red and ache, my fingers tremble and throb, old bones broken years ago complain when I try to sleep, in whatever position; my back twinges when I move swiftly and when I do not move for long stretches of time, my breath is short and foul, and my kidneys give sharp expressions of protest every day just before dawn, even though I piss five times or more during the night. I am old, that is all, and nothing can be done for it – my physician seems to have no inkling of what exactly ails me and mumbles about my humours being out of balance and the unfortunate alignment of the stars, the damned ignorant quacksalver, before taking a pint of blood from me, and a purse of silver, too, for his trouble.

I am hampered in my efforts to set down this tale, not only by my failing health, but by the presence of my grandson and namesake, Alan, here at the manor of Westbury, in the fair county of Nottinghamshire. The lad is now eighteen years of age – a fully grown man and a trained knight, skilful with sword and lance. But he has lost his place with the Earl of Locksley at Kirkton Castle. He trained there as a squire for five years or more and last year the Earl did him the honour of knighting my grandson himself – he did this, I believe, not for any prowess that young Alan showed at arms, but as a mark of respect for the long friendship I had with his father, Robert Odo, who was my lord before him and who is now, sadly, in his grave. The young Earl has a great respect for tradition, and as I loyally served his father, it seemed he wished for my grandson to serve him as a knight. But something has happened, I know not what, and young Alan has returned to Westbury in disgrace. He refuses to tell me what is amiss and I must summon up the vigour in these old bones to ride up to Kirkton, in south Yorkshire, and find out for myself what has caused this grave rift between our two families.

Meanwhile, young Alan has decided to fill his life with noise and merriment. He has invited a pack of young, well-born louts to stay at Westbury – he calls them his comrades-in-arms, though neither he nor they have ever fought in real battle – and they spend their time hunting deer, hares, wild boar (anything that moves swiftly), all over my lands, and then returning to Westbury, filthy with mud, their horses blown, and with a thirst that would rival a Saracen's camel train. Since they arrived, a week hence, they have been working hard to drink my wine cellars dry night after night. I have already had to place a fresh order for another two dozen barrels with my Bordeaux merchants, the second one this year, and it is not yet October. I will need to order again before Christmas, I make no doubt.

Their wild antics, their drunken bellowing, their endless inane laughter keep me awake at night, even though their revels take place in the guest hall fifty yards from my quarters; and, poorly rested when I rise at dawn, my irritation grows with each passing day and my rising bile prevents me from concentrating satisfactorily on my labours on this parchment with quill and ink. I should admonish him, I know, but I love him – he is my only living issue, his father, my only son Robert having died of a bloody flux more than ten years ago – and I too was young once and enjoyed a cup of wine or two with friends, and a little mirth. So I believe I can endure a measure of youthful rowdiness for a little while longer.

And for now, at this hour, Westbury is mercifully quiet, praise God. It is not long after dawn, a pleasingly chilly, misty morning, and young Alan and his friends are sleeping off their surfeit of wine. I must seize this opportunity and begin to scratch out my tale, the tale of the great battle, perhaps the greatest battle of them all, a long and truly terrible siege, that I took part in forty-odd years ago in Normandy; and the part played by my lord, my friend, the former outlaw, the thief, the liar, the ruthless mercenary, Robert Odo, the man the people knew as Robin Hood.

The great hall of Nottingham Castle was warm and dry and, for once, adequately illuminated against the shadows of the raw spring evening. A large rectangular building in the centre of the middle bailey of the most powerful castle in central England, the hall had been the scene of many uneasy moments for me over the years. I had been insulted, mocked and humiliated here as a youngster; I had fought for my life several times in its shadow. This beating heart of the castle had once been a place that I feared and avoided. But on this day, on the ides of March, in the year of Our Lord twelve hundred and one, I was a privileged guest

6

within its embrace. It was bright as noon within, with the cheerful yellow light of scores of fat beeswax candles held fast on spikes in a dozen iron 'trees' – six along each long wall – and a leaping blaze of applewood logs in the centre of the open space. Had it not been for the presence of fifty English and Norman knights standing awkwardly in murmuring clumps and dressed in all the finery they could muster, it might have been a cosy, domestic scene.

Clearly the newly appointed Sheriff of Nottinghamshire, Derbyshire and the Royal Forests, Sir Hugh Bardolf, the constable of the castle, wished his most honoured guest to be at ease, and wisely so: for this guest was none other than the King himself – John, only living son of old King Henry, and lord of England, Ireland, Normandy, Maine, Anjou, Poitou and Aquitaine.

I must admit I despised the fellow, King or no. To my mind, John was a cowardly, cruel, duplicitous fool. He had tried to destroy me on several occasions and I had survived only by the grace of God Almighty and the help of my friends. I had no doubt that if he ever brought himself to recall some of our past encounters, and he thought there would be no repercussions, he would seek to have me dispatched forthwith. I felt the same about him. Indeed, I would have happily danced barefoot all night on his freshly filled grave. But I continued my existence on this earth, as a minor knight of the shires with only one small manor to his name, because I was just too insignificant for the King to notice. I was, indeed, beneath his royal contempt. I also had a powerful protector in the form of my lord, Robert Odo, erstwhile Earl of Locksley, a man who, at this very moment, was kneeling humbly before the seated King, his arms outstretched, palms pressed flat together as if in prayer. My lord, I knew for certain, hated King John quite as much as I did. And yet here he was on his knees in humble submission before him.

Robin was bareheaded and unarmed, as is the custom for these ceremonies, dressed only in a simple grass-green, ankle-length woollen robe. His light-brown hair was washed and neatly cut and combed, his face freshly shaven. He looked solemn, meek and pious, almost holy – if I had not known him so well, I'm not sure I'd have believed that this clean and spruce and humble fellow was once the famous thief and murderer Robin Hood. I was still having difficulty encompassing in my mind what I knew was about to happen. My lord, once good King Richard's most trusted vassal, and more recently the scourge of wealthy travellers in Sherwood, was about to swear homage to the Lionheart's cowardly younger brother. Incredibly, before my eyes, Robin was about to make a solemn vow that he would always be King John's man.

I was shaken to my boot soles when Robin told me, a month earlier, of his decision to give up his outlaw life in Sherwood and make his peace with the King.

'I'm tired of all this, Alan,' Robin said, over a cup of wine in the hall of my own small manor of Westbury, half a day's ride north of Nottingham. His clothes were little better than greasy rags. His hair was shaggy, hanging past his shoulders and I could see burrs, twigs and clots of dirt in it. A fuzz of brown beard hid the lower part of his lean, handsome face – but his eyes blazed silver in their intensity as he told me his plans.

'It was wonderful when I was a youngster,' he said. 'I was truly happy – living free of all constraints, doing whatever I wished, whenever I wished to do it. The danger was a tonic to my soul. I danced each day on the edge of a sword blade – and adored every moment. But, now . . . now, I miss my wife and my children. I think about Marie-Anne and Hugh and Miles far away in France. I want to see their faces and hold them. I want to watch Hugh and Miles grow tall. I want to live at Kirkton – all of us together. I want the quiet life, Alan, the dull life of the good man; I want to husband the Locksley lands, see the sheep sheared in spring and the crops brought in in summer; I want to bring justice and peace to the people who live there, and sleep safe in a warm bed at night. I don't want to be constantly in fear that I will wake looking up at the killing end of a spear-shaft, surrounded by the Sheriff's men. I don't want to end my days on a gibbet, rough hemp around my neck, slowly choking out my last breaths in front of a jeering crowd. I want . . .' He huffed out a breath, lifted his chin and straightened his shoulders. 'I want, I want, I want – by God, I sound like a whining brat. My apologies, Alan. I must be getting old.'

That was exactly my interpretation, too. Robin, by my calculation, had now seen thirty-six summers – a goodly age, and one at which a man has one eye fondly on his wild, adventurous youth and the other on the loom of his dotage. I understood my lord's impulse. I was ten years younger than Robin, but I too felt the lure of domesticity and secretly hoped that my years of battle, bloodshed, constant fear and mortal danger were behind me.

'William is going to fix it,' Robin said. 'My brother is well with King John, it appears. He has spoken to Bardolf, who seems a decent man – for a damned sheriff – and although I must pay an enormous bribe and bring myself to kneel and do homage to King John, I will eventually be allowed to take up my lands and titles again in Yorkshire, and Marie-Anne and the boys can finally come home.'

'Eventually?'

'Yes, eventually. John, for all his many faults, is not a total imbecile. He wants me to serve him faithfully in France for three years – he has even drawn up a charter to this effect – and then I will be allowed to retire to the Locksley lands. He's also giving me the lands in Normandy that Richard promised – do you remember? – as a sweetener. It's a good arrangement for both of us. Three more years of fighting, then home with Marie-Anne and the boys. Don't look at me like that, Alan; while John might not be, let us say, the most palatable fellow, he is still our rightful King.'

I breathed in a mouthful of wine, coughed, spluttered and mopped my brick-red face with a linen napkin.

'Not the most *palatable* fellow? Our rightful King? Are you quite well?'

Robin looked annoyed. 'Don't climb up on your high horse, Alan. What am I supposed to do? Spend the rest of my days living alone like a hunted beast in the wild? Staying outside the law because John behaves like a petty tyrant from time to time? He's the anointed King of England, sovereign over us all, he's entitled to be a little high-handed. And I can change him. I can. If I'm at his side, I can curb his excesses, guide him, help him be a better man, a better King . . .'

I said exactly nothing. I cautiously took another sip of my wine.

Robin frowned. 'Damn you, Alan, I am doing this whether you approve of my actions or not. The King wants me to raise a mercenary force in Normandy, nothing too unwieldy, two hundred men-at-arms or so, some archers and cavalry, too. The money is very good, and . . .' Robin cleared his throat and smiled slyly. 'Well, I wondered whether you would care to climb down from that lofty horse and agree to serve for pay on a hired mount on the continent. Good wages for a knight: John is paying six shillings a day; there would be the usual spoils, too. It might be fun . . .'

This was a most generous offer from Robin. I held the manor of Westbury from him, as the Earl of Locksley, and

I was, in truth, obliged by custom to serve him as a knight for forty days a year, if he called upon me to do so. But Robin had never asked me to fulfil this obligation and, although I had served him in many a campaign and fought many a bloody battle under his banner, it was always out of love and loyalty rather than duty.

'By your leave, sir, I will remain here at Westbury,' I said formally. 'The manor is in poor condition and urgently needs my attention, as does baby Robert. But, more than that, I believe my fighting days are behind me at last. I've had enough of pain and bloodshed, enough of foul food and festering wounds, of good men dying for bad reasons. I would be a lord of the land from now on.'

'As you wish, my friend,' said Robin. 'I will not force you. If you change your mind, there will always be a place for you in any force that I command. Just don't go around speaking ill of our noble king. Apart from being most offensive to those of us who would be his loyal vassals, it's treasonous. John is very alive to threats of treason. Royalty should be shown the proper respect.' Robin grinned at me to show he was jesting, and I could do nothing but smile back.

I tried my hardest to show the proper respect to royalty, and to Robin, to the extent of donning my best clothes and attending this royal ceremony of homage at the great hall in Nottingham Castle that cold March evening. Yet in the peacock swirl of the nobility of all England, I felt very much like a drab nobody. I was not nobly born myself and had very little wealth in either lands or silver – my father Henry Dale had been a monk, then a musician, then a peasant farmer before his early death – and I earned my knighthood on the battlefield with King Richard. On this day in the great hall, I was conscious of the fact that my only good cloak had recently been torn on a nail, then mended by one of my elderly female servants. The stitches were crude and lumpy; they showed up like a stain, proclaiming: look, this gutter-born oaf cannot afford a new garment even for a royal occasion.

The mending of my cloak made me long once again for my sweet wife Goody, who had been killed in a terrible accident the year before. My lovely girl would have repaired it, quietly, efficiently and no one would have been the wiser. But it was not only for her needlework that I missed her. I had known her since we were both children; we had, in a way, grown up together, and I had loved her with all my heart – her loss was sometimes overwhelming. I still wept from time to time, alone in bed, when I suffered the lash of her memory.

'I never thought I'd see the day Robert of Locksley would bend the knee to King John,' said a deep voice at my shoulder, shaking me from my sad reverie. I turned to see a tall, gaunt form, with grizzled grey-white hair, muscular shoulders and big scarred hands. He was dressed richly, in silk and satin and velvet, as befitted one of England's richest men, and yet on William the Marshal,

Earl of Pembroke, the outfit looked absurd, like a broad-shouldered, hairy soldier got up in a woman's dress for a fair-day lark. I felt that he'd have been much more comfortable in well-worn iron mail from top knot to toe, a garb I had seen him don on countless occasions on campaign.

'Why is he doing it, d'ye know, Sir Alan? You know him best of all. What's cunning old Robin Locksley up to this time, eh?'

'He says he's tired of sleeping in the woods. He's getting old, he says. He wants to retire to his lands in Yorkshire and live in peace.'

'Hmmf,' said the Marshal. 'He's barely a stripling. He's not even forty. I hope he hasn't gone soft. We need him; we'll need all our good men in Normandy before long, you mark my words, Alan.'

Just then we were joined by two men. One was a neighbour of Robin's, a stiff-necked baron called Roger de Lacy, who held Pontefract Castle for the King, and of whom I had always been slightly in awe. He was short, square, with fierce dark eyes, and his manner was habitually brusque, bordering on rude. De Lacy had a reputation as a fearsome fighter, a man with contempt for any weakness in others and himself, but he was said to be as true as Damascus steel once he had given his oath.

'Pembroke,' he said, with a curt nod at the Marshal. Then: 'Dale – didn't bother to dress up for the occasion, I see.'

14

I wrenched up a smile but made no reply.

The other man was a tall, smiling, open-faced stranger, clearly a knight by his garb and manner, but with a gentleness and humour shining from his eyes that seemed oddly unwarlike. He was accompanied by a girl. Not just a girl, in fact, but a vision of such beauty that I had difficulty paying full attention to the stranger's name and rank, when the Marshal introduced him.

'I beg your pardon,' I stammered. 'What name did you say?'

She was about eighteen or nineteen, I judged, with skin so pure and white it seemed like the palest duck-egg blue, glossy sable hair under a snow-white headdress, a heart-shaped face, wide mouth, small nose and happy blue-grey eyes.

'Are you deaf, Alan – what ails you?' said the Marshal. 'Here is Sir Joscelyn Giffard, lord of Avranches in Normandy, and his daughter the lady Matilda.'

'Everyone calls me Tilda,' said the girl, in a low, smoky voice, and when she smiled I felt a delicious rush of blood through my veins. She reminded me of Goody – her colouring was entirely different, Goody had been peach-pink and golden whereas this lady was swan white and midnight dark, but there was a calm joy in her perfect face that put me in mind of my beloved. I tore my gaze from her and, my head reeling like a drunkard's, I bowed to Sir Joscelyn and bid him a stammering welcome to Nottinghamshire.

A blast of trumpet saved me from having to make conversation with these men. A young and spritely bishop entered the hall bearing a tiny golden casket on a plump purple cushion. Many of the more pious assembled knights fell to their knees as the bishop and his burden passed – for that bright little box housed a sacred relic, a toe-bone from the body of the blessed forerunner of Our Lord Jesus Christ, John the Baptist himself – but I remained standing when the holy man went by, as did William the Marshal. I had had some experience of so-called relics in recent years and, as a consequence, I was no longer so swift to afford them all deep reverence.

The bishop stopped beside the kneeling form of Robin and the seated form of the King and stood between them. There was a second trumpet blast – ordering silence in the hall – and John spoke, his voice rusty, harsh, almost a frog's croak.

'Good. Right. Everybody quiet. Let's begin.' The King glanced down at his right hand where I could see he held a scrap of parchment. He cleared his throat.

'Are you willing, Robert Odo, son of William, Lord of Edwinstowe, to become my man?' The King squinted down at his hand. 'Do you choose to do so with a pure heart in the sight of God and in the absence of all deceit, false-hood and malice?'

'I am willing,' said Robin clearly.

King John tucked the parchment under his thigh and placed his two hands over my lord's, and holding Robin

16

almost captive for a moment, he looked at him and said, 'Then from this moment forth you are my sworn man.'

And he released his grip.

The bishop spoke then: 'This homage that has been made in the sight of God and Man, and in the presence of this holy relic, can never be unmade. Thanks be to God.' Then he said, 'Are you now willing to swear fealty to your sovereign lord for the lands and titles of the Earl of Locksley?'

'I am willing,' said Robin, and he placed his right hand softly on the little golden box on its rich, velvet cushion. 'I swear, by my faith in Our Lord Jesus Christ, that I will from this moment forward be faithful to my lord and sovereign King John and that I will never cause him harm and will observe my homage to him against all enemies of my lord in good faith and without deceit.'

Robin lifted his hand and, knowing what I did about my lord's larcenous nature, I half-expected the little golden box to have disappeared into his palm, but it was still there, gleaming on that purple cushion.

To his credit, John also seemed to play his part in a true and honest manner. He raised Robin to his feet and they exchanged the ritual kiss of peace. The trumpets flared again. John said loudly, 'Fare you well, my true and trusty Earl of Locksley!' Then he handed Robin a roll of thick parchment, very softly patted him on the cheek and whispered something into my lord's ear. Robin bowed low in one graceful, fluid movement and backed away from his new master.

17

Amid much slapping of his back and many a shouted word of encouragement, Robin made his way through the crowds of knights and nobles and, still clutching the roll of parchment, he came over to our group, to Sir Joscelyn, his daughter Matilda, Roger de Lacy, William the Marshal and myself.

I congratulated my friend, as did the Marshal, and Robin smiled ruefully, humbly and said little. De Lacy said, 'That's an end to all your damned Sherwood nonsense, Locksley. You are the King's man now and you'd best not forget it.' Robin smiled and inclined his head in agreement. Then Sir Joscelyn gripped him by the right hand and pumped it firmly.

'The King is fortunate indeed to have a good man such as you as his vassal,' he said, beaming at Robin. Tilda, I noticed, kissed my lord softly on his cheek and asked after Marie-Anne and his children. Robin answered her briefly but with great kindness and courtesy. I asked Tilda if she knew Marie-Anne well – a silly question, given that she had just asked after her health, but for some reason I wanted her to give me her attention. She said that she did and that they had been together in Queen Eleanor's court in Poitiers for some time the year before. I asked a few questions about the court, again just for the pleasure of hearing her speak and having her lovely eyes fixed on mine, and then she surprised me.

'Your name is well spoken of there, Sir Alan,' she said.

'Some of the Queen's ladies are avid for music and your name has been mentioned as one of our finest *trouvères* – perhaps you will play something for me one day. Or better yet, perhaps you will even write one of your famous *cansos* about me! Something terribly scandalous – I hope.' She poked the tip of her pink tongue out of the corner of her mouth an instant after she said this, to show that she was not completely in earnest. It was the most enchanting thing I'd seen for an age. And I found myself shocked and aroused at the same time. A *canso* was a song, usually about love, about *adulterous* love, between a knight and a lady. By God, by all the saints, the minx was actually flirting with me – and Goody not yet a full year in her grave.

I blushed beetroot red and mumbled something about being delighted, if time and my duties permitted, then I turned to William the Marshal and asked him in a gruff voice for news of the war on the continent. With one part of my mind, I wondered what it would be like to touch Tilda's pitch-black hair, to run my fingers through it. Would it be coarse? What would it smell like? I had to wrench my mind back to what the Marshal was saying.

The Lusignans were stirring up rebellion in Poitou and Aquitaine, the Marshal said – and the other men huddled in to listen, too – but it was nothing serious, a little looting and livestock theft, no more; and King Philip had his envious eyes on Normandy, as usual, although in this seasoned warrior's opinion the treaty signed recently at Le

Goulet, a solemn compact between the kings of England and France, ought to restrain him for some months to come.

'There is not all that much going on just at the moment,' sighed the Marshal. 'Even Duke Arthur of Brittany has dropped his claim to the Angevin lands. Philip made him do so – in the name of peace between England and France.'

'There seems to be a terrible danger of a long-lasting peace breaking out,' said Robin, to much knightly guffawing. I stole a glance at Tilda, and from under her long dark lashes she caught my eye and smiled shyly. I blushed again, looked away, and resolved to restrict my thoughts to proper masculine affairs.

'There can be no real peace until Philip is defeated,' said de Lacy, thrusting out his chin. 'While he can still field a force of two thousand knights, and twice as many men-at-arms, Normandy will not be safe. And God help the man who doesn't understand that. Philip must be crushed. Utterly destroyed.'

Sir Joscelyn coughed. 'It might well be possible to have peace, if the King were to agree to hand over a small part of Normandy to the French. The Vexin, perhaps, some of the eastern castles . . .'

'Nonsense!' De Lacy's interruption was an axe blade cutting through Giffard's words. 'The King must hold his patrimony, every part of it. It was given to him by God, and it is his sacred duty to guard it for his heirs and successors. Every castle, every town, every yard of land. If he shows the slightest weakness, he will lose the whole damn lot in double quick time.'

I kept my eyes on Robin's face as the talk of war and peace, of alliances and shifting loyalties rolled over me. There was something a little strange about my lord's demeanour this evening. On the surface he seemed perfectly happy, now reconciled with his King, no longer an outlaw, and once again restored to the title of Earl of Locksley – even if he had three years of service yet before he could fully come into his lands. He should have been contented, joyous even; this was his day and, indeed, he appeared happy. He was witty, irreverent; he seemed serenely in command of his life. Yet I knew in my heart he was furious. I had known him half my lifetime then, and I could tell, if nobody else in that bellowing throng could, that he was boiling with a suppressed and very violent rage.

After perhaps an hour, Robin took me by the elbow. 'Let us take some air,' he said. We disengaged ourselves from the gathering and walked out of the hall into the middle bailey. Robin looked up at the night sky, scattered with uncaring stars and lit by a low silver moon.

I waited in silence for him to speak.

'He did not set his seal on this,' said Robin finally, lifting the rolled parchment that he was holding. 'My rights, my obligations, the extent of my lands – it's all here in an elegant clerkly hand in beautiful Latin. But it

21

means nothing without his seal. It's just a scrap of animal skin with no force in law.'

'I'm sure he'll set his seal on it when your three years are up,' I said.

'Are you? I wish I were.'

I said nothing.

'I do not see what else I could have done,' Robin said. There was an oddly plaintive tone to his voice that I did not much like. 'Surely Marie-Anne and the boys must have a home?'

There was no ready answer to this, so I remained mute.

'Are you sure you will not come with me to Normandy?' he said after some little time had passed.

'I cannot,' I said. 'Truly, I cannot. Westbury is greatly impoverished; I have sorely neglected it of late. And little Robert has been motherless since Goody died. I must raise him and the fortunes of Westbury together. I am sorry, my lord.'

'A shame. I could have done with a good man at my side, one of my own people,' said Robin. 'Someone I can actually trust,' he added with a sideways smile.

'What did the King whisper after you had made the oath?' I asked, not expecting that he would tell me.

He didn't, for a long time.

'It was nothing,' he said, finally. 'Nothing at all important.'

'What did he say?'

Robin looked at me, and I could see the silver sheen

of his strange grey eyes in the darkness: 'He said four words, Alan. Only four – but I think I will be hearing them in my head for the rest of my life.'

'What did he say?'

'He said, "There's a good boy."'

Chapter Two

The harvest was bad that summer in Nottinghamshire. Towards the end of August, when the wheat was just beginning to turn gold in the fields, angry violet clouds massed like demon armies, came charging forward and dumped an ocean over Westbury. The harvest died in the fields, trampled flat by a deluge that would have sunk the Ark. For two solid weeks the pouring Heavens battered the standing corn. I stood in the doorway of the hall day after day, under the steady gush of the eves, and looked out over the grey sheets dancing across the Westbury fields. After the second week, a break in the clouds briefly raised our spirits – perhaps, I said hopefully to my steward Baldwin, with a few dry days we might be able to salvage some of the barley and the oat crops, which were due to be brought after the wheat. But the next afternoon the clouds returned, the waterfall resumed.

I gathered the villagers of Westbury into my hall in early September, more than a hundred dripping folk and, as the lightning cracked across the slate-grey sky and the rain pounded my sodden thatch, I told them all that they need not fear starvation, come wintertime. We would build large brick ovens and dry some of the grain, I told them, and that way we might salvage something of the summer's bounty. We had some stores of wheat, barley and oats from the previous year, not much admittedly, and most of it needed for seed, but we would eat it rather than starve, and I was prepared to spend my own silver on more seed grain from other parts of the realm, or from Normandy or the Low Countries. There was nothing to fear, I told my people.

But there was.

In the autumn a murrain broke out among my flocks, rotting their feet and blistering their mouths, and more than half of the sheep of Westbury died within two weeks. Four of our milk cows went down too, their mouths creamy with froth.

A herd of fallow deer broke through the fences of the bean and pea fields in late September and ate or destroyed much of that harvest before they could be chased away by the local children. And the fruit crop from my orchards was meagre that season – no catastrophe here, it just happened, as it sometimes does, that the apples and pears were thin on the branches, small and hard. A bad year.

Each of these setbacks would have been endurable in itself but the cumulative effect was disastrous. The local people muttered that God was punishing Westbury.

If God were indeed punishing Westbury, He was also punishing the rest of Christendom. For when I tried to purchase grain to fill the barns and tide us over through the winter months, I found that harvests had failed all over the country and across the seas, too. The price of wheat – in an ordinary season four shillings a quarter – doubled, then trebled; the price of barley and rye, too. Oats were three and half times their previous value. A hen, which might be worth a half-penny in ordinary times, was now two pence or even three – if you could find a man willing to sell. I bought as much food as I could – but a fire the year before had destroyed my hoard of silver and necessitated the complete rebuilding of Westbury, and despite Robin's generous help, the cost had been very high. I now knew for certain there was not enough grain in my barns to feed everyone in Westbury until the first crops of the next summer could be brought in. Without grain the people would starve.

My knightly neighbours thought me a fool to spend my own precious coin on the Westbury peasants. I had a duty to protect them in war, certainly, but not to fill their lazy bellies. They told me I should allow God to decide whether they lived or died. But that has never been my way – perhaps I am a fool, perhaps it is the result of my own peasant upbringing. For I had known hunger as a child; my two sisters had died of it. I could not sit snug in my hall while my hollow-bellied villagers died.

So I spent what little money I had on sacks of grain shipped from the Low Countries and the village baker and I organised a distribution of loaves to every household in the village once a week. Every Sunday after church, the manor servants served out a hot meal in the courtyard to all who wished it. Simple fare: a soup, perhaps a very thin stew of root vegetables, and bread, if we had it. I hunted as much as I could on my lands – deer, boar, hares, even wood pigeon – and turned a blind eye to local poachers trying to fill the family pot. But the game soon became scarce, killed by the villagers or by my own hounds or just wisely moving away to safer, more remote corners of the Sherwood wilderness.

I shared the meagre diet of the Westbury folk, as I felt it my duty to set an example, as did all the servants at Westbury and my half-dozen men-at-arms. But I made an exception for my son Robert, who was then a little more than a year old. He might have as much milk and bread as he wished, I told his nurse, and she seemed pleased, no doubt thinking that while her charge ate well, she would not go hungry.

But many did that long winter. The villeins butchered their oxen, horses and donkeys and ate them hooves, hides and all; the dogs and cats of Westbury mysteriously began to disappear, and no one enquired too closely after them.

My own hunting hounds grew rake thin and ill-tempered and fought over bones already boiled white for their juices. Eventually, I sent them onward, gentling each animal, fondling its ears and slitting its throat with my own knife. Their carcasses went to make soup for the people of the village, and for two weeks we ate relatively well. But hunger was ever-present, hovering like a shadow or an evil spirit. I could see it in the eyes of my servants, and the folk I met in the lanes. I could smell its chalky bitterness on their breath. The villagers scoured the woods around and about for nuts and nettles and roots. Some boiled half-rotten acorns to make a bitter mush; others went so far as to strip bark from the trees and chew it. There were tales of cannibals loose in the forest who'd eat any travellers they came across.

In January the old and the very young began to die. They sickened, a racking cough settling on their lungs and refusing to depart, and then they quietly passed beyond this hungry world, perhaps, with God's forgiveness, to a better place. Babies and old men, mostly. But others too. In early March I came across a young woman, thin as a yearling ash, her limbs but pale twigs, lying dead beside the road not two miles from my hearth. Her mouth had been stained green as a result of her attempt to eat her fill of grass and weeds like a beast of the field. A living baby lay in her cold arms and I gathered it up and took it to the village to find a foster mother for the poor starveling creature. But no one would take an extra mouth into their home and so I brought it to the manor, and with the help of Ada, one of my late wife's maidservants, I tried to feed it warm sheep's milk. It died a day afterwards, silently, and though I was no kin to the poor mite, I was heartbroken.

The spring came and, while the warmer weather lifted our spirits, our stocks of food were utterly exhausted – by then, even we privileged folk in the hall were eating nettle soup and bitter acorn bread, and drinking nothing but cold water – but with the April sunshine came a letter from Robin in Normandy.

It said simply, 'Alan, stop trying to be a damned farmer and come and fight.'

With the letter came a fat purse of silver.

We must have made a poor impression as we disembarked at the quayside in the town of Barfleur on the afternoon of the first day of May in the year of Our Lord twelve hundred and two – myself and my only accompanying man-at-arms, Kit, a bold freeman from Westbury, both of us thin, queasy and grey-looking from the rough sea journey. Indeed, I heard the sound of mocking laughter from the throats of several watching men as we led our horses down the gangplank and on to the stone jetty of the harbour – the beasts looking as ill and miserable as we did – and I straightened my spine and looked angrily to my left to see a crowd of rough-looking men-at-arms mounted and heavily armed and waiting beside the customs house. At the head of the group was a huge figure on an equally massive horse. He wore a short-sleeved iron hauberk that seemed too tight for his vast chest, and under a plain steel cap, dirty yellow hair tied in fat plaits framed a large battered red face. When I caught his eye, he bawled out, 'Move along, you beggar-men, there are no alms for you here today! Move along! Knock at the church door yonder and you may get a few mouldy scraps to keep body and soul together. Ha-ha-ha! But only if you both get on your knees and offer to suck the priest's cheesy cock!'

The men-at-arms behind him duly guffawed at his cudgel wit.

We did indeed look shabby. Under a patched and faded red cloak, my own hauberk hung loosely on me; my boots were scuffed; the shield slung over my back was sorely in need of repainting. My bay horse's coat was dull and his eyes rolled with the remnants of his seasickness, and he skittered unhappily on the unmoving ground. I pointed his nose towards the group of men-at-arms and walked him slowly towards the blond giant. 'It is true. We are hungry, you fat greasy capon. And, if you don't mind your manners, I'll eat you and your horse whole,' I said. 'Spurs, saddle, boots – and I'll spit your cracked bones into the midden!'

My horse was shoulder to shoulder with the big man's, and at my words he opened his arms and threw them around my back. 'God's great dangling gonads, Alan, but it's good to see you,' said Little John, squeezing me almost hard enough to snap a rib. 'Let's go and get a bloody drink or two under our belts – there's a tavern not far up the road – and I'll tell you what's what and who's who in Normandy.'

I pushed him off me and grinned happily into his scarlet face. 'As long as you are paying, John, I'm your man,' I said.

'In truth,' grinned the warrior, 'I am your man. And so are these rascals.' He gestured at the pack of three dozen smirking men-at-arms crowded behind him.

'Robin's orders. I am to serve you as I would him, he told me, and I am to try my very best to keep your dainty feet out of the shit.'

The tavern had food – fresh bread, soft cheese, smoked ham and the light floury yellow apples of Normandy – and we ate outside at a scatter of tables in the spring sunshine, drinking flagon after flagon of tart cider as the shadows lengthened.

'Robin is in Rouen with the King,' said Little John. 'The Wolves are scattered about Normandy – either patrolling the marches or kicking their heels doing garrison duty in the frontier castles.'

'The Wolves?' I asked.

'These ugly buggers,' said John, jerking his head at the men-at-arms who were by now dispersed around the tavern yard in various states of relaxation, some sleeping, some rolling dice, others merely drinking and talking. A couple of them, hearing John, threw back their heads and gave a fairly good imitation of a wolf's howl. I noticed then that many of them had scraps of grey fur attached to armour and clothing, and some had wolf tails hanging from shields or helmets. But they seemed a disciplined lot, on the whole, for what they were – paid mercenaries. I could not sneer at them for I was now one too – Little John had presented me with another purse of silver from Robin and shown me a strong-box in the baggage that contained a hoard of coin I was to use to pay the men – two shillings and sixpence a day, for each mounted man.

'They are calling him the Wolf Lord,' John continued, smiling fondly. 'On account of his banner. It's his new *nom de guerre* – and so his men are the Company of Wolves. You remember Vim? Well, Robin found him in a tavern in Calais, drunk and penniless, and sobered him up and set him to recruiting fighting men.'

I remembered Vim – or Wilhelmus of Mechlin as he was more properly called – a leathery Flemish mercenary who had taken part in a bloody adventure with Robin, John and me in the southern lands two years before. 'I thought he had his heart set on becoming a wealthy Bordeaux wine merchant,' I said.

'Maybe he did,' replied John, 'but he found he had no head for the trickeries of trade, and he liked drinking his wines much more than selling them. He's one of Robin's lieutenants now. A good fighting man – when he's sober.'

'How is Robin?'

'He's all right – given that he has to lick that royal bastard's crusted arsehole day and night. He's set things up so that he's making a little bit on the side, with various, um, enterprises.'

My heart sank at this. I knew Robin of old. We had fallen out several times over his 'enterprises' – a polite name for outright robbery and extortion. I had hoped that now he was no longer an outlaw, that he was once again a well-rewarded royal servant, he would have given up these ruthless money-gathering games. Something of this must have shown in my face, for John said, 'Don't get all high and mighty, Alan. We all fight for money these days, even you. None of us has lily-white hands. I don't. I know damned well you don't either. And if Robin can accumulate a pile of silver, we will all benefit when he comes in to his own as Earl of Locksley. He wants to give you another manor, did you know that? No? I didn't think so. Somewhere plump, and closer to him in Yorkshire. Bear that in mind when you scowl so reprovingly at his actions.'

'So what exactly is he doing?' I asked, keeping my tone neutral. John smiled like a cream-fed cat. 'Oh, it's good, it's very much our Robin's old style: he is generously offering his personal protection to Holy Mother Church, and all its vast properties, across Normandy. If a rich monastery or abbey wants to avoid being ravaged by roaming bands of Godless men-at-arms, packs of lawless mercenaries, for instance, it has to pay Robin a fee in silver. Good, isn't it?'

'And what does the King have to say about this?'

'Oh him,' said John, with deep contempt. 'That ginger shit-weasel doesn't care what Robin does as long as our lord provides him with plenty of fighting men. Doesn't trust his barons, see, but he does trust his paid men. Robin has carte blanche, as far as he is concerned – although there was a little unpleasantness recently from the Abbess of Caen . . .'

'What happened?'

John chuckled fondly. 'She was a spirited old bird, that one. Plenty of guts, but not enough brains. She refused Robin's kind offer of protection, rashly – threw him out of the Abbey, if you please – and called him a blackguard to his face. But then, sadly, an unknown group of ruffians – fearsome, desperate fellows, it seems – completely stripped her lands of livestock and grain. There wasn't so much as a billy goat left untouched. She ended up paying the King forty marks to give her protection from future attacks by these unknown marauders – silly old duck. And John was well pleased, you'd best believe it, Alan. He was forty marks up on the game.' Little John laughed like a delighted child.

'No, Alan, you can be sure that our esteemed King doesn't care a jot what Robin does. So long as he gets a buttered slice of the loaf and there are enough loyal swords at his command when the real fighting comes – as far as he is concerned, Normandy, and all its abbesses, barons, knights and peasants, can go hang.'

'Doesn't seem right,' I said. 'I know Robin has no love for the Church, but to extort money from an old lady, a holy person, too . . .'

'Where do you think the money comes from to pay your wages, Alan – to pay for this fine meal, this liquor?' said John, sloshing his cup of cider under my nose.

I had nothing to say to that.

The next morning we rode south – thirty-four Wolves, Kit, myself and Little John, heading for the Castle of Falaise. I was impressed with the Wolves: they did not drink themselves into insensibility the night before, as many a company of hired killers might have done, although there was drink enough and to spare; and they were all up before dawn, saddled and ready while I was still yawning and scratching and fumbling about for my boots. Kit was doing duty as my squire and had brought a breakfast of apples and cheese, and I munched them in the saddle as the sun rose and we jogged along the sunken lanes through the well-kept fields and pretty orchards of upper Normandy.

Little John and I rode at the head of the column. He explained that we had been assigned to garrison duty in the formidable Castle of Falaise under its haughty and high-born castellan Hubert de Burgh.

'I'd better warn you, we probably won't see much action,' Little John said with a grimace. 'Lord de Burgh's men and our lot are there only as a threat to stop the Bretons invading Normandy from the west. The war – what little of it there has been so far – is happening in the east. Or in the south . . .'

'Let me see if I have this correctly,' I said. 'To the west

35

we have the Bretons, loyal to their own young duke, Arthur – who despite being lord of all Brittany thinks he should be Duke of Normandy, too . . .'

'And King of England,' John said. 'He is the son of Geoffrey, King Henry's fourth son, now both rotting in their graves, and you might argue that he has as much right to the throne as our John, who is old Henry's fifth and youngest son. But who has more right to the throne – the grandson or the son of King Henry? I don't think anyone truly knows the answer . . .'

'The man who is rightful King is the man who has the main strength to hold the kingdom,' I said, and then paused, a little shocked by my own cynicism.

'Very wise, young Alan,' said Little John, nodding seriously, 'very wise – and very bloody obvious, too. Have you noticed that the sky is blue? And that patch of grass over there – what colour would you say that was, O wise one?'

We rode on for a few minutes in awkward silence, and I said, 'So, we have Duke Arthur in the west, and in the east we have King Philip of France, who wants Normandy for himself and nothing more than the destruction of all the Angevin holdings on this side of the Channel all the way south to the Pyrenees.'

'That is so,' said John.

'And in the south, what?'

'In the south we have the Lusignans, a powerful old family – sure you've come across them before, some were in the Holy Land with us: cruel fighters, fond of women

– theirs and other men's – and vassals of King John nominally. They will side with Arthur or Philip, or whomever suits them best at the time.'

'And now?'

'Now they are in rebellion, supporting Arthur's claims to the dukedom. But they are being held in check in the south by William des Roches – remember him from the Great Pilgrimage? Red hair? A madman with a mace . . .'

'I remember him – but I thought he was loyal to King Philip, or was it Arthur?'

'Used to be. Used to be Arthur's man. He's just like the rest of them – interested first and foremost in himself and his family. King John offered him cartloads of silver, more Norman lands and a permanent seat on his royal council, and William came running as swift as a hound. He did make one condition to our John, though. He insisted that if Arthur were defeated he be treated honourably – apparently, he's a bit sentimental about the lad. Genuinely fond of him, if you can believe that.'

'So he does have some honour?' I said.

'Honour? You've come to the wrong shop for honour, Alan. The barons on both sides in this war will go with whoever offers them the best price. The knights, too. Honour be damned. It's cash that counts. Robin's got it right, you know, fill your boots while you can – for God only helps those who help themselves.'

Chapter Three

The Castle of Falaise was the birthplace of William the Bastard, conqueror of all England – as the local Normans never tired of pointing out back in my great-great-great-grandfather's day. It stood on a raised plateau above and to the south of the bustling town, and consisted of a massive square stone keep – ten times the height of a man and as wide as it was high – at the north-west corner, and a round tower of similar height attached by a fortified passage to the square donjon. A fifteen-foot-high curtain wall looped around a wide area stretching two hundred yards to the east, encompassing barracks, blacksmiths, bakeries, a deep well, cookhouses, storeroom and stabling for two hundred horses. It was an impressive fortification – not as fearsome as, say, Caen or Rouen or Château

Gaillard, the Lionheart's mighty castle that stood guard over the eastern marches of Normandy, but enough to daunt Arthur of Brittany if he showed his nose west of Dol. And with a garrison of some four hundred and fifty men-at-arms, knights, squires and sergeants, it could do more than daunt. If Arthur came across the frontier and attacked with all his forces, Falaise could hold out for months until help could be mustered by King John. If Arthur tried to bypass the powerful castle and venture further into Normandy, even perhaps to link up with Philip surging in from the east, a couple of hundred well-mounted, well-armed warriors could sally out and cut up his supply lines and ambush any stragglers in his army. Falaise was at the very centre of Normandy: if Rouen was the brain, the capital, the home of its mercantile activities, Caen thirty miles to the north, with its stalwart fortifications, might be said to be its heart; but Falaise – birthplace of its greatest Duke – was the loins; it was where people felt the most Norman. From Falaise, an army could swiftly march south into Maine or east into Brittany, but that army could also do valiant service by staying where it was.

Lord Hubert de Burgh greeted me in his lavish audience hall on the middle floor of the keep. Rich tapestries hung from the walls; the furniture was carved with fantastic faces of animals and demons, painted in blues and reds and, though not yet dusk, the room blazed with light from a pair of trees holding good beeswax candles. Lord de

Burgh stood by the fireplace on the far side of the hall, feeding scraps to an enormous gyrkin, a black-and-white spotted falcon two feet in height, that perched on his arm. The bird looked at me with flat, black eyes over a viciously curved beak, and then returned to gobbling flesh from its master's hand. Lord de Burgh looked across the hall, appraising me from my boots to my brows in a manner similar to that of the bird, and in a similar silence. He wore a long black woollen robe with sable at the collar, gathered at the waist by a leather belt decorated with seed pearls, and observed me with dark-brown eyes, closely set above a long nose. His hair had once been black, but was now flecked with grey and white, and his broad moustache and beard were similarly speckled. With all this, his beak-like nose, the cruel stare and the jut of his body, he looked extraordinarily like the bird on his gauntleted fist.

After three leisurely days on the roads of Normandy, sleeping under the stars, laughing and joking with Little John and the Wolves, and getting to know them a little, I felt suddenly unnerved to be in an elegant castle hall in front of a fine Norman lord. I knew I did not look my best: my hair was disordered and dirty, and I wished I had taken the time to get out of my stained travelling clothes. My hose were marked with spatters of dried mud from riding and my only warm cloak was tattered at the hem. I had not even thought to wash my face and hands.

Beside me Kit was openly gawping at his surroundings, and in a most unfair flash of anger, I wished that my old squire Thomas, a wondrously efficient young man, was still with me.

'You might have reminded me to change my clothes,' I whispered to Kit.

'I'm sorry, sir, I didn't think. It's all so new and confusing.' The boy looked set to weep. 'I've let you down, sir; we've not been here a sennight and I've already shamed you.'

'Shh! Hold your tongue.'

Lord de Burgh was beckoning us over to the fireplace.

I crossed the room and bowed low before the Constable of Falaise and said, 'My lord, I am Sir Alan Dale, a knight in the service of the Earl of Locksley, and I present myself to you, at his orders, and those of the King, bringing an augmentation to your garrison.'

I tried surreptitiously to smooth my hair and found a long straw stuck in it from the barn we had slept in this last night. I plucked it out and examined it briefly, and as I looked at it saw that my fingernails were black with grime. I swiftly hid both hands and the bumpkinish straw behind my back.

'One of Locksley's men – ah, that would explain your extraordinary . . . that is to say your . . . Sir Alan Dale, you said? Hmm. And you serve the King for pay? You are what they call a *stipendarius*? Interesting. Well, I must bid you welcome to Falaise Castle. Tell me, Sir Alan, how many paid fellows did you bring with you?'

He summoned his falconer, who had been standing in

a corner, and handed him the gyrfalcon. The man took the bird gingerly, as though afraid of it.

'Thirty-five men, sir, and Master John Nailor, my lord of Locksley's master-at-arms.'

'Thirty-five – good, good. I can always use more men. Tell me, Sir Alan, do you like my gyrfalcon? She is called Guinevere.'

'She is indeed a noble bird, my lord,' I said.

'Isn't she. First-class hunter. I've had her since she was a chick. She will feed from no one but me. A proud but loyal creature, you might even say honourable. Do you suppose that birds can have honour, Sir Alan?'

I shrugged, and immediately regretted it.

'You don't? Men claim to have honour – I dare say I would claim a little for myself. And women, too. So why not a bird? Guinevere is a creature of violence, but controlled violence – she kills at my command and at my command only. You might say she chooses to serve me, like a knight. And she does so loyally. She could not be induced to serve another man. Why should she not be called honourable?'

I summoned my wits. 'I would say, sir, that honour stems from a freedom to act in one way or another – for good or ill. And I did not think that a bird can act in any way that is not part of her nature, or instilled by months of training.'

There was a silence. The lord of Falaise stared at me over his beak of a nose. The silence stretched out long and painfully thin. I felt an overwhelming urge to fill the quiet. 'And a bird, the Bible teaches us, has no soul,' I said. 'Can a creature without a soul have honour?'

As soon as I said it, I wished the words back in my mouth.

'All men have souls,' said de Burgh. 'But many of them have no honour. Some so-called men look only to their own advantage without the slightest regard for oaths to their rightful lord, for their avowed loyalty . . . For example, a mercenary such as your good self fights only for silver' – I could feel blood rushing to my cheeks – 'can you truly trust someone like that? Would you, for instance, sell your sword elsewhere, to Duke Arthur or King Philip, perhaps, if offered a fatter purse?'

His question was a whisker from a mortal insult. He was saying he thought I had no honour and that soldiers such as me were little better than greedy merchants.

'I serve the Earl of Locksley,' I said, through clenched teeth. 'I swore an oath a long time ago that I would be loyal to him until death. I will never break that oath. His enemies are my enemies, and I will serve no other. That is my honour.'

'But he, too, fights for silver, does he not?'

I had had enough of this conversation. I remained silent.

'Well,' said Lord de Burgh after a long pause, 'I mustn't keep you. Your men will no doubt be hungry – better feed them before they steal all the bread from the pantry. Ha-ha! Bertier, my steward, will see them housed and fed, and their horses stabled. You will find him in the kitchens at this hour. Down the staircase and take the passage to your right. You will find quarters suitable for you and your servant in the East Tower, on the other side of the courtyard. Perhaps you would be so good as to dine with me and the other knights tomorrow. At noon.'

I bowed silently and made to leave. 'One more thing, Sir Alan. The bath house is in the east of the castle. Perhaps you would care to visit it before you next present yourself to me. I must not question your honour but the knights of this garrison, both hirelings and those who serve out of a sense of duty to their lord, are expected to maintain certain standards. Remember that.'

I walked out of the hall with my guts seething and, as I approached the head of the stone spiral stairs, I turned to Kit to say something further about his failure to do his duty by me as my squire – and was knocked flying by a man sprinting up the stairs and smashing into me with his shoulder. I leaped back to my feet, my hand reaching for the dagger at my waist and glared at the man.

'Mind where you are going, oaf,' he said coolly.

I was an instant from burying the blade in his belly.

'You, sir, knocked into me,' I said icily.

'You dare to answer back, cur – don't you know who I am?' said this fellow, a tall, big-boned fattish creature dressed in a fine red satin tunic, with a sword and a jewelled dagger at his belt. He was a knight at the very least, more

44

likely a lord, but he seemed to me very young, not yet twenty. His lank black hair was greasy, though well combed and a rash of pimples adorned his plump cheeks and ample chin. He, too, had his hand on his dagger hilt.

'Cur?' I said. I was past boiling point by now, and if he wanted a fight . . .

'He doesn't know who you are, Benedict,' said a calm voice behind me. 'How could he? He only arrived this hour.'

Hubert de Burgh was at my shoulder.

'May I present, Sir Alan Dale, a knight in the service of the famous Earl of Locksley. Sir Alan, this is my nephew Sir Benedict Malet, who loyally serves me,' said the lord of Falaise.

We stared at each other for a few moments, but the tension was seeping away. I was honour-bound to be courteous to de Burgh, and doubtless I would be thrown into company with this rude nephew often enough, too. I gave him a stiff bow of greeting.

'He's a knight? Why, he looks as if he's been sleeping in a pig-pen for a week!' said this spotty lard-arse.

'Benedict, where are your manners? Sir Alan might be a sell-sword but he is a member of our household. Tell him you are sorry and that will be the end of it.'

The ill-mannered lordling said nothing, just stared at me with contempt.

'Benedict. You will apologise to Sir Alan this instant!' Hubert de Burgh's voice cracked like a whip.

'Apologies,' muttered Benedict, dropping his head, a black forelock falling over his eyes.

I nodded curtly but said nothing; Kit and I moved away, past Benedict, down the spiral stairs and out of their sight.

I met up with Little John in the vast courtyard of Falaise Castle towards dusk, after Kit and I had found our quarters in the East Tower and made ourselves as comfortable as we could in the spartan circular room there. The Wolves had been assigned space in the wooden barracks that lined the southern wall, and they were taking a meal of tripe soup and bread at a long table in the big hall in the middle of the courtyard when I joined them.

John was in a cheerful mood. 'We have landed on our feet here, Alan,' he told me with a genial slap across my shoulders. 'Good food, dry lodgings and nothing to do but a few patrols from time to time to make sure the Bretons don't try to sneak across the border and bugger our beautiful Norman sheep.'

'You find this post to your liking, then?' I said a little sourly.

'Do you not?' he replied. 'What ails you? You look like a kicked dog.'

'Perhaps you are right. A foul-mannered knight called me a cur earlier today.'

'You didn't kill him, did you?' said John, scratching his groin. 'There are rules about not fighting among ourselves. Robin's orders. Who was he anyway?'

'He calls himself Sir Benedict Malet – he's Lord de Burgh's nephew. And yes, I refrained from killing him, this time.'

'No point sulking over it. I've heard of this Malet fellow. One of the castle sergeants mentioned him. Fat lad. He commands a *conroi* of the castle guards. Unsure of himself, or so they tell me. Doesn't want to appear weak or inexperienced, though he is both. A big puppy – not dangerous, just incompetent. I'd forget all about him, Alan, if I were you. Have something to eat.'

Kit and I helped ourselves to the thick soup from the cauldron hanging over the hearth, then sat back down with Little John and the men.

'We're going on patrol tomorrow at dawn,' I told the Wolves. 'Just a short ride to get the lie of the land. Back by mid-morning.'

There were a few nods.

'One more thing. The lord of this castle seems to think that as sell-swords we are less trustworthy than the other soldiers here, that we have less honour. He is wrong. And we will demonstrate to him that we are the equals of any man here in skill, loyalty, honour and discipline. You are not to get blind drunk or brawl with the other men-at-arms, or rape the local maidens, or go absent without leave, or misbehave in any way. Any lapses in discipline will result in severe punishment. I will not be shamed by you. Does everybody here understand me?'

Murmurs of acknowledgement from the faces around the long table.

'If I could just add a little something, Sir Alan,' said Little John, his red face sober and deadly serious. 'I will rip the dangling balls off any one of you sorry bastards who steps out of line. I will then cook 'em and feed 'em to you personally.'

Chapter Four

We travelled south on patrol the next morning in the cool, pink air of a Norman dawn, riding into the gently forested hills between Falaise and the County of Maine. I slightly regretted my intemperate words to the men the night before because, while the Wolves might have looked a rough crew – dirty and unkempt, with patches of animal pelts sewn on to their mail, and armed any old how with a variety of swords, long knives, poleaxes, spears and even the odd spiked cudgel – they were, in fact, very competent soldiers. Robin had been training them for a year or more and they obeyed orders immediately and without question. They knew how to patrol, with scouts on each flank, and a pair of riders ahead and behind the main column, and they were alert and reasonably quiet as they rode – very little banter or raucous laughter. Solid, professional men, doing a job they knew well. Their leader and Little John's deputy for keeping order in the troop was a vintenar called Claes, whom I knew as one of Vim's original men. He was a steady, fair-haired fellow with one eye – the other had been lost two years before in a desperate battle at the fortress of Montségur, where he had fought at my side. I was comforted by his presence: he knew his men and he knew me, and a hard-earned respect existed between us.

Claes told me that in the past year the Wolves had seen little fighting – a few skirmishes in the eastern marches against the French there – and the men were eager for battle and the promise of loot from a defeated enemy or the prospect of a rich knight captured for ransom. They were almost all Flemings, with a scattering of Normans, some French and even a German or two, and it was the threat of starvation, one bad harvest or a crop destroyed by war, that had driven most of them to sell their swords to Robin. Some were veterans, such as Christophe, a scruffy grey-beard nearly fifty who before I was born had served as a man-at-arms with lionhearted Richard in his days as a rebellious prince in Aquitaine. He was nicknamed 'Scarecrow' by the other men for his perpetually raggedy clothes and odd hair that stood out stiffly from his head in random clumps, and had fought everywhere, it seemed, and knew the many aspects of battle as well as he knew his own calloused hands. He had been a cavalry trooper, a crossbowman, a spearman, even a miner – gouging into the bases of besieged castles to bring down walls. Some of the men were relative newcomers to war, such as Little Niels, a tiny joker who resembled a hedgerow bird, all quick jerky movements and bright inquisitive eyes. Niels was not yet seventeen and he seemed to think the soldier's life was a grand adventure. He had been an apprentice in a wealthy cloth town, had hated it, and had run off to seek his fortune. Now he was a Wolf.

As we rode out, Little Niels moved his horse up alongside mine, and with much tugging of his forelock, smiling and bobbing nervously in the saddle and other outward semblances of respect, humbly begged if he might ask me an important question.

'What is it?' I asked, looking down into his cheery little face. I could hear Little John just behind me growling like an angry bear at the intrusion, but I stilled him with a hand.

'Come on, man, speak up.'

'Well, sir, it's like this. We was wondering, all of us, like, about the spoils, and how they might be divided among us.'

Some of the men in the column had quickened their pace and I could sense their horses at my back and ears straining to hear my words.

'A very good question,' I said. 'It will be like this. Any spoils of war, goods that we take as legitimate prizes – cattle, gold or jewellery, fine cloth and the like – will be

51

sold in the market at Falaise, or elsewhere, and the coin will be divided among all of us. Ransoms, too. But I do mean *legitimate* prizes. I don't want the Norman people preyed upon. That is an iron rule. Understand? But we may find ourselves in enemy territory, and if we do, the pickings might well be rich. As your captain, I will take a share of one fifth, Claes and Little John, as my officers, will take a one-fifth share between them, and the rest – three-fifths – will be divided equally between the men.'

'Can't say fairer than that, captain,' said Little Niels. 'Two-fifths for our three officers, three-fifths for all thirty-three men.'

I looked at his bright-eyed red-cheeked face to see if he was making mock of me. It was impossible to tell: his expression was quizzical but perfectly respectful.

'Just one more question, captain.'

'Go on,' I frowned at him.

'How would I go about becoming an officer?'

His question was greeted with a roar of laughter from behind us and Little John's bellow: 'Niels, you get back in the ranks, you impertinent little shit, or I will person-ally tear you several new ones. Get back here where you belong, lad.'

I turned in my saddle and addressed the horsemen. 'Any man here might one day become an officer. If you obey my orders, keep my rules and fight with the valour of lions when the time comes – any one of you might rise to become a vintenar.'

I paused for a heartbeat. 'Even Little Niels.'

My quip was met with more laughter, genuine as far as I could tell. And for a mile or so Little Niels was subjected to some gentle ribbing from his fellows who called him 'the captain-general' and 'my gracious lord'. They seemed a contented group, to my eyes. Spirited but not lawless. There was no doubt that a few of the Wolves were genuinely bad men – bandits by trade, or murderers on the run from their manors – but most were poor men driven to take up arms to put food in their bellies. I liked them, to be honest, and for the most part they seemed to like me.

The patrol returned to Falaise without event a little before noon, and I had ample time to wash and be dressed by Kit in the best clothes that I possessed: a decent blue silk tunic and grey hose – which were clean but a little saggy at the knee as a result of their advanced age and Kit's clumsy laundering – good kidskin shoes, and a black felt hat with an eagle's feather fixed in place with a blue enamel broach. Kit had laboured long and hard over the outfit and, while I was never going to be mistaken for a prince of royal blood, I hoped for his sake and mine that I would not disgrace myself with my apparel.

The meal was a dull one. I was placed far from Hubert de Burgh and his fat nephew Benedict, at the end of the long table – which did not displease me in itself except that it emphasised the point that as a paid warrior I was scarcely respectable; indeed not much better than a servant. There were a dozen other knights at the meal, little wine was served and only a dozen platters of food emerged from the kitchens for the twenty or so guests. There was no music, and the only entertainment was a sad-faced juggler standing in the corner, who did amazing things with three, four and five silver balls that he kept aloft with great skill; although his air of abject misery prevented me from enjoying the performance overmuch. I spoke little and, apart from a chilly nod from de Burgh at the beginning of the repast, I was ignored by the company. Young Benedict refused to recognise me at all – indeed he paid little attention to anyone and seemed determined to eat as much as he possibly could – but I cannot say it grieved me sorely.

I returned to my chamber in the East Tower mid-afternoon, sober and reflecting that I had not impressed my new lord, nor yet made any friends in my new home. So be it, I told myself. I would keep my head down, attend to my duties with the Wolves and wait for Robin's call to arms.

So the days passed in an uneventful, repetitive parade. I went out with the Wolves three or four days a week, patrolling the countryside south to Maine and west as far as the Brittany border. We spent long chilly nights on the battlements, doing our share of the sentry duties, staring into the empty darkness hour after hour. One night when making my rounds of the sentries, I came across Christophe crouching down behind the parapet. His face was pressed against the wall but he was easily recognisable by the clumps of hair jutting out from under his helmet. I thought at first that he was asleep, a grave crime for a sentry, and a surprising lapse for a soldier as experienced as he. But when I came closer I saw he was on one knee picking with a dirty finger at the mortar between the massive stones of the curtain wall.

'What are you doing, Christophe?'

'It's too dry, sir – look!' He held out a handful of grey powdery sludge. 'It hasn't been mixed right.'

By the light of my pine torch, I peered at the crumbly melange of sand and lime in his big paw.

'Look at it, sir! It's a bloody disgrace, sir, and no two ways about it. Too much sand, not enough water. A rush job, I'd say. Done on the cheap by some bandit who is no more a mason than he is a merman. If the Bretons ever got serious about taking this place, we wouldn't last a week.'

Christophe's words alarmed me somewhat.

'Is the whole curtain wall like this?'

'No, sir, if it were, not a stone would be standing on another. It looks like a repair job. A shoddily done repair job. Just this section here, I reckon.'

'You think if the Bretons were to bombard us it would fall?'

'If they knew where to strike, sir. But that's not the problem. The problem would be the mines. If they knew this mortar here was so weak they'd dig their bloody great mines right under our feet, and then there'd be the Devil to pay.'

I thought about his verdict for a few moments.

'Well, Christophe, the Bretons aren't here, are they? They are still in Brittany, as far as we know. And even if they did come and besiege us they wouldn't be able to tell that this section of wall was weak just by looking at it, would they?'

He looked doubtful. 'No, sir. Not unless they got close and looked real careful like at the joins. Or if some rascal were to tell them about it.'

'Well, we'd better hope the Bretons don't have your sharp eyes. And I think you'd better keep those eyes of yours on the outside of the walls from now on.'

'Yes, sir.'

I dined infrequently with the lord of Falaise, about once every ten days, but he seldom troubled me with his conversation. I went to Mass in the castle church every day, if my duties allowed, and practised my sword and shield work in the courtyard with Little John – a master of all weapons – as often as I could. I tried to write a tune or two for my vielle and wrote some very poor poetry, which I soon abandoned as unworthy of my voice. I kept to myself, engaging with the other knights of the castle only when duty demanded it and, in my leisure hours, eating, drinking and playing dice with the Wolves, or throwing quoits with Little John.

It might sound as if life was dull – and, in a way, it was. But there was a tension in the castle that made rest difficult. A weight pressing down on us. It was like the feeling before a thunderstorm, an itchy uncomfortable heaviness. Battle loomed, everyone could feel it. You could smell it on the wind.

From time to time we had reports from the east, where King Philip was still knocking away ponderously at the thick screen of castles guarding the marches. The French army would occasionally besiege a small castle, the sort of isolated tower only defended by a couple of knights and two dozen men-at-arms, eventually either taking it or being forced to withdraw when one of King John's mobile relief forces arrived. But they made little progress. Château Gaillard stood like an iron mountain at the centre of the defences of eastern Normandy, a mighty rock occasionally lapped by the tides of Philip's armies but never submerged, and as long as King John held that puissant bastion, Philip and his barons could not get a firm grip on the duchy. It was an almost impregnable stronghold – as I knew well, for I had been Château Gaillard's castellan for a few months some years previously. King Richard had lavished much labour and many riches upon it and, as well as choosing the perfect position high on a crag overlooking the Seine valley, he had designed layer upon layer of defences that would keep even the most determined aggressor at bay. He and Philip had traded words and worse over its construction. The King of France boasted that he could take it, if he so wished, even if its walls were made of iron; King Richard retorted that he could defend it, even if its walls were made of butter. And, it was true, Philip's army might capture a lonely fort or two along the borderlands, but they did not dare to attack Château Gaillard – the Iron Castle.

I had not realised how far my spirits had been pressed down by the monotony of life in the Falaise garrison until one day in the middle of July. I was waiting in the great hall to report to Lord de Burgh about a routine patrol out to the Brittany border. I had been served a cup of wine and was waiting for the attention of the castellan, who was busy with his bailiff, when there was a flurry of activity as Sir Benedict Malet clattered up the stairs calling shrilly, 'My lord, my lord!' He burst into the hall, followed by two burly sergeants hauling on the arms of a terrified fellow in tattered leather armour, who was clearly their prisoner.

'I have come to report a severe case of insubordination, my lord,' said Benedict.

'Yes?' Lord de Burgh looked up from the parchment he had been poring over.

'This fellow has been grossly insolent. He insulted me!'

'How so?' De Burgh seemed irritated by the interruption.

'He . . . he . . .' I saw that Benedict was blushing and reluctant to speak.

'Speak up, Benedict. Don't waste my time.'

'He made mock of me in front of his fellow men-at-arms.'

'What exactly did he say? Come on, spit it out, man.'

'He called me . . . he called me "Sir Eats-a-lot" and made noises like a . . . like a giant pig feeding. I happened to be passing by the barracks when he and his fellows were drinking ale and heard this disgraceful insolence with my own ears. I want him punished, my lord, severely punished. I won't have my own men laughing at me.'

I was trying not to laugh myself. I took a deep swig of my wine.

'Well, he is under your command, you have the right to punish him, if you truly think his crime merits it.'

At that moment a loud snort of laughter escaped me that, most unfortunately, might have been interpreted as the noise a hog makes at the trough. Sir Eats-a-lot looked over at me, his eyes murderous, his face flushed a purplish red.

'You have something to say, sell-sword?' Benedict stared at me like a madman.

'Oh no, Sir Benedict, it is just that *this wine* went down the wrong pipe.'

'The swine? You mock me too!' He took a step towards me, hand on hilt.

'Peace, Benedict, peace,' said de Burgh. 'Sir Alan meant no insult. Did you?'

'No, indeed, my lord,' I said, my face a mask of solemnity.

'Very well,' said de Burgh. 'Benedict, I suggest you give your funny-man his punishment and allow me to return to my labours.'

Benedict was still glaring at me. He half-turned away towards the prisoner.

'I will teach you to laugh at your betters,' he said, and I was not entirely sure if he was speaking to me or his wretched man-at-arms. Then he said, curtly, 'Day after tomorrow. At dawn. Nose slit, tongue cut off, ears cropped, and after his just punishment, he is to be expelled from the garrison without pay. Take him to the cells to think about his insolence – and the reward it has brought him.'

The prisoner gave a moan of absolute horror, before the guards dragged him from the hall, and I heard his desperate shouts echoing up the stairwell long after he and his two captors had disappeared.

'Benedict,' I said, crossing the room towards him, 'come now, man, that was unduly harsh. Surely, it was only a soldier's crude jest—'

'*You* do not speak to me about this matter.' Benedict was still furious. He waved a shaking finger at me then turned on his heel and left the hall.

I turned to Hubert de Burgh. 'My lord, surely this is grossly unjust.'

But de Burgh was not interested. 'Sir Alan, this is not your concern. That man served under Sir Benedict, and my nephew has the right to punish him in any way he chooses, save by the taking of his life. I cannot interfere – how would you like it if I oversaw how you disciplined your men? He will be punished for his insolence, and that is an end to it. Now, if it please you, I must get on with my accounts.'

He turned back to his parchments and his waiting bailiff.

I was appalled but there was nothing I could do. Worse, it seemed my own teasing of Benedict had made matters harder for the prisoner.

The next day, summoned for a feast at noon, I was standing by the window in the great hall, looking out over the pretty town of Falaise. My mood was black. I was bored and lonely and I felt guilty about the poor man in the stinking dungeon below my feet. What was I doing in Normandy? The war was a sham. The enemy were far away. I was stuck in the middle of nowhere doing garrison duty in the midst of men who despised me – and whom I despised – and for what? For Westbury? I should beg Robin for another loan to feed my villagers, and go home. I was just pondering some comfort I could bring the wretch below before his sentence was carried out, a kind word, a meal, a drink of wine infused with poppy juice for the coming pain, perhaps, when I heard a voice behind me say, 'Greetings, Sir Alan, how wonderful to see you again. But what is it? You look awfully grim. Is everything all right?'

I turned and looked into the lovely face of Tilda Giffard, who was smiling up at me with her blue-grey eyes. I felt something turn over in my belly at the sight of her, and, for a moment, it was as if I had no wind in my lungs.

Then I beamed, all thoughts of returning home and of the wretch in the dungeon below my feet forgotten. I was so pleased to see her that I was within an inch of throwing my arms around her and hugging her to my chest. But, thank God, I did not. Instead, I said much more formally than I meant, 'Lady Tilda, what a great pleasure to see you. I didn't know you were in Normandy. And what brings you to Falaise?'

'Oh, Daddy has been at the castle at Avranches for months now, keeping the border against the savage Bretons. He recently had fresh news from his scouts . . .'

Her voice had the same smoky timbre that I remembered well. And her lovely eyes sparkled with mischief. I had thought of her from time to time since our meeting in Nottingham, mostly at night alone in my blankets when my troubles kept me awake, but she had been very far from the forefront of my imagination. Seeing her now was like the sun coming out from behind a dark cloud. She looked perfect: her hair black as midnight under a stark white headdress; white skin and blood-red lips; a few delicate locks hanging before the perfect swirl of her ears; a long, slim neck and a hard, determined chin; her body encased in a tight gown of some shimmering white material that emphasised the narrowness of her waist and the inviting swell of her breasts . . .

I realised I was staring at her chest and lifted my eyes guiltily.

'. . . and so we came here to pay our respects to Lord

de Burgh, and of course to take council over this news from Brittany.'

I realised I had not been listening to a word she said. Something about Duke Arthur's movements along the border. But before I could apologise or ask her to repeat herself, a trumpet sounded and we were summoned to the feast.

'I do hope you will be sitting near me at the high table,' said Tilda, squeezing my forearm with her hand. Her touch was like a hot coal against the material of my tunic.

'I fear not, my lady,' I said. 'I shall be with the lesser knights.'

'Well, we must have a proper talk afterwards. You still have not played me any of your wonderful music,' she said, with a smile that punched through my ribs. Then she was swept away with the other high lords and dignitaries to the places at the table on either side of Lord de Burgh.

I watched her all the way through that meal, eating and drinking mechanically, and wondering what it would be like to put my hand on her warm naked white skin, to kiss her lips. I could feel my member thickening in my braies and tried to concentrate on Goody, holding an image of my dead wife and our love together in my mind as I crumbled a piece of bread between palsied fingers. But in my mind Goody's face became Tilda's – the image of my wife and I entwined in our bed changed subtly. It was Tilda whispering in my ear; it was Tilda's white hand between my legs gently stroking, teasing; it was Tilda's buttocks curved into the cup of my pelvis . . .

'Mother of God,' I muttered, 'get a hold of yourself. Goody is barely cold in her grave. Would you desecrate her memory?'

This was absurd. I barely knew this girl. I had met her twice and I was already ravishing her repeatedly inside my head.

'Are you quite well?' asked my neighbour at the table, an elderly monk from Caen.

'No, brother, I fear I am very far from well,' I said. There was a sprinkling of sweat on my upper lip, and my chest felt tight and heavy. I excused myself and slipped out of the hall.

I recovered my poise outside the keep and, after dunking my head in a bucket of water and standing in the brisk wind on the battlements for several moments cursing my weakness of mind and my sinful lust, I slunk back to my place on the bench.

'Feeling better?' said the old monk.

'Yes, brother. A passing malaise, I am sure.'

But it was no passing malaise. I was possessed, heart and soul, by one notion. I must have Tilda Giffard as my lover, my mistress, my wife – I did not care which as long as she was mine. I wanted her with a passion, a physical pain that I had not felt since my early days with Goody. I felt that I would go mad if I could not have her. She called to me inside my head, in my heart, and in those lower, baser places, too.

Indeed, perhaps I was already mad.

After the dinner, I was invited by my Lord de Burgh to play my vielle for the company. I had offered to display my musical skills to the castellan long before, during my first few weeks at Falaise, but he had declined my offer brusquely. That afternoon, it seemed, he was disposed to be more friendly.

'The Lady Matilda has told me you are a *trouvère* of great renown at Queen Eleanor's court and elsewhere, Sir Alan. Perhaps you would honour us with a song today, if your duties permit.'

They permitted. Little John had taken the men out on a long-range patrol south to the Maine border some twenty-odd miles away, and would not be back before nightfall, and Kit was engaged in a thorough overhaul of my equipment and weapons – cleaning, oiling and mending them – in the East Tower. He had also told me he intended to repaint my shield with its image of a wild boar in black on a blood-red background. So I was a man of leisure that lovely afternoon and the thought of playing my finest music before Tilda made me a little light-headed.

And though Almighty God will no doubt judge me for the sin of pride, I have seldom played better than that afternoon in the hall in the keep of the Castle of Falaise. I started with a *canso* – a classic tale of doomed love between Lancelot and Guinevere, the wife of King Arthur. It was roundly applauded by my audience. Then I made them laugh with a bawdy tale about a hungry fox and a timid rabbit, a cheeky cockerel and a wise old owl. After that I took a chance and gave them a crude soldiers' song that mocked King Philip and compared his royal mace to his intimate bodily parts: they roared with laughter, and I gave a sigh of relief. Finally, I brought them all home with the well-known lay of Roland and Oliver – a tragic piece about brave warriors slain in the pursuit of their duty, dying nobly with a ring of dead Saracens at their feet. The cheering and stamping from the audience of mainly fighting men seemed almost to shake the massive stone keep itself. Then, wisely, I bowed out, refusing to play any more and claiming that my voice was sore and weak.

'Oh, Alan, that was so moving, so infinitely sad,' said Tilda afterwards, as I was receiving plaudits from the crowd of knights.

'Did you really like it?' I asked her.

'It was . . . truly lovely,' she said, and once again she put her burning hand on my arm and squeezed lightly.

I felt as if I were walking two feet above the ground after hearing her words – and I believe that my status in the de Burgh household shifted significantly that day. Knights who had barely spoken to me before came and shook my hand or pounded me on the back and congratulated me on my skill. Even Hubert de Burgh offered his polite thanks and a few words of lukewarm praise. I felt accepted into the Falaise company, at last. And it was all Tilda's doing.

Sir Joscelyn Giffard approached after my performance. He praised me knowledgeably, even going so far as to compliment the Spanish-style fingering on the vielle that I had attempted during the Arthurian *canso*, and then, out of a cloudless blue sky, he said, 'Sir Alan, do you have children?'

I was slightly thrown by his question, but I admitted that I had a son, Robert, a lusty two-year-old.

'You are fond of him,' he asked.

'I love him more than life itself,' I said.

'And if someone were to harm him, or to dishonour him in some way, what would you do?'

'I would slaughter them.'

'I, too, would kill anyone, absolutely anyone who harmed my daughter – or who dishonoured her in any way,' he said. 'She is a lovely girl, and very friendly, sometimes foolish and, dare I say it, a little forward at times. Doubtless I should have beaten her more thoroughly when she was a child. But her mother is dead, she is my only daughter, and I love her, I have no doubt, as much as you love your son.'

He smiled at me, a little sadly. 'I truly did enjoy your music,' he said. 'Thank you for that.' Then he walked away.

Well, I had been warned. Tilda's father was not blind,

neither was he a fool. He had just threatened me with death if I made any advances on his darling girl. But, strangely, given that I do not care to swallow threats of any kind, I could not think harshly of him. Indeed, the manner of his message – honest, firm but not hostile – caused me to respect him. I did not fear him, but he made me reconsider. What was I thinking? Tilda inflamed me, mind and body, I was mad for her, but she, too, was another man's daughter. I vowed to myself, then and there, that I would never dishonour her. I would not let my lust master me. I would not seek her out, I would not pester her for favours. I would banish her from my mind. Indeed, for a good many days and nights, I did just that.

For the next morning, I rode out to war.

Chapter Five

Lord de Burgh mustered his knights and captains in the courtyard a little after dawn, all of us armed and armoured and ready to ride.

'Arthur, Duke of Brittany, and several thousand of his men have crossed the border far to the south and are now ravaging the Loire Valley with fire and sword,' de Burgh said briskly. 'Our war has truly begun.

'We have this intelligence courtesy of Sir Joscelyn Giffard.' De Burgh nodded benevolently at the lord of Avranches, who was standing a couple of paces from me. 'He is to ride to Rouen to reinforce the garrison there against the threat from the east. I must remain here to hold Falaise – but Sir Benedict Malet will lead a force of fifty of our men south to join up with the King on the road to Le Mans. You, Sir Alan, will take all your men with him and offer what support you are able. When you join with the army, you are to place yourself once again under the Earl of Locksley's banner. But on the road, Sir Benedict is in command, is that clear?"

I nodded, with a sinking heart, vowing silently that I would never let Benedict have dominion over my men. The wretch who had so foolishly mocked his superior had been mutilated earlier that morning in the dungeons and, while I had not witnessed it, I had heard his screams and seen the poor fellow, his head a mass of black blood, stumbling out the main gates not an hour since. I would not allow any of my Wolves to be treated so, even if it meant murdering the lardy knight myself.

Around mid-morning, we clattered out of the gates of Falaise Castle and took the road heading south-east, aiming to cut John's line of march at Alençon. Benedict gave me no orders before we set off, save for an insolent instruction to try and keep up with his men and not to get in their way.

So, we ate his dust all that day and rested the night in Argentan. My men and I camped apart from the Falaise force, in the pretty orchards outside the town. But I made certain the Wolves were ready well before dawn and we formed up behind Benedict's force the next day without a single word being exchanged between us. We rode all morning and joined the main road from Rouen at midday. I noted with deep satisfaction the obvious signs of a passing army – a big one. By nightfall we could see the campfires of the host in the fields outside the Castle of Alençon. We broke from Benedict's column, without bothering to take our leave of its commander, and walked our horses through a small town of green tents and rough brushwood shelters, before arriving at a black pavilion, which I saw, by the light of two flaring torches planted by the entrance, was topped with a large white flag with the snarling mask of a wolf depicted in bold lines of black and grey.

'Ah, Alan, here at last. Well met, my friend,' said Robin, as I pushed through the woollen flaps of the tent – and then I was being embraced by my lord.

It felt like coming home.

'You remember Vim, of course,' said Robin, waving vaguely at a big blond-grey man seated by a large table in the middle of the tent. 'Some wine?' I gratefully took a cup from my lord's hands.

'All well with Little John and the men?' he said.

'Yes, my lord,' I replied. 'He's seeing they get themselves sorted out. He'll be along in a moment or two. What news from the south?'

'Oh, Arthur's burning his way up the south bank of the Loire – he's already taken Saumur. His Bretons are having a high old time: looting, raping and slaughtering those who don't flee. We have to teach them some better manners.'

Despite the levity of Robin's words, there was a grim timbre to his voice.

'What's wrong?' I said. I knew the answer before the words were out of my mouth. 'Where are Marie-Anne and the boys?'

'They were at Fontevraud with Queen Eleanor. But, with Arthur and his men twenty miles away and advancing rapidly, they fled. Now – anybody's guess.'

'But they will be safe with Eleanor, surely?'

'You think?' said Robin. 'Eleanor has, what, forty or fifty Gascon men-at-arms? There are a dozen of my bowmen under Sarlic's command with Marie-Anne, a guard of honour, no more than that. Arthur has a thousand heavy cavalry alone in his main force. How long do you think they would last in a pitched battle?'

'But Eleanor is Arthur's grandmother—'

'And the Queen backed John's claims against him. That makes her his enemy, grandmother or no. Although that might spare her some humiliation. Marie-Anne's fate is another matter entirely.'

I could see his point.

'Where is King John?'

'He's up at the castle, dithering as usual; doing a bit of moaning and whining too, I would imagine. He's come all this way but doesn't want to go any further. He says we must defend the Norman border, the half-wit. I was just going up there to see him. You'd better come, too.'

The King was pacing up and down the length of the hall on the second floor of Alençon Castle. I had not seen him for more than a year and he had aged alarmingly. His shoulder-length reddish hair had fine streaks of silver in it, and cruel lines were cut into his face on either side of his nose. His brow was well lined, too, and his mouth wrinkled in the corners. He was no older than thirty-seven. When Robin entered the chamber with myself at his shoulder, the King whirled suddenly, as if afraid.

'You, Locksley,' he called out in his harsh, frog-like voice. 'Are your men alert? Are they watching the roads?'

'Yes, Sire,' said my lord. 'I have sent out night patrols. There is no enemy within twenty miles of this castle.'

'Hmm. So you say. Sometimes there are enemies where you least expect them, sometimes those who cry friendship the most loudly are the ones to fear most!'

Robin said nothing; he merely inclined his head slightly in a gesture that could have meant agreement, or nothing at all. The King resumed his pacing, his footsteps short and jerky. He reached the high window at the far side of the hall, spun on his toes and began back towards the door. The walls either side of this path were thick with barons and knights. He looked like a beast in a menagerie, caged by invisible bars, with most of the barons of England and Normandy gathered to watch the spectacle of this strange creature stalking up and down inside his cage.

'Count Robert.' The King had stopped. He poked a finger at one gloomy face near the wall that I knew well from my previous time in Normandy: the Lord of Alençon, the castellan of this very castle. He was a good man, loyal, honest and fearless in battle, though prone to savage bouts of melancholy. 'You will post double guards on the walls,' said our noble sovereign. 'I shall sleep safely in my bed this night, if it is all the same to you. Double the guard!'

'Sire, I have already doubled the guard, as you ordered me to not an hour since.'

'Do you dare to answer me back? Do as I command. I am your King!'

'My lord, if I may make so bold,' said Robin in his most calming tone, 'would you be so good as to tell us what you plan to do?'

'Do? *Do?* I will fight! I will crush these contumelious bastards – these men of Arthur's, these vile, traitorous curs, I will destroy them, I will grind their bones to dust, I will drown the fields with their blood . . .'

'An excellent plan, Sire. And no more than they deserve. But could you be a little more specific. Should we ready our men to march south to confront—'

'We are not going anywhere. I will fight them here. Here in Normandy! Here in the home of my ancestors where I am safe from spies and traitors!' The King stamped his foot on the rush-strewn floor, sending up a little puff of dust.

'But, Sire, begging your pardon,' said Robin, soothingly, 'the Queen Mother is in the south and, for all we know—'

A blast of trumpets interrupted Robin and a tall man of middle years strode into the hall. He was dressed in a dusty cloak over a surcoat splashed with mud and under it could be glimpsed a full suit of mail; two bushes of flaming red hair jutted from either side of a sunburned head that was otherwise as bald as an egg. Two knights entered behind him, equally travel-stained. The tall man knelt stiffly before the King.

The herald, who had announced his presence with the trumpet, now said in an unnecessarily loud voice, 'Sire, the Senechal of Anjou, Lord William des Roches!'

'I know who he is, you fool. William, get up man, get up. What are you doing here? Have you forsaken Le Mans?'

'No, Sire, my men hold it yet,' said des Roches 'But I bring grave news.'

'More bad news. I knew it!'

'It concerns your venerable mother, Sire,' he said, then, catching sight of Robin, he added, 'and the Countess of Locksley, as well. It seems they have been caught between the Bretons and the Lusignans. Queen Eleanor was at Fontevraud Abbey when news came of Duke Arthur's advance. She fled south, hoping to find sanctuary at Poitiers. But, alas, the Lusignan forces came north from their lands in Poitou and the Bretons pursued her from the west, and she was caught at . . .' He turned to one of his knights. 'What's the name of the wretched little place again?'

'Mirebeau, sir,' said the knight.

'Mirebeau, yes. Well, the ladies were forced to seek refuge at Mirebeau Castle, and there they remain; but they are now besieged by the forces of Arthur and by those of

Hugh and Geoffrey de Lusignan. Sire, they cannot hold out for long – their enemies outnumber them ten times over. We must ride now, with all our strength and relieve the castle, if we are to save your lady mother from death or captivity.'

'Ride? South? Now? Are you mad? I have King Philip in my rear, gobbling up eastern Normandy piece by piece, and you want me to gallop a hundred miles away and throw my army into the jaws of Duke Arthur's savage Bretons and all the massed knights of Lusignan. You've taken leave of your senses.'

I looked at Robin's face. He was smiling serenely as if he had just had some pleasant, idle thought – he did not look like a man who had just heard that his wife was surrounded by a horde of enemies intent on rape and slaughter. But, by his next words, I could see that he was indeed determined to effect a rescue.

'Sire, this is our one chance, this is our moment, I swear it. If we are swift. If we act decisively, now, we can smash this southern rebellion once and for all. We know exactly where our enemies are – and that they are weak. The main force will be at Mirebeau but at least half of their men, half their strength, will be away ranging the lands between Saumur and Poitiers looting and burning. They are weakened and spread out. I know Mirebeau Castle well. It will not fall easily, not for several days, a week perhaps. If we act fast, if we ride now, in secret, we can reach Mirebeau in two days with all our strength and deliver a killer blow. They will not expect us so soon. With speed, surprise and maximum strength, we can destroy them utterly, and then, before Philip even has word of our movements, we can be back in Normandy and, in turn, bring our whole force to bear upon the east.'

'The Earl of Locksley is right, Sire,' said des Roches. 'We can do this.'

'I don't know,' said the King. 'It is late and I am tired. It seems very risky, to me. Perhaps we should take counsel on this matter tomorrow.'

'It is indeed a bold stroke, Sire,' said Robin, 'and men will tell their grandsons, and their grandsons' grandsons the tale of your courage and cunning, but for it to work, we must leave now.' Then, rather quietly, he delivered the *coup de grâce*. 'It is most certainly what your noble brother Richard would have done.'

I saw John's red head lift at the mention of his older brother. His hopeful, watery blue eyes fixed on Robin's certain silver ones.

'Do you truly think it is what Richard would have done, were he alive?'

'Yes, Sire, said Robin. 'It is a masterstroke of war – worthy of another Lionheart.'

'Very well,' said John, a smirk cutting his aged face in half. 'We ride!'

An hour later I found myself a-horse, in the dead of night, and heading south for Le Mans, with Robin at my side and Little John, Kit and Vim trotting behind us, and behind them came two hundred and fifty overexcited Wolves.

Word had spread swiftly through the ranks that Robin had forced the King's hand, and the men were proud of their lord's sway with his sovereign.

'Do you think it will work?' I asked my lord after a mile.

'No idea,' was the terse reply. 'But I will not sit idle in Normandy while Marie-Anne is at the mercy of our enemies. That royal bullfrog would have done nothing and squandered his chance. It might work, it really might, with a bit of luck.'

'I didn't know you were familiar with Mirebeau,' I said.

'Never heard of the place before tonight,' said Robin, and in the moonlit darkness I could just make out his crooked smile.

We rode all through the night and by dawn had reached Le Mans, where the bulk of William des Roches's men were quartered. We stayed in that town only long enough to eat a hurried meal, feed and rub down our horses, and before the sun was a hand's breadth above the horizon were back in the saddle.

It was a hellish journey – indeed, as with so many unpleasant experiences, I cannot recall the full details of it now. I just have a vague memory of aching thighs, battered knees and bruised buttocks; numb fingers and a crushing weight of exhaustion pressing on my shoulders; the stink of sweat, both from horse and man; the constant jingle of metal accoutrements and the creak of leather. We rode without Robin for much of the time. My lord felt it wiser to be at the King's elbow, in case the wretched fellow changed his mind or his resolve failed him.

Little John and I rode side by side, with Kit and Vim on our heels and the uncomplaining Wolves behind us. Hour after hour we rode. The sun arced across the Heavens before us. We crossed rivers great and small, by bridge and ford, but tiredness blurred the hours, day and night, into one seamless agony of protesting bodies and jolting move-ment, of orders passed up and down the column. My head felt as if it was being squeezed in a vice, yet still we rode, endlessly pushing southwards. But William des Roches, who with Robin led the army on that awful, endless march, knew that we must rest our horses and ourselves. It would do no good to arrive at Mirebeau without the strength to fight.

We stopped a few miles before the city of Tours, at a small castle still loyal to des Roches whose name I never learned. We had been riding for almost twenty-four hours without cease, and there we slept for four short hours. The King commandeered fresh horses for every man, some two hundred knights and three times as many mounted men-at-arms: we must have taken up every rideable beast within miles – and a good thing too, for my bay was nearly dead with exhaustion, his neck lathered with foam, his eyes rolling, his feet unsteady, legs shaking. I was not in a much better state. When I collapsed into my blankets in the straw of the castle stables, I slept immediately and, it seemed, had to stagger to my feet immediately, rouse the men, snatch a mouthful of cold porridge and a cup of water from Kit, and mount an unfamiliar horse, for the nightmare to begin all over again. Twelve hours of ceaseless riding later, twelve hours of agony, at a village a little to the west of Châtellerault, an hour or so after dusk, we stopped again, and once more fell into slumber like dead men. This time, however, with a sense of accomplishment in the back of our exhausted minds. We had ridden more than eighty miles in forty-eight hours. We were a handful of miles from Mirebeau.

Robin summoned me from my blankets a little after midnight, and I cursed him as I struggled to stand. My back was one long sheet of pain; my thighs were chafed raw, the thick woollen hose worn away against the saddle to expose inflamed skin; my head felt as if it had been stuffed with burning wool.

'The King wants to see all the commanders of his contingents in the church – now,' he said. I saw the bulk of Little John standing in the blackness behind Robin.

'Come on, Alan, we've done well, very well indeed to get here so fast, with all our men,' Robin said. 'But we need to be clear about the attack on Mirebeau, and how we should proceed. William des Roches's scouts are back with news of the enemy dispositions. Come on. Wake yourself up, man.'

A score of senior knights and barons stood yawning in

the candlelight of that rustic church. I saw Sir Benedict Malet leaning against the far wall, his eyes closed, his face greyish and seemingly a little thinner. Little John, Robin and I stood near the altar and John handed me a beaker of wine with a manchet balanced on the top. I tore into the small round loaf like a ravenous wolf and washed the sweet bread down with the wine. I was awake now. The sight of the King, strutting jerkily about the church, talking, joking with his barons, amazed me. He was filled with a desperate, manic energy that crackled about him like lightning. I had seen its like before – around his brother – and, although I hate to admit it, he did indeed have something of the Lionheart's air.

Nevertheless, it was William des Roches who called the gathering in that church to business. 'Gentlemen, my advance men have reported back from Mirebeau,' he said. And all the sluggish chatter in the church stopped.

'It appears that Queen Eleanor and her party are holding out. The town has fallen, its east gatehouse has been burned to the ground, and the Bretons have looted the place pretty thoroughly. They have also managed to take the outer defences of the castle, the curtain wall and the outbuildings, but not the keep; the Queen still defies her enemies from the safety of the keep, praise God. Duke Arthur is there. His personal standard has been seen. Hugh and Geoffrey de Lusignan, Raymond de Thouars, Savary de Mauléon and a good many more of the most prominent rebels are also there. My scouts estimate their forces in and around Mirebeau to be about one thousand two hundred men, with more scattered across the whole county. After some losses on the ride – accidents, falls and fatigue – we have some seven hundred effectives. So they outnumber us. So what! We are easily a match for them. But the best news of all, the most important consideration' – des Roches paused here for greater effect – 'is that they do not know we are here. Gentlemen, we have surprise on our side.'

'We will catch them sleeping in their beds!' crowed the King, bouncing on his toes with excitement. 'We will slaughter them before they can pull their dirty braies on, let alone their armour. Ha-ha. I will have that brat Arthur hanging from his neck from the battlements by sundown.'

William des Roches frowned at this last remark. 'Sire, you promised me. You gave your word.'

'What?'

'Sire, you swore to me, when I rallied to your banner, that Duke Arthur of Brittany – your nephew – would be treated decently, if captured alive. You gave your solemn word of honour. He is an excitable lad, and evil friends have persuaded him to take up arms against your Highness but, by the laws of chivalry, if he is captured . . .'

'Yes, yes, all right, William. I won't hang the traitorous little rat.'

'Sire, I want your assurance that you will heed my advice when it comes to Arthur. I want your assurance that you will not harm him in any way.'

'And I have given it to you. Enough of this matter. Let us proceed to the plan of attack. Locksley, what is your counsel?'

Robin took a couple of steps into the centre of the gathering, where all could see him. 'Speed and surprise – these are our allies. If the east gate is destroyed, I'd say that is our attack point. I doubt there will be much to obstruct us. We go in hard and fast, straight into the town and punch through to the castle. We don't stop until we have linked up with the Queen and her people in the keep. If it goes badly, we can regroup in the castle and, if necessary, defend ourselves best there. But I do not think it will. Indeed, quite the reverse. I think our true problem will be making the most of our victory . . .'

I felt a quickening of my body at Robin's words. For the past two excruciating days and nights, I had been concerned solely with the ride, the condition of my horse and my aching body, and keeping the men together on the road. I had had no thoughts of the coming battle. Now, hearing Robin speak, I felt a shiver in my bones, a fire being kindled in my blood. Once again I would be riding into battle, into the clash of steel and the cries of men. My fatigue, my aches, my pains, all seemed to dissolve like a dream upon waking.

'. . . and accordingly, I would suggest we detach a small force – say a dozen knights and a hundred men-at-arms – whose task it is to capture any of the enemy who try to flee. If they set off now, before the main body, and circle west of Mirebeau, they should be able to catch any of the rebels as they try to run.'

Robin had finished. The church seemed to be brimming with the same wild joy as was burning in me. Eyes sparkled, cheeks glowed, faces were animated – nobody was yawning now.

For battle was upon us.

Chapter Six

William des Roches and a dozen of his knights led the
charge and behind him came the Norman contingents,
led by William de Briouze and Sir Benedict Malet, then
Robin, Little John, Vim and myself and the Wolves – five
hundred mounted men in all. King John, at the last
moment, had decided prudence was the paramount virtue
in a sovereign and he and his closest companions held
back from the attack, forming a small reserve of forty
knights a mile or two behind the advance force. As the
golden rim of the sun was rising directly before us, we
came trotting over a small rise and saw the little town of
Mirebeau slumbering at the end of the empty, dusty road.
A thousand thatched roofs were packed inside a stone
wall twice the height of a man, and in the middle of the

town I could see the spike of the church spire and beyond it the block-like grey masonry of a keep, a tiny red-and-gold flag fluttering from its roof.

The order was given for the canter. A hundred yards out, we came up to full gallop, heading straight for the charred ruin of a wood and stone fortification that had once been the eastern gatehouse of Mirebeau. A thick surging column of armed and mailed men, a fat iron-clad snake, poured down that road towards Mirebeau – riding to glory. A trumpet sounded on the battlements of the town, and I could see a dozen black heads peering over the stone walls. We thundered forward, a vast jostling crowd of men and horses aimed like an arrow at the heart of our enemies. My own beast was snorting with excitement; I had my sword, Fidelity, in my right hand; my left arm was slotted through the loops of my shield and gripped the reins; and I used my spurs to drive my unfamiliar mount forward without mercy. I could hear shouts of alarm, of fear, from the gatehouse, and saw a low, makeshift barrier of sheep hurdles, boxes and bales had been set up, no higher than a man's shoulder.

At the head of the column, des Roches bellowed, 'For God and King John!' and the horde of five hundred galloping men behind him roared approval. Then he and his knights were at the flimsy barrier, their bodies leaning forward eagerly and their horses leaping high to clear it. They poured over in a glittering cascade of steel and iron, crashing down into the soft bodies of sleep-fuddled men the other side, swords swinging, dipping and rising red. The handful of terrified men-at-arms who had charge of the ruined gatehouse had little chance – they were chewed to ragged bloody pulp by our iron-clad men and their huge, plunging destriers. The press of our mounted Wolves coming up fast behind des Roches's foremost knights – Robin laughing with joy just ahead of me – swept the remnants of the barricade away like a river in spate, hurling defenders on foot and mounted attackers all together down the street with the force of a mighty sluice gate being opened. We were swept along into the streets of Mirebeau – and Hell was washed along with us.

I was hemmed in on all sides by horses and men. I looked down to my left and saw a whey-faced enemy man-at-arms running by my stirrup. He looked into my face, his mouth wide with fear, and I smashed my shield into his forehead and he disappeared beneath my horse's hooves. We surged forward inexorably, swords high, screaming our war cries. A spearman on my right, with his back to the wall of the narrow street, lunged his point at me, missed, and I split his face with Fidelity. The Wolves were still all around me – there was Claes up ahead, hammering his sword down on to the shoulder of a running man-at-arms. I saw Christophe casually lop the wrist from a half-naked madman who lunged at him with a dagger. Little Niels was on the ground, stabbing a wounded enemy with a long dagger. The defenders of the gate were all dead or gone under our hooves, and a crowd of mostly townspeople, men, women, children, fled before our snorting beasts. A man in a bloody-butcher's apron waving a cleaver hurled himself at me from out of a doorway and I killed him with a straight lunge through the throat before he could strike. But most of the folk were in full flight, and by and large we let them be. I shouted, 'Westbury!' and spurred after a fleeing man-at-arms who darted down a side-street, slashing wildly at him. But I mistimed the blow and merely scored the back of his scalp, and he ducked and dodged away, streaming blood. I found myself, with a dozen of the Wolves, out of the press of the main surge, in a narrow cobbled street with white-washed walls and dark timbers on either side.

And suddenly in a real fight.

A dozen men-at-arms on foot came round the corner and charged us. There were horsemen hard behind them. A spear jabbed at my face from the right. I saw the twinkle of steel and ducked and the blade screeched across the top of my plain, dome-shaped helmet. I lashed out with my sword and hacked into the arm of a man-at-arms in a padded gambeson, cutting deep, and he screamed and fell. A half-dressed knight, mounted but bare-chested and carrying mace and shield, shouted something in the Breton tongue as he charged me from the left. His spiked mace swung at my head but my guard was up and I took the blow safely in the centre of my shield, the force of it shaking the bones of my forearm. I saw then that he had outlandish blue tattoos marking his snarling face. Fidelity lanced out, over the top of my horse's neck, and plunged down into his naked hairy belly, punching through and through, the tip of the blade jarring against the high wooden cantle of the saddle behind his back. He looked shocked, almost offended, red mouth wide open, fierce blue tattoos suddenly seeming oddly childlike, and swung again weakly at me with his heavy mace, but I smashed the weapon aside with my shield, tugged my gory sword from the suck of his innards and spurred forward. As I passed, the shoulder of my horse crashing into his, he screamed high and wild in his barbaric tongue and slid from his saddle.

We pushed forward into a bigger street, wide enough for two carts, and rejoined the rest of the Wolves in a wild free-for-all with a group of Poitevin knights. Kit was at my right by now, his young face eager, his sword flecked with red. I saw Vim, the mercenary captain, two horse-lengths ahead, killing a knight with an effortlessly skilled backhand blow. And, a yard or two to my left, there was Robin dispatching a crossbow-wielding footman with a sword thrust through his yelling mouth; and Little John beside him, surrounded by half a dozen enemy squires his great axe swinging and spraying blood with every wide arc. As I watched, a man-at-arms wielding a poleaxe with a long vicious spike at the end ran forward from behind John and slammed the point deep into the big man's lower back, punching through his mail just above his kidneys. I saw John flinch from the blow, then turn, swing and sever the top of the man's head with a backhand sweep of his own huge axe. The noise was deafening: the screaming of men in mortal pain, the crack and crash of metal on wood, the shouts of outrage, the neighing of frightened horses. The stink of opened bowels, horse sweat and hot blood poisoned the air.

'Sir!' Kit grabbed my arm and was pointing to a knight in the black-and-white surcoat on a beautiful horse, who was advancing on me down a side alley. He had a golden coronet fixed atop his open-faced helmet, and his shield bore the arms of the ducal house of Brittany. There were a pair of household knights just yards behind him. 'Sir,' yelled Kit, 'it's Arthur, it's Arthur! It's the Duke!'

The three knights rode at me and I spurred away from my friends to meet them with only Kit at my shoulder. Duke Arthur, if it were truly him, came on at a canter; he swung at me with his sword, quick and hard. I caught the blow on my shield, and returned it, hacking overhand at his head. But the man was lithe and fast, and his black-and-white shield took the blow that would have opened his skull. I had a glimpse of a pale young face screwed up in anger, a boy's face framed with ginger locks, and then he was past me and the household knight behind him was lunging at my face with his sword. I ducked, his blade clanging against my helmet, and I snapped up and punched him in the teeth with the crossguard of Fidelity as he passed. He rocked back bloodied, stunned, and Kit knocked him out of the saddle with a vicious sword chop that crunched sickeningly into the side of his mailed neck.

I looked around for Arthur with one blazing thought in my mind: his ransom, a duke's ransom, it would be more money than I could ever need. The fight had taken us into a small square with an elegant stone fountain in the centre. The whole town now echoed with the yells, the mad shouts and screams of combat. Somewhere a dog was barking. I saw the Duke on the far side of the square, with the second knight, and he saw me and lifted his sword in salute. He spurred back, aiming to come at me again, but after a dozen yards the knight managed to get hold of his bridle and halt his progress. He was shouting something urgent at his lord. To my left I saw what the household knight had seen: the square was filling with Wolves and men-at-arms in William des Roches's colours and King John's livery, too. The knight was tugging at the Duke's bridle urging him to come away. I shouted, 'Fight me, Your Grace!' and I imagined I saw a look of regret in the young man's face as he allowed himself to be pulled away by his vassal. I spurred towards him, but my path was blocked by a rush of jubilant Wolves who came in from the side pursuing a pair of fleeing enemy footmen, then my horse and I were swept to the far side of the square by the press of mounted men. A small window popped open from the wall just beside my head and I found myself staring from a distance of about two feet into the terrified face of an elderly woman in an elaborate white headdress. She hastily withdrew and slammed the shutter behind her.

'On me, the Wolves, on me!' Robin was shouting. His bannerman was waving Robin's snarling-wolf standard above his head, calling the men to his side. My lord's horse was drinking from the fountain forty yards away. And his men obeyed. Wolves were coming in from all quarters, some bloody from their wounds, but most laughing with battle joy. Kit and I spurred over to him. They came in dozens and scores. Little John was there, chalk-faced, thick blood sheeting his right leg, but still in the saddle. On the other side of the square, I saw a gang of unhorsed men-at-arms in the surcoats of Hubert de Burgh's castle garrison battering at the doors of a tavern with axes and hammers, and I heard the desperate screams of women and children coming from inside. Brave Sir Benedict Malet, I noticed, was personally directing their labours.

'The castle, we must reach the castle,' Robin was still shouting to his men, at me. 'There beyond the church.' He was pointing up the narrow street, now empty of living enemies but strewn with bodies. Beyond it men scurried past. A knight rode by, looked at us for an instant and spurred quickly on. We trotted over blood-wet cobbles, fifty of the Wolves, war-grimed and savage. Vim beside me had a bad cut on his gaunt cheek. The heavy stench of burning thatch caught in my throat. I coughed, spat thickly and rode on. We emerged into a wide oval space, the centre of the town, I judged, and into the shadow of a handsome yellow-white church with a tall spire. And there were the enemy, drawn up in good order on the far side, blocking the road to the castle, a dozen knights on horseback, Lusignan men to judge by their surcoats, and some thirty footmen with long spears and big round shields crouched in two ranks before them.

'They will not stand!' said Robin, gripping my shoulder as he passed, and he pointed his long sword at the ranks of men, and shouted, 'Locksley!' then thrust back his spurs and charged directly at them. The Wolves howled their agreement, throwing back their heads and imitating the eldritch call of the pack, and fifty bloodied, battle-happy sell-swords barrelled towards the line of enemies in a screaming mob.

The enemy fled. The men-at-arms dropped their spears and shields and squirmed away through the shifting legs of the horses behind them, but the well-born men, too, the Lusignan knights, were turning their mounts, refusing the engagement – but not nearly fast enough. Robin was in among them, his sword slicing and plunging, hacking and biting into the backs of the knights as they split apart and spurred up the street back towards the castle. I killed a wounded knight as I passed him, slicing Fidelity across the bridge of his nose, cutting deep into both his eyes. But most escaped, galloping desperately, the iron of their horseshoes striking sparks on the cobbles, disappearing like scurrying rats in ones and twos down the warren of streets. We followed, striking at men's unguarded backs and horses' rumps. A few knights dropped their weapons and raised their hands in the air, shouting, 'Quarter, quarter. I yield, sir!' to delighted mercenaries, who grabbed their horses' bridles, physically laying claim to these valuable prisoners.

And then we were outside the high curtain wall of the Castle of Mirebeau.

Inside, I could hear the foul shrieks of battle, curses and shouts of joy and agony and the ringing of metal, the cracking of wood, and saw a black column of smoke rising above the walls with a scattering of orange sparks. Twenty yards ahead of us were the gates of the castle, a pair of massive wooden squares reinforced with strips of hammered iron and studded with broad iron nails.

'Axes, axes – who has an axe?' Robin was searching the faces of his men. He called to Little John, slumped low in the saddle on the edge of the crowd of jostling bloody mercenaries. 'John, can you break that gate for me? I must get inside.' His voice was filled with an almost desperate urgency. I kicked my horse over to Little John and pulled the massive double-headed axe from his limp hand – the big man smiled into my eyes, a wan acknowledgement. I paused for a second – the sounds of battle coming from inside the walls had ceased, apart from a lone voice alternately screaming and whimpering his way into the next life; smoke and sparks still poured from a burning building, but it seemed the battle, whatever it had been, was over. I paused and looked uncertainly at Robin. He shrugged. And then, like a miracle, the big black gates began slowly swinging open. The Wolves were frozen in their saddles; scarcely a man coughed or shuffled. Even the horses were strangely stilled. A dark-haired much-scarred man stepped out from behind the gate into the street, a bloody sword in his right fist and an axe in his left, a look of grim triumph on his face.

Robin rode forward and reined in a yard or two from the man, who bowed before Robin's horse with a flourish.

'How does my lady, Sarlic?' said Robin.

'She has not been harmed, my lord,' he said.

'I thank you, Sarlic, truly I am in your debt.'

And just then, a slight figure in a blue dress, with long uncovered chestnut hair, stepped daintily through the now wide open gate, with a dozen green-cloaked men hurrying just behind her, yew bows in hand, arrows nocked on strings.

Robin vaulted off his horse like a tumbler. He took two steps towards her, pulled her in and enfolded Marie-Anne in his arms.

Chapter Seven

It took four hours before King John could be cajoled into entering Mirebeau. But when he finally summoned the courage to enter the recaptured town, he was delighted with what he saw. The enemy had been comprehensively beaten. Taken completely by surprise, many of Duke Arthur's men had indeed been asleep when the royal army smashed through the east gate just after dawn. Many died in the streets under the thundering hooves of the attackers and a goodly number managed to flee, some avoiding the screen of men that William des Roches had put out to the west. But as many as two hundred knights and barons were captured – including Duke Arthur himself, who surrendered to William de Briouze after being surrounded by his men near the western gate, along with Hugh and

Geoffrey de Lusignan, Raymond de Thouars, Savary de Mauléon and dozens of other important men. I cursed my luck that I had missed capturing the Duke myself, but I had survived the battle more or less unhurt and we had achieved a famous victory, and perhaps even won the war. In one extraordinary *coup de main*, the King had decapitated the rebellion in the south and quashed the cause of Brittany – with the majority of his enemies in the south and west now bound or caged and awaiting his pleasure.

Robin's man Sarlic, a tough English outlaw-turned-mercenary, and his small force of Sherwood bowmen, along with Queen Eleanor's Gascon guards, had been holding out in the keep for four days now while the Bretons and Poitevins ravaged Mirebeau town and the surrounding countryside. But when Sarlic observed the attack on the eastern gate, and picked out Robin's standard among the throng, he sallied out of the keep with his whole strength immediately and he and his bowmen cut down the half-asleep force of Duke Arthur's men inside the castle walls, trusting that Robin would fight his way through before Breton reinforcements could join the fray. It was a gamble and it paid off handsomely. Queen Eleanor was safe, and so, most importantly, was Marie-Anne, Countess of Locksley, and her two boisterous young boys, Miles and Hugh.

In the aftermath of the battle, I was stricken, as I so often am, with a deep sense of melancholy. The rage of combat seeped away and left me feeling cold and empty.

As I washed the blood from my hands and face in a basin of hot water in the courtyard of Mirebeau Castle, I saw Robin and Marie-Anne sitting together on the far side of that open space, talking quietly and holding hands. As Wolves and Sarlic's bowmen bustled about putting out fires, tending to our wounded, I watched Robin and Marie-Anne construct their own private bubble of happiness in the centre of all the hubbub. It was then that I felt the loss of Goody most keenly, as an actual pain like a blade in my gut. I felt like weeping at the unfairness of the world: Robin had his Marie-Anne, while my beloved lay cold and still in the graveyard by Westbury church. I think I might even have wept, had it not been for Kit. He seemed to sense that I was in the darkest of humours and his solution to my unhappiness was to bring me food and drink. Though I had no appetite at all, he brought me hot chicken soup with fresh bread.

At first I waved away his offerings and buried my face in my hands. Then he surprised me by taking a stern line.

'Now listen to me, sir,' he said. 'My nan always used to tell me that a killing casts a shadow over your soul, and the Lord knows we've done our share of killing today. The best cure for a soul-shadow is pottage and ale and a good night's sleep. Now we haven't got no pottage, nor no ale. But I have got this here hot cock-a-leekie, and you'd best eat it up. And I have got you this nice skin of wine. So you be a good master and eat that soup while it's hot and drink this wine, and I'll go and find you a place to sleep.'

The soup was mostly bones and gristle, and the wine not far from vinegar, but I got them down me to please Kit, praising him lavishly for his valour in the battle. His old nan was quite right, of course. I felt a good deal better after dinner. Then slept like a stone for fourteen hours and I was a new man.

We did not tarry long in Mirebeau. When the wounded had been gathered up, the prisoners collected and the fires in the town and castle extinguished, we rested for one full day only, before we were back on the road north. We travelled much more slowly this time, setting off mid-morning and stopping by mid-afternoon. King John was eager to show his ducal prisoner in every small town on the way back to Normandy, and he displayed the wretched Duke, with heavy metal fetters on his thin wrists and ankles, in each market square before crowds of gawping yokels. Arthur, stripped of his fine armour and battle fierceness, proved to be a thin, gingery, freckled lad of only fifteen summers. The poor boy was forced to stand on the back of a cart – guarded by two royal bachelors, unknighted young men of good families, who served in John's personal retinue. These two were a pair of syco-phantic bastards, it was said, who crawled to King John and bullied anyone they felt beneath them, trusting in their relationship with the King to keep them out of trouble. Neither had fought at Mirebeau. They were called Hugo and Humphrey and while John harangued the miserable Duke from his horse a few paces away, mocking everything from his bodily parts to his prowess in war, Hugo and Humphrey moved through the crowds encouraging the peasants to throw rotten vegetables, dung or even stones at the hangdog young prisoner. The small-town folk found this bewildering, I noticed, to see two such great persons – a Duke and King, one being the uncle of the other – behaving like a hedge-school bully and his hapless victim.

I was glad we travelled slowly – not only because I was still worn with fatigue from my exertions over the past few days but because our own wounded would not have survived a hectic pace. At least thirty of the Wolves sustained serious wounds during the battle for Mirebeau, and many of them would die of their injuries on the journey – but I was most concerned with Little John. He lay on his back in a straw-filled ox-cart oozing blood from the wound in his back as we jolted along the rough roads. His eyes were tightly closed, his face running with sweat, but he made no sound except for the occasional whispered groan when the wheels of the cart hit a particularly deep rut.

Somewhere near Chinon, I gathered the courage to ask Robin if he thought our friend would live. My lord's happy face – he was touchingly delighted to have his wife and children with him and directly under his protection once more – grew sombre. 'It is a bad wound, Alan, and deep. I think it would have killed a lesser man than John already.

But John is very strong, in spirit as well as in body. And so . . . we will have to see. But if you wish him to forgive you for anything, if you have a peace to make with him, the time to do it is now, not later.'

Robin's words chilled me. I had known Little John all my adult life and while I had seen him take some hard knocks in battle, I had never seen him laid low like this. He had always been like a rock – a bawdy, crude, battle-hungry mountain of a man. I could not imagine life in Robin's company without him. I went to see him when we stopped the next afternoon, bringing a jug of wine for his comfort, and found Marie-Anne there. She and her maid-servant Constance, a petite pretty girl, had stripped the soiled clothes from his enormous body and were tenderly washing the caked blood away with soap and hot water.

The sight of his pale naked body was a shock. His face was waxy and the weight had melted off him over the past few days on the road. At first I thought he was dead, there and then, and the two women were laying out his corpse. I choked back a sob and Marie-Anne glanced at me and smiled sadly.

Then John opened one blue eye and whispered, 'Do you mind, Alan. A little privacy, if you please. It's not every day . . .' He coughed out a gobbet of blood and his face screwed up with pain. 'It's not every day that I can persuade a pair of beautiful youngsters to soap my hairy cock and balls.'

He coughed bloodily again, laughing weakly at his own wit.

Constance blushed beetroot. Marie-Anne lightly slapped his naked thigh and said, 'That's enough out of you, John Nailor. You lie quiet and behave yourself.' Then she turned to me. 'He needs peace and quiet, Alan. Let him rest.'

I nodded and stumbled away, unshed tears burning beneath my eyelids.

I walked blindly – we were camped that afternoon in a broad hayfield near a fair-sized hall King John had commandeered for the night – and somehow found myself standing next to a stoutly built ox-cart, roofed and with thick wooden bars on all sides. And a voice spoke to me: 'Sir, of your mercy, give me something to drink. I am faint with thirst.'

I looked up and found myself gazing into the face of the young Arthur, Duke of Brittany. The jug of wine was still in my hand and, wordlessly, I passed it to him through the bars. The boy tipped back his head and drank greedily.

Then he thanked me and said in a puzzled tone, 'But you were the one I fought, in the square at Mirebeau.'

'I was indeed, Your Grace.'

He nodded and said, 'I'm very sorry that I could not accept your challenge for a second passage of arms, but Sir Raymond insisted we try to escape—'

'Hey, you, get away from the prisoner!' came a rough voice, in Norman French. I turned and saw two young men: the taller man thin, with jet black hair and dark

102

stubble and a sallow, yellowish skin, like some of the men I had seen in the Holy Land; the shorter man, who had spoken, was wider in girth and had copper-coloured hair slicked back from his narrow head. Both had swords in their hands.

Despite their rudeness, I tried to be conciliatory, for I knew these men as Humphrey and Hugo, the King's bachelors.

'I merely gave His Grace a drink of wine, what harm is there in that?' I said, with a friendly smile.

'We will decide when the traitorous brat eats and drinks – and no one else,' said Humphrey.

'Which is never!' snapped Arthur. He was standing at the bars of his cage, his face flushed, his right fist gripping one of the wooden poles, the knuckles white. 'I believe you mean to have me starve or die of thirst. I have had nothing in two days.'

Hugo swung his sword hard, the flat of the blade cracking against the boy's knuckles, and the prisoner stumbled back into his cage with a cry, his left hand nursing his right.

'There is no need for that,' I said. 'Let the boy alone.'

'You mind your own affairs, sell-sword,' said Hugo. 'He is lucky we do not stick him full of holes.' And he lunged at the boy through the bars with his sword, causing Arthur to scramble to the far side.

'I said, leave the boy alone.' My voice had hardened. 'He is the Duke of Brittany, a prisoner of war. He should be treated with respect until he is ransomed.'

103

'King John himself gave him into our charge and we will treat him as we wish – indeed, like the disloyal dog he is.' Humphrey was standing at my shoulder. He was half a head taller than me, though not as strongly built, and he looked down at me with black eyes, trying no doubt to intimidate me. He put a heavy hand on my shoulder and squeezed hard, his fingers digging into my flesh.

'You will not fill your purse, hireling, by trying to molly-coddle this scum. Be on your way or we'll teach you to keep your nose out of the affairs of gentlemen.'

I slumped under the weight of his hand, my arms by my side, as if in agreement. Then I dropped my knees an inch or two and smashed my right fist, with all my strength, into the fork between his legs. The blow lifted him, temporarily, off his feet, crushing his soft testicles against the bone of his pelvis like a hammer crunching walnuts on an anvil. He let out a swift whoosh of air, but no sound, and crumpled like a baby on the ground at my feet.

Hugo still had his sword between the bars of the cage. I stepped forward, trapped his right arm with my own, grabbed him by the scruff of his mail hauberk with my left and crushed his face against the poles of the cage, pulled him back, smashed him once more against them, then hurled him sprawling to the ground. My right boot crunched down on his right wrist, the hand still holding the sword. I heard a click of snapping bone. My left boot went to the top of his chest, half on the collar bones, half on his soft throat. If I moved it an inch I could crush his windpipe just with my body's weight and so end his days.

I looked at the man pinned beneath my feet.

'Listen to me very carefully,' I said. 'I will seek you out tomorrow at noon and, at that time, I will bring food and wine for the prisoner. If during the intervening hours, he has been hurt, even the merest scratch, even a splinter, even if his hair has been rumpled, I will kill you and your friend with a great deal of ease and – I may honestly tell you – pleasure. It's important you understand this. Am I being clear?'

Hugo's face was as florid as his hair but he gave a tiny nod of his chin against my boot.

'All right then,' I said. 'I will see you at noon tomorrow.'

I did not see either Hugo or Humphrey at noon the next day. Instead, I was summoned to Robin's tent after dusk by Sarlic.

'The man wants to see you,' said Marie-Anne's bodyguard when he found me taking my ease with Kit and my own little contingent of the Wolves under a spreading oak. I was entertaining the men with one of the bawdier country songs that I had picked up on my travels, but I laid my vielle aside and followed him to the big black pavilion that housed my lord.

The tent was dark, lit only by a couple of tallow rush lamps on a folding table, and I could smell the meaty stench of the burning mutton fat that fuelled them. The rest of the space was bare except for a straw-filled pallet and a couple of stools. As ever, Robin travelled light, just his weapons and armour and a few spare clothes. The Earl of Locksley himself was sitting on a strongbox, sipping a goblet of hot, spiced wine.

'What's all this about you assaulting the King's bachelors?' he said without the slightest preamble.

'They were mistreating a prisoner – Duke Arthur, to be precise – and they were rude to me when I gave the boy a drink of wine. I taught them a lesson.'

Robin sighed. 'So it's true, then. Well, one of your victims has a broken nose, a broken wrist and his neck injuries have rendered him incapable of speech; the other has balls the size of Spanish onions and cannot walk. King John is livid. He wants me to hang you forthwith.'

'Truly?' I said, my stomach turning cold. 'He would hang a man over a disagreement between soldiers? I didn't even touch my sword. And it's not as if I killed either of them.'

'They are his men, Alan. His favourites – they do all his dirtiest work for him and now they are both out of action.'

I put my hand on my hilt. I wasn't going to allow myself to be hanged – by the King, by Robin, or anyone else for that matter. I saw that Sarlic had his hand on his hilt, too; he was watching me dark-eyed, the way a hawk watches a field mouse.

'Calm yourself, Alan, I talked him out of it . . . in the end. But you've got to be punished, do you see? So I'm docking you a month's pay. I am now admonishing you, Alan: you are a naughty fellow. Hear me? And you're being sent away from the army, back to Falaise. And, since you have incapacitated his guards, your duty is to look after our most important prisoner – the Duke. Take him to Falaise and lock him up there until the King decides what to do with him. If he escapes, it's your head on the block. No excuses. Chop. You are responsible for him. You alone. Understand?'

I nodded, relief rushing through my whole body. I do not think I am a coward, I have proved myself often enough, but hanging holds a special terror for me.

'Thank you, my lord,' I said.

'Don't thank me, just don't make my life any more difficult than it has to be.'

I turned to go, but at the flaps of the tent, I turned back.

'Robin,' I said, 'remind me – why do we serve this King?'

'I serve him because I swore a solemn oath to do so. You serve me for the same reason. Is that good enough for you?'

'I'm not sure,' I said and pushed my way outside.

I left the next morning, accompanied by a score of the Wolves, our spare horses and baggage and the ox-cart that held the cage of Arthur, Duke of Brittany, heading north. I went to visit Little John before I left but he was deeply, unnaturally asleep on his bed of bloody straw and I did not care to awaken him. He looked worse than the night before – painfully gaunt, with white strands mixed in with his yellow hair, and blackberry bruises under his eyes. But when I bent down and put my ear to his lips, I felt the tiniest waft of his breath.

I prayed to God as we rode away from the column that He would spare Little John's life, but I do not believe He heard me. A dozen miles out, I halted the march and burst open the prisoner's cage and allowed Arthur to stumble into the warm August sunlight. He was very weak – from despair at his capture, mostly, and from lack of food over the past few days since the battle at Mirebeau.

I said, 'If you will give me your word of honour not to try to escape, I will let you ride to Falaise as a member of my company. We will feed you and give you our fellowship. But you must know that if you do try to run, these men will hunt you down and I will bind you and drag you the rest of the way at the tail of my horse.'

'I will ride,' said the young man. 'I give you my word of honour that I will not try to escape.'

The Duke of Brittany was as good as his word. For the next three days he rode with the Wolves, he ate and drank with us, and he made no attempts to run for freedom. My squire Kit, and Christophe, Richard the Lionheart's greybearded veteran, kept a close eye on him at all times, even when the Duke went into the woods to relieve himself, but it proved unnecessary. The boy quickly realised I would not mistreat him and there stood a very good chance his countrymen would soon raise the colossal sum necessary for his ransom, and he would be freed. After a couple of days riding beside him, I began to like the fellow. He had shown himself brave in the fight at Mirebeau, and though he was rather undernourished, he had the strength, speed and enthusiasm of youth. He was not as haughty as he might have been for the grandson of a king, and once he had had a couple of decent meals, his natural good humour shone out like the August sunshine. We had stopped in a woodland glade, just inside the borders of Normandy, to breathe our horses and to take a drink from our wine-flasks, when I noticed him watching a pair of squirrels play-fighting in the branches above our heads. As the two nimble animals squabbled and chased each other through the leaves, I saw him laughing with pleasure at their antics. When we rode hard and fast for long periods, he never complained of fatigue. On the other hand, he clearly never forgot his exalted rank and position, and one evening as we ate round the camp fire, he tried to buy my loyalty.

'Are you a wealthy man, Sir Alan?' he asked, when I had a mouthful of roast hare.

I laughed and shook my head.

'Would you like to be?' he said bluntly. 'I could grant you lands and titles in Brittany, if you so chose. Instead of heading for Falaise and a prison cell, we could all ride west to the Brittany border and I would reward you – all of you – handsomely.'

'Watch your tongue, youngster,' I said, swallowing the meat.

'No, I suppose not,' he said sadly. 'You are King John's loyal man. A good and decent knight, I can tell. You have chosen his side in this contest and taken oaths, no doubt, and it is wrong of me to try to tempt you from the path of honour.'

I was glad I had finished the mouthful of hare. It might have choked me when he called me one of King John's loyal men. He did not mention the subject again but in my heart of hearts I did actually, for a few moments, consider his offer – and I asked myself once again why I was fighting for a King I despised.

On the ride north, as we trotted through the pretty woodlands, well-kept barley fields and apple orchards of lower Normandy, I noticed Arthur and Little Niels seemed to spend a good deal of time riding beside each other. They were as far apart in rank as it was possible to be, but close in age and they both seemed to find amusement in the same small things. Little Niels taught the Duke some of the rough Flemish slang the Wolves used, mostly concerning sex and excretion. And I admit I was rather shocked when Duke Arthur burned his hand on a camp-fire coal to hear him cursing and using the word for a lady's most private parts in a thick Flemish accent. Little Niels thought it the funniest thing imaginable and nearly made himself sick with laughter. The other Wolves seemed to have a high regard for our prisoner, too, and I overheard grizzled Christophe remarking to Claes that it seemed a pity the lad was to be incarcerated when we arrived at Falaise.

Claes said, 'He might be a charming lad, Scarecrow, but he's our enemy and our prisoner, and don't you forget it. He and his Bretons would have carved you into butcher's meat at Mirebeau given half the chance.'

I thought a good deal about Tilda on the ride. I wondered if she would be at Falaise when I got there, a vain wish as she was far more likely to be in Rouen with her father or back home in Avranches. But I allowed myself to hope. I was still determined not to dishonour her in any way, although I must admit I longed to glimpse her face, even for only a few minutes. She seemed to find me pleasing company. Or was I mistaking a natural friendliness for something more?

Sadly, a match would have been impossible: her father was a wealthy lord and I was an impoverished knight forced to sell his sword. There was no possibility of Sir Joscelyn agreeing to a marital connection with me, I realised gloomily. And I would not take her in a base fashion, much as I wanted to. I tried, therefore, to put her from my mind, as my horse steadily ate up the miles beneath us.

I thought about Robin instead. I was grateful to him for saving me from the King's hangman. I did not care much about the month's pay being docked, nor about being ordered to become a gaoler to a Duke – but I did care about being sent away from the main army. Little John's fate was in my mind a good deal and I feared I would never see him again in this world, but also the prospect of a return to dull garrison duty in Falaise had little appeal. I would have enjoyed it if Robin and I could have served together in the east – on the marches where King John must surely project his full strength now the south was pacified. If I was stuck in Falaise, I would miss out on the final victory, and the loot and ransoms that would entail.

We arrived at Falaise in the middle of the afternoon, four days after leaving the army, and I reported directly to Hubert de Burgh and informed him of the identity of my illustrious prisoner and of the King's order that he be safely housed in the castle.

'We'd better put him in the cells below,' he said. 'It's not really a fitting place for a Duke, but we dare not let him escape. He will not lack for company – Benedict is already back, and he has brought Hugh and Geoffrey de Lusignan with him. So the three of them can roost down there until the ransoms are arranged. See they are safely installed, would you, Sir Alan, with all reasonable comforts due their rank.'

Before I left the lord of Falaise, I rather timidly asked after Sir Joscelyn Giffard and his household.

'Oh, he's back in Avranches, keeping the border safe. The Bretons are apparently furious about the loss of their Arthur and they have been raiding, looting and burning the farms within half a day's ride. Sir Joscelyn and his men will soon have them back in line, though, I have no doubt.'

112

He paused and scratched his grey beard. 'It's remarkable how much stock they put in the Duke, given that he's not much more than a boy. Strange. Must be because of his name.'

As I gathered up the Duke of Brittany and ushered him to the lowest depths of the keep, I reflected on de Burgh's words. The songs and stories about King Arthur were popular throughout Christendom but, in certain places, Wales for example, and Brittany in particular, they had assumed an almost religious aura. The Duke, despite his Angevin blood, was half Breton, and perhaps his people believed he really was the great Arthur of legend reborn and restored to them.

The real, flesh-and-blood Arthur tried to hide his dismay when I showed him down the stone steps at the base of the castle, some twenty feet below ground, along a right-angled corridor, passing storerooms, the armoury, the pantry and buttery, and into a low, dark, square space in the bottom of the keep. The windowless room, lit only by a pair of cheap tallow candles, was perhaps ten paces on each side, but about a third of it had been separated off with a square latticework of iron bars set firmly in the ceiling and the floor and the walls on either side. This third was again divided into three cells, each perhaps three yards square. Two of them were occupied: I could make out pale faces in the gloom, at the bars and looking out. Geoffrey and Hugh de Lusignan, uncle and nephew, heads of the powerful clan. The two prisoners said nothing as the gaoler, a shapeless oaf called Rollo, and his assistant, a scurrying rat of a boy, showed Arthur into the cell in the corner of the room and clanged the door behind him, locking it with a big iron key. Two castle guards sat yawning on stools beside an unlit brazier. On the wall, heavy chains and manacles had been fitted and hung down, each set a couple of yards apart, and a wooden rack held the implements of torture: knives, saws, long iron pincers . . . I looked away quickly. Each cell held only a basic cot – a wooden box resembling a coffin filled with none-too-clean straw, a stool and an earthenware jug, filled with water presumably. Once again the pale face of the Duke of Brittany looked out at me from behind stout bars.

I turned to the gaoler. 'Do you feed them regularly?'

'Yes, sir,' he said smartly. 'Bean pottage every day at noon – with a nice piece of bacon in it on Sundays. As much water as they can drink.' He smirked at me. 'There's many a free man who'd be grateful for as much in these troubled times.'

I merely grunted. He was right, a peasant might well consider this an adequate diet; many folk managed to survive on much less – we had at Westbury. But for a young lord of gentle upbringing it would be a hardship. God knew how long he might be here while the ransoms were arranged. It could be a year, or two, even ten.

'I will be bringing food and wine for the prisoners from time to time,' I told Rollo, 'when my duties permit.' He looked uncertain at this. I fumbled in my pouch, pulled out several silver coins and gave them to him.

'They are not to be mistreated, hear me? I shall be angry if they are harmed.'

The coins had disappeared and the fat little man was beaming at me. 'Yes, sir, whatever you wish, sir.'

I turned to go. That dank, dark place was corroding my soul.

'Sir Alan,' said the Duke. 'I thank you for your kindness – in this foul place and on the road with your men. God will surely reward you, even if I cannot.'

I merely nodded at him, unable to speak. I could not wait to get out of that fetid dungeon and into clean fresh air and sunlight.

Chapter Eight

The summer that year was glorious. Long golden days with little work to do except for the odd patrol around the surrounding countryside with the Wolves. I visited Arthur about every other day, bringing him wine or cider and a piece of meat or cheese, sometimes fruit. I hated to go down those stone steps and enter that dark place, but I forced myself to. The truth is, I felt sorry for the boy. I sat with him for an hour or so, and sometimes we played chess to while away the time – he was an awful player and I beat him so easily the first few times that I was forced to play without a queen and a castle, just to make a decent game of it. I still won almost all the time. He was not a bright lad, certainly brave and good-humoured, but not bright.

One conversation I had with him, however, stuck in my mind. We were playing chess one day and he was playing so badly that I had no need to concentrate very hard on the game. I said, idly, 'Tell me, Your Grace, do you truly believe you are the rightful King of England?'

He looked up from the board, surprised. 'But, of course.'

'How so?' I said, taking his queen with a pawn.

'My father was Geoffrey, Duke of Brittany, as you know, and he was granted the duchy by his father, my grandfather, King Henry of England, Duke of Normandy. I never knew my father, alas; he died in a tournament before I was born.'

'I'm sorry to hear that.'

'I'm sorry, too, but it was God's will. Yet I feel his spirit with me wherever I go.'

Unwisely, he advanced a pawn to threaten my knight. My bishop sliced down diagonally and took his castle. He took my knight.

'When old Henry died, Richard, my father's elder brother, became King of England,' he continued.

I moved my castle. 'Check.'

He stared at the board blankly and said, 'And when the Lionheart died, my father would have become King, had he been alive but he was already with God. And so I believe that I, as his son, am the rightful King in his place. The rights pass from King Henry, my grandfather, through my late father to me. So, by the laws of God and man, I am King of England and Duke of Normandy. John is the usurper.'

He said this with such firmness and passion that I was a little taken aback. He truly did have a royal glow about him despite the rags he wore and the filthiness of his surroundings. For a brief moment, I allowed myself to wonder how things would have been if he had been made King on Richard's death.

On the board, he moved his king to the left.

'King John is both the brother of King Richard, and the son of King Henry, so surely he has a stronger claim than you?' I moved my bishop back into the centre and murmured, 'Checkmate.'

Arthur glared at me. 'I should be King of England and Duke of Normandy! And no other. It is God's will. It has been so decreed by God and the Church.' Such was the ferocity in his young eyes that I dared not contradict him.

On the days when I was busy, or could not face the dank misery of the dungeon, I sent Little Niels down with food and instructions to tell Arthur the gossip of the castle and what scant news we had of the war. The little fellow always returned to the surface with a cheery smile on his face and a tale of the jests they had shared through the bars. I was glad he was able to provide some moments of levity for the Duke in his misery.

There was no word of the ransom negotiations at all.

The months passed and summer became autumn. I had sent some money to my steward Baldwin and received a letter telling me the harvest in Westbury had been bountiful that year and all was well with my little son Robert.

I exercised daily in the courtyard at the wooden paling there with Kit, working on his sword and dagger combinations mostly, and practised tilting at a quintain to keep myself sharp. I had entertained hopes in the first few weeks after my return to Falaise that I would be recalled to the army. After John's stunning victory at Mirebeau, he had a perfect opportunity to summon all his men to the east and push Philip out of Normandy for good. If he had been his lionhearted brother, I think he might have done it. Instead, he was cautious, making small gains against the French on the march, but no clear, decisive moves. He basked, though, I heard from many lips, in the glory of Mirebeau, claiming he devised the plan and fought heroically in the battle. Those who were there knew differently, but kept their silence.

I was puzzled by John's relative inactivity. One day I summoned up the courage to ask Lord de Burgh what the King had in his mind. He looked stern. 'It is not my place nor yours to question the strategy of our divinely appointed King.'

I dropped my gaze, scolded. But, surprisingly, de Burgh relented and said quietly, confidentially, 'He fears treachery, Sir Alan. He does not trust his barons and so he cannot move freely. I fear he is right to do so. Word reached me yesterday of a great blow to the King's cause. Did you know William des Roches has lately turned traitor and gone over to Philip's side?'

'But why? He fought bravely at Mirebeau; indeed he

was, along with the Earl of Locksley, the cause of our victory there.'

'He claims he was promised charge of Arthur if the Duke was captured. He says he does not trust John to deal with him honourably. That is why, he says, he will serve the King no longer. Because of his treachery, now Anjou and the whole of the south is once again imperilled. William des Roches fights for Philip on the Loire, and Aimery de Thouars, too, has forsaken the King and ravages his lands down there.'

I admit I was shocked at the news that William des Roches had gone over to the enemy. But, to be honest, I could not feel the proper sense of outrage at his choice. Once again I wondered how the world would be if Arthur had become King.

'Surely,' I said, 'if King John doesn't trust his barons, doesn't that make them more likely to be distrustful of him in return, and more likely to depart?'

'It is quite simple, Sir Alan, an honourable man does not change his allegiance for any reason, whatsoever. None. He does not pick and choose his lord according to the way the wind is blowing that day, or by what he eats to break his fast. He makes an oath, a sacred promise; he keeps it, till death. Either his death or the death of his lord. Else he has no honour at all.'

Towards Christmas a courier from Robin arrived with a welcome chest of silver for my Wolves and me – and a sad message. Little John still lived, Robin wrote, but he was weak and growing daily weaker. He was not expected to rise from his bed again. He was being cared for at Fécamp Abbey, thirty miles down the coast from Dieppe. Apparently, the monks who cared for him considered his continued existence these past few months a genuine miracle – but they knew he could not last much longer. Tears blurred my eyes then, and I had to look away from the parchment for a moment. Robin's other news, however, was almost as dismal – the Wolves had been dispersed across Normandy to hold some castles in their own right, to bolster the garrisons of some others and, he wrote cryptically, in some cases to ensure the loyalty of the castellan. With winter almost upon us, it seemed likely the fighting would grind to a halt. Nothing of note had been achieved after the summer victory at Mirebeau. Indeed, the situation was almost exactly the same as before, with Normandy ringed by enemies to the south, west and east. King John himself, Robin informed me, would hold the Feast of the Nativity in Caen and Robin would be accompanying him. If I could be spared from my duties in Falaise, Robin urged me to spend the days of Christmas with him there.

Caen lay only twenty miles to the north of Falaise, one day's ride, and I stressed this proximity to Hubert de Burgh, when I asked his leave to spend Christmas with my lord. I would leave the men here under Claes and take only Kit with me. If he had need of me over the celebration period, he had only to send a rider and I would return forthwith. Hubert de Burgh grumbled a good deal but finally, grudgingly, agreed to my leave of absence.

So I found myself, with Kit at my side, walking our horses through the muddy slush on the road north to Caen on Christmas Eve, with the snow softly falling all around, making the air hazy. I had bid farewell to Arthur and made him a gift of a roast capon, two loaves of fine-milled white bread, a milk pudding sweetened with honey, a dozen apples, a bag of walnuts and a small barrel of wine, so that he and his fellow prisoners, now gaunt, stinking, filthy and close to despair, could keep the feast of Our Lord's Nativity themselves with a decent meal. I told him I would be back within two weeks.

'Do you think I will ever leave this cell?' Arthur asked piteously, after he'd thanked me with tears in his eyes for the food.

'Of course, the negotiations must be well advanced by now,' I said cheerily. In truth, I was not sure. 'I will ask Robin if there is news,' I said. 'Perhaps he can persuade the King to hurry things along.'

It was a strange Christmas: cold, crisp and melancholy. The happiness I usually felt at this holy season was entirely absent. I felt hollow, woolly headed and purposeless. We heard Holy Mass in the freezing abbey church of St Stephen on Christmas Day and afterwards feasted joylessly all afternoon in the great hall of the castle. I went to bed that night sober and restless.

As well as Robin, a great number of barons and knights attended the King and Queen Isabella at Caen, including William de Briouze, William the Marshal, Roger de Lacy and Robert d'Alençon. And a few days after the Christmas Day feast, to my delight, Sir Joscelyn Giffard arrived at Caen. I had not dared to hope that I might see Tilda this Yuletide, but now the prospect seemed imminent. Sir Joscelyn greeted me as an old friend and asked for an account of the battle of Mirebeau and my news of Falaise. I gave it to him and we spoke for a while about music. Then, diffidently, almost timidly, I asked after his daughter.

He looked at me happily. 'I have some wonderful news about Matilda,' he said. 'She has agreed to become a Bride of Christ; she is with the Abbess of Caen as we speak, taking instruction, and is set to become a novice at the abbey soon after Christmastide.'

My stomach went cold. My Tilda was to be a nun, a woman taken out of the world of the flesh, away from the love of any man – and she would live a chaste life of prayer and sanctity until, old, wrinkled and dry, she was finally called to God.

'How wonderful,' I said, my voice shaking. 'You must be very proud.'

'I am, Alan, I am. Her mother would have liked the idea very well. She was wed to me when she was young, and happily so, I believe, but before the marriage it had always been her dream to live a holy life, a life in the service of God. I think she looks down on Tilda from Heaven with loving pride and approval.'

I nodded and said nothing, feeling dizzy and sick.

Sir Joscelyn put a hand on my arm. 'I know you were fond of her, Alan, but she has chosen a better life, a far better life than she would have had as somebody's dutiful wife, and a mother to his children. Can you understand her decision?'

'Of course, sir,' I said, smiling gamely. 'She has chosen to devote her whole life to God. It is an honour for you and . . . and a great blessing for all mankind.'

He patted me kindly on the shoulder. 'It is, Alan, it truly is.'

I saw Tilda only once that black Christmastide – and behaved dishonourably. I saw her walking with a group of other holy women in the street of parchment-sellers near the abbey. She looked perfect, quite perfect: swathed in a black fur-trimmed cloak, her beautiful face peeking out from under the hood, glowing with the cold, her grey-blue eyes bright, lips blood red, her soft cheeks pale as snow. She was walking perhaps twenty paces from me, across my path, noticed me, stopped and waved happily. Seeing her was a physical shock. Like a horse-kick to the stomach. I turned my back on her, without returning her greeting and hurried away, my cheeks burning with shame. I regretted it later, of course, and consider it to have been a cowardly act, but I knew I could not look into her perfect face, knowing I would never have her, and keep my dignity as a man.

I had one other less-than-heroic encounter in Caen that wretched Christmas. It was during a lavish dinner hosted by the King on the feast day of St Thomas à Becket, and I was returning to the hall after a visit to the garde-robe, when I found myself confronted by the tall, dark form of Humphrey and his shorter russet companion, Hugo.

'You!' said Humphrey. 'I haven't forgotten you!'

They had both fully recovered, it seemed, from the lesson I gave them in the summer, and I saw with satisfaction that Hugo's nose had been badly set and bore a knobbly bump in the centre.

'Well, thanks to the mercy of God, I have managed to forget both of you. And I do not wish to be reminded. Now, get out of my way,' I said.

I wore no sword, it being the dinner hour, and neither did they, but I had my misericorde, and I was fairly certain I could put the two of them down without too much difficulty. Going by our last encounter they had little prowess. But, more importantly, it seemed unlikely they would try to knife me in the corridor outside the hall where the King himself was feasting. The prospect of either of them challenging me to a duel was laughable. Still, I kept my hand on my dagger and watched carefully as they shuffled to the side to allow me to pass.

'There will be a reckoning between us soon,' Hugo hissed as I slid past. I was so close I could smell his rank breath. 'A reckoning for you, hireling – and that traitorous child you play gaoler to in Falaise.'

125

'It's a pity,' said Humphrey, 'but that disloyal Breton whelp will never see his own children at play.'

Hugo cackled at his companion's words as if he'd said something clever.

I did not care. I was beyond them by now and heading back into the warm hall – but that last exchange rang oddly in my ears. Why did Hugo find it so funny?

I got drunk with Vim, the mercenary captain, on my last day in Caen. Robin joined us briefly in the Wolves' tower, but he slipped away when it became clear we were both planning to go at the wine in a determined, warlike fashion. Robin almost never drank to excess and he was busy with the King day and night in those days. I was drinking hard because I had behaved so boorishly towards Tilda and I was fairly certain I would never see her again. The nuns of the Abbey were very well protected against the sinners of the world, and particularly against rough and lustful soldiers. Vim drank, he told me, out of boredom. His men were well-trained, he only had a handful of them with him in Caen, and he had two competent sergeants to do the day-to-day organisation, food, pay, discipline and so on.

'We have not seen a decent battle since Mirebeau, Alan,' he slurred at me. 'We are men paid to fight – and there is no fight!'

'In the spring . . .' I began.

'Yes, in the spring we might see a little movement, but for now we trot merrily around from castle to castle with the King and his cavalcade of overbred silk-soft fools, while the Earl of Locksley holds John's cloak hem and wipes his bum after he takes a shit, then feeds him his warm milk at bedtime. Our lord tells the King he must take swift action against Philip, against William des Roches and against the Bretons – not that John listens. Maybe I should sell my sword to Philip, he seems a far better King than our one. More like a man. They all hate him, did you know that?'

'King John?'

'No, Robin – yes, they hate John, most of them anyway, how could you not? But they do not like our own lord either. He has no lands in Normandy – so he has no stake in the ruling of the duchy. And he has the King's ear. John trusts him, you see; he trusts him because he pays him, and he gives more and more of the castles over into our hands, with the lands that support them. In the spring I am to recruit and train another five hundred men – had you heard that, Alan?'

'That is good, surely,' I said. 'It will mean more silver for Robin, and for us, too. The pay is good, is it not?'

'I do not complain about the money – money is good. But it makes you soft. The more money I have, the more wine I drink. The more wine I drink, the softer I become – like an old man. I want to feel a bright sword in my hand, a swift horse between my legs and an enemy's neck under my blade.'

I rode back to Falaise leather-tongued, my breath

stinking of half-digested wine and unfulfilled lust – with Kit frowning and tutting all the way at my uncouth state.

In the second week of January, in the year of Our Lord twelve hundred and three, two riders entered the Castle of Falaise. It was a blue, clear, cold day, and Kit and I were raising a sweat in the chilly courtyard, sparring hard with each other with sword and shield, battering and blocking, lunging and parrying. The riders were hooded and cloaked against the weather and I paid them little attention – I was concentrating on keeping Kit's blade from my body. They dismounted by the stables, gave their horses over to the castle grooms and went directly into the keep. At the gatehouse one of the men turned and looked at me, noisily clashing arms with Kit, and smiled. I held up a hand to stop the bout and saw Humphrey smirking at me. I met his look with a cold glare, then turned back to Kit. Humphrey followed his companion into the keep. Doubtless, they have dispatches for Lord de Burgh from King John, I said to myself. I will avoid them and they will soon be on their way. But something about their arrival troubled me. And as Kit and I were sluicing the sweat away in the wash-house, a half hour later, I felt a cold wind on the back of my neck and shivered. I recalled the words Humphrey had spoken: *It's a pity – but that disloyal Breton whelp will never see his own children at play.*

Then I was afraid. Not for myself, for Arthur.

I pulled on my linen chemise over my wet and soapy

body, grabbed my sword belt and strapped it on, tucked the misericorde into the back, pulled on my boots and told Kit to dress himself as swiftly as he could and then find Lord de Burgh and bring him to the lowest level of the keep. Then I hared across the courtyard, and clattered down the stone steps, through the kitchens, down again another floor – I could hear the shouting by then – ran past the armoury and stores, and burst into the dungeon.

Chapter Nine

The dungeon was as hot as Hell itself. And seemed to be as full of tormented souls as the Devil's domain. Shouts of rage and cries of sheer terror split the smoky air. The brazier had been lit and the heaped charcoal was glowing cherry red. Rollo and his rat boy stood by the far wall and the rack of implements, and two men-at-arms were by the nearest two cells, those holding Geoffrey and Hugh de Lusignan, and these two captive lords were standing at the bars of their cages and shouting defiance with all their might. In the middle of the room, King John's two bachelors had stripped off their tunics and chemises and wore thick leather aprons tied around their naked torsos. Humphrey, nearest the brazier, held an iron poker, its tip glowing like the dying sun. His face was covered with sweat and his hand was protected against the heat of the metal by a filthy rag. Hugo held a pair of sheep shears, two viciously sharp long triangles of iron connected by a U-shaped rod. Behind them, by the open door of the empty cell, stood Sir Benedict Malet. On the wall to my right, naked as a babe, was pinned Arthur, Duke of Brittany. His hands had been manacled above his head to short chains hanging from the wet black wall a yard apart. His feet were similarly widespread and chained to the floor. His emaciated body was milk white, but for a scattering of scabs and sores and an angry red mark in the shape of St Andrew's cross that had been burned on his hairless chest. His skinny ribs were heaving with agony but his mouth was open, round and soundless.

I pulled Fidelity from its scabbard and roared, 'What is the meaning of this?'

An absolute silence fell over the ten men in that small room – the Lusignans ceased their shouting, Arthur suddenly closed his mouth, Benedict opened his and gawped at me like a dying fish, and the King's bachelors glared at me with undisguised loathing. Then everybody began to speak at once.

'Oh, Sir Alan, oh, thank God, sir—'

'How dare you burst in like—'

'This is a filthy outrage, by all the laws of chivalry—'

'Sir Alan, this is really no concern—'

'Silence!' I bellowed. To my surprise I was obeyed instantly.

131

'You, sir' – I pointed my sword at Hugo, who still held the shears in his right hand – 'what designs have you on my prisoner?'

Hugo pulled back his plump shoulders. 'We have been charged, by our sovereign lord, and yours, King John of England, rightful Duke of Normandy, to render this foul traitor seedless and sightless, so that he may never shatter the King's peace again with his contumelious rebellions.'

'What!' The phrase 'seedless and sightless' fluttered around inside my head.

Humphrey spoke: 'The King himself has charged us with the castration and blinding of this traitor. I warn you, sir, you impede us in our duty at your own peril.'

I glanced involuntarily at the shrivelled genitalia of the chained Duke, which bore a mere wisp of ginger hair above his tiny member and tightly bunched sack. Before I could reply, I heard the patter of boots outside the door and Kit came into the room. He was alone.

'Where is Lord de Burgh?'

'Sir,' said Kit, 'he would not come. I told him you desired him to come to the dungeon but he dismissed me and said he was too busy for my nonsense.'

'Do you think my uncle does not know what goes on in his own castle?' Sir Benedict spoke. 'These men have a warrant from King John himself. They do his express bidding. Carry on, Hugo, do your duty.'

Hugo took a step towards Arthur and lifted his iron shears. Fidelity lashed out, almost of its own accord and smashed the shears from the man's hand; the clatter they made on the stone floor seemed deafening.

The two Falaise men-at-arms drew their swords, a rattling rasp of steel blade against wooden scabbard.

I turned and pointed the index finger of my left hand at them. 'If either of you men move so much as another hair, I will kill you both upon the instant. You hear me?' The two froze. I turned back to the room. 'This man, this duke of royal blood, is my prisoner. I have responsibility for him. Those were the orders I was given by my lord, who received them from the King. I will not allow him to be harmed. I swear, upon my honour, that I will kill every man in this room before I will allow him to be touched. Do you understand this?'

Nobody said a word. But I heard Kit drawing his own sword behind me – a warm, comforting sound when a man is in a tight spot.

'Sir Benedict,' I said, 'go upstairs right now and fetch Lord de Burgh down here. Tell him if he does not come then he is a coward, a churl and a man without honour. And tell him that when I have finished slaughtering these scum I will come upstairs and tell him so to his face.'

'Sir Alan, be reasonable, this is none of your concern. The King—'

'Go and get your uncle. Now.'

It cannot have taken more than the time it takes to say ten Hail Marys before Hubert de Burgh marched into the room – but it seemed like a month in winter. No one moved, the only sound a whisper from Hugh de Lusignan, who murmured, 'God bless you, sir', from behind his bars, and a groan from Arthur, who had closed his eyes and hung his head against his chest. The dungeon air was as thick as sour curd.

'What the Devil do you think you are playing at, Dale,' said Lord de Burgh, stepping into the room. 'Why are you improperly dressed? Put your sword away this instant. That's an order.'

I looked down at my body and realised I wore no more than a wet, partially transparent white chemise. My bare legs were shoved into an old pair of leather riding boots. I could feel a cold breeze around my nether regions. I suddenly felt quite ridiculous and sheathed Fidelity with fumbling hands. Arthur gave another low moan. I saw then that Lord de Burgh had half a dozen men-at-arms at his back. One of them was pointing a loaded crossbow at my heart.

I drew a breath of hot, stale air.

'My lord,' I said as calmly as I could. 'This man here is my prisoner, he is my responsibility—'

'No, sir, he is not. I am the castellan of this castle. I am the lord here. He is my prisoner and my responsibility. You men carry on' – he gestured at Hugo and Humphrey – 'continue your work. Fulfil the task you have been given by the King.'

I lost myself then. 'If you claim it, then you must take

full responsibility for the Duke's safety, my lord. You call yourself a man of honour, you pride yourself on your honour, you boast of it ceaselessly' – I realised I was yelling at de Burgh – 'yet you would close your eyes and let a helpless man, a prisoner who surrendered to our forces in good faith, be horribly mutilated in your own castle. You, sir, have less honour than any man here, for you have the power to prevent this crime against all the laws of God and man, but you lack the courage to do anything about it.'

Lord de Burgh sucked in a gasp. I thought he would order his men to take me and I had a tight hand on Fidelity's hilt.

He glared at me for a long time, his breathing hard and heavy.

'You shame me, sir,' he said. 'You, a low mercenary, a raggedy sword-for-hire, would put me to shame – you of all people dare to question my courage and my *honour*.' He bellowed this last word.

Then he said quietly, 'You are right to do so. God's blood. God's holy blood. Benedict, release the prisoner from his chains and secure him back in his cell.'

'Uncle?' said Benedict.

'Do it now, boy. And you fellows,' Lord de Burgh jerked his chin at Hugo and Humphrey, 'you men have no more business in this place. I suggest you return to your master forthwith and tell him the lord of Falaise will not permit this sort of barbarity to take place in any castle that he has the honour to hold.'

'But, my lord,' said Humphrey. 'We—'

'Go now!' said Lord de Burgh. 'Go quickly before I set you in the Duke's place and use these instruments upon you myself.'

I thought that my relationship with Hubert de Burgh would have been destroyed by our clash in the dungeon that day, and by my intemperate words. I had called him a coward and a man without honour to his face, and I truly expected him to take his revenge on me, or at the very least challenge me to fight him for his good name. Instead, he thanked me. At dinner the next day he placed me beside him at the high table, in the position usually occupied by Benedict. His nephew was banished beyond the ornate silver salt cellar with the lesser knights, and spent the whole meal stuffing meat and bread into his mouth and glaring at me while Lord de Burgh helped me to the choicest cuts of beef and praised my courage and integrity.

'I fear I misjudged you, Sir Alan,' he said. 'You have shown me the path of honour and I thank you for it, from the bottom of my heart. I cannot imagine what the King was thinking to send those two poltroons here. I expect it was a fit of bad temper, an imbalance of the humours; unfortunately the King is prone to these rages, as you may have heard, just like his blessed father was before him. He does not see clearly what is right and wrong when the red rage descends. So I thank you myself for preventing

136

this foul crime from taking place, you showed great bravery, and I believe that King John will thank you, too, when he realises his mistake.'

I doubted it. But I was content to enjoy being in Lord de Burgh's good graces for a change.

Arthur thanked me, too, with tears running freely from his eyes, when I brought him a pair of roasted pigeons and a flask of cider the next day.

'You are an angel, Sir Alan, an angel sent from God to deliver me . . .' the boy was sobbing with relief and gratitude; he made me feel uncomfortable. For I had only behaved as any decent man would, and poor Arthur was still a prisoner in a stinking cell. Furthermore, at the back of my mind I knew that this passage of events was not over. Whatever Lord de Burgh thought about King John, I knew from my own experiences with him that he did not like to be thwarted in anything. And Hugo and Humphrey would surely not forget their second humiliation at my hands.

A week or so later the castle was thrown into turmoil by news brought by a courier from Rouen. Queen Isabella had been surrounded in Chinon by the rebels and John, urged by Robin, it seemed, had ridden south with half the Wolves to her rescue. It might have been a repeat of the Mirebeau triumph, except that as soon as John left Normandy, Robert d'Alençon – that gloomy yet, I had sincerely believed, decent and loyal lord – went over to King Philip, offering the French King his castle in exchange for confirming him in possession of his lands. At the same time Ralph of Beaumont, a Norman knight from the east, had done the same. King John, alarmed at this double treachery, had retreated back to Argentan by a circuitous route to avoid the Castle of Alençon, now in enemy hands, and Robin had gone on alone to Chinon to rescue the Queen.

A rumour, no doubt based on knowledge of the orders given to Humphrey and Hugo, was spreading that Arthur had been tortured and murdered in Falaise – and it was this false news that triggered the defections of the lords d'Alençon and Beaumont. Worse, the Bretons, enraged that their Duke had been dispatched in such a cowardly fashion, had broken out of their duchy once again and the borders of Anjou and Maine were aflame.

Hubert de Burgh himself was incandescent with rage. He paced about the great hall, calling down God's vengeance on traitors and liars. 'He lives, the Duke lives, by God's blood. He lives and we all know it. You most of all, Sir Alan. Why do people not believe that Arthur still lives?'

'Perhaps, sir, if you were to show him to the people, then the word might spread . . .'

De Burgh spun on his heel. 'I cannot have Arthur carted across the breadth of Normandy to reassure fools and silence rumour-mongers. The risk is too great. He might be rescued, or seized by another Norman traitor to be used as a bargaining counter. He might escape! God forbid. No,

I have issued a proclamation and sent it east and west, swearing by my sacred honour that Arthur lives and is well. That shall suffice. The Duke of Brittany must remain under guard at Falaise.'

That was not to be, for a month later another courier arrived with orders from the King himself. Arthur was to be brought to Rouen immediately – in chains.

And I was to bring him there.

I took my leave of Hubert de Burgh at the end of February. Duke Arthur of Brittany, along with Hugh and Geoffrey de Lusignan, were to be escorted to Rouen by myself and two dozen Wolves. On my own authority, I decided to forgo the chains and made Arthur and the Lusignans swear an oath not to try to escape. I need not have worried, all three were too weak to run far. Despite my attempts to feed him, Arthur was no more than skin over bones, and the Lusignans were not much fitter. We travelled slowly, taking six days to ride the eighty miles across Normandy, stopping frequently to eat and rest at inns, castles and religious houses. The three prisoners seemed to enjoy the journey, a wonderful change from their hellishly cramped abode in Falaise, and Arthur in particular seemed happy. He saw this transfer to Rouen as the first step in his ransom and return to Brittany. The Lusignans were more cautious – they knew King John lay at the end of the road, and their futures were still uncertain. We slept at the Castle of Neubourg on the last night before we arrived at Rouen,

139

and out of my own pocket I provided three new modest suits of woollen cloth for my charges, which were run up by a tailor in the town overnight. They had been dressed in stinking rags, I had plenty of money in my pouch – the Wolves' wages were paid regularly every quarter – and it seemed appropriate that they present themselves to the King attired as decent Christians rather than starveling beggars.

The King received us in the great audience hall of the Castle of Rouen with apparent delight. The hall was packed with barons, knights, mercenaries and hunting hounds – a colourful sea of creatures and every man talking at the top of his voice, arguing passionately and drinking from big clay cups constantly being refilled by an army of servants armed with deep leather jugs. After so many days in the open air, the smell of stale sweat, wet dog and hot spiced wine was so strong as to be almost visible. The King leaped out of his throne as we were announced by the herald, pushing roughly through the drunken throng of his courtiers, and came to stand before the Lusignans with hands on hips, a beaming smile on his wine-reddened face.

'Ah, my dear Geoffrey, and Hugh, you are both quite well, I trust?' said the King as though greeting favoured relatives, rather than the captive heads of a treacherous enemy family. The surprised Lusignans admitted to being in reasonable health considering the circumstances and enquired civilly after the King's wellbeing.

'I have glad news for the House of Lusignan,' said the King. 'I have magnanimously decided to restore you to my good graces. You shall swear an oath of allegiance to me, and there are some minor legal matters that we must agree upon – my clerks will sort that out – but you shall be restored to your lands within the month. What do you say to that?'

I noticed that Arthur, who was standing beside me, was smiling with joy. The King ignored both of us, and congratulated the Lusignans fulsomely on their soon-to-be-achieved liberty. Duke Arthur took a step forward: 'My lord, might I make so bold as to enquire if, in your gracious magnanimity—'

'You, traitor, shall be silent!' In an instant the King lost all his oily bonhomie. His face was a livid mask of rage, his voice a harsh snarl. It was an extraordinary transformation – from sunshine to storm in the blink of an eye.

'And you, Locksley's lackey, Dane, Dale, whatever your name is, you dare to bring this vile wretch before me? Get him to the dungeon. Get gone, this instant!'

I saw Robin pushing through the crowd, with Vim at his back and a couple of Wolves. Two mercenaries took Arthur's skinny arms and led him to the stairs. He looked back at me, despair in his eyes, and all I could do was shrug helplessly. Robin put an arm around my shoulder and led me from the King towards the side of the room. Behind me I could hear John commiserating with the Lusignans about the poor quality of their attire and

141

promising to make them a gift of velvets and silks and the finest gold thread.

'What's going on?' I asked Robin. 'Why are the Lusignans being treated like prodigal sons, while Arthur is slung back in the dungeon?'

'Carrot and stick. He's trying to buy peace in the south,' said Robin tersely.

'What?'

'He's releasing the Lusignans – the carrot – to show he can be merciful, if he chooses. He's treating Arthur harshly – the stick – to show he is not weak.'

'That is idiotic. By releasing the Lusignans he will just make the southern rebels stronger.'

'I know, Alan, I know. I have tried to reason with him time and again but he won't listen on this matter. Someone got to him – I don't know who, some agent of King Philip or a Lusignan-paid spy most probably – and whispered into his ear that freeing the Lusignans would show the world what a noble fellow he is, a generous lord, a magnanimous king, all that. He swallowed the idea whole. He wants to be loved, did you know that? Underneath all his cruelty, his disloyalty, his treachery and suspicion, our royal mountebank wants his barons to adore him for the kindly man he thinks he is.'

'And do they?'

'Of course not. They don't trust him. Half are already in secret talks with Philip and the other half are thinking about it. It's a snake pit here, Alan. A nest of damn vipers.

Almost every week, Philip takes another castle on the eastern march, often surrendered without even a token fight. John's holding on to Normandy by the skin of his teeth.'

I digested that for a few moments.

'And what am I doing here?' I asked.

Robin looked into my eyes. 'I want someone beside me I can trust. With Little John on his death . . . in his sick bed, I need you. I can't do it all on my own any more. The more his barons edge towards Philip, the more responsibility the King gives to me and the other mercenary captains. Truly, we are the ones holding Normandy for him. We're the only ones he trusts.'

'And my duties are?'

'You are going to be training up a new batch of recruits for the Wolves.'

I said nothing.

'Don't look so glum, Alan. In a way, the worse it gets for the King, the better it is for us. More responsibility means more power. And more money. Anyway, let's get something to eat at home with Marie-Anne and the boys and I'll tell you all about it.'

Chapter Ten

I set to my new duties with as much determination as I could muster. I handed over my own little band of Wolves to Vim, saying farewell to Claes, Christophe and Little Niels and the others with some regret, for we had grown close in our time together, and in return I was given a company of two hundred new recruits.

Like my Falaise Wolves, they were from Flanders, Brabant and Hainault, the flat lands to the north-east, peasants mostly, some of whom had never held a sword before. And after some months of relative inactivity, I found I was as busy as I had ever been in my life. I had to feed, clothe and arm the men, and I lodged them in hastily built barracks to the west of the city walls on the banks of the Seine. I divided the company into ten squads of twenty men, each under a vintenar – usually a man who had some little experience of warfare, sometimes a seasoned campaigner, although there were few of those. King John was prepared to spend lavishly on their armament and so each man received a new sword, a dagger, a spear and a kite-shaped shield, as well as a short-sleeved hauberk of iron mail that covered them from elbow to knees, and a round steel cap with a nose guard. As the saying goes, blacksmiths never go hungry in time of war, and we had the smiths and armourers of Rouen working night and day to outfit this new host. Each man also received: two linen chemises, two pairs of braies to cover their loins, two pairs of green woollen hose, a green woollen tunic, a sleeveless padded gambeson to wear under mail, or instead of it, and a new green woollen cloak. The drapers, dyers and tailors of Rouen were busy, too, that spring.

We trained each morning, beginning at dawn, and I was alarmed to see on the first morning just how inept the men were with arms. After choosing the vintenars, and setting them at their heads of their squads, I began at the very beginning with the basic sword and shield manoeuvres: one, block, and two, cut, and three, step forward, and four, lunge, and so on – and I had each squad of men-at-arms repeating these moves and chanting the numbers out loud. It was how I first learned to fight, long ago, in a remote manor deep in Sherwood. I thought it ridiculous then, but now I knew the benefit of learning by rote. The parries and strikes of the sword become second nature to a man after repeating them many thousands of times, and in the chaos of battle, his life could be saved by instinct. When the men had mastered the basic moves, we moved on to the six lateral strikes of the sword – neck, waist and knee, from left and from right, and the six blocks that countered them. I taught them several easy set manoeuvres, sword and dagger combinations that would become instinct after many hours of practice. For example, a forehand slash with the sword in the right hand to distract the opponent, step in and thrust with the dagger in the left, aiming to catch the enemy under the ribs, then step back out of range. A simple killing manoeuvre, but it needs to be done very swiftly, and with perfect timing. One-two, three-four. Sword-slash, step in, dagger-thrust, step back. Feint and step in, strike and step back.

When they were reasonably comfortable with several individual combat patterns, we moved on to simple infantry formations such as the hedgehog – a ring of men several ranks deep with a bristling hedge of spears pointing outwards, an effective defence for infantry against cavalry – and the boar's snout, that running wedge designed to punch through a shield wall, and so on.

We laboured from dawn until noon, the dinner hour, when I would return to the castle to eat the main meal of the day, sometimes with the other knights and nobles with King John in the great hall, and at others just with Robin and Marie-Anne in his narrow three-storey house near the cathedral. After dinner, we resumed our training until the bells of Vespers rang out the end of the day, and I would retire to Robin's house for a light supper, a little music and singing on occasion, and my bed.

Kit was particularly helpful in these days. He acted as my aide, relaying orders and instructions to the vintenars. He seemed to have a natural rapport with the recruits. Without my noticing, during his time in Falaise the lad had picked up a decent command of the rough tongue these men spoke. While I had no grasp of their language, save a few filthy curses, Kit seemed quite comfortable chattering away in Flemish and explaining to them the incomprehensible orders of their new knight-commander.

We held competitions between squads, games, trials of speed and strength, and mock duels between individuals and, after only a month, I realised we had the beginnings of an *esprit de corps*. I noticed the men began to attach scraps of wolf fur to their clothing and armament; God knows where they got the material, as we hunted no wolves. And, as a special mark of our company within the Wolves, some acquired boar tusks and affixed them to their helmets or hung them around their necks – an homage to my own device of a strutting black wild boar on a red background. I was truly flattered by these little gestures and began to feel a regard for the men, green as they were, and the beginnings of a mutual respect.

The progress of the recruits was noted with approval

by Vim. Indeed, the captain of Robin's mercenaries stole a dozen of my more promising men-at-arms in early April. He needed them, he told me, to add to the veterans he already had because he had been ordered to take a hundred men to Château Gaillard to reinforce the garrison there, and he was short-handed. A score of experienced Norman knights and their mounted sergeants were going too, but mercenaries were needed to make up the numbers. King Philip still did not dare attack Château Gaillard's powerful fortifications, yet some of the surrounding fortresses, part of the Iron Castle's broad network of lesser defences, had been overrun, and King John understandably wished to strengthen the rock securing his eastern flank. I was angry at first that he should seek to break up my company so soon after its formation, and just when we were beginning to set like a jelly into a coherent fighting unit, but Robin soothed me and pointed out that Vim had sore need of the men and I was a victim of my own success. It was a compliment to my training methods, he said; then he reminded me that the men were not mine to dispose of but, indeed, his. So Vim took my dozen best recruits and I bit my tongue.

I dined with the King a few days afterwards. It was a depleted gathering, a score of knights, Robin and myself – and Humphrey and Hugo. I had seen this ugly pair around Rouen often, in the castle and in the streets of the town, but decided it was prudent to avoid them. The King was drinking hard, as was usual at that time, and seemed angry at everything and everyone. One of the squires serving the meal spilled a drop of gravy from a brimming platter of venison on to the white tablecloth. King John flew into a rage and knocked the hot serving plate from the boy's hands, then he slapped the boy down with a round-house across the face and began kicking at him as he lay curled on the floor. After a dozen blows, the King was gently restrained by his household knights, and the bruised squire was allowed to scuttle away.

'That boy is some Norman baron's child,' I said quietly to Robin. 'Do you think his noble father will love the King more or less when he discovers how his son and heir has been treated?'

Robin merely shrugged. I felt the glow of irritation at my lord. He seemed utterly indifferent to decency.

The drinking had begun in earnest, with Hugo and Humphrey and King John sinking goblet after goblet of good red wine, and calling out toasts. Most commonly: 'Death to all traitors!'

Some of the knights began to make their excuses – it was late afternoon by then – and slip away from the long table, pleading other pressing duties. The King seemed content to let them go and called for more wine for those man enough to take it. After a while, Robin rose to his feet. This time the King objected, calling out loudly, 'You are not leaving us, Locksley, surely. Come, sit by me, drink a cup. It will do you good. Get your singing-boy, whatshisname, to play us some of his famous music.'

I froze in my chair. My head blossomed with red fury. I could feel my eyes starting from my head. I had not been called singing-boy for many a year. I wanted to knock the King's teeth down his throat; I could see the action clearly in my head; and feel the sharp, cutting impact across my knuckles as the royal incisors snapped under my blow. Then I felt Robin's heavy hand on my shoulder. 'Just do as he says, Alan. Go and get your vielle, calm down, and play a tune or two for his highness. He'll soon be too drunk to hear you, anyway.'

I left the hall, shaking with rage. In the little alcove just outside I splashed my face with cold water from an earthenware bowl set in an iron stand. The beaten squire, seated on a stool beside it, was snivelling to himself. I could hear the drunken shouts clearly from the hall as I dried my face on the linen towel he offered me.

'Death to all traitors!' bellowed Humphrey.

'May they all learn to fear my wrath,' shouted the King.

'May the Devil take them all back to Hell!' Humphrey again.

'Yet, at this moment, we have one dirty traitor residing in this very castle!' Hugo, this time.

Then a burst of drunken laughter and mumbled conversation.

'Teach him a lesson. Make an example of the bastard!'

I heard Robin speaking low and urgently, but I did not catch the words. 'Stay then, Locksley, if you have no stomach for our sport,' the King's harsh voice cut through

Robin's murmurings. Then the scraping of tables and benches, the sound of a heavy man falling over, curses, laughter and the snap of boot leather on stone. King John strode past the alcove without seeing me, and on his heels came Humphrey and Hugo, red-faced, sweaty and grinning like demons. Heading down the spiral staircase to the dungeons.

I stood there considering all that I had heard, trying to explain away their visit to the lower reaches of the keep. I could not, and I knew that I could not stand idly by. I had to act. I saw Robin at the head of the stairs looking hard at me.

'Alan, it's not our affair. This can only end badly. Let it go.'

But I was running by now. Robin tried to stand in my path, his arms spread wide as if to catch me. Without thinking I dropped my shoulder and smashed my lord aside with my hurtling body. I leaped down the spiral of stone steps, jumping three at a time, following as swiftly as I could after the drunken King and his blood-hungry bachelors.

'Alan, wait!' Robin's cry was breathless, far above me.

Near the bottom of the stairs, I stumbled, tripped and fell the last few yards, knocking my head painfully against the damp walls outside the cell that I knew housed Arthur. My vision was streaks of red and gold and black and, when I got to my feet, the dim anteroom seemed to swim. I recovered soon enough; but precious moments were wasted.

The door to the cell was open, and when my head had cleared, I steadied myself with a hand on the jamb and looked in on a scene from a Devil-spawned nightmare.

Arthur was standing in the middle of the little cell, dressed in the rags I had bought him more than a month earlier, his wrists manacled. Hugo knelt before him and held him around the waist, pinning his arms to his body; Humphrey held his upper body from behind, one arm curling around Arthur's thin chest, the other holding a long dagger to the Duke's throat. King John sat on a wooden stool. He was smiling, his lips slack and stained with wine, his head lolling between hunched shoulders. But his eyes were fixed firmly on Arthur.

'Now then, nephew, be so good as to tell me, – who is the rightful Duke of Normandy and King of England?' he said, and giggled, wiping his wet mouth with the back of his left hand.

Arthur, Duke of Brittany, straightened his emaciated body as much as he could in his captors' tight grasp. He lifted his chin, and said, in a loud, clear voice, 'By God Almighty, by His son Jesus Christ, by the Virgin and all the saints, I am.'

I knew Robin was at my back. I could feel his breath on my neck, a powerful restraining hand on my shoulder.

King John nodded as if agreeing with the boy. 'Yet if you truly were the rightful Duke and King, then God Almighty, His son, His mother and all the saints would not let this happen to you.'

The King shifted his gaze to meet that of Humphrey. 'Do it!' he said. In one swift movement, Humphrey drew the keen blade across Arthur's neck. Blood jetted from the terrible wound, arcing into the air in thick, pulsing spurts.

Robin took his hand off my shoulder. I fumbled at my waist but found no weapon there except a small eating knife. Nevertheless, I drew it and made to step forward into the cell. I felt Robin's arms lock around my arms and chest, and his voice hiss in my ear. 'Alan, if you love life even a little, and if you want to continue to enjoy it, I tell you in all earnestness – walk away from this now and never think or speak of it again.'

Arthur had fallen to the floor, the blood still pumping from the yawning gash in his throat, a red pool swiftly forming beneath his pale cheek. King John leaned forward on his stool, fascinated; a tiny river of blood wended its way across the stone floor towards the kidskin-shod royal foot. Both Humphrey and Hugo stepped back to keep their feet clear. The blood trickle reached John's immobile shoe and seemed to try to bury itself under the sole. Arthur was still, at the other end of the blood trail connecting him to the King, lying in his own gory lake. I gave a cough of rage and sorrow, a wordless noise, like the expression of a dumb beast, and Robin lifted me off my feet and turned me around so that I was facing the upward curve of the stairs. Then he released me. 'Go now, Alan, for all our sakes,' he said quietly, giving my back a gentle shove. 'Go now, and do not look back.'

I ran from that bloody chamber, away and up the staircase almost as fast as I had tumbled down it. But I was not fleeing in horror from King John and his butchers in that blood-splashed dungeon.

I was running to fetch my sword.

Chapter Eleven

I ran from the castle, through the narrow streets of the town, directly to Robin's tall house by the cathedral. I burst through the doors and pounded up the stairs to the chamber at the top that Robin and Marie-Anne had put at my disposal. As I strapped Fidelity around my hips and tucked the misericorde into my right boot, tears ran freely down my cheeks. Duke Arthur had not been my friend, indeed he had been my enemy, but the tragedy of his last few months on this earth had wrung my heart, and his murder at the hands of his drunken captors filled me with a fury that could be quenched only by blood.

I knew what to do. White-hot rage and bull-at-a-gate stampeding would not achieve it. So, half an hour later, back inside the castle, I made myself calm, loitering in the long shadows by the well-house in the courtyard, the hood of my cloak hiding my face, drinking from time to time from the dipper in the bucket, watching the entrances to the keep. It was near dusk by then, and the bells of Vespers were ringing mournfully across town, but I had to wait another full hour in the growing darkness before I saw two men, carrying a large, long object wrapped in blankets, emerge from the side door to the keep. I stepped into the deepest shadow behind the well-housing and forced myself to breathe easily, in through the nose, out through the mouth.

Humphrey and Hugo marched their burden straight out of the western gate of the castle, unchallenged by the guards thanks to their status as the King's bachelors. They passed across the lowered drawbridge over the moat and took the road heading west along the right bank of the Seine. At the gatehouse I told the guards I'd be sleeping in the barracks with my recruits that night and was grudgingly allowed through, although it was well past the curfew hour.

I stayed some fifty yards behind the murderers and I doubt if they noticed me once we left the lights of the castle and the town of Rouen behind. We passed the barracks of the Wolves – I saw the gleam of tallow candles leaking through the cracks in the structure and heard the sound of ill-tuned singing. It crossed my mind, only for a moment, to summon some of the recruits to aid me. Then I dismissed the notion: I would do this alone. I would not taint my new men with this night's foul work.

There were few folk about then; the day was dead and well-earned slumber beckoned all good Christians to their beds. Some passed me on the road, going east, heading to the gaggle of huts that had spread outside the walls of the town, refugees from twenty years of bloody fighting across Normandy who had made their own encampment in the shadow of the capital city. But these were wary, dirt-poor folk, who minded their own affairs as a matter of survival, and not one so much as gave me a second glance. They trudged past, eyes down, hoods pulled forward like mine, mute as mice. A pair of noisier fellows passed, too, men-at-arms swaggering in drink, but they also ignored the bachelors and their limp burden fifty paces ahead of me – or did not notice them in their inebriation – and I stepped off the track and into a dark stand of trees to allow them to pass.

When the soldiers had been swallowed by the gloom, I strode forward again, silent as a shadow. I was a dark wraith behind the two men and their cloth-wrapped load on the road by the Seine – only locked inside my heart was the bright hot flame of rage.

About half a mile outside Rouen, Humphrey and Hugo stopped and laid down their parcel. They looked before and behind them, but nobody else was on the road by then, and the nearest boat on the Seine was more than two hundred paces hence – a wherry pulling away from us and heading for the far bank. I was thirty yards behind them, unseen behind a rowan bush, crouched on one knee.

I stood tall, then slipped Fidelity from its scabbard and stepped on to the road. As I approached them on fairy-light feet, they bent to the long bundle, hoisted it between them and swung the body, once, twice, three times, and hurled it into the Seine, where it splashed noisily in the black waters and sank almost immediately. I realised they must have weighed it down with iron chains from the dungeon. Thus disappeared the mortal shell of Arthur, Duke of Brittany, claimant to the throne of England, a brave man, a man of honour. May his immortal soul rest with God.

I was ten feet from them by now and still unnoticed.

I called out softly, 'Hold, you murderers. Hold there, my bold assassins.' Humphrey spun round and peered at my shape in the darkness. He saw the wink of my long blade and gave a cry and fumbled for his own sword. Hugo, likewise, a short round shape in the gloom, was drawing his own weapon.

Good, I thought, arm yourselves. It should not be black murder.

'Did you think yourself brave, Humphrey, when you slew a bound man? Did you? Did you feel like true men when you cut Arthur's throat, when you killed a prisoner who could not defend himself? Would you boast to your friends of your valour? No? I thought not. For you have none, cowards.'

The bachelors separated, each with a drawn sword, going left and right, Hugo on to the road, Humphrey along the riverbank. They meant to attack me at the same time – the right move for them, more dangerous for me – but I cared not. They would die this night. I knew it in my bones, in my blood, in my vitals. They could have had a dozen comrades with them and I would have felt not the slightest trepidation. My rage warmed me and made me invincible – at least to scum such as these.

'I shall feel very good about cutting your throat,' said Humphrey. 'That pleasure is long overdue.' Even as he uttered these words, his companion hacked at my head with his sword. I was distracted momentarily and saw the movement only by God's grace out of the side of my eye – I ducked, as Hugo's blade sliced through the air an inch over my skull. I came up, leaning back, towards him, and drove my elbow hard into his face. He was coming forward, impelled by his strike, and I was going backwards, and my elbow crunched into his nose like a padded mason's hammer. He sat down heavily as if his legs had been cut from under him. Then Humphrey was on me, aiming to split me from crown to crotch with a fast, vertical blow, but I was already moving, and had slipped half a step right and twisted to the side even before his blow was halfway done. These men are not fighters, I thought. Cutting the throats of bound prisoners was the limit of their skill: they were executioners, not warriors.

As I was.

Humphrey swung his sword at my neck, and I blocked it easily, our blades ringing out like hammer on anvil in the darkness. He pulled back, then rushed forward again, flailing at my head, backhanded this time, from my right, a wild swipe with his sword gripped in both hands. I swayed back out of reach and, when the tip of his blade had whistled past my nose, and he was off balance and as wide open as a country barn door, I stepped in and hacked Fidelity into his waist. My blade sliced deep, above his left hip, through bowel and belly and kidney, and I felt the jar of bone as sword was halted by spine. The air came out of his lungs in a long, soundless blast and he dropped to his knees. I planted a boot on his chest and tugged Fidelity out of him, kicking his half-severed frame to the turf as my blade came free.

I turned to attend to his friend.

Hugo was still down, half-stunned and trying to scramble away on all fours. I walked after him and stamped on his back, knocking him flat to the ground. He pushed himself up again with his short arms, still trying to scuttle free. I carved Fidelity straight down through his neck, set his head rolling free of his body and buried the tip of my sword into the earth. The torso remained at a crouch for five or six heartbeats, blood gushing from the neck over my blade, until his elbows relaxed and it thumped down on the riverbank. I pulled Fidelity free and strolled over to Humphrey, lying on his back in a pool of black liquid. He still lived. His pale face looked up at me beseechingly, his mouth open and oozing blood, his eyes wide and dark. I hawked and spat, showering his cheeks with spittle.

'That is for Arthur,' I said.

He looked bewildered. As if he had never heard the name before.

'And so is this,' I said.

I lifted my sword, double-handed, point downward and drove it into his chest with all my strength, piercing him through and through, pinning him to the turf.

When my heart had calmed itself, I looked left and right, and saw we were still alone, praise God. I dragged their corpses to the river's edge, although I had some trouble finding Hugo's head in the dark. Then I kicked their mortal remains over the lip of the bank into the dark, memoryless Seine.

Arthur was avenged, at least in part.

Robin was waiting up for me when I returned to his house. Marie-Anne, Kit and the servants were all in bed, but my lord was sitting at a trestle table by the hearth with a jug of wine at his elbow. He said nothing as I clumped in in my muddy boots and sat beside him at the table. But I saw him eyeing the blood on my tunic and hose. He poured out a big cup of wine and shoved it over to me.

'Feel better now?' he said.

'Not really,' I said. 'But it needed to be done.'

Robin nodded absently and took a sip from his own cup.

'I'm sorry for knocking you down in the castle,' I said.

'It is no matter. What did you do with the bodies?'

'They are in the river. No one saw me do it.'

'Good. When their disappearance is noted, I will say to the King that I have long had my suspicions of the pair of them, and I have heard rumours they have gone over to Philip's banner.'

'The King,' I said dully.

A vast exhaustion suddenly came over me. I finished my wine, longing for the oblivion of sleep.

'Do not even think about harming the King, Alan. I am serious. I will not support you, do you hear me? Leave the King be or risk my wrath.'

His silver eyes bored into me. I stood, all my limbs weighted with weariness.

'Remind me, why do we serve this King?' I said.

Robin let out a hot breath. 'I swore an oath to him, and you . . .'

'Oh yes, our sacred oaths. I recall now. Good night, my lord, sleep well.'

For the next few months I avoided the King as much as I could. It was not difficult, he spent a good part of the spring and early summer on the move, and I was planted in Rouen training the recruits to the Wolves. But, whenever he was in Rouen, and I might have been summoned to the hall to dine with him and his barons, I found some excuse not to attend. I went out on exercises in the Norman countryside with the recruits, long, exhausting patrols, or feigned a sickness of the stomach. I did not trust myself in his presence. I did not trust myself not to attack him with my bare hands or rip his scrawny throat out with my teeth. How Robin could stand it, I do not know – or perhaps I did understand a little when I saw him at training with Miles and Hugh in the courtyard of the house.

Hugh was then thirteen years old, a solemn lad who adored his father and strove in all things to be like him. He took his training to be a knight extremely seriously, practising with sword and shield, and with lance on horseback, in any spare moments that he had outside the hours prescribed by the master-at-arms who had been hired to instruct him. But, for all his hard work, he was not a natural swordsman; he was clumsy and slow, and when he fought his attacking moves were dangerously predictable. While he strove to be as much like his father as he could, copying Robin's dress and habits of speech, he bore absolutely no resemblance to the Earl of Locksley at all. He was short and dark, while Robin was tall and fair. He had no time for mischief and whimsy, while Robin sometimes seemed to live for both. He loved books and studied as hard at his schooling as he did on his training for war. But he was no milksop – he could take a hard blow from a wooden sword without weeping – and he had a determination that many older men might have envied. I liked him, and I spent some time with him each week working on his sword play. While he might not be a gifted warrior, he was dogged, and I was able by patient repetition to

163

teach him some of my own tricks that I hoped might save his life when he went into battle.

Miles was, in looks, character and temperament, the very opposite of his brother. Although not yet nine years old, Miles was almost as accomplished a fighter as Hugh. He did not have the strength yet, but he was nearly as tall as his sibling, and much faster and more inventive with a blade. He was lively and quick-witted, fair and willowy in build – one of the laziest boys I have ever met, yet also one of the most energetic. Hugh would often rise before dawn and practise his sword work in the courtyard before the household was awake. Miles had to be dragged from his cot with curses and blows, and if not supervised minutely, he would find a quiet corner to curl up in and take a nap. On the other hand, of an evening, while Hugh was sitting in his chamber with a candle and his nose in a book of Latin grammar, Miles would have escaped the house, ignoring the curfew imposed on Rouen by King John, and by his father on him, and be running about the darkened streets and scrambling over rooftops with a gang of wild friends. With a sword, even at his tender age, Miles could surprise his master-at-arms with a cunning new trick that he had invented, some unheard of combination that slipped like quicksilver past his teacher's guard. Then he would lose interest and be easily overcome by his adult opponent. Miles was frequently beaten for his misdemeanours; Hugh almost never. Yet the two boys, for all their differences, were devoted to each other.

Robin doted on them both, and when his duties permitted would take them out hunting in the woods and come back bone tired, happy and with a couple of bloody deer carcasses across their saddles. Robin played chess with them; he worked on their sword skills when he had time; he sang with them and Marie-Anne after supper, occasionally with me providing the musical accompaniment on my vielle. He had been away from them far too much, he confided in me, while they were growing and he was outlawed or on campaign, and he had refused to send them off to some other knight's household for training as was customary for most lads of their age and rank. It would have been a little dangerous, to be honest, in his outlaw years, for his enemies might have taken it into their heads to capture them and hold them for ransom. But the truth was that, unlike so many powerful men in the King's court, he loved his sons and wanted to spend as much time with them as he could.

'If I die in battle, I want them to remember my face,' he told me. 'I don't just want them to inherit my lands and title.'

This, of course, was the reason why Robin served King John; this was why he had sworn an oath to be his loyal man. Why he put up with John's behaviour. For them. He wanted to make a home and a future for his boys, and for Marie-Anne.

'Only one more year to go, Alan,' he told me a few weeks after Arthur's murder. 'One more year of nurse-maiding the

165

King and I shall take Marie-Anne and the boys to Locksley and never stir from there again.'

'If John keeps his word,' I said nastily. Robin scowled at me.

'He'd better. For, if he doesn't, I'll set you on him.'

There were no repercussions from the deaths of Humphrey and Hugo, which I found a little strange. The King seemed to accept the premise fed to him by Robin that they had gone over to the enemy, as had so many other men already, and the next time the King was drunk, Robin told me, he fell on his neck, crying that Robin was his only true follower and wailing on about treachery in those closest to him.

The murder of Arthur was another matter. Word spread fast that the Duke of Brittany, John's nephew, had been slain – some said by John's own hand – but, of course, there was no proof of his murder. The only living witnesses to the crime were Robin, myself and the King. Robin had impressed on me the importance of keeping silent on this matter, and I had agreed reluctantly. So the disappearance of Duke Arthur remained a mystery. The Bretons were certain that John had killed him, or ordered his death, and were incensed. Their depredations on the western border of Normandy, and in the south, where they had joined forces once again with the Lusignans, increased in violence and frequency. Worse than that, any chance John might have had to make peace with them, even a temporary truce, so that he could concentrate his force against King Philip in the east, was long gone. In Rouen, and in English court circles, the name Arthur was never mentioned. Not once. But King Philip, the sly dog, from thenceforth insisted that before there could be any negotiations over Normandy, John must produce his prisoner and demonstrate to the world that Arthur was alive and well.

This was plain mischief-making on Philip's part – the French King knew well enough that Arthur was dead; he had scores of spies in Normandy, according to Robin, and even if he had not, the steady stream of knights going over to his side must surely have told him much about the rumours of the young Duke's fate.

With Norman support for John seeping away, and the opinion of Christendom against him for the murder of his nephew, and with the Bretons and the Lusignans resurgent in the west and south, King Philip felt strong enough to make his move. In the middle of August, a travel-grimed horseman on a lathered horse clattered into the courtyard of Rouen Castle. Robin and I were giving his sons a lesson in swordsmanship, when the messenger arrived. And Robin hurriedly sheathed his blade, strode over and seized the horseman's bridle.

'What news?' my lord said.

'I must speak to the King,' the man said.

'He is still abed. Tell me, and I will wake him.'

The man looked surprised for it was long past dawn, almost midday.

167

He stammered, 'The King must know . . .' and stopped. 'What is it, man?'

The messenger mastered himself, swallowed and said, 'King Philip is marching, with all his knights, all his strength.' He stopped again. 'Philip is in the Seine Valley, not twenty-five miles from here, outside Château Gaillard with thousands of men. This time he is in earnest. This time he truly means to take the Iron Castle.'

Part Two

Chapter Twelve

I returned from Kirkton yesterday, a sadder and wiser man. I have discovered the nature of young Alan's disgrace and the reason why he was expelled from the Earl of Locksley's household. It is over a woman – not a villein or a common trull, not some drunken tavern slut, but a yeoman's daughter from Stannington. Her father, Godwin, is a freeman of some property; he holds several decent-sized sheep pastures, and according to the Earl is a most respectable fellow, strong, healthy, sober and hard-working and much liked by his neighbours; his wife is a large woman, cheerful and kindly. His only daughter Agnes is, like her name, as mild as a lamb, but as beautiful as the dawn, with golden hair of surpassing brightness and a loving disposition. Apparently, young Alan met her while out hunting with the hearth knights of Kirkton – some of the drunken louts who now infest my guest hall – and he was charmed by her grace and beauty. He visited her several days running with his fellows and she gave the young noblemen some refreshment after the heat of the chase – ewes' milk and bread and cheese – but behaved entirely modestly, her family insist. The Earl told me my grandson formed some sort of attachment for this girl, who cannot be more than seventeen, and took to visiting her in the evenings, over several weeks, riding miles across the Locksley valley to spend a few moments speaking with her, feigning to have a great fondness for her ewes' milk.

Well, it seems that they did a little more than talk and drink milk. For the girl is now six months gone – and her father is a very angry man.

Godwin came to see the Earl a few weeks ago with the complaint that one of his knights had besmirched his daughter's honour and got her with child. He threatened to take the matter to law, to the King himself, if necessary. It was clear from the guilt written on his face that the culprit was young Alan – and he swiftly admitted it. Godwin suggested sensibly that the young couple be married, and the Earl gave his blessing to the match, but Alan flatly refused to take the girl as his wife. When the Earl insisted that Alan reconsider taking this Agnes as his bride, Alan was apparently extremely discourteous to his lord, grossly rude, in fact, and gathered his belongings and left the Earl's service the same day.

I pondered this problem over a late supper, saying nothing to young Alan, and retired to bed. Not long afterwards I heard the drinking songs begin in the guest hall, the calling and shouting of young men sounding strangely like the cries of fear-maddened farmyard animals. I tried to stop my ears to their youthful din. In vain.

A little before midnight, when sleep had eluded me for several hours, I finally released my temper. I pulled on my boots and an old cloak and went out into the darkness. I ripped open the door of the guest hall and found my grandson and his playmates in a disgusting state of drunken disarray. The young men were evidently playing some game that involved repeating a long and complicated series of phrases, and the punishment for any mistake was to down a brimming beaker of wine. Naturally, the more wine consumed, the harder it is to remember the phrases – a deeply stupid pastime, in my opinion. Alan himself was declaiming something about a cardinal as I burst through the door roaring for them, in the name of God, to be silent. I am not proud of myself, but after a good deal of shouting, all of it from me, and mostly concerning the state of affairs in the guest hall night after night, the embarrassed giggles turned to sheepish looks in the circle of young men. I told the boys that, while it had been a pleasure to be their host – a damned lie – it was time for them to leave Westbury, and I would be most grateful if they would pack up their traps and leave by noon the next day.

At which point Alan stood up and complained that I was being most unfair. These were his bosom friends, he told me, and if I did not treat them with the honour due to noble guests, then I was also slighting him.

To my shame, I told him to shut his stupid mouth – what did he know about honour? I asked. Nothing. I told him that when he inherited the manor of Westbury – if ever he did – he could do as he liked, he could carouse himself to death, and play silly drinking games for as long his liver could stand it, but while he remained under my roof . . .

To cut an embarrassing tale short, I made a spectacle of myself – a foolish and ranting old man, his skinny, scarred and wrinkled body clad only in boots and braies and a billowing cloak. The only excuse I can offer is that I was truly angry, and with the last of my midnight ire, I ordered Alan to come and see me the next day the moment he had bid farewell to his unwelcome friends. We had grave matters to discuss, I said. Then I retired to my hall and my bed.

Silence reigned.

I was rich, I was young, I was a warrior at war – and so, after sending a goodly amount to Baldwin at Westbury, I took some of the hoard of silver that I had accumulated in the past year and commissioned a full suit of mail from the armourers of Rouen. I took possession of it at the beginning of August: chausses that covered me from toe to thigh in a mesh of round iron links and attached to a belt around my waist. The belt and the leather straps that held up my chausses were covered by a knee-length mail hauberk, which protected my thighs, belly, chest and the full length of my arms; the hauberk even included leather-palmed mittens to protect my hands. A separate coif, a metal-link hood that laced up at the back and attached to the neck of my hauberk, protected my skull, and a new flat-topped steel helmet went over the top of that, secured by laces under my chin. The helm covered my entire head with just a pair of slits for the eyes and a breathing grille over my nose and mouth. It was formed in the shape of a boar's mask, and had engravings of boar's tusks on either side of the short tubular snout. I loved that helmet – although it was rather heavy – it looked bold and fierce and offered almost complete protection for my head in battle.

I also had three new triangular shields made up, oak-framed and faced with slats of flexible elm, light and strong, and covered in tough ox-hide and painted with my device of the walking boar in black on a red field. I ordered a dozen twelve-foot wickedly tipped lances and purchased a new long sword and dagger for Kit. I had a new delicate edge ground on Fidelity and the blade oiled and polished, and a new handle fitted to my misericorde, as the old one had begun to rattle loosely on the tang.

When I strapped Fidelity around my hips and admired myself in a mirror of polished steel that belonged to Marie-Anne, I hardly recognised the pig-faced monster who glared back through the eye slits of my helm. Here is the true warrior, I said to myself proudly, let his enemies tremble.

Kit was even more enamoured of my new warlike finery than I was, which was just as well, as he would have charge of it and the responsibility of keeping it clean, oiled, rust-free and ready for battle, and I am certain that when I was engaged elsewhere he would try it on and strut and pose as I had in front of the mirror.

The only drawback was the weight – in full mail, I was carrying forty pounds of metal on my body, and while cinching the hauberk tight at the waist distributed it more evenly, I was still slower than usual when I moved; indeed when Kit and I exchanged a few passes in the courtyard of Robin's house, I was hard-pressed to keep his blade from slipping through my guard. I was used to fighting in only a hauberk and a plain light helm, but the new chausses and the fancy head-covering added twenty pounds in weight to my ensemble. However, even if an enemy did pierce my guard, he was unlikely to be able to pierce my flesh, protected as it was by a thick skin of fire-hardened iron and steel.

I wore ordinary clothes – a woollen tunic, hose and boots, and a dark-green cloak – but slung Fidelity at my side, when I went with Robin to a conference called by King John for his senior commanders the day after we heard the news that Philip had marched. I had protested to Robin that I had no wish at all for the society of the King, but my lord insisted.

'You must let the Arthur thing go, Alan. Really, it has been four months now. I need you with me – you are my right hand; if I fall, you need to know all our plans and stratagems in the minutest detail so you can command the Wolves.'

Reluctantly, I agreed, though I vowed not to speak to the King.

We met in the great hall of Rouen Castle, which had been emptied of all furniture save for a broad trestle bearing a square box filled with sand. The King was peering at the sandbox with that old warhorse William the Marshal at his side pointing out several features contained within it. A few of John's household knights were gathered round, as well as several of his mercenary commanders, men I knew by sight but generally avoided on principle as their reputations for brutality and vice were even more unsavoury than Robin's. The King was speaking when Robin and I entered the hall, and I caught the end of his sentence.

'. . . just like Mirebeau. Fast and deadly, the two arms acting together as if controlled by the same mind.'

The Marshal scratched his grizzled head. He was frowning down at the sandbox.

'Sire,' he said, 'these things can be very difficult to execute in the field. I know from experience. Perhaps if we devised something a little more simple . . .'

'Nonsense,' huffed the King. 'It will be child's play to accomplish for any half-decent commander. Ah, there you are Locksley, just in time. I have had a superb idea to remedy the situation at Château Gaillard. Marshal, perhaps you would care to explain it once again now everybody is here.'

I walked over and looked into the sandbox and saw a crudely drawn model of the lands around Château Gaillard, with the Seine snaking through the middle. The Iron Castle was marked in the centre by a square block of limestone the size of my fist, and to the west of it, a tongue-shaped piece of land, made by a loop in the Seine, appeared to lick at the stone battlements. The Isle of Andely, a boat-shaped island in the middle of the Seine a few hundred yards downstream, or north, of the castle was marked, as was the walled town of Petit Andely, just to the north of the stronghold; and, as a line of pebbles, a bridge that linked town and Isle and the tongue of farmland. As I looked at the map, a host of memories came flooding back. I felt the loss of Richard most keenly then, and not for the first time I cursed the cruel fate that had taken him and left us with this murderous creature for our King.

'As we all know,' William the Marshal began, 'Philip has brought his army up the left bank of the Seine, in an attempt to capture Château Gaillard. His host, some two thousand men, was encamped here initially.' The Marshal poked a calloused finger into the tongue of land to the west of town and castle, the broad flood plain on the other side of the Seine.

'We believe,' the Marshal said, 'he aims to throw a noose around the castle, cut it off from all help and starve it into submission over weeks and months.'

There were a few mutters and mumbles of assent from the knights around the sandbox. It was the wise thing for Philip to do.

'Roger de Lacy, who commands Château Gaillard and the surrounding defences, is, as I'm sure many of you are aware, a most brave and competent knight. He has not been idle: when Philip's host was first sighted, de Lacy destroyed the bridge connecting the Isle and the east and west banks, which meant that for some days Philip was blocked by the river, unable to cross the water and attack either the small wooden fortress on the Isle or the town of Petit Andely, or indeed Château Gaillard itself. For a while, the Seine acted as a huge moat keeping the French on the western bank, away from our walls. But Philip's a competent fellow, too, and it seems he is serious about taking the Iron Castle.'

'That cannot be allowed to happen,' interrupted the King. 'All of you must understand this: Château Gaillard cannot be allowed to fall to the enemy!'

'Quite right, Sire,' said the Marshal. 'Quite right. If we hold Château Gaillard, we hold Normandy. But if it falls . . .'

'Explain my plan, Marshal,' said the King. 'Go on, tell them. Tell them.' His face was alive with enthusiasm, like a child who thinks he has been especially clever.

'To replace the bridge that de Lacy destroyed, King Philip has constructed a pontoon using flat-bottomed river craft mainly, lashed together, but with larger ships on each end, on which he has raised defensive towers. Our scouts report that the new floating bridge is positioned here.' The Marshal indicated a point beyond the northernmost end of the Isle of Andely. 'And since its completion, Philip has been able to cross the river with his best troops and invest the fortified town of Petit Andely, here.'

The knights and barons all leaned forward to peer at the sandbox.

'As far as we know, the town is holding out, aided by some brave knights from the castle garrison, but when Philip gets the bulk of his troops across the river, the town will fall and our men must retreat to Château Gaillard itself.'

The assembled men muttered and huffed at this open talk of defeat. But the Marshal was still speaking: 'That mighty fortress, however, will not fall. Château Gaillard can stand firm for months under siege because it was designed to do exactly that. It has layer upon layer of defences to ensure that no attacker can even get close – furthermore, Roger de Lacy has sworn on his honour to hold it in the King's name until the sky falls. He says he will not quit the castle until he is dragged out of there by his feet at the tail of King Philip's horse. And he will hold it, too, because apart from his courage and determination, he has large stocks of food, plenty of water and a full garrison – forty knights and some three hundred men-at-arms, but—'

'My plan, Marshal, tell them my plan!'

'Yes, Sire. His Royal Highness has wisely decided to fight hunger with, um, food. He intends to send a relief convoy of seventy barges filled with wheat, barley, oats, cheeses, oil, wine and so on to Château Gaillard. If the provisions can be got into the castle, the siege is over. If the barges get through, there would be enough food for the garrison to hold out for a year or more, and even Philip with all the resources of France at his fingertips cannot sit outside the walls that long, the risk of disease is too high – his men would soon be dead or dying of the shivering sickness or the bloody flux if they were to sit there for a year twiddling their thumbs. Desertion would be a worry as well – his proud knights would grow bored and impatient after months of inactivity. Many would go home, promising to return if battle loomed. Philip's army would drain away like water from a leaky bucket. He would look like a fool, too, sitting there doing nothing month after month, waiting for de Lacy to feast his way through his vast piles of stores. Philip cannot stay before the walls of Château Gaillard for a year. So, if the convoy gets through, he will most likely pack up and go immediately. Food is the key. If the food convoy gets through to the castle, at one stroke we will have won the battle.'

'But if the French hold both banks of the Seine,' said Robin, speaking for the first time, 'and this ingenious bridge of boats blocks passage of the river here' – he pointed with his finger to the thin line in the sand north of the Isle of Andely – 'how can we possibly deliver these vital stores to the defenders?'

'Good question, Locksley, very good question. And to answer that the King has come up with a bold plan. It is this: a dual attack on the French positions by land and by water, at the same time. I will lead a small force, four hundred men in total, south from Rouen by land, overnight, down the left bank of the Seine. We will march fast and attack the main French camp on the tongue of land to the west of the river, here. If we are swift, we shall be among them before they know we are coming. By all accounts, Philip's best knights are across the river attacking the town of Petit Andely, and we face a camp full of *ribaldi*, hangers-on, washerwomen, merchants, whores, beggars and other rascally types that follow an army wherever it goes. It will not be difficult for us to prevail. We aim to smash through the camp and swiftly capture this boat-bridge – and utterly destroy it. Leaving Philip's knights on the eastern bank cut off from supplies, servants and baggage. Meanwhile, the river convoy, with three hundred men under your command, Locksley, will be approaching upstream and once we have cleared the bridge of the enemy and destroyed it, you will sail south of the Isle and moor the food barges at the quay directly below Château Gaillard. The garrison will come down to meet you and help unload the stores. The French at Petit Andely may try to interfere, but you will have your famous Company of Wolves to hold them off until the cargo has been safely delivered. Once the castle is filled to the brim with provisions, it can easily hold out until . . . oh, I don't know, until Judgment Day, or at least until Philip realises he has lost this contest and slinks back to Paris.'

I looked at Robin. He was frowning at the King.

'Sire, have I this scheme correctly?' my lord said. 'You plan for two small forces, a few hundred men in each, one coming overland and the other upriver by boat, to depart Rouen and arrive – simultaneously – a few hours later at a spot twenty-five miles away as the crow flies, and twice that distance by water, in the dead of night. Is that it? And the rendezvous you have chosen is a heavily fortified bridge held by hundreds, perhaps thousands of French knights, who also hold both banks of the river. Have I grasped the essence of it, Sire?'

'Exactly, Locksley – it is a stroke of genius, don't you think?'

It was a stroke of lunacy, to my mind. Robin seemed to agree.

'Sire, would it not be better, perhaps, to make a simpler plan. If we took all our combined strength and attacked Philip on land and in daylight, I am certain we could surprise him, destroy his camp and drive his men off without too much—'

'This is the plan,' interrupted the King, his voice becoming harsher. 'It is a most excellent plan and it will succeed. You will make it succeed, Locksley, or I shall hold you responsible. I will be obeyed in this matter. Do you understand me?'

Robin let out a hissing breath. 'As you command, Sire,' he said.

The King nodded once, decisively, and stalked from the

chamber, followed by his closest household knights. It felt as if, with his departure, a window had been opened and clean, fresh air were rushing in to fill the room.

'We will go tomorrow night,' said the Marshal. He looked around the room at the doubtful faces of the remaining knights and the mercenary commanders, and his eyes narrowed. 'A word of caution to everybody. Do not speak of this to anyone but your most trusted comrades. We do not want word getting to the French. We must have surprise. Right. Dismissed. Locksley, would you stay? I need to discuss a few fine details with you.'

I left Robin and the Marshal in deep conversation and went back to my lord's house alone. I told Kit we'd be taking a journey by river, and there would be some hard fighting but, although I trusted my squire with my life, I followed the Marshal's instruction and was vague about the exact particulars of our mission.

I had a cold feeling in my stomach the rest of the day.

The next night, at a little after midnight, I found myself crouched in the bow of a sixty-foot trading barge at the head of a vast convoy of some fifty or so boats, large and small, being rowed very slowly up the Seine by three hundred Wolves. On the prow of the boat, Robin stood, peering into the darkness, his green cloak fluttering out behind him in the breeze off the water. He was lightly dressed for one going into battle: a simple domed helmet with a nose guard, a knee-length mail hauberk, kite-shaped shield, leather gauntlets reinforced with iron and riding boots. At my shoulder sat Kit, who was fidgeting with the toggles of the padded gambeson that he wore as much for warmth as for protection. Around his waist were strapped the new sword and dagger I had given him. I was resplendent in full suit of mail, with heavy boar's mask helmet in my hands, but I was feeling less like a glorious knight and more like a nervous nun or a stripling going into a fight for the first time. We had until dawn to reach the bridge of boats under Château Gaillard, perhaps another five hours, but we were still more than thirty miles away and while the oarsmen heaved valiantly, our progress against the heavy current was snail-like.

Just before dawn, the Marshal had decided, was the perfect time to attack the French camp. The enemy would be asleep, and he and his knights, and an attached force of mercenaries, should find it easy, he said, to carve through them and reach the bridge by first light.

But we in the food convoy were going too slowly, the pull of the river flowing towards the sea was too strong. We had only just passed the town of Orival and the first great bend of the river, seventeen miles upstream from Rouen – one third of our journey – while we had used up half the time allotted to us. When I mentioned this to Robin, he smiled serenely.

'I'm sure it will not matter if we are a little tardy, Alan. Once the bridge is destroyed and the river cleared, we can sail past whether it is dawn or noon.' But I noticed that he passed orders down the convoy for the speed to increase.

Hour after hour we slogged, the river black around us save for a speck of light here and there from a small castle or watchtower on the bank. As the first streaks of grey touched the eastern horizon, I could make out the bridge at Pontjoie directly ahead and knew with a sinking heart that we still had five long miles to row. By the time it was fully light we could make out the tinny sounds of battle, distant cries and clashes, and see a thread of smoke rising to the south – for the convoy was running north-east along the river on the tongue of plain where the Marshal's men, only a mile away overland, were engaging the enemy.

It is rare that I have the chance to observe a battle as an impotent spectator. As we rounded the bend of the river, with only two miles to go, I saw the Marshal had been as good as his word and the French camp on the western bank was ablaze – I saw little stick figures of men on foot and a-horse running hither and yon between the burning tents and rough shelters. Clumped bodies littered the green turf.

Horsemen surrounded the few groups of armed men still resisting and mercilessly cut them down; a stream of raggedy folk, many of them women with infants, was already fleeing west. The smoke billowed thick and black, jewelled with bright red and orange sparks.

It seemed we were winning the battle for the camp.

The Marshal's men were fighting on the bridge, too. It was an extraordinary structure, as I could now see, with boats of every description lashed together in a solid barrier directly across our path, and two high towers mounted on round sailing ships at either end. I could make out hundreds of tiny figures struggling at the centre of the bridge, which bucked and writhed under their stamping feet. I could hear the ring of steel, the shouts of combatants and the screams of the wounded. Dead and dying on both sides tumbled from the bridge, sucked into the water, never to be seen again. Horses screamed and plunged with their hapless riders into the pinkish foam. French crossbowmen from the tower on the sailing ship at the eastern bank were raining down quarrels on to the middle of the pontoon, on to the heads of the struggling men, it seemed indiscriminately, killing both the attacking Normans and their fellow Frenchmen.

Then the deadly crossbow assault abruptly ended and a thirty-strong *conroi* of French knights, on big horses with bright pennants fluttering from couched lances, shouldered their way on to the eastern end of the bridge and came to a clattering canter on the wooden pontoon. I could clearly hear their war cries as the *conroi* surged forward and ploughed into the knot of struggling men, driving them back, skewering mail-clad bodies on the tips of their long weapons. The charge of the knights was halted by the heavy press of men – but only briefly. Spurs gouged horses' flanks, drawing blood that showed crimson on the pale cloth trappers of the French mounts. The long lances reached out, lunging and stabbing at the enemy. More Frenchmen cantered across the jouncing bridge, adding their weight to the writhing pack at its centre. Which was slowly, slowly being driven backwards. The Marshal's brave men held on, and more of their comrades charged on to the bridge to add their weight to the mêlée. For a few moments they held the French counter-attack, even pushed it back a few yards. The dead were falling like scythed barley, toppling and splashing into the blood-churned river. But there was soon no doubt about the outcome: the Marshal's attack had been halted, checked and was now slowly being repulsed. Like a plug being popped from a flagon of wine, the French horsemen surged forward, shouting triumphantly, sweeping the living and the dead out of their path. The Marshal's men were no longer hurrying on to the bridge to join the fray; indeed, with a cold pool forming in my belly, I could see the hindmost men were beginning to turn and run, skirting the inferno of the French camp away into the fields beyond.

We were still half a mile away – and the golden orb of the sun was clear of the hills to our left.

'Faster men, row for your lives!' Robin was bellowing to the convoy that straggled out behind our lead boat. I stood and loosened Fidelity in its scabbard. And to my dismay saw the last of the Normans being pushed off the bridge by the irresistible charge of the knights. And more

188

enemies on foot rushing on to the bridge from the French side, scores of them. I could make out William the Marshal's personal standard, a red lion rampant on a split field of yellow and green, and a tall knight roaring and trying to rally the last of his men, screaming for them to join him in one last desperate attempt on the bridge. But it was too late: the pontoon was intact, and once again in French hands.

'Robin,' I said. 'Do we go on? Do we go back? What?'

'We'll just have to take the damn bridge ourselves,' my lord said.

'Are you serious?'

'The King has commanded it. You heard him. He will be obeyed in this matter. It's time for us to earn our pay.'

The French were all the way across the bridge and flooding back into their burning camp. I saw the Marshal's flag departing westwards with a handful of other mounted men, and scores of running foot soldiers discarding weapons and fleeing for their lives. There were cries of jubilation from the victorious French. And the sound of singing. The land-based attack had failed to take the bridge.

Our river-borne attack was about to begin.

Our approach had hardly gone unnoticed. It was full daylight by now. We were two hundred yards from the bridge, with our exhausted rowers at the last of their strength, hauling on long pine oars to bring us into battle as swiftly as they could. The French men-at-arms, shouting defiance, now lined both banks. The bridge, too, was packed with men, and the gleam of steel danced across the water towards us in the morning sunshine.

Then the crossbow bolts began to fly.

A man on the port side just behind me screamed and slumped over his oar, an evil black shaft sticking out from his neck. Another quarrel skittered on the wood of the deck at my feet. Missiles were boring in from both sides of the river, and from the bridge before us. Men were screaming as the quarrels struck; others were shouting war cries. Our craft were still pulling forward on both sides of my barge and I saw a horde of eager faces in the prows of the leading boats, as the Wolves readied for battle. Axes and swords glittered. Here and there a man dropped back, an ugly quarrel sprouting from his torso. Kit beside me was shivering from cold or fear or both; he had his drawn sword in his hands.

'Sir,' he said, his voice shaky and high, 'we can do this, can't we? We can take that bridge? There seem to be so many of them.'

I gave his shoulder a squeeze then swiftly pulled on my new boar's helmet. Immediately, my vision was narrowed, my peripheral sight extinguished, by the two eye slits. I felt Kit's fingers fumbling with the leather laces to secure the helm under my chin. I could see nothing but the looming bridge directly ahead and the hundreds of enemies, some bloodied from combat with the Marshal's men, jeering, waving swords and spears. A hundred yards to go. Robin was standing high on the prow like a pirate, sword sheathed and a long yew bow in his hands. As I watched, he drew a shaft from the quiver at his waist, nocked it and loosed and I saw the black line of the arrow arc up and down and slam into the chest of a man-at-arms on the pontoon, knocking him back into the press of his fellows. Robin loosed again, and another Frenchman died. Other bowmen among the Wolves were loosing too, dozens of shafts soaring high and smashing into the waiting ranks of the enemy. But the French were taking their toll on us, too. Crossbow bolts whipped and cracked all around, swooping down from the high tower on the eastern bank of the pontoon bridge – now just fifty yards away. I got to my feet and felt my own legs trembling. Thirty yards to go. A quarrel thwacked into my shield and I tucked my shoulder and as much of my body as I could into the lee of its protection. Another iron-tipped missile screamed off my helmet. Twenty yards. I mumbled a prayer to St Michael, the warrior archangel, begging him to keep us safe. Ten yards. Five. Then, with a crash of timbers and a deafening roar from defenders and attackers alike, the prow of our boat smashed into the lashed craft of the bridge.

Robin leaped on to the pontoon, his bow abandoned, and his naked sword swinging like a scythe, taking the head clean off a yelling Frenchman. Wolves were jumping from their vessels to get at the French above them. But just as I readied myself, a boat from our own convoy racing in behind hammered into our stern, and I was knocked from my feet. The boat swung round, side on to the bridge, and as I scrambled to my feet, almost blinded by my helmet, a screaming man-at-arms jumped down onto the deck and lunged at me with a spear. I took the point on my shield and Kit cut the legs from under him with a sweep of his sword to the back of his knee, a move we had practised endlessly in the courtyard at Falaise.

I struggled to the prow, my movements slow, my armour weighing down my limbs. I felt as if I was wading through cold honey, as in one of those dreams where everything moves at a crawling pace. I bent my knees and leaped upwards, landing heavily on the deck of a wherry lashed in its position in the bridge. Two men were jabbing at me with spear and sword. I killed the swordsman, Fidelity breaking his neck, but the spear crunched hard into the iron mail guarding my belly. I was winded but not pierced, thank God. I stepped past the spear shaft and killed the man at the other end, crushing his skull with one heavy blow through his thin helmet. I shoved another man backwards with my shield, trying to make room for the Wolves to come up beside me on to the bridge, and stepped into the press, stabbing, cutting and slicing into the wall of men. There were enemies shouting and jostling all around me. But there were cries, too, of 'Locksley! Locksley!' coming from behind me that fired my spirits. I was dimly aware of Kit to my left, his sword jabbing forward again and again. I cut down a man-at-arms on my right;

I blocked a savage mace blow from a knight behind him, shoved the tip of Fidelity through his open visor, punched it home, and he fell away screaming. I felt my familiar battle rhythm coming to my rescue: cut and shove, and thrust and slice; sword and shield acting together in a perfect marriage, as the good Lord intended them to, to batter and pound other lesser men into submission. I hacked and cut. I cursed at my enemies as I killed them, and trampled their bodies under my mail-shod feet as my bloody sword rose and fell.

I glimpsed Robin not three yards away, protected by four Wolves who held off a wall of enemies as my lord sliced with an axe at the cables connecting the bridge of boats. A man leaped at me screaming and I dropped him with a straight lunge that cracked through his ribs and into the bloody cavity beyond. He fell gurgling, dragging my sword arm down. But there were two more of his fellows behind him. I ducked the first sword strike, blocked the second with my shield, hauling Fidelity with some difficulty free of the chest of the dragging corpse. And then . . .

And then something heavy smashed into the side of my helmet – I knew not what – and I staggered back a pace or two. My vision dipped and swam; streaks and flashes of red and black. The world was slowly revolving. Something shoved hard against my shield-side. My bloody sword was flailing madly in empty air. I stepped back another pace . . . and into the void. And, dream-like again, I felt myself falling, falling for eternity. For hours I hung between the wood and the water, or so it seemed, before splashing into the cold, shocking embrace of the river. My helmet filled with water, my eyes, nose and ears terrifyingly awash. Down, down I plunged, sucked swiftly, head first into the cold, the darkness, into a frigid Hell. I managed to shake loose my shield, but kept a death-grip on Fidelity's hilt. My heavy mail pulled me down as if I was roped to a millstone. I kicked my legs in desperation, clutched at the river with my free hand, grasping, scooping, trying to lift my body, but to no avail. I sank deeper, my lungs burning for air, the pressure unbearable but growing ever more powerful. My belly twitched; I had to breathe. My whole body craved the air with a desperate, total necessity. But the icy darkness had me firmly in its possession. The ancient waters claimed me. And I yielded to them. I opened my mouth, the river rushed in and all the world turned black.

Chapter Thirteen

'Be silent,' hissed Robin. 'Be silent or you will get us all killed. Be quiet, Alan, or I swear that I will cut your miserable throat myself and quiet you for good.'

I realised I had been babbling, shouting even. I coughed weakly, then vomited a scalding gush of brown water out through my nose – but as quietly as I could. The sunlight dazzled my eyes and my head was thumping like a war drum, but I could just make out the scowling face of my lord, inches from my own. And someone else supporting me under the armpits. I turned my head painfully and saw Kit's anxious young face peering into mine. I was shoulder-deep in water, I realised, but I could feel mud and loose stones under the soles of my feet, and there was a greyish wall of bare chalky earth before my nose. Above me drooped the thin branches of a young ash tree, and long nodding strands of yellow grass and mature nettles forming a canopy, with the sun shining through and making weird patterns on Robin's face. We were at the riverbank, and I was not dead. I opened my mouth to ask why – and Robin put a hard hand over it and glared at me from his slate-grey eyes; ordering me silently to save my breath. Above I heard the quiet chink of metal on metal, a heavy footfall and a squeak of leather. A horse whinnied softly. Two yards to my left a sword suddenly slashed through the covering foliage from above, once, twice.

'There is nobody here, sir,' said a voice in thickly accented regional French, barely comprehensible as that language at all.

'Be quiet, Gerard, I thought I heard a cough.' This voice was refined, educated, a knight's for sure. It was strangely familiar.

'The bastards must have drowned, sir. If they fell off the English boats they would have sunk like stones in their mail. No man could have made it this far alive.'

'Maybe Gerard, maybe. I just had a feeling, you know, as if a goose walked over my grave. Perhaps I am wrong.' The knight moved in his saddle and again I heard the leather protest at his shifting weight.

'There's no one here, sir, I'd swear it before God himself.' A sword stabbed downwards through the ash leaves inches from my nose and disappeared again.

'See? Nobody here, sir.'

'Very well, Gerard, we'd better get back to camp.'

I was certain then that I knew the owner of the knightly voice.

As the sound of horse and man receded, I removed Robin's hand from my mouth and gently parted the leaves very slowly, just a little, enough to catch a glimpse of the rider – blond, youngish, bareheaded, straight-backed, in a suit of costly mail – walking his horse away along the path by the riverbank.

It was my cousin Roland.

The appearance of Roland was less of a shock than being alive at all. It added to the weird dream-like air of that waterlogged morning. In the next few days, indeed, I wondered whether he had merely been a phantom of my half-drowned mind. Robin, if he recognised my French kinsman, whom he knew well, made no comment on the matter, and neither did Kit. But it was perhaps not so bizarre to encounter Roland at this place. I knew he served the French King; his father, my uncle, the Seigneur d'Alle, was one of Philip's more powerful barons. And we knew that Philip was here with his best men. But I had prayed I would never meet Roland again in battle; both of us knew our duty to our lords outweighed our duty of kinship. It had been agreed between us many years before that if we were to meet in these circumstances, despite our affection, indeed, our love for each other, we would each fight with all our strength to overcome the other in a fair and honourable fight.

However, all thoughts of Roland were gradually washed away in the course of that long, pain-filled day. We dared not stir in daylight hours, for the French were patrolling the riverbank looking for survivors, and every few moments, it seemed, another party of marching men-at-arms or a *conroi* of cantering knights passed only feet away from our hiding place. We spoke in whispers as we waited – hour after hour, up to our necks in cold water and shivering beneath the cover of the ash tree – for the sun to go down. My headache seemed to grow ever worse, a white-hot spike through my temple, and I was dizzy and weak and fought the urge to vomit almost constantly. A day has never seemed so long in my recollection. It crawled. I suffered. The sun seemed to be nailed in position, fixed high in the blue sky.

I had the story of my reprieve from death that day, in short hurried whispers from Robin, between passing patrols. A French knight wielding a poleaxe had struck me a savage blow from behind on the side of my helmeted head – I could feel the tender egg-sized lump above my ear – and I toppled off the boat-bridge into the water. Fortunately for me, I fell near a sandbank where the river was not more than ten feet deep, and even more fortunately, Kit saw me fall. He called out to Robin, who was being driven slowly and surely back to the boats by the ferocity of the defenders, and my squire quickly divested himself of his gambeson and dived in after me. It took some moments of desperate groping in the mud and muck of the riverbed to find me and haul me to the surface, and when we were both in the blessed air, floundering on the surface, and sinking again under the weight of my mail, Robin spotted us and leaped from a departing boat to help my squire keep my unconscious body afloat in the churning, corpse-clogged waters of the Seine.

The convoy had been seriously mauled, with more than half of the men killed or wounded, Robin told me. When it became obvious there was no more to be gained, that the French were too many, my lord had given the order for the few boats that remained intact to withdraw. Even that did not stop the slaughter; for the enemy followed in captured vessels, and from behind and from both river-banks poured volley after volley of crossbow bolts. It was, Robin told me frankly, a catastrophe. Hundreds of our men dead or wounded, a fortune in provisions destroyed or captured, and absolutely nothing achieved.

I was deeply touched that Robin had given up his chance of escape to rescue me from drowning, but when I told him so, with sincere gratitude, and tried to thank him properly, he looked away and merely said gruffly: 'What would I tell Marie-Anne? That I sat in the boat taking my ease and calmly watched you drown? She'd never forgive me. Besides, if I went back to Rouen, the King would likely make me shoulder the blame for this bloody shambles – he'd have my head on a spike. It seemed a much more pleasurable option to take a refreshing dip in the river with you two.'

He could joke all he liked: I knew that Kit could never have saved me alone and that, once again, Robin had risked his life to save mine.

So here we were, huddled under a young ash on the eastern bank of the Seine, up to our armpits in muddy water, exhausted after a long night and a short battle, and my head feeling as if it were about to split in two. We had been swept some five hundred yards north of the pontoon bridge, seven hundred yards downstream of the Isle of Andely and its brave little wooden fort, and about a mile distant from Château Gaillard, which could be glimpsed through the grass like a great greyish-white mountain rising to the south-east. It happened that I knew this landscape well – I knew that between us and the safety of Château Gaillard lay the besieged town of Petit Andely.

The town was well defended, however. The Gambon and the Andelle flowed into the Seine at that point and Petit Andely had been built between these two rivers so that it was bordered on all sides with water. A stout stone wall surrounded the town, too, inside its flowing natural moat. With a determined commander and enough men, it should be able to hold out against the French for some time. But, in the end, it would be no match for Philip's artillery, his feared trebuchets, mangonels and assorted heavy petraries, the stone-flinging engines known collectively as his castle-breakers. Once the French set their minds to it and began a concentrated bombardment, Petit

Andely would fall in a matter of days. However, Château Gaillard, half a mile south, was another matter. Even though we had failed to deliver the convoy of food, it remained a mighty fortress, well defended by nature and man; I was confident that even without fresh supplies it could still hold out for many months against the wrath of King Philip. We would be safe there.

Robin seemed to be thinking along the same lines. 'We must wait till nightfall, then make straight for the castle. Vim is there with some of the Wolves – we will be among friends. But we must loop inland around the town, avoiding the enemy before its walls. Are you fit for a night march, Alan? A couple of miles and then spiced wine and a heaped platter of roast pork with old comrades inside the walls of the Iron Castle. How does that sound?' He smiled devilishly.

I tried to shrug nonchalantly. But I was shivering so hard I am not sure if Robin recognised the gesture. When I tried to nod my head, it felt as if my brain was about to shoot out through my eyes. Yet I was fit enough for the march, I told myself, I must be: I had merely taken a knock to the head. I had suffered far worse in the past. I was, however, curious about two shallow wounds under my chin, dagger cuts they felt like, to my questing hand, and still bleeding.

'I beg your pardon, sir, I truly do. But that was me,' said Kit. 'I had to get your helmet off and the quickest way was to cut the ties with my knife. You were unconscious, sir, but we were being thrown about in the water something

201

awful. I am most sorry, sir, and I confess I dropped the helmet, too. Your lovely helmet . . .' My squire looked heartbroken.

'I could not give a fart for that helmet,' I lied. 'Or a few scratches. I owe you my life, Kit. You have rendered me fine service and I will never forget it.'

'Well, while we were rolling about in the water, I did just manage to keep a grip on this, sir,' said Kit, brightening a little, and he lifted a dripping hand above the surface to display a magnificent sapphire encased in a silver ring, a wire-wrapped handle and a steel crossbar, and the top of a blade, shining wetly.

'Fidelity,' I murmured as if greeting an old friend – and, in a way, I was.

After an eternity of shivering, cramping and red waves of pain between my ears, when it seemed I had spent most of my life in the water, I saw by the sun that it was almost noon. But the sky I noticed was darkening. I wiped a hand across my eyes and wondered if the blow to my head had affected my vision. Then I saw it was smoke. A thick grey plume, boiling upwards from the south and filling the sky. Robin cautiously poked his head out of our hiding place and reported back that the small fort on the Isle of Andely, a few hundred yards upstream, was ablaze. 'You see, Alan, there are worse places to be trapped than at the water's edge. I'll wager any of those fellows roasting in that fortress would swap places with us in a heartbeat.'

I tried not to think about the score of poor souls caught in that inferno. But all afternoon we smelled the acrid smoke and heard the screams of pain and the distant almost musical clash of metal. And it seemed the French were not content with having seen off our botched attack; nor with reducing the island fort to smoking rubble – they were determined to take all the outposts of Château Gaillard in one fell swoop. For at the close of day, only a little before Vespers, I judged, we began to hear the distinctive crack of flung stone on wall, and after another cautious reconnaissance by Robin, learned that Philip's engineers had two big mangonels set up, playing on the town of Petit Andely.

At long last, night fell. Yet we waited another full hour in the water, at Robin's insistence. And as the moon began to rise, when we finally crawled from our hideout on to the rough dry grass of the path, I found my legs had lost all feeling. With Kit's help, in a thick patch of cover a hundred yards back from the river's edge, I finally stripped off my chausses, hose and hauberk, and set them on a low hanging branch to drip, while we all took turns massaging each other's icy legs and feet. I could have slept then and there for a week, but at Robin's gentle urging I struggled to my feet and, swaying, only half-aware, dizzy with pain from my head, I stumbled after my lord as he led the way due east up a chalky path to the crest of a low hill that overlooked the town. To the south and south-east, I could see the campfires of the French in a ring around Petit

Andely. Across the black river, a ribbon of orange torches marked the span of the pontoon, and on the far bank the main French camp sparkled with a hundred pinpoints of light. A broad, sullen red glow in the centre of the Isle was the only memorial to the men who had died in the defence of its fort that day.

The hours that followed have mercifully leaked from my memory. I followed Robin's broad back, blindly, silently, stopping when he commanded, starting to march again at his order. Kit came behind me, carrying my heavy mail armour bundled up in a wet cloak, and my weapons too: Fidelity and my old misericorde. I travelled almost naked and unarmed, barefoot and wearing only braies and a chemise, like a trusting child; but I do not think I could have fought off a petulant field mouse in my state of feverish exhaustion. At one point I recall crouching numbly in a patch of tall marsh reeds as a French patrol passed across our front. I had a powerful, insane urge to call out a cheeky greeting to the enemy as if we were playing some harmless school-boy's game, but mastered it, just. Next we were splashing through water up to our waists and I thought we were back in the Seine. But no, we reached dry land soon enough and were climbing a steep rocky road, deeply rutted with the tracks of many heavy carts, and the castle walls looming impossibly high and black before us; then came a sentry's shouted challenge and Robin was calling out his name and rank, and there was the blaze of blinding torches and friendly faces, and the jostle of mailed men, and hard slaps of welcome on the back. And then nothing.

Chapter Fourteen

I watched the fall of Petit Andely from some four hundred feet above it, from the north tower of the outer bailey, which also happened to be its easternmost, two days after Kit, Robin and I were admitted to the Iron Castle. I had slept for most of the intervening time, and eaten like royalty, and I had finally managed to, shake off the monstrous headache that had bedevilled me since the day in the river. I was, in fact, feeling reasonably fit. The top of the tower was crowded – not least because most of it was filled with a large war machine affectionately named Old Thunderbolt.

Eight feet long and three feet wide, Old Thunderbolt was a kind of gigantic crossbow, known as a springald, which could hurl a lethal yard-long iron bolt weighing a good five pounds. It was powered by two bow arms, encased in twisted sinew, which were winched back by its handlers, before the bolt was slotted into its groove and loosed at the enemy. It was big and clumsy and slow to load – but I was entranced by it. Aaron, the sergeant of engineers who was its master, a dour Yorkshireman who barely spoke, muttered two words to me, when I asked about its purpose: 'Knight killer,' he said, and nodded as if that were plenty of information for the time being.

Philip's mighty castle-breakers – massive stone-throwing machines with twenty times the power of Old Thunderbolt – had been set up on the far side of Petit Andely, about three-quarters of a mile away. From there they systematically destroyed the northern walls of the town. I had slept through the worst of the bombardment, but the steady crack-crack, crack-crack of boulders smashing against the remains of the town's flintstone and mortar walls could clearly be heard even from my vantage point. The broken walls crumbled at each strike and the rubble toppled and rolled down the slope to fill the waterway that was the town's main protection. I could see battles of men-at-arms, hundreds of them, forming up in the open fields beyond Petit Andely, not far from where Robin, Kit and I had spent that long, awful, water-logged day. The foremost ranks of Frenchmen carried vast bundles of straw or great baskets of loosely woven twigs filled with earth – and it was clear that very soon they would be given the order to advance and would hurl their burdens into the moat before the town and create a temporary bridge. Behind the footmen were several *conrois* of knights and mounted men-at-arms, perhaps a hundred riders in total, the colourful trappers covering the horses' bodies and the fluttering lance pennants giving these well-mounted killers a surprisingly festive air.

The town itself was in turmoil, the narrow streets and small squares filled with panicking people hurrying about with large packages; there seemed to be a profusion of handcarts, too, piled high with bundles and being wheeled every which way, creating blockages by their sheer numbers. The bells of St James were ringing out in alarm, as if the townsfolk needed to be told that the end was near.

'Vim's down there somewhere,' said Robin, who had appeared beside me. 'And fifty of my Wolves.' I merely nodded but I could see there were still disciplined soldiers huddled bravely on the battered ramparts, tucked down tight with shields over their heads, and men-at-arms collected together in squads of ten or so below the walls, waiting to repulse the attack when it finally came. In the square next to the church, a small group of mounted men had collected and I could see they were being instructed by a knight in a red surcoat. It was too far to make out the face of the knight but something about him struck a chord. Robin must have seen me frowning and peering at the distant figure, for he smiled at me knowingly and said, 'You know that

Sir Joscelyn Giffard has been given command of the town, don't you?'

I looked at him in astonishment. He continued to grin at me as I asked. 'His daughter, the Lady Matilda, is she in Caen or . . .'

'She's not in Caen. And she's not down there among the ville folk, Alan. Do not worry yourself.' And because he had a cruel streak that I knew all too well, he let five heartbeats pass before he said, 'She is snug right here in the castle. I saw her in the great hall this very morning. I must say she seemed to be glowing despite our difficulties, in very fine looks indeed, in my opinion.'

I was saved from having to reply by a faint roar from the assembled ranks of the French beyond the town. I could hear trumpets and drums and the thin notes of whistles, as the whole mass of men, perhaps five hundred in all, began to move forwards towards the River Andelle, their bundles of straw and baskets of earth brandished before them. The attack on Petit Andely had begun.

I do not know what I was expecting. A heroic defence, perhaps, with the remaining men-at-arms in Petit Andely bravely rushing to the breaches now the artillery bombardment had ceased, filling the gaps with their bodies, their courage and their naked steel, and stemming the screaming horde of Frenchmen as they hurled their burdens into the moat and splashed across the makeshift causeway to climb the piled rubble that had once been the town walls. In fact, I was indeed expecting something like that. Or at least some sort of attempt to resist the enemy. What happened left me gaping in surprise. The moment the French signalled the attack, the gates of Petit Andely on the southern side, furthest from the assault, swung wide open; the drawbridge was swiftly lowered to cover the river-moat on that side, and the *conroi* of knights and men-at-arms I had seen in the square rode out of them. Then these thirty or forty men lined up on either side of the road to the castle and turned to face outwards. Through the gates of the town poured the entire citizenry of Petit Andely: men and women, grandmothers and tiny children, servants and squires, craftsmen, peasants, beggars, priests, whores . . . The whole population flooded out, hundreds upon hundreds of people, with their bundles and baggage, handcarts and packhorses, and this vast herd of humanity began to scramble up the winding chalk road towards the castle. A surprising number kept on coming, steaming through the gates, between the lines of mounted men who stood guard over them against roaming French cavalry, scrambling, running, pushing and shoving, every soul making his or her way up towards the safety of Château Gaillard.

Beyond the waves of refugees surging up the hill towards us, in the centre of the town, there was some sporadic fighting. Here and there swords flashed and knots of men struggled against the French who were pouring into Petit Andely through the breaches in the northern walls. I saw patches of grey wolf fur and knew that Vim's men formed the rearguard, and those brave men I had known in Rouen and Falaise were dying by inches to allow the townsfolk to escape.

Robin had disappeared from my side, and I saw him striding across the courtyard of the middle bailey towards the gatehouse, roaring at the men-at-arms there to open the gates. I looked back at the town of Petit Andely and saw that it was almost completely overrun by the enemy now. Wolves and a few mounted men-at arms were urging the last of the stragglers through the open gates, fending off the bolder foes who menaced them. But, for the most part, the French men-at-arms let the townspeople depart in peace, quite unmolested; they seemed content to revel in their effortless possession of this rich Norman town. For once the fires that invariably accompany the sack had not been kindled, the French could be seen rushing here and there, their arms filled with booty, kicking down doors, no doubt marvelling at what they had captured at so little cost. They had stormed almost undefended walls and earned themselves a town devoid of souls but filled with costly goods: household furniture, fine tableware, rich cloths and draperies, silver pots and copper pans, barrels of wine, dried hams, wheels of cheese and all that could not be easily carried away.

In contrast, when I next looked down at the middle bailey of Château Gaillard, it was a babbling sea of humanity, packed as tight as a shoal of fish caught in a purse net. Almost all the former denizens of Petit Andely, some two thousand souls, had come to claim their right of protection in their lord's castle.

I must tell you a little of the dispositions of the Iron Castle, its precincts and halls, its walls and towers, its tricks and secrets. For in those days I knew it as well as I know Westbury. One must remember that this castle was the pride and joy of King Richard: perhaps the greatest achievement of his short and glorious lifetime. He built it fast, in a little over two years, but he built it well. The lionhearted king lavished more treasure on this one castle than on all the others combined. It was the jewel in his crown; he loved it, and even playfully referred to it as his daughter – and he used all the vast store of military knowledge he had accumulated in thirty years of warfare from Aquitaine to Acre to make it impossible to conquer.

First, its positioning: it was perched high on a great limestone outcrop, fully three hundred and fifty feet above a broad loop of the Seine. The outcrop ran north-west to south-east, with the wide river below the north-western battlements. There was no attack possible from that side as sheer cliffs dropped from the battlements to the grey waters of the Seine. Indeed, the land fell away from the castle steeply on all sides, but the gentlest slope was at the far end, the south-eastern face, no more than a saddle of land between the walls and a low hill. This being the most obvious point of attack, King Richard had doubly fortified it with an outer bailey roughly triangular in shape and separate from the main castle. This outer bailey had five high towers and eight-foot-thick walls, and just by itself this bastion was as tough a nut to crack as many a fully grown castle. It was connected to the castle by a retractable wooden bridge, the idea being that if this bastion were to fall, the enemy would be no further forward in conquering the rest of the castle. This outer bailey was where Robin and I – and Vim, who arrived grinning and without a scratch after the retreat from Petit Andely – and eighty surviving Wolves had been lodged on our arrival by Roger de Lacy, Château Gaillard's constable.

The retractable bridge over a deep dry moat led from the outer bailey to the middle bailey. This formed the defences of the castle proper and was roughly circular in shape, though the circle was a little flattened; again it had been built to take a battering, with thick walls and high towers and a formidable square gatehouse in the east, which formed the main entrance to the castle as a whole. The courtyard of the middle bailey held a well that provided an inexhaustible supply of sweet water; and it had deep and spacious underground storehouses clawed out of the soft limestone, and many wooden buildings erected around the walls to provide shelter and accommodation for a multitude of horses and men-at-arms. There was also a latrine block and, rather scandalously, a small chapel that King John had caused to be built on top of it, as well as blacksmiths' forges and huts for armourers, fletchers, brewers, a bake house, several kitchens and even a wine seller's counter under a striped awning that proved popular with off-duty knights.

If the middle bailey was deemed a difficult fortification to take – and, believe me, it was the envy of the greatest castle-builders of the day – the inner bailey was even more formidable. Set to the rear of the middle bailey, and protected not so much by very thick solid stone walls as by a series of linked D-shaped bastions – so constructed as to shrug off the pounding missiles from enemy petraries like water off a duck's back – the inner bailey was the kernel of the castle, its core. But even that was not the final redoubt, for inside the inner bailey was a tall, high tower, with the thickest walls of any in the castle: the keep. This was built *en bec*, that is shaped like a teardrop for extra strength, and it was where the defenders could finally seek shelter if, by some malign trick of fate, the outer bailey, the middle bailey and the inner bailey were all somehow to fall. The keep had its own stock of food and water in casks sealed with lead and wax – enough to keep fifty men alive for three months.

This was why Château Gaillard was the greatest fortress in Christendom: as well as the great difficulty of attacking the place due to its formidable natural features, it had an astonishing four layers of defence that an enemy had to batter through before it would fall. King Richard was justly proud of it; King Philip justly in awe. You will remember that Philip had boasted he could take it if its walls were made of iron; and Richard had boasted he could hold it if its walls were made of butter. Yet they were not butter, but two layers of vast, well-cut, oblong-shaped limestone blocks, an inner and an outer wall, with the gap between them filled with flint, chalk and rubble, and the whole bound together by a strong sand, lime and clay mortar. The walls of Château Gaillard could easily stand up to months of cruel battering by the mightiest castle-breakers and, more importantly in my view, they were defended by good fighting men who understood their business as well as any.

Lord de Lacy gathered the inhabitants of the castle together in the open air of the courtyard of the middle bailey the day after Petit Andely was lost. With the massive influx of folk, there was not room enough for every man to find a place to stand and men hung from cresset hoops in the walls and perched on the roofs of the stables, kitchens and barracks to hear his words.

'People of Petit Andely,' he bawled, to make himself heard over the tumult of the crowd. 'I bid you welcome to this castle and say this to you all: fear not the anger of the French. Our fighting men are most valiant. Our walls are impregnable. Our storerooms are full. They shall never subdue us – never!'

He paused to allow the shouts from the multitude to subside a little. And they did become quiet – or as quiet as any crowd of two and a half thousand souls can be.

'We have the strength, we have the will, we have

the courage to hold this castle and, by God, we shall hold it until this French rabble before our walls is dispersed.'

Roger de Lacy raised a hand in the air and pointed a finger north-west. 'Our sovereign lord, King John himself, will never allow us to be defeated. Even now, he is mustering his armies, gathering his loyal men, and he will ride to our aid and crush our enemies like ants beneath his boot heel. Our task, and the task of every man and woman here, is to stand fast, to keep our courage high. We must keep the faith, keep a good watch from the walls, and put our trust in God and good King John!'

It was a short speech, plain but powerful – much like its maker. I must admit I was more than a little moved by it. Kit, standing beside me, had tears in his eyes when it was done. I noticed even Robin was smiling quietly as he listened to de Lacy's stirring words.

Afterwards de Lacy paid us the honour of a visit in the outer bailey. He strode into the circular hall on the second floor on the big south tower, the largest chamber in the bailey, which Robin had appropriated as his headquarters, and formally bid us welcome before briskly making it quite clear what our duties would be.

'This bailey is your responsibility, Locksley, you and your rascally Wolves. I can give you a few extra men-at-arms from the garrison, and some engineers for the springald, but you must defend this bastion against all they can throw at you. You must hold it.' He fixed Robin and me in turn with his hot brown eyes to make sure we understood.

'This, most likely, is where the hammer blow will fall,' he said. 'And you must suffer it, and repel them with all your strength. I'm counting on you – both of you. For if we can hold this bailey, if we can hold out *here*' – he stamped a mail-shod foot on the wooden floor planks – 'I truly believe we can hold Château Gaillard for the King until the Heavens fall.'

The constable's words were put to the test the next day. For the French, flushed with pride with their victories on the pontoon, against the little fort on the Isle of Andely and by the easy capture of the town itself, came eagerly to attack our walls.

Chapter Fifteen

They did not attack the outer bailey, as we expected. Indeed, when they came they did so without science or skill, straight up the path to the main gate in the middle bailey in a sprawling horde. I believe a good many of the men who came against us that day were drunk, either on wine looted from the town or merely on the joy of victory.

The first I saw of it was a crowd of men-at-arms gathering and being harangued by a pair of energetic young knights in the wide hollow between the river and the gates of the town, at the bottom of the chalk track that led up to the castle. King Philip was not present; I am not certain he even knew about this attempt on our walls, for I could see his banner flying in the French encampment on the far side of the Seine.

Nonetheless, many hundreds of men-at-arms had been collected together and were milling about at the north-eastern base of Château Gaillard, a mere four hundred paces away as the eagle flies, and a hundred paces beneath us. Many were drinking from looted earthenware jugs and big leather mugs; some quaffed straight from small kegs of wine, splashing their faces red with the liquor. The two knights took turns to speak, standing on a barrel so as to be seen, their arms waving towards the castle but their words indecipherable. Priests and monks passed through the throng, giving out blessings and anointing the men with holy water. I could easily imagine the well-worn message the knights and clergy were delivering – that all the vast riches of the town, wealth beyond the dreams of avarice, was now inside the castle; that the English defenders were demoralised, broken and weak after their recent defeats by French prowess; and that God, of course, and all the saints in Heaven were on their side.

I was looking down on them once again from the north tower of the outer bailey, the tower that guarded the narrow oak door that was the only way into our detached bastion, with Robin, Kit and two dozen archers from the Wolves. Aaron and his engineers had, on Robin's instructions, dismantled Old Thunderbolt and moved the unwieldy springald and its stand of massive iron bolts to the south tower, which formed the apex of the triangular shape of the outer bailey, so as to make room for the Wolves, who were now stringing their six-foot war bows and selecting their straightest, sharpest and best-fletched arrows.

After more than an hour, in which I watched the enemy drink and shuffle around each other and shout out threats and curses and occasionally listen briefly to the exhortations of their betters, they began to straggle up the hill towards us around the middle of the afternoon. Drunk or sober, they were still brave men. The two knights came first, with fifty well-mailed followers in a tight pack around them, and then came the rank-and-file men-at-arms in a loose and disorderly mob several hundred strong. Among the foremost of the tight knightly group, I spotted ten men carrying between them a large, iron-capped tree trunk, with crude handles carved into the wood, and six men wielding long axes.

They began to die a hundred yards from our walls. Before they had even reached halfway up the chalky track, the arrows and crossbow bolts of the garrison were falling thickly upon them in a killing rain. There had been no attempt to disguise the point of attack nor to provide the attackers with any more protection than their armour and the shields they carried, and they died in their scores as the steel-tipped yards of ash from Robin's bowmen punched through mail as if it were linen, and the quarrels driven by powerful crossbows from de Lacy's men in the middle bailey sank into arms and legs, piercing torsos and skulls, and nailing fallen men to the earth. From my post, I could clearly see blood gouting from almost every strike, and a handful of men dropping, wounded or dead, at each beat of my heart as they slogged up the steep path, still shouting and waving their weapons, through a dense cloud of destruction. Every half-decent bowman in Château Gaillard, that sunny September afternoon, killed and wounded and maimed to his heart's content. I even heard Robin's archers calling out targets to their fellows and wagering on a hit or miss. By the time the French came within thirty yards of the main gate, their numbers had been thinned by perhaps half, and skewered bodies and broken men were sprawled everywhere, and still the black missiles whizzed and thumped home and the running men spun and dropped, coughing blood from pierced lungs, tugging at transfixed limbs and crying out to God. The lead knight, a bold fellow if ever there was one, was thickly feathered, sheeted in his own blood, yet he urged the men onward to attack the gate. The bravest man among brave men. But the gate was narrow, built of foot-thick oaks reinforced with five fat strips of black iron, and de Lacy had more than a hundred men-at-arms on the walls above it, in the gatehouse itself and in the two round towers on either side, hurling javelins and spears and huge rocks down on the unfortunates below. More than a few able-bodied townsmen had joined them, taking revenge for the loss of their homes. Skulls were crushed like dropped eggs, strong backs were impaled by spears, bones snapped and flesh was ripped by spear and quarrel. From the outer bailey, Robin's archers poured one withering volley after another into their flanks, the destruction truly terrible to see; they nailed enemies' bodies one to another with their wicked shafts.

Through a murder hole directly above the main gate a gallon of boiling oil sizzled down on the half-dozen souls below who were desperately battering at the oak with the ram. The men around it screamed like the souls in Hell as oil many times as hot as boiling water splashed down upon them and seeped through their ring-mail to scorch the skin beneath. They dropped their burden, stumbling blindly away, the skin of their faces sloughing off like melted butter from a skillet. Then the French force broke; they ran blindly from the pain and death, falling down the track, jumping, tumbling, down and away, leaving more than a hundred bodies in the lengthening shadows below our walls.

We lost one man, a young townsman killed by an enemy crossbow at the fiercest pitch of the fight. Another half-dozen took scratches, bruises and minor cuts – some of them inflicted accidentally by comrades in the fever of battle.

Morale is a strange beast. Before the French assault, I had seen the strain of fear etched on many of the faces of the Petit Andely refugees. After the attack failed, with the French lying in bloody, writhing mounds before our walls, the faces of the townsmen shone with joy and our men-at-arms walked with the swagger of merchant-venturers whose ships had just come safely home.

Robin did not seem affected one way or another. When I complimented him on the performance of his archers, he shrugged and said, 'Yes, they did well, kept their discipline. We'll see how they fight in a real battle.'

'You do not consider that battle to have been real?' I said, surprised at his dismissal of a bloody action, in which a hundred brave men had uselessly died.

'King Philip is over there,' he said, pointing across the river to the French encampment. 'He – the King of France himself, God's duly appointed prince on Earth – came here to take this castle, and he is not going to let one petty skirmish and the deaths of a handful of his men alter his intent. I think, Alan, you will find that we have many hard months ahead of us; with fighting of such ferocity that this little dust-up will one day seem like a jolly summer picnic.'

I looked at the heaps of dead and wounded before the walls, at the crushed heads, staring eyes, broken limbs and puddles of blood, and acknowledged the truth of Robin's words. This, I knew, was only the beginning.

'Be a good fellow, Alan, and take a squad down there,' my lord said, nodding at the carnage before the gatehouse, 'and gather up as many unbroken arrows as you can; cut them out of the bodies, if you have to. We are going to need every one.'

The French sent a pair of heralds the next morning, and two trumpeters as well, all dressed in blue and yellow and under the banner of the King of France, a gorgeous azure field covered in golden fleurs-de-lis. The party picked their way up the track on horseback, unmolested by our bowmen, and halted at a spot some twenty yards from the main gate, and the trumpeters formally announced their presence with an elegant but unnecessary fanfare – the walls of the castle were already thick with gawping men and Roger de Lacy himself was standing in the roof of the gatehouse, resting his hands on the breast-high parapet and looking out at the advancing foe.

'His Royal Highness, Philip Augustus, King of France, by the Grace of God Almighty, lawful overlord of John, rebellious Duke of Normandy, sends you his greetings,' intoned one of the heralds.

'And I, Roger de Lacy, Castellan of Château Gaillard, vassal of His Royal Highness King John of England, Duke of Normandy, return them,' said de Lacy. 'What is His Highness King Philip's pleasure this day, my noble lords?'

'The King instructs and commands you to take up your arms and all your goods and chattels, your servants and your animals and to quit this place and surrender it willingly to His Royal Highness by the end of this day. In doing so, you will earn his everlasting gratitude, and the favour of God Almighty for the lives saved and the blood not uselessly spilled over this matter. You will be allowed to ride from this place as free men, untroubled by our forces, with all your arms and your honour intact. But if you refuse, mark this well, the King bids me to tell you that his wrath will know no bounds and he will surely expel you and all your men by force of arms and there shall be no guarantee that any life shall be spared, nor that any man-at-arms however noble or exalted shall go unpunished.'

De Lacy frowned at the heralds. In truth, despite the dire threat to slaughter every man in the castle if it fell, it was a generous offer; a free pass to leave with honour. Many a man would have grasped at it; but de Lacy was cut from finer cloth.

'That, my lords, I shall not do,' he said gravely. 'My master King John has commanded me to hold this castle in his name against all-comers, and hold it I shall. I will never willingly surrender this place until I am dragged from it by my heels at the tail of the King's horse. That is my last word on this matter.'

The heralds nodded solemnly. 'If that is your last word, so be it. But first, our noble King craves a truce for this day, and this day only, until the hour of midnight to remove the bodies of his dead for burial and the wounded for their succour.'

'So be it,' said de Lacy. 'A truce until midnight.'

All that day parties of Frenchmen came up to the walls and carried away the dead and the few wounded who had survived the night. I saw the enemy men-at-arms stepping among corpses and looking curiously, perhaps fearfully, at our walls and more than a few jeers and jests were exchanged. But I had no time for taunting our foes, as I was busy as a bee at a task set for me by Robin – an examination of the defences of our outer bailey and an accounting of the stores of food and weapons at our disposal.

In the outer bailey we had one hundred and seventeen fighting men under Robin's command. They were mostly Wolves – and I was pleased to see so many familiar faces: Vim, Robin's mercenary captain, who had shed the drunken lassitude I witnessed at Christmas and seemed filled with a deep happiness by the imminent danger; one-eyed Claes, the vintenar who had fought with Robin and me in our southern adventure a few years before; Christophe Scarecrow, veteran of so many of Richard's wars. Little Niels, who was hanging off the battlements watching the French clear away their dead and wounded, called out to me as I passed through the crowded courtyard below with a vast armful of bloody arrows.

'Looks like we've won the battle, sir. Does that mean we can all go home now?'

'Everyone else can – but not you, Niels,' I replied. 'Get down here. Your job is to clean and sharpen these arrows. I want them spotless, properly dried and stacked in the armoury by sundown.'

'And if I do a right good job of that, sir, will you make me an officer?'

'No, Niels, I won't make you an officer yet – but I'll tell you what I will do. If you don't make a decent job of this task, I will shove my right foot so far up your little arse you'll be smelling my boot leather from now till Christmas.'

About half of Robin's men were archers; we also had thirty-one men-at-arms from the castle garrison, and half a dozen engineers who answered to Aaron. This would have made the outer bailey a snug billet in ordinary circumstances but, as well as the fighting men, it was crammed to the rafters with more than two hundred men, women and children from the ville. Each side of the outer bailey's triangle was only fifty paces long, and while there were three floors in each tower, and several wooden buildings in the courtyard that could be used to house folk, much of the space was occupied by armour, weapons, baggage and stores. In order to move around, I had to squeeze through men, women and children sitting on their possessions, not knowing what to with themselves. It was my job to feed them, find them places to sleep, and keep order. It was no simple task, I may assure you.

To begin with, I organised all the townsmen of military age into work parties and set them to clearing the rubbish and rubble from the moats around the outside of the outer bailey, and to deepening these dry ditches until they were at least three times the height of a man. There was a good deal of grumbling from some of the softer-bellied townsfolk, those whose previous occupations had not necessitated hard outdoor labour, merchants, shopkeepers and the like, but I put it to them in the most simple terms: if they did not work, they would not eat.

The women and older children were put to cleaning the outer bailey from top to toe, scrubbing every table and stool, every nook and store cupboard, even the stones of the floor and the walls themselves, with hot water and vinegar. For I knew that in such a crowded stew one of the worst dangers we faced was disease. The older folk, less nimble on their feet, and the halt and the lame, were set to mending the clothes of the soldiers and making bandages from old clean linen rags.

I divided the fighting men, excluding the engineers, into three watches of forty men. Several townsmen with a small amount of military experience had volunteered to join the defending force, taking our numbers up to more than a hundred and twenty men. I mingled the castle men-at-arms and the volunteers with the Wolves, and divided each watch into 'tower squads' – three squads of ten men, who were to man each of the three large towers, and two squads of five men for each of the two small towers. When their watch was on duty, they were required to man the roof of their towers and keep a sharp, sober lookout. Any man caught sleeping or drunk at his lookout post would be hanged, I assured them earnestly. It was Lord de Lacy's decree, not mine, but I meant to enforce it. So, at any moment of the day or night, one watch was on duty in each of the five towers, the second watch was in reserve, on stand-by, and the third watch was off duty, resting, sleeping or eating.

Each day every fighting man was issued a small loaf of

bread, a quarter pound of cheese, a quarter pound of butter, a cup of dried peas or beans and a pint of wine. Once a week they were given a pound of salted meat or fish and, of course, they could draw as much water as they liked from the well, which had been sunk an astonishing four hundred feet through the limestone rock, right down below the Seine. Each family of townsfolk, regardless of their number, received the same as one fighting man, but without the ration of meat or fish and with an extra loaf of bread. It was not a lavish diet, to be sure; we would be in no danger of growing too fat, but it should be adequate to keep us alive, active and in reasonable health.

I received a shock when I first reported to the quarter-master in his little shack in the southern part of the middle bailey's courtyard – for it was none other than Benedict Malet. I had not known that Hubert de Burgh's ill-favoured nephew was in Château Gaillard at all, let alone that he had been entrusted with such a position. For during a siege the role of quartermaster was crucial: he would control the distribution of the food supplies that would determine how long the castle could hold out.

It was an unpleasant shock to come face to face with the big, pimply fellow, particularly as I was there cap in hand to beg rations for the outer bailey.

He was sitting at a small square table inside the three-walled hut outside the underground storeroom, with a brimming cup of wine by his wrist. Half a dozen burly men-at-arms lounged beside the entrance to the store-cave, sneering at the crowds who thronged past – for the middle bailey, the heart of the castle, was even more crowded than the outer bailey – and Benedict looked up at me as I approached with a faint smile on his face. 'Ah yes, Sir Alan Dale,' he said, 'the common hireling who thinks he's a knight. And what can I do for you today?'

I swallowed my irritation. I would have to deal closely with this irksome fellow every day for the foreseeable future. I could not afford to let my temper get the better of me.

'Good morning, Sir Benedict,' I said, smiling amiably, if a little stiffly. 'I trust you are well. I have come today for the allocated rations for the outer bailey.

'Have you now?' he said, looking down at a sheaf of parchments on the table. 'What are you asking for exactly?'

'I have a hundred and twenty-one men-at-arms and forty-three households from Petit Andely in my ward, which means I need two hundred and six loaves of bread—'

'I have one hundred and seventeen men-at-arms here. What sort of game are you playing? Are you trying to hoodwink me?'

'No, four new men volunteered as men-at-arms—'

'If they are not on the list they do not receive rations. I'm surprised at you, Dale. I have had a number of grasping fellows trying it on already this day and it saddens me that you should think me such a fool as to fall for your exaggerated claims. I will not tolerate this sort of greediness.'

I knew he was being deliberately unhelpful. I gritted my teeth. 'I have a hundred and twenty-one brave men-at-arms serving under me—'

Benedict was rapping repeatedly on the table in front of him with the handle of his dagger. 'One hundred and seventeen men it says here on this list. No more, no less.'

'Who makes up the list?' I grated. I had a growing urge to snatch the dagger and jam it hilt-deep into his fat belly.

'The official list is made up by the bailiff of the castle, Lord de Lacy's right-hand man. Sir Joscelyn Giffard himself. And Sir Joscelyn has entrusted me with the important task of issuing the rations according to his official tally of fighting men.'

'Oh, Bennie, I'm sure Daddy wouldn't mind if you made an exception,' said a low, deliciously smoky voice behind me. 'Just this once. After all, we're only speaking of four extra men.'

I was then granted the stomach-churning spectacle of Benedict's expression changing from that of stern counting-house clerk to lovesick fool. His tongue slid out to lick his wide lips, his nostrils flared like a stallion scenting a mare in season, he flicked a lank strand of hair off his spotted forehead. His voice dropped and he said rather huskily, 'My lady, what an unexpected pleasure!'

I don't think I have ever wanted to stab someone more. The lady wisely ignored him. 'Sir Alan, what a wonderful surprise to see you again.' I turned to see a vision of loveliness beside my shoulder.

'Lady Matilda,' I said stiffly.

'Tilda, please,' she said, putting a small, cool hand on my sleeve and, as usual, roasting the bare flesh beneath the cloth. 'After all, we are old friends.'

She smiled. I lost all the breath in my body.

'Come now, Bennie, could you not unbend a little and grant Sir Alan his request? As a favour to me. I'm sure we can sort it all out with Daddy later.'

'Very well,' grumbled the clerkly oaf. 'Tell me again – what number of men are you claiming for, Dale?'

I walked from the store-cave with Tilda's hand still on my arm and Benedict's solemn promise ringing in my ears to have the stores delivered to the outer bailey within the hour. As we strolled around the corrugated walls of the inner keep, Tilda prattled on about 'Bennie' and what a fine fellow he was, but I only half-listened, merely gazing at her perfect face and the line of her white neck.

'. . . such a help, even if he is rather odd-looking. Daddy says he doesn't know what he would do without him. Certainly Bennie is always most obliging . . .'

'I thought you were going to join a nunnery,' I said, cutting through her prattle a little more abruptly than was polite.

'Oh yes, I am still destined for a life of service to God, everyone absolutely insists on it. But personally I feel more inspired by that famous prayer by Saint Augustine. Do you know it? "O God, make me chaste and celibate – but not yet!"'

She looked at me out of the side of her eye and I felt a stir in my loins at the thought of her being neither chaste nor celibate. I felt giddy: I did not know if I were more astounded by her outrageous comment or by the fact that a girl of nineteen could already quote the works of Saint Augustine by heart.

'So what happened?' I asked. 'I heard you were all set to join the sisters of Caen Abbey. Did you change your mind?'

'They expelled me before I even had a chance to take my vows. And all over a tiny little party. Can you imagine? At first I was such a good girl, so good – praying for the souls of the abbey's long-dead benefactors day after dull day, rarely indulging in red meat or decent wine, hardly ever skipping Mass. And then, after some months of this dreary existence, I decided I needed a little treat to raise my spirits. It was April and the anniversary of the day of my birth, and I crept out of the cloisters with two good friends of mine, novices like me, and we went to a tavern in Caen for a secret feast at midnight. It was so exciting!'

I was shocked. I knew she was forward, I knew she did not abide by the normal rules governing a lady's modest behaviour. I had seen that by her over-familiar behaviour towards me. But for a young girl, a novice nun at that, to go off to a low tavern unaccompanied – it was breathtaking. I gazed at her in admiration.

'Oh, Sir Alan, how we ate and drank and laughed; we made absolute pigs of ourselves – it was all perfectly innocent, just us three having a little fun, but then some musicians joined us – not grand *trouvères* such as yourself, Sir Alan, but a couple of jongleurs, handsome local boys who made up funny rhymes and sang naughty songs about love-making. We had a simply wonderful time and were back in the dormitory before Matins with no one the wiser – but do you know what? One of my friends on this jolly escapade, a silly goose called Emmeline, she took a fancy to one of the jongleurs, and she started writing him little notes and got back the most adorable love poems from him, really quite saucy. Soon she was arranging to meet him behind the chapel after Compline, that sort of thing. Well, never mind, a little harmless flirtation, you might say. But the stupid chit came to believe she had fallen in love with this penniless jongleur. She went to the Mother Superior a few weeks later and asked to leave the abbey. But what is worse, she confessed all. She told the Mother Superior about her lover and how she met him at my anniversary feast. Quick as lightning, all three of us novices were summoned, briskly interrogated and promptly expelled the very next day. Just for having a little party. It was so silly and unnecessary.'

'So have you given up the dream of a monastic life?' I tried to keep all signs of my soaring hope out of my voice.

234

Tilda sighed. 'My father has his heart set on it, and I want him to be happy, so I expect I will have to take the veil before too long. Your lord, the rather dashing Earl of Locksley, has been talking to Daddy about finding a place for me in a Cistercian priory in England. Somewhere in Yorkshire – Kirklees, I think the place is called. Do you know of it?'

I muttered that I had heard of it, and privately vowed that I would speak to Robin and make sure this little plan did not come to fruition. I had lost Tilda once to Holy Mother Church and I would not lose her again, not if I could help it.

We promenaded around the middle bailey and, like a foolish braggart, I tried to impress Tilda with tales of my adventures in the Holy Land and elsewhere. She listened attentively, but I was distracted, for it became clear to me that I was not the only man in Château Gaillard entranced by Tilda. A least a dozen of the men-at-arms grinned broadly at her as we walked past, calling out friendly greetings, winking and snatching off their headgear; and three of the garrison knights bowed low as we passed, one of them – a Gascon, I believe – even going so far as to kiss the tips of his fingers. Tilda responded beautifully in a friendly, sober, courteous manner.

For my part, I glared at them and wished them all to Hell.

Chapter Sixteen

After the initial botched and bloody attack at the beginning of autumn, there was little fighting for almost a month – a few exchanges of arrows from the battlements when the French approached too near, and a party of knights who rode up to the walls and challenged our best men to single combat. But de Lacy said he would hang any man who took up their offer and the French rode away disappointed, calling us cowards.

However, King Philip was far from idle during this time. Indeed, he and his men stirred themselves to great feats in the art of warfare – which, in truth, meant great feats of digging.

A small hill to the east and slightly to the south of Château Gaillard, just out of bowshot, suddenly became a hive of activity in the second week in September. Hundreds of workmen, or perhaps men-at-arms stripped of weapons and mail, swarmed over it and began to dig a trench a dozen feet deep around its circumference. I was watching them from the top of the south tower of the outer bailey with Aaron, the engineer, who was busy oiling the big ratchet on Old Thunderbolt. Their fervour was striking; I'd never seen workmen so possessed.

'Teams. Competing,' said Aaron and went back to his springald.

Vim strolled over from the other side of the tower where he had been joking with the members of the watch on duty. 'It's not just that Philip's barons have them divided up into teams competing with each other. They know that we have a few engines like this one' – here he gave Old Thunderbolt a slap, and earned a black scowl from Aaron – 'and the sooner they get those earth walls up, the safer they will be.'

'Could Old Thunderbolt reach them from here?' I asked Aaron.

'Waste of iron,' the Yorkshireman said.

'But we could attack them? We could impede them in their works?'

Aaron stared hard at me. Then he grunted at one of his assistants, who immediately came over to his side. As I watched, the two of them slowly and laboriously winched back the thick horsehair cord with a long lever, the pawl clicking loudly as it engaged with the ratchet. The two thick bow arms bent back towards the engineers, as they grunted and hauled, and it seemed to me that the entire wooden structure of the springald was quivering under the immense strain in the bow arms. Then they ceased their labour, mopped their brows, and Aaron set a yard-long bar of iron with a sharpened end, a thick ugly shaft, in the groove before the cord.

Aaron sighted along the groove, through the hole in the centre of the two bow arms. He said, 'Two spans left', and his assistant lifted the butt of the machine by an iron spike and moved it about ten inches.

I tried to peer along the groove to see exactly where the springald was pointed but Aaron said, 'Clear!' and Vim put a hand on my chest and moved me back out of the way.

'And loose,' said Aaron. The assistant tugged on a line, there was a sharp crack, the cord leaped forward and the bolt disappeared in a black blur. I saw it sail in a long arc and thump into the turf on the forward slope of the hill two hundred yards away, burying itself up to half its length about two dozen yards wide of a pair of workmen jogging towards the earthworks with spades on their shoulders. One of the men glanced round as the bolt landed but they didn't break step and carried on to their place in the diggings.

'Fifty, seventy yards,' said Aaron. 'Beyond that – pfft!'

'He could shoot at them all day,' said Vim, 'use up maybe two score of iron bolts, probably all his stores, and kill one or two men, if he was lucky. It's not accurate beyond fifty yards; beyond seventy you'd be fortunate to hit a barn door. You wait till they get a bit closer, Sir Alan – and they will come closer – then you'll see what he can do.'

I left the tower feeling chastened and went to join Tilda at Mass.

The chapel was a wooden cube perched atop the stone privy block on the south side of the middle bailey. It was reached by a set of stairs beside the latrines. Vim once joked that it was a perfect arrangement as one could attend one's bodily needs below and the needs of one's soul above. It was lit at night by fine beeswax candles and during the day the large barred wooden window shutter was flung open, allowing the sunlight to stream in and illuminate the handsome golden cross on the altar. It was unusually quiet inside, a place of peace, as only knights and senior officers were permitted to worship therein: rain or shine, the common people were ministered to in the open air of the courtyard.

It was a sunny Sunday morning. I stood next to Tilda in that calm and holy place, very conscious of her warm presence and the faint smell of roses that came from the perfume she wore. I tried to concentrate on what the priest, Father Pierre de la Motte, was saying but found I was distracted merely by the girl's presence. It was a saint's day, though I forget which one, and the priest was speaking about the poor man's particularly gruesome martyrdom long ago at the hands of a pagan Roman Emperor. Father de la Motte was a refined and aristocratic fellow from Rouen whose family's extensive lands stretched from Boulogne to Burgundy. I had met him only a few times and he seemed a rather ferocious character, tall, lean with hooded bright blue eyes that seemed to pierce your soul.

As the good Father droned on about the ultimate sacrifice every Christian must be ready to make for his faith, I snatched a glance sideways and caught Tilda looking at me with smiling, mischievous eyes. I looked away quickly, then back again to find that she was still eyeing me, with a slightly amused uptilt in the corner of her mouth. She discreetly mimed a yawn, rolling her eyes towards the priest. I fought the urge to laugh, almost successfully.

'And are you prepared, Sir Alan? Are you fully prepared?'

I tore my gaze from Tilda and looked towards the altar to find that Father de la Motte was addressing me. I had no idea what the priest's question meant. My mouth was opening and closing soundlessly like a fish.

Tilda saved me. 'Of course Sir Alan is prepared to die in battle for the sake of Our Lord Jesus Christ and the Christian faith. Of course he is. He proved his valour many times in the Holy Land during the Great Pilgrimage.'

I smiled gratefully at her.

De la Motte ignored Tilda entirely. His blue eyes seemed to be boring into my head. 'Are you truly ready to sacrifice yourself, my son?' he said.

'Oh yes, Father,' I said. 'Absolutely. Very keen.' I thought for a moment about what I had just said. 'Well, no, not actually *keen*; rather reluctant, if the truth be told. But, you know, if it were unavoidable, I suppose . . .'

The priest frowned at me. Tilda was now giggling uncontrollably, muffling her laughter with a lace kerchief.

The rest of the service was a blur of embarrassment. Tilda kept nudging me with her elbow and every time I looked at her we both broke into hysterical giggles. Mercifully it soon ended, and just as I was heading for the wooden staircase with Tilda, Father de la Motte called me back and asked to speak with me. I expected to be reprimanded for my unseemly behaviour, and I confess that I was more than a little nervous. He was more than a priest; his aristocratic background had earned him a place on the high council of the castle, the spiritual and temporal overlords of every soul inside its walls. Indeed he was third in the chain of command after Lord de Lacy and Sir Joscelyn Giffard.

In the event, Father de la Motte made no mention of our childish giggling and nudging. He asked about my family circumstances, my service in the Holy Land, and my duties in the outer bailey. When he found out that I had been charged by Robin with a thorough examination of the state of the defences there, he became deeply interested.

'And what, in your opinion, Sir Alan, is the condition of the mortar in the walls of the outer bailey?' de la Motte asked. 'I have heard it is as wet as custard in some parts. Is that so?'

I understood why he asked. A section of the walls in the outer bailey had recently been strengthened and when the outer shell of stones were removed by the castle masons, the mortar that bound the rubble in-fill between had been found to be still slightly moist. Indeed, just as in Falaise, it had been Christophe Scarecrow who had brought this substandard work to my attention. He blamed the masons who built the fortifications, at King Richard's orders, in such a tearing hurry. But he also told me the outer shells were perfectly solid. And he admitted it would probably stand up to a French assault, with a bit of luck.

I passed all this craft wisdom on to Father de la Motte.

'So in your opinion, they will hold when Philip manages to set up all his heavy artillery and the bombardment begins?' the priest enquired.

'On the whole, the Lionheart built this castle well, sir,' I told him. 'It should hold against the castle-breakers, or so my man assures me.'

Father de la Motte grunted and moved on to question me about the morale of the Wolves, the watch system I had instituted, the state of our weapons and armour, and the number of sheaves of arrows at our disposal. He even asked about the effectiveness and range of Old Thunderbolt.

The French dug and they dug. High earthen walls appeared around the little hill, pierced in only a few places by wooden gatehouses flanked by strong wooden towers. They were, in effect, building a crude mud castle in the hill.

We saw King Philip's blue and gold banners entering the earthen camp a few days later, now that it was fully protected from our missiles, and construction began of more permanent shelters than the damp, sagging woollen tents of the men-at-arms: barracks made of nailed planks and thatch. Next, timber stables and storerooms popped up like mushrooms after autumn rain inside that walled expanse of mud.

I expected the digging to cease then, but it did not. Our enemies were not content with protecting themselves with their earthworks, they also sought to hem us in by digging a long ditch and accompanying wall from the western end of Philip's Hill, as we now called it, all the way to the Seine; and another from the south face of the hill looping around to the south of Château Gaillard and joining the river there. These walls were manned day and night and high towers watched over us as well. We were cut off. Even if we had wanted to leave Château Gaillard, there was little chance of that now.

When the French earthworks were complete, around the first week of October, the heralds once again came to our gates with trumpets blaring and a flag of truce flapping in the chilly breeze. I did not hear the exchange, for I was on duty in the outer bailey, but Robin told me the sense of it was the same as before: Philip offering us one last opportunity to leave with honour and Roger de Lacy telling him he would not go from this place until dragged out by his heels.

I applauded the castellan's stand, but in my heart a seed of doubt was growing. I did not doubt we could defeat our enemies when they next came charging at our walls – but I was concerned that there was an invisible enemy already inside our fortifications whom we could never defeat: hunger.

It was Sir Benedict Malet who delivered the bad news to me in the second week of October, the day after the heralds' visit, when the first of the icy, autumn rains were lashing the castle walls.

'All rations have been halved, I am sorry to say,' admitted the pimply fat-boy, wrapped in a warm cloak, sitting snug and dry in his hut by the store-cave. He did not sound in the least sorry and I was not sure if I should believe him or whether this was, in fact, another of his attempts to irk me.

I snarled wordlessly at him.

'It is not of my doing, Dale. It is my Lord de Lacy's express command. With all these extra mouths to feed we have depleted nearly one third of the castle stores in a single month. If we continue like this we'll be starving by Christmastide.'

When I told Robin the news, he wasn't in the least surprised. 'Simple counting could have told you this already, Alan,' he said.

He had a bad head cold that day and was in a foul mood. 'We took in some two thousand people from the ville, and this castle was originally stocked with rations

244

for a garrison of three or four hundred-odd for a twelve-month. I'm surprised Lord de Lacy did not consider this earlier.'

Quite apart from his cold, Robin had another reason to be out of sorts. Despite his status as an earl, he had been excluded from the private discussions of the castle's high council: Roger de Lacy, Sir Joscelyn Giffard and Father Pierre de la Motte. While Robin was extended every courtesy due his rank – and had been given the outer bailey to defend on his own – he was not included in the major deliberations about the castle, Roger de Lacy told him, because he had no official status in the hierarchy. De Lacy, Giffard and de la Motte had been in the castle for some months before the siege began, and had formed an efficient triumvirate for its governance, while Robin, as well as being a despised mercenary captain (this went unsaid), was as much of a refugee as the townsfolk who flocked here a couple of days after we arrived.

I was mostly too busy to worry about Robin's nose being out of joint. As well as organising the Petit Andely folk in their tasks, and the fighting men's duty rota and over-seeing the distribution of the rations, I was determined to keep the sentries up to the mark. My secret dread was a surprise night attack by the French. I had had a dream in which a horde of dark, demonic, many-legged creatures swarmed up the walls of the outer bailey in the dead of night before the alarm could be raised.

I made a tour of the sentries every night before retiring,

reminding each of the dire consequences if they fell asleep. One night I came across Stefan, a blacksmith from Petit Andely who had volunteered to serve with the Wolves, and who was doing sentry duty in the small eastern tower. His four fellow members of the watch were in the chamber below huddled around a brazier, for the nights were chilly, and Stefan, a hairy man with forearms as thick as my thighs, was alone on the top of the tower. He was leaning out into the darkness, peering intently towards the French camp. When I came silently up behind him and tapped him on the shoulder he jerked in surprise and nearly fell over the parapet. When he had calmed himself, I asked if he had anything to report.

'I can't be certain, sir,' he said.

'What do you mean? Either you have something to report or you do not.'

'I think there is somebody out there, sir, but I can't be sure.' He pointed to the saddle of land between our walls and the French encampment on Philip's Hill. 'There, sir.'

I peered into the darkness and could see . . . nothing.

'What did you see?' I asked Stefan.

'I thought, sir, I saw something. A man, a hooded fellow, crawling towards us. Just a glimpse when the moon came out from behind a cloud and then it was gone.'

I strained my eyes and I was about to suggest Stefan took a turn beside the brazier, when I saw it. A long dark shape scuttling like a huge rat over a small rise and down into a hollow. And then it was gone.

246

I wondered if I had imagined it, and then knew for certain that I had not. It was a man, alone, as far as I could tell and he was heading stealthily towards us.

I shouted, 'Who goes there!' into the blackness, but received no response. I went to the far wall of the tower where a pine torch was burning, plucked it from its becket and, whirling it around my head, hurled it as far as I could. It sailed down and landed on the bare turf about twenty yards from the castle walls, creating a pool of orange light as it sizzled on the damp grass. As it landed I saw, once again, a shape moving swiftly at the very edge of the circle of light further into the shadows.

'What is it, sir?' asked Stefan. He looked extremely nervous.

'It is a spy, I think, scouting our walls. But I think we have scared him away for the time being. There is nothing to fear. I will send someone up to watch with you, two pairs of eyes are better than one, and if you see more of them sound the alarm.'

I trotted down the stairs and went to seek Robin in his chamber and ask his advice. But, though I searched the whole of the outer bailey, room by room, then went across to the middle bailey to enquire for him there, I could not locate my lord. After two hours of fruitless search in every hall and chamber in the whole of Château Gaillard, every nook and cranny, I was certain of just one thing.

The Earl of Locksley was not inside the castle.

Chapter Seventeen

The next morning he was back. I discovered Robin in one of the storerooms of the outer bailey, deep in conversation with Vim about the construction of makeshift javelins from old kitchen knives and arrow-straight willow wands, of which the grey-blond mercenary captain had discovered a bundle in the stores.

When I told him about the spy and my search high and low for him in the castle, he was irritatingly vague.

'I was here and there. I had some people I wanted to talk to. We must have missed each other in the darkness,' he said.

'But where exactly were you?' I pressed.

'I don't answer to you for my whereabouts, Alan. You serve me, remember. And you can't keep running to me whenever you see a ghost in the night. In my absence, you're in charge of the bailey. You have to learn to make decisions for yourself.'

I was nettled by his words but I could see he had no intention of explaining himself, and so I was forced to let it drop. And, anyway, soon his mysterious absence was completely driven from my mind.

I was sitting on a bench with Tilda at the wine stand in the middle bailey on a pleasantly dry but cloudy afternoon, taking a cup of wine and, at her urging, telling her all about my exploits at Mirebeau, when the first French missile sailed over the eastern walls and shattered against the inner bailey.

The middle bailey had been quiet, for it was the height of the afternoon and many people were sleeping after dinner, but there were still some two hundred people aimlessly moving about as there always were in our crowded community. When the stone ball smashed itself to shards against the wall above our heads, the air was suddenly filled with falling debris and flying splinters of sharp rock, and my immediate, unthinking response was to throw myself at Tilda, to shield her. My fifteen-stone body smashed into her slighter frame, knocking the wind out of her, and the two of us were carried off the bench to thump to the sandy floor of the bailey. I tried to land on my knees and elbows, but I still ended up with my body pressed hard over hers and the two of us lying one on top of the other, face to face, in the dust. Once she had got over the shock and surprise, Tilda began to laugh.

I looked around, still lying atop Tilda, waiting to see if there would be another missile impact, and found myself staring at a pair of mailed feet with silver spurs attached. I looked up the mail legs, past the flowing surcoat, and into the furious face of Sir Joscelyn Giffard. His hand, I saw, was clenched on his hilt.

'You, sir, will get off my daughter this very instant,' he said.

I did so hurriedly. Tilda was laughing harder than ever, almost weeping with mirth, as the knight reached down and took her hand and pulled her to her feet.

'Sir, I can explain,' I said.

'I will hear no excuses. I know what was in your mind! You filthy dog.'

'No, sir, you misunderstand; I was merely—' but I found I was talking to Sir Joscelyn's retreating back. He marched across the courtyard towards the gate to the inner bailey, where he and his daughter had their chambers, pulling Tilda behind him, the girl still laughing helplessly.

That single missile, lobbed by Philip's massive castle-breakers, was the only one to fall inside the middle bailey that day. I believe that something may have broken in the mechanism after that first loose, or the aim may have been changed, for we were not troubled inside the walls again for some days. But the outside walls began to receive a brutal pounding from that day onward.

From the north tower of the outer bailey, a little while later, I could look out at the tops of the three engines of the French over the earth walls on Philip's Hill, and also two smaller machines set up due east of us behind the earthworks that surrounded the castle. They loosed at us with a ponderous regularity, but without haste, each machine discharging its burden perhaps one or two times per hour, which was a rather slow rate compared with that which these machines are capable of. The French were in no hurry. They had time on their side. Sometimes an hour or two would pass without a missile being fired, usually around the middle portion of the day, at the dinner hour. In the later part of the afternoon the bombardment ceased all together. It was a somewhat lackadaisical way of proceeding against us, and I was reminded in contrast of King Richard's capture of the Castle of Loches in a single day, nine years before. But the Lionheart had twenty well-oiled war machines, huge numbers of missiles, and he urged on his engineers to loose as often as they could – and Loches was not nearly as strong as Château Gaillard.

Over the next few weeks some of the missiles fell short, a very few of the lighter stones sailed high over the ramparts and exploded against the walls of the inner bailey, but most crashed with dull regularity against the outer walls. Chips of stone would fly, a dent might be made in the limestone shell, but despite concerns about the mortar, the walls stood firm. Yet with each blow I could feel the castle become just the tiniest bit weaker, just a little more tired. People no longer strolled carelessly around the enclosures; they scurried, faces turned nervously towards the sky, hurrying across the open spaces. The most dangerous strikes – mercifully rare – were when the stone balls struck the wall-tops, splintering the galleries fixed there. When this happened there was a great danger of impalement by a shard of wood, some many feet long, not to mention being crushed by the missile itself. Whenever I walked along the top of a wall, I wore my shield on the outer side as an extra protection, although as Father de la Motte pointed out in a lesson one Sunday, it was all in God's hands. We lived or died according to His will – and it was arrogance to assume that we knew better than the Creator of the world.

Towards the end of October, when we'd endured two weeks of bombardment and about a dozen people, mostly townsfolk, had been killed or injured by flying splinters of wood or chips of stone, I was summoned to a meeting of all the knight commanders in the great hall of the inner bailey, tucked behind the keep.

As I entered the hall, Sir Joscelyn waylaid me, catching my arm. I blushed to the roots of my hair and was about to protest my innocence in the matter with Tilda in the courtyard, when he took the breath from my lungs with these words: 'Sir Alan, I have an apology to make to you. I have wronged you.'

I stammered something to the effect that it was a matter of no importance but Sir Joscelyn continued. 'No, I have been at fault. I believed the worst of you and I was wrong. Tilda has explained the matter fully to me and I see that you were acting solely from the most chivalrous of intentions, putting your body between her and mortal danger. I should have known you were a man of honour with no disgraceful designs on my daughter. I hope you will find it in your heart to forgive me.'

I assured him he was forgiven, but I could not look him in the eye when I said so. For the moment when Tilda's soft body was pressed under mine had been in my head and heart since that day, and at night I had been harbouring a host of disgraceful thoughts about this good knight's daughter. Yet we clasped hands and I told him I was happy there was no longer a misunderstanding between us.

There were about thirty knights in the hall that day, most of the men in mail and all serious-faced, as Roger de Lacy addressed us.

'Good sirs, I thank you for coming at this hour. But fear that I have some sad news to impart. We must cut the rations once again. From now on they will be issued every second day and there will no longer be a butter ration. The meat and fish issue is also discontinued, as from today. The meagre stocks of butter and meat that we have left will go to the sick and injured. It's clear that Philip means to remain before our walls all winter to starve us and we must ensure—'

'King Philip is no longer before the walls.' Robin's voice hacked through de Lacy's speech. 'He is back in Paris preparing for a fresh campaign in the south in concert with the Lusignans and he is organising support for the Bretons in the west.'

'But his standard—' de Lacy began.

Once more Robin interrupted him. 'Yes, the French royal standard still flies above Philip's Hill – but it is a ruse. The King departed in secret nearly a week ago. But your premise is correct. The French do intend to remain here all through the winter. They believe we will succumb to hunger long before spring.'

'How can you know this?' Roger de Lacy seemed utterly astonished by Robin's revelations. In truth, I was, too.

'I have been inside their camp, several times; I have sat by their fires and gossiped with their men; I have eaten their pottage and drunk their wine. I have listened to their complaints, laughed at their jokes and shared all their tittle-tattle.'

'Why did you not inform the high council that you were undertaking these irregular and, if I may say so, ignoble activities?' De Lacy was angry and he showed it. He had been made to look a fool. 'You have acted no better than a common spy.'

'I have brought back valuable intelligence,' said Robin. 'If you will not include me in your deliberations with regard to the fate of this castle, I do not see why I should include you in mine.'

The air in the great hall was as taut as a drawn bowstring. I was certain that at any moment something would be said that must cause bloodshed between de Lacy and my lord. I fingered my sword hilt and looked at the knights around Robin, wondering which I would have to strike down first. But the castellan of Château Gaillard was no fool. He knew we could not afford discord in our camp in our present situation. And, wisely, he was not above playing the peacemaker.

'Then, if it would please you, Lord Locksley, would you be so good as to impart to us this "valuable intelligence" that you have gathered on our behalf.'

The room leaked a breath of relief.

Robin began. He outlined the forces ranged against us – some fifteen hundred men-at-arms in total – their dispositions, the number of mangonels and trebuchets aligned against us (five) and the smaller fry, onagers, springalds and the like. He revealed they had a shortage of missiles for these stone-throwing engines, but a consignment was expected upriver from Paris in the next month or so. He told us the French were commanded in Philip's absence by a Lord Simon de Montfort, a fairly decent fellow by all accounts, and a competent soldier who fought in the recent pilgrimage against the infidels of the East, and that they had plenty of grain and wine and no disease or sickness in the camp at present.

'I also understand there is a general distaste among their high command for the indiscriminate bombardment of the castle – the French know their petraries are killing innocent townsfolk inside these walls and that is the reason why we have been spared a harsher rain of their missiles.

They are reluctant to make war on the non-combatants from Petit Andely, the old, the sick, women and children and' – Robin paused significantly here – 'I think I can see a way in which we can benefit from their fine scruples.'

There was a profound silence in the hall and thirty knights raised eyebrows or scratched their heads. They began to mutter.

Robin sighed. 'We must let the townsfolk out of the castle. We let them go and I am fairly certain the French will allow them through their lines, to make their way to freedom. We let the old, the sick, the weak out – and they will no longer be a burden on our limited supply of stores.'

De Lacy gave a great roar of understanding. He strode over to Robin and grasped his arm. 'Do you think so? Do you truly think so? They'll let them get through unharmed?'

'I believe they will,' said my lord.

The three hundred people gathered in the middle bailey two days later were a collection of some of the most miserable specimens of humanity I have ever seen. They looked like an army of beggars: thin, sick, ragged folk, mostly elderly and infirm, but with a few younger men and women scattered among them, and all visibly too feeble to fight. I do not know who spoke the phrase for the first time, but this company soon became known, cruelly, in the way of soldiers, as the 'useless mouths'. For good reason: not one of the three hundred souls gathered in the yard could have lifted a bread knife in anger, yet each had need of his daily bread.

We had agreed an hour-long truce to begin at noon and, when the Useless Mouths were assembled, de Lacy blew trumpets to alert the French and the gates were thrown open and the raggedy procession allowed to exit the castle. They shuffled along, coughing, staggering, limping, holding on to each other for support as they filed slowly out and down the chalky path towards the river and the earthworks of the enemy a quarter of a mile below.

We watched the painfully slow progress of the Useless Mouths from the walls, and it seemed as if the whole garrison were holding its breath when the pathetic procession advanced towards the gates set in their high earthen walls outside the town of Petit Andely. On the other side of the walls were hundreds of armed foes, and we had only Robin's assurance that they would not fall on these unfortunates and slay them where they stood. The Useless Mouths halted at the bottom of the slope, a dozen yards from the deep ditch before the earth wall, and voices cried out to the French for mercy and protesting their good faith and status as good Christians and non-belligerents. And, to my great relief, the big gates swung open and the Useless Mouths surged forward and disappeared through them into the town beyond that had once been theirs.

Five days later we mustered another group of Useless Mouths in the middle bailey – some four hundred wretched souls this time – and they too were allowed to pass safely through the enemy lines.

Robin was, in a reasonably quiet and modest way, cock-a-hoop. Thanks to his efforts the castle was safely rid of some seven hundred people who, merely by continuing to breathe, would have been an intolerable burden. He was now a full member of the high council, with full responsibility for intelligence gathering and, with Roger de Lacy, Sir Joscelyn Giffard and Father de la Motte, one of the four lords who held all our lives in his hands. I was pleased for him – it was no more than his due as an earl and a man of his cunning, skill and experience.

I must confess, though, I was not overly fond of the idea of Robin being in charge of 'intelligence gathering' – I had had some bad experiences in this corner of the battlefield in the past – and my heart lurched against my ribs when he took me aside one day, in a quiet corner on the ground floor of the outer bailey, and said, 'Make sure you get plenty of rest this afternoon, Alan. I need you to be fresh tonight.'

'My lord?' I said.

'We are going beyond the walls, just you and me, to see what we can see.'

Chapter Eighteen

We dressed ourselves in warm, dark clothing and smeared a mixture of soot and hog grease over our faces and the backs of our hands, and as silently as cats we crept out of the postern gate at the foot of the north tower and gingerly stepped across the long plank bridging the deep ditch at the foot of our walls.

I wore no mail, for speed of movement and so that there might be no telltale chink of metal on metal, and reluctantly I had left Fidelity in the care of Kit, and carried only my misericorde in a leather sheath at my waist. Robin similarly lacked proper armament, except for a hunting knife jammed down his boot.

'We are not aiming to hurt anybody tonight, Alan. If we have to fight, we have failed in our mission and are probably as good as dead,' said my lord. For a man who knew well how to raise his followers' spirits, I found his words disquieting.

It truly was a black night, with only the faintest sliver of moon peeking very occasionally through the blanket of clouds – which was, of course, why Robin had chosen it. We crawled due east through mud and loose rock and tussocks of wet grass, for about two hundred yards by my reckoning, moving on elbows and knees with infinite slowness, and pausing every yard or so to listen for the enemy, using techniques that a dear Bavarian friend of mine had taught me long ago. Robin led and, as I inched along after him, I wondered what we were doing out here in no man's land between the walls of two mighty forces when we might be tucked up snugly in bed. My thoughts turned to Tilda as we made our snail-like progress across the ground. Her smile, the way her eyes danced with light when she laughed, and how easily she found joy in the world; perhaps one day . . .

'Alan!' Robin's voice was not even a whisper, but I caught a glimpse of his steel eyes in the darkness. I realised my forearm and all my weight was pressing down on Robin's boot. I shook myself free of Tilda's embrace and concentrated on placing one elbow and one knee in front of the other as silently as I could. We saw and heard nothing, wrapped in the blackness, the night dense around us. At least I saw and heard nothing until I felt Robin rise up on his knees a yard ahead of me, cup his hands together and make the sound of a barn owl hooting, three times.

To my surprise, his signal was repeated back to him twice, and up ahead there was a patch of darkness fuller than the rest. The earth wall. And was there someone there? I heard a click of trodden stone on stone and Robin rose silently to his feet. I got to mine, put my left hand on his shoulder and followed him and soon I could make out the shape of a man greyer than the surrounding gloom. I put my right hand on the handle of the misericorde, but remembered Robin's ominous words and did not draw the weapon. The man was standing by a stout wicker gate in the earth wall and, as far as I could tell, he was alone.

The gate opened just the width of a man, Robin and I slipped through and I found myself face to face with a small, very ugly middle-aged man in a dark hood. 'This way, monsieurs,' he said in a rough regional French accent. 'You are late. I expected you an hour ago.'

Robin made no excuse. He clapped the man on the arm and said, 'Lead us to him, Gerard!'

As we walked on, into the light of campfires and standing torches – almost blinding after the darkness – I realised we had just strolled, well, crawled, into the heart of the French camp. We were paid no mind by the few figures we saw crouched around campfires murmuring to comrades, nor did we interact with the men walking between the shacks and tents; no challenges were issued, we were merely three more shadows moving through the night.

In the time it would take to say ten Hail Marys, we were outside a simple white oiled-linen tent, illuminated from the inside by the light of many candles. Gerard said, 'One hour, and I'll be back. That is enough?'

Robin nodded and gave him a coin from his purse. Then my lord held back the flap of the tent and indicated I should go inside.

Mystified, curious and not a little nervous, I stepped through the gap between the folds of the fabric with my hand on the hilt of my dagger and there, seated on a camp stool cleaning a long sword with an oily cloth, was my cousin Roland.

He stood, and we embraced. Then he held me at arm's length and we looked fondly at each other. Apart from that glimpse at the riverbank, I had not seen my cousin for four years. He looked healthy, fit and only a little older. A tall, blond man, similar to myself in colouring and looks, except that he had a large shiny scar on the lower left side of his face.

'Well, you don't seem to be starving just yet,' said Roland amiably. 'This siege seems to be agreeing with you, Alan.'

'I would find it more agreeable if you would persuade your master Philip to leave us in peace,' I said.

'That will never happen in a thousand lifetimes,' he said and turned away to fill a goblet with wine for me. I turned to say something to Robin but to my astonishment he had disappeared.

Roland handed me the goblet. 'He has gone to snoop around our camp like a dirty spy,' he said with a grimace of distaste. 'My lord of Locksley likes to talk to the men-at-arms, though God knows what he hopes to discover. The truth is plain. We are here, we are staying here, and soon you will be forced to surrender your walls.'

I shook my head. 'We will outlast you, cousin. I promise. But I pray we will not meet on the battlements because . . .'

'Yes, if that happens we must fight. I know it. We must do our duty. But for now, for this night, let there be a private truce between us – what say you, cousin?'

'For tonight,' I agreed. 'But how comes Robin to know your serving man, to be met by him and to be guided like an old friend to your tent? And what am I doing here?'

'As for the first part, I do not wholly know. My lord of Locksley appeared, like a revenant, one night some weeks ago. Just popped into my tent like a country neighbour paying a friendly call. I was too surprised to sound the alarm, and then he gently reminded me of our comrade-ship and the great service he had done me when I was captured by Richard's mercenaries after Gisors – do you remember? – then he wanted a cup of wine and something to eat, and, well, soon it was too late to call for my men without looking a fool – not that I wished to. He stayed, we spoke of this and that, we drank a cup of wine, ate a little. He swore not to cause harm to any of our men in his wanderings. I asked after you and he promised he would bring you to me at the next dark of the moon. So, though honour demands we must be enemies in this unfortunate business, there is no need for us to forget our kinship, for this night at least.'

I smiled at him. I was fond of Roland, and while it was fantastical, absurd even, to be sharing wine with a friend in the heart of the enemy camp, I was very happy to be there.

We talked for a while, comfortably, quite naturally, about his family – the Seigneur d'Alle who was in Paris at the King's side, and his beautiful mother Adele, who very much wanted to introduce me to a young unmarried cousin of hers. We shared a few sorrowful words about the death of my lovely Goody, too. He asked after my little son Robert, and Thomas Blood, now a knight, who had shared our adventures in the south in pursuit of the Grail. And I told him the sad news about Little John and the terrible wound he had taken at Mirebeau. We drank to his speedy recovery but without much true conviction. Before too long the hour was nearly up and, suddenly, Roland was all briskness.

'Alan, I have something that I must tell you – I do not think I am betraying any great confidences by saying this, and I believe it will save the world a great deal of misery if I share it with you. The King has heard about the wretches you released from the castle and whom our men allowed to pass. He is extremely angry. The message I have for you is this: we will allow no more of the occupants of Château Gaillard to leave. You must all surrender, or none. That is the King's word. We are all aware these people are mostly women, children and elderly folk, but they are your responsibility and we have been giving an advantage to you in this bloody game of ours by allowing them to pass. No more shall be allowed through, do you hear me? No more.'

I could see his point. I nodded slowly.

'I have one more thing to tell you. Please listen carefully, cousin. King John cannot come to your rescue. He is even now making plans to withdraw to England, our spies tell us. You must persuade Roger de Lacy to surrender the castle to us, to avoid unnecessary bloodshed. Simon de Montfort will accept his capitulation, despite de Lacy's insults. You need have no fear, Alan, you can surrender to me and I will guarantee your safety; your life will be as sacred as my own.'

'If King John is truly going to England, as you say, he must be going to gather fresh men. He will come to us; he must come to us.'

'Monsieur!' The ugly little fellow was at the flap of the tent. 'It is time. We must away. The other monsieur is outside.'

'King John cannot save you,' Roland said. 'You must trust me on this.'

I said angrily, 'Is this a ruse? Is this Philip's way of sowing

265

discord behind our walls? I think this is most dishonour-able of you, cousin – that you should seek to trade on our kinship to gain advantage over your enemies.'

'I do not lie. On my honour. Stay here with me, I beg you, or surrender very soon, or we will be forced to face each other in the fire of battle and only God knows what that outcome will be. I do not want to have to kill you, my dear Alan.'

'You could not, even if you tried!' I snarled at him.

I had no more to say and strode out of the tent without thanking him for his wine or his company. With Gerard and Robin, and feeling like an ungrateful boor, I hurried across the silent camp and back towards the wicker gate.

A little before dawn, when I was back in the outer bailey and wrapped in my blankets, I thought deeply about Roland's words. It must be a ruse, I thought, it must be. King John, bad as he is, could not abandon Château Gaillard to the enemy. It would spell disaster for him. Roland had lied. But, even so, I could not hate him for long. He was honour-bound to serve his King, as I was to serve mine. It was his duty to persuade me to surrender by whatever means, fair or foul.

I informed Roger de Lacy the next day of what Roland had said, along with my conviction that it was a ruse, and also passed along some scraps of information Robin had gathered from his campfire chats with the French soldiery.

'It is a murky game you and Locksley play, Sir Alan,' said de Lacy. 'But I believe you have fathomed your cousin's intent. Do not fear. King John will come. He might take a few weeks to muster all the available forces from England but he will come. He knows well that if Château Gaillard is lost, then so is Normandy. Also, he gave me his word of honour that he would do so. He will come and he will sweep these dogs from our walls. We must be patient, hold true to our purpose, and the King will surely come.'

I was cheered by the castellan's words. Not because John had given his royal word to de Lacy but because it was in truth unthinkable for the King to abandon the Iron Castle and, so, Normandy. King John, in his own sweet time, when he had mustered sufficient strength, must come to our aid or lose all.

I gave de Lacy Roland's message about the Useless Mouths.

'Hmm,' said the castellan, 'we shall see about that, too.'

Two days later I slept late after a night watch on the north tower and, rising at nearly noon and climbing to the battlements, I was puzzled to see a vast gathering of townspeople, mostly mothers and their children, but a few elderly men and women as well, in the courtyard of the middle bailey. By chance the man standing next to me was Stefan, the former denizen of Petit Andely who had spotted Robin's nocturnal antics outside the walls. I asked what was happening. 'They are sending them out,' he said. 'The last of them. My grandfather is down there, with my wife and baby son. I am so glad this is over for them, they will be safe at last.'

I looked at him in amazement. Surely de Lacy could not have misunderstood the information I gave him. Surely de Lacy could not be expelling them when he knew what he knew? My head was spinning; I wasted precious moments cudgelling my brains to unravel the castellan's true intent and, as a result, was far too late to do anything – for as I looked on, the gates of the castle creaked open and the last of the Useless Mouths, many hundreds of souls, eight hundred, nine hundred, perhaps as many as a thousand, limped out of the gate and began slowly to make their way down the path towards the river and the town.

I raced for the stairs, tumbling down them, knocking a man-at-arms flying as I charged across the open space. Up the steps I went, across the drawbridge separating outer from middle bailey, and skidded to a halt in the middle of the courtyard just as the last of the Useless Mouths was shuffling out of the gate, and the doors were swinging shut behind him.

I sprinted for the gatehouse, spotting de Lacy's broad back high up on the gallery above the portal, the man himself evidently looking out on the departing folk. I managed to calm myself and climb the stairs. A deep feeling of dread filled my bowels. When I reached the gallery, I saw that Robin was standing beside de Lacy, with Vim beyond him. I half-expected my lord and de Lacy to be whispering darkly like murderers but both stood perfectly still, their shoulders square, heads up, watching the raggedy procession wend its way towards the French ramparts. Vim nodded at me, but his face was grim, and he took up a position at Robin's shoulder, facing me, as if he wished to prevent me from coming close to my lord. I went to the stone rim of the gallery, a few yards from Robin and the castellan, and looked at the stream of humanity filing down the path.

When the first of the Useless Mouths came within fifty yards of the French, my wildest hopes were dashed. The gates set in the earthen hill remained firmly closed and the heads of half a hundred men-at-arms appeared on the ramparts. The foremost of the pathetic horde called to the enemy and indistinct replies were made, but the gates stayed shut.

Then, to my horror, I heard a shout of command in French, and an evil cloud of bolts flew up from the earthen walls, hung in the sky and came down upon the unfortunate herd of frightened, unarmed, unarmoured women, children and old men. As the Useless Mouths were crowded together, almost every bolt found a mark. People staggered and dropped as the deadly bolts punched through their miserable rags and into vulnerable flesh. They cried out piteously, mewling and calling that they were not belligerents but harmless citizens of Petit Andely seeking mercy. Mercy! The French reply was another flight of missiles. Again the bolts soared, hung and dropped – I saw a child of no more than five years spitted through its skeletal arm, and heard his mother's howl as she snatched him up and ran to the ramparts shouting madly and holding out her wounded child so the crossbowmen could see the results of their work. Yet more quarrels lashed the crowd, plucking souls from the earth, here and there, maiming others, pinning yet others to the ground, and at last the mob splintered and the people dropped their meagre belongings and fled back up the slope, leaving more than two dozen still on the ground before the French walls.

I was frozen, aghast. The wretches scrambled up towards us, some on all fours in their haste to escape, ignoring the winding path and coming straight up the hillside, clawing at the rock and turf like scurrying animals, hundreds of souls, many wounded, trailing blood, surging upwards, crying out for us to open the gates and let them back inside, begging for the protection of the Iron Castle.

A mass of humanity soon formed outside our main gate, hundreds upon hundreds of bewildered men and women, their lined faces and wide, rolling eyes looking up at Roger de Lacy as he stood like a statue above the gate – which also remained firmly shut. They called to their lord, begging him to re-admit them. De Lacy looked down on them, his face a mask of implacable calm.

He raised his hands to still the babble of the Useless Mouths. An uneasy quiet descended over the multitude below.

'I cannot admit you. I cannot feed you,' he said. 'Your fate is in God's hands.'

A chorus of howls broke out. I could see old men and women I had passed the time of day with in the castle courtyard; I could see children I had watched at play on the ramparts with our men-at-arms. Now they were shouting that they had been tricked; that it was de Lacy's duty to protect them.

'I cannot admit you,' de Lacy said again. 'I cannot. You must depart these walls. Go with God!'

The confused shouting broke out once more.

'Go from here,' said de Lacy. 'You must go hence from my walls or face the consequences.' He made a gesture with his right hand as if plucking a low-hanging apple from a branch above his head. On the top of the towers to both left and right of the gatehouse, I saw men standing up and stringing bows. It was the archers. It was the Wolves.

The Useless Mouths saw them and wailed.

'Go,' said de Lacy. 'Go with God!'

The archers had nocked arrows and were beginning to draw the hempen strings back on their bows.

'Robin,' I said, 'you cannot do this. These are our people. We owe them our protection. Not . . . this!'

Vim was standing before me. Big, grim, calm-faced. 'Let this go, Alan.'

I looked the mercenary hard in the eye. 'Get out of my path, Vim, right now. I would speak face to face with my liege lord.'

'No, Sir Alan.' Vim sounded oddly sad. 'I cannot. He is my lord, too, and he has asked me to make sure that you see sense.'

'Out of my way, Vim. Last chance.' My fingers were on the handle of my sword, and I believe I would have used it and taken the consequences, but I was distracted by a wild shout from inside the walls. Stefan was running across the courtyard of the middle bailey. He had a sword in one hand and a dagger in the other and was waving both madly as he ran towards the guard post where the men who operated the opening mechanism stood watch. He was calling for them to open the gates and yelling that if they would not he would slay them and undertake the task in their stead.

He got within a dozen paces of them before he was felled by four arrows that thumped into his belly and chest simultaneously, dropping him stone dead. I made to draw Fidelity, but felt a grip of iron on my wrist, and now Robin's face was inches from my own.

'Let this go, Alan. Think, just think for a moment.'

His extraordinary silver eyes were looking into mine with such an intensity that I was forced to close my own. I let out a great, shuddering evil breath, my shoulders dropped, my soul sagged, and I released the grip on my hilt.

'Come with me,' said Robin, and he half-pulled and half-guided me off the gallery into the little space at the top of the steps to the courtyard.

He stared into my face. 'Have you mastered yourself?'
I nodded.

'Do you understand why we cannot let them back in?'

I nodded again. I was on the lip of disgracing myself with childish tears.

'I will tell you anyway. So that we are as clear as crystal. We cannot hold this castle and feed those hungry mouths. It is a cruel choice. King John will surely come to our aid. But we must do our part. We must hold this castle until he comes and we cannot do so if we are dead of hunger. We cannot feed them and also feed our fighting men. We cannot hold even another week against Philip if we must nourish those wretches down there. It is the castle or them. Tell me you understand.'

I nodded a third time.

'Tell me in words. Say to me the words: "I understand".'

'Robin, you tell me, why do we serve this King?'

'You know why, and if we are not true to our oaths, we are nothing. Our oaths are our honour. Now, tell me you understand.'

'I . . . understand.'

'Good, now go and find Kit and explain matters to him. And get yourself something to eat. But not too much. From now on, every morsel is a precious jewel.'

Chapter Nineteen

The Useless Mouths – oh, how I came to shudder at that name – built pathetic homes on the steeps slopes of the hill below Château Gaillard, to the north-east of the citadel, between the castle walls, the banks of the Seine and the earth ramparts of the French. It was a pitiful encampment: a few scrapes in the chalk to make shallow caves to keep the children out of the worst of the weather; a few shelters of crudely hacked out turfs supported by mud walls, sticks and stones; no food but what could be scavenged from the bare hillside – herbs, roots, a berry or two – and nothing to keep them warm but the rags on their backs.

It was early November then, cold and windswept, with a constant threat of rain or worse. After a few days the weakest among the Useless Mouths began to die.

Even inside the castle we had scant stores left. We had fed the people of Petit Andely for nearly two months, a dull and meagre diet, to be sure, but the vastly swollen population of the castle had eaten its way through nine-tenths of Château Gaillard's stores. Winter was coming. But we had the fighting men to hold until John came and all those inside the walls shared the grim determination that the sacrifices made by the Useless Mouths would not be in vain. Or so our leaders told us.

De Lacy addressed the whole garrison from the wall of the inner bailey on the day after the last of the Useless Mouths had been expelled. It was a rousing speech, once again, about courage and fortitude, mentioning the strength of our walls and the rightness of our cause. He assured us once more that King John was even now collecting fresh men-at-arms from England to ride to our rescue. I did not pay much attention, to be honest. I could hardly bear to look at the castellan, let alone swallow his foul nonsense about the Christ-like sacrifice of the noble citizens of Petit Andely.

'We have thirty-one valiant knights here,' de Lacy said, 'full of honour and prowess and armed with a determination that can never be conquered; we have two hundred and fifty-three brave men-at-arms. And we have a hundred and four strong and willing men who have bravely volunteered for this fight . . .'

And one brave woman, I thought to myself.

I looked up at the ramparts where Roger de Lacy was ignoring the drizzle and exhorting his garrison to fight on, and looked to his left at Robin, Father de la Motte and Sir Joscelyn Giffard standing there stern and silent – and at Matilda Giffard, who seemed to be smiling down only at me.

The rations were cut again, to a quarter of a loaf of bread per man per day and a piece of rock-hard cheese no bigger than a dove's egg. A cup of dried peas or sometimes beans and a few shreds of salted beef were issued to each man once a week, and in the outer bailey we made big cauldrons of soup from it and all the members of a watch shared it equally. It was a watery, bland-tasting slop, but it was hot and, at least once a week, with our bread and cheese ration we could feel almost satisfied. The rest of the time we were hungry. Hunger crouched darkly beside us all day, every day, like our own shadows, ever-present, never forgotten. The weight began to fall from my body; I bored another hole in my belt, and then another. I dreamed of food; the men seemed to talk of it all the time – great feasts they had enjoyed, the feast they would like to have when the siege was over. It only made things worse. But, if there was little food and no wine to be had, there was at least plenty of water. I took to drinking it hot, in large beakers with dried herbs infused in the brew to give it some taste. Pints of it. It made the stomach feel, for a while, that it was full. The faces around me began to look gaunt. My belly skin became looser.

But, if we suffered hardships within the walls, it did not bear comparison with the fate of the Useless Mouths.

The weather grew colder; in December the rain turned to snow. The calls for mercy from the folk outside our walls never seemed to cease, day or night. One of the volunteers threw his bread ration down to his aged mother who called out to him piteously from the bottom of the east wall – the poor old woman was crushed to death in the riot as her fellow unfortunates, now thin as wraiths, stick-like confections of rags and burning, febrile want, fought each other tooth and nail for the crust. They had to be driven from the walls with crossbow bolts. Roger de Lacy had the volunteer hanged in the courtyard as an example. Wasting food became a capital offence. We closed our ears to the cries of the Useless Mouths, but hideous stories began to circulate – among these wretches, Kit told me, a woman had given birth to a stillborn child only to see it ripped apart and devoured still warm from her body by her own family and friends. I drank my hot water and herbs, munched my crust of bread and nibbled my nugget of cheese – and gave thanks for it to God.

Our one piece of good luck was that, in the middle of December, a few days before the Feast of the Nativity, the bombardment, which had slowed to a trickle in the previous weeks, a few missiles loosed a day, stopped altogether. Perhaps the siege-machines had broken down; perhaps they had run out of missiles. Perhaps the engineers who manned them had gone home to their families for

Christmas to feast on roast goose and fat pork and fruit pies with thick cream, and to make merry with wine and cider, the Wolves muttered, eyes murderous with jealousy.

On Christmas day, Vim, Robin, Kit and I dined on a pair of fat rats that Kit had trapped in the storerooms, killed, skinned, gutted and stuffed with crumbled bread and herbs, smeared with a little oil and salt, and roasted. They were, I must confess, absolutely delicious. Robin begged, bought or borrowed, but most likely stole, a skin of good red wine from somewhere. My lord and I sang some of the jollier English folk songs together; Vim told us some blood-curdling stories of his life as a mercenary; Kit became dizzy and gigglesome on the single cup of wine he drank; and we were able to celebrate the birth of Our Lord in decent style.

One piece of bad luck in that bad time, was that Tilda took up a post in the underground storerooms acting as an unofficial clerk to Sir Benedict Malet. Her ability to read, write and calculate numbers meant that although, being a woman, she could not fight on the walls, she was valuable to the castle in the recording and husbanding of our dwindling stores – not that she would ever have been expelled as one of the Useless Mouths. Her father, and for that matter I, would never have allowed that to happen. But this also meant that, while I saw her twice a week when I went to collect the rations for the outer bailey, I could never be alone with her for any length of time.

Benedict, that lardy pimple-garden, was always interrupting us in our private conversations and sending Tilda away on errands when I dropped by, asking her to fetch this sack or that box, to take a message to the guards in the keep or other such excuses to keep her out of my company. And I could not see much of her when she was not employed with the store work, for now she was the only woman in the castle, Sir Joscelyn kept an especially close eye on her and she was cloistered in his quarters in the inner bailey for many hours of every day, and for all of the hours of darkness.

I made matters worse between us by embarrassing her and making a fool out of myself on the third day of Christmas. I went to the storeroom in the middle of the afternoon meaning to ask her to take a stroll with me around the battlements, for the snow had made the surrounding countryside quite beautiful – and since the French bombardment had ceased, it seemed safe to do so.

I asked the man-at-arms who guarded the door where she was and he smirked knowingly and told me the Lady Matilda was in the back of the store-cave. I didn't like his grin and pushed past him roughly, entering the cool limestone cave with its weird greenish walls. My heart sank to see the depleted state of the stores. Three months before this place had been packed tight, with boxes, barrels and sacks of grain piled high against the walls – now those near the entrance were bare and reflecting a ghostly light from outside, and one had to enter deep into the dim recesses, down wide tunnels that twisted and turned, to find anything worth consuming. I did not want to alarm Tilda, and so I called her name only softly, as I advanced.

After a dozen yards I saw a shape moving on a mound of grain sacks. Bigger than a woman, but I could definitely see arms and legs. I called Tilda's name again and heard a sharp cry of terror as her face came into the light. It was my beloved and there was a man grappling with her, assaulting her, or so it seemed.

I took three fast steps, grabbed a handful of cloth with my left hand, and pulled the fellow away from Tilda. My right fist, with my full shoulder behind it, smashed into the man's large, pale face – a beautiful punch, perfectly timed and containing all my strength – and he was hurled away to crash against the walls and fall limply to the floor.

At the instant of my hitting him, I realised the obvious. It was, of course, Sir Benedict Malet, and he had been trying to defile my beloved girl with his filthy fat-boy lust. I pulled Fidelity from its sheath and was preparing to slaughter the half-conscious dung-heap as he lay bleeding on the floor, when Tilda jumped on me and grabbed my sword arm with both her hands.

'Do not do it, Alan, for my sake. Do not hurt him any more!'

'After what he was trying to do to you? He needs to die.'

'No, no, you mistake the situation. He was helping me. He was trying to help.'

I looked at her in confusion. She released my sword arm.

'It is all just a silly misunderstanding, Sir Alan,' she said, smiling prettily at me through wide, teary eyes. 'Bennie would never hurt me. There was a spider caught in my hair; it had crawled in under my headdress, and I stupidly cried out and Bennie gallantly came to my aid. He was trying to help me get the spider out. That is all.'

I stood there feeling like the biggest fool in Christendom. Benedict was shaking his bloody head and trying to get to his feet.

I said formally, 'Sir Benedict, I must crave your pardon. I acted rashly and without thought.' I took a step towards him and held out my right hand to help him to his feet. He cringed away as if I had offered to strike him again. His nose streamed with blood; from its misshapen look, I guessed it to be broken.

I did not know what to do.

'I hope you can forgive me, Tilda,' I said. 'I am truly sorry.'

'Well, yes, I forgive you, Alan. But perhaps you might leave us in peace now and I will tend to Bennie's hurt. Can't you see you are frightening him?'

'Ah, yes . . . Benedict, I am very sorry, old fellow, you see I thought that—'

'Alan. You will leave us now. This instant, if you please,' said Tilda, with more than a little steel in her tone.

I left.

The next day, when I went to receive the rations, I tried once again to make things right with Benedict. His nose was hugely swollen and there were purplish-red marks under both his eyes. Tilda was nowhere to be seen.

He accepted my apology brusquely and said, 'It was a mistake, Sir Alan. Yes, I understand that you behaved like a brute with your cowardly surprise attack and I accept your contrition. But I would prefer if we did not speak of the matter again.'

I did not care much for the word 'cowardly', and it was on the tip of my tongue to ask him whether he wished me to give him satisfaction for the blow. I would have been most happy to meet him with sword or dagger at any time he chose to name. But I managed with some difficulty to hold my tongue. Slaughtering the porky bastard would not get me back into Tilda's good graces.

The siege wore on. My new suit of mail which fit me perfectly in August now sagged alarmingly. By January our stores were nearly exhausted. The snow fell almost every day. There were few rats to be found in the castle, and the dogs and cats had long since disappeared. Then Roger de Lacy gave the order that the war horses should be killed, one by one. A truly desperate measure – for a good war horse was worth two or three times the annual revenues of Westbury. We were eating money, or so it seemed. They started with the least expensive animals, cutting their throats and saving the gushing blood to make puddings. The meat was salted – we had plenty of stocks of salt, for some reason – or made into stew with the last of the beans. But four hundred men-at-arms take a lot of feeding and the horse was eaten up, hooves, hide, the lot, inside a week. Towards the end of January, Robin went out of the castle and into the French camp in the dead of night. He acquired a leg of mutton, a bag of onions and a loaf of stale bread, which Kit, Vim and I ate with him – guiltily on my part, for I knew I should be sharing it with the other men. But Robin pointed out that it was his meat, he had risked his life for it, and he would share it with whomever he chose. Nevertheless, I palmed a slice of the meat and later gave it to Tilda, who told me she would share it with her father. I saved the bone, onion skins and scraps to make soup for the sick of the outer bailey, for they were many. Months of bad food had taken their toll on the entire garrison, and we had scores of men down with various fevers, fluxes and agues. A dozen had died already. But, as always, our lot seemed comparatively good when one looked over the walls at the huddled shapes down the slope towards the Seine.

The Useless Mouths were mere ghosts now, no longer wholly human. Most lay unmoving in crude shelters, listless, dying or dead, but a few wandered the snow-covered slopes like ragged black skeletons, skin over bone, their eyes huge with suffering, searching for anything that might fill their bellies. They ate each other – horrible as it is to contemplate, it is true. Flesh was stripped from the newly deceased by a mob of ghouls with flashing knives and swallowed down in thick purple gobbets. I saw this obscenity with my own eyes. More than a few souls killed themselves, or asked their fellows to cut their throats for them. Some drowned themselves in the Seine. Whenever possible, I kept my gaze averted from that terrible hillside and I prayed their suffering would soon be over.

In February His Royal Highness King Philip of France returned to Château Gaillard with his mighty host. I stood on the north tower of the outer bailey, swathed in two thick woollen cloaks over my mail, my legs wrapped in old blankets, for hunger made me feel the cold as keenly as if I were naked, and watched his royal banners, and those of his closest barons and counts, ascend the hill opposite the castle and stand erect over the fortification. It was a beautiful day: a wide blue sky and pale golden sunshine that reminded you of happier times, but with an icy wind to tell you that spring was not yet come. I could hear cheering coming from the enemy camp, the cheering of men scenting victory, now the King was here and they were reinforced. The entire encampment was alive with warlike vigour, and it came to me that, despite all our suffering, we had been slumbering during the long winter and it was time to awaken. We had been huddled like bears in a state of sad hibernation, and our enemies, too, had been sleeping all winter long. But, with the sunlight, with the promise of spring, the bears must come out of their caves – and fight.

Robin put it another way that evening when we were sharing a bowl of watery bean soup, a lump of stale maslin bread the size of my fist and two beakers of hot herb-water. 'Philip has come to finish us,' he said, with a wry smile at me. 'We have had it nice and easy till now, Alan. Now we're truly going to earn our silver.'

Chapter Twenty

The King of France's first act on his arrival at Château Gaillard was one of mercy. He caused the gates set in the ramparts before the town of Petit Andely to be flung open and allowed the surviving Useless Mouths to pass through. He even fed them lavishly with white bread and roast meats and cheeses from the royal stores, I heard later. He gave them wine, too, and sweetmeats. Most died as a result of his largesse, their shrunken stomachs unable to digest the rich food. A grim jest, that.

Philip stirred his men-at-arms into action, too. The digging began once again.

The French started two parallel trenches heading from Philip's Hill, aimed directly at the eastern side of the outer bailey. The men dug day and night, protected from our arrows and bolts by thick, square, sloping, wooden shields on wheels, which were faced with wet ox-hides. The spoil the diggers threw up went to build a causeway between the two trenches, a wide earthen road that crossed the saddle of land between Philip's Hill and the outer bailey, the loose earth packed down hard by more workmen, as well protected by mobile wood and ox-hide shields as the diggers in their ditches. A great tongue of earth seemed to be rolling out, slowly, slowly, a few yards a day, from Philip's Hill to our battlements. I knew what would come next. They were building a road along which to assault our walls with siege towers. The road was aimed like an arrow, almost due west, at Robin's bastion.

This, of course, was exactly what the outer bailey had been designed for. The Lionheart had realised that the only practical way to attack the Iron Castle was from the south or south-east. The other sides were too well protected by the fall of the land. So he caused the outer bailey to be built, a separate and powerful castle all of its own that must be overcome before the real fortress could be assaulted. I knew how strong the outer bailey was: its walls were eight feet thick, it had five mighty towers from which we could pour down destruction on the attacking enemy men-at-arms, and the defenders were Robin's Wolves – iron-hard mercenaries who had hardly grumbled at the severe privations they had suffered during the long winter. And if by some quirk of fate these defences were overcome, which I did not believe could happen, we could always retreat in good order to the middle bailey.

Nonetheless, we did all we could to impede the progress of the earthen causeway and harass the workmen. Robin picked out the two finest archers in each watch, and these six men were declared the only ones allowed to loose arrows. They received a dozen a day. We had a goodly store of them – some four thousand shafts, if I recall correctly – but they must be kept in reserve for the assault, Robin decreed. The six marksmen's task was to sow fear among the diggers and to thin their ranks when the opportunity presented itself. The favoured technique was to wait until the diggers grew careless – which they did after some time without an arrow being loosed – and began to show themselves, or parts of themselves, outside the shield. For these archers, some of whom I knew from the old days in Sherwood, all they needed was the sight of an arm or leg, displayed only for a heartbeat, to skewer it with a yard of ash. When they had pierced an unfortunate digger, his comrades would huddle together behind the shield and the archers would loose shafts high in the sky to drop vertically behind it. So we killed a dozen men a week, and kept them fearful. But the causeway advanced and the French responded by beginning the bombardment once more. This time there was nothing lackadaisical about their methods. All five siege engines focused their venom on the outer bailey and from that day, the crisp, repetitive ringing of stone ball on stone wall was only silenced by the fall of night.

Carpenters' hammers rang out, too, on Philip's Hill and

before long we saw the bones of a monstrous structure rise up on the horizon: tall, square-built, with five platforms constructed one on top of the other and connected by ladders. It was roughly the same size as the tower on which Robin and I stood.

'A belfry,' said my lord. 'That clever devil. I have not seen one of those in an age. Philip is building himself a belfry.'

I threw him a puzzled look. I was not familiar with this type of siege engine and a little surprised by Robin's respectful tone.

'It has been used in battle since the days of the Ancient Greeks but, because it requires a good deal of shaped timber and hundreds of fresh ox-hides and many skilled engineers to construct, it is a very expensive contraption to manufacture. Many lords do not have the depth of purse to build one – Philip does, of course – but it can be devastatingly effective. Richard used one at Acre, don't you remember?'

I looked at Robin and shrugged.

'No, no, of course, you were sick and delirious at the time. Forgive me. Well, it is not much more than a series of big boxes, one on top of the other, all set up on two pairs of wheels,' he continued. 'You fill it with fighting men and wheel it to the castle walls. A door drops down on to the battlements from the topmost box and the fighting men charge out directly. There is none of that murderous unprotected scramble up the ladders you get

289

when you are trying to take a fortress in the usual way. Though, of course, you have to build a causeway, perfectly flat, that leads right up to the walls, but Philip is doing just that, isn't he? The devil. Oh, this is going to be a real fight, Alan, you mark my words. A proper all-or-nothing dust-up.'

The hammering continued for several days, insect-like men crawled all over it, and wooden flesh was put on the bones of the belfry. It looked formidable, intimidating, even from four hundred yards.

I found it deeply frustrating to watch the French preparations for the assault, standing impotently by while the diggers excavated deep trenches on either side of the causeway, which reached closer and closer every day. Fresh ox-hides were nailed to the exterior of the belfry, which I knew would make it impervious to our arrows and to fire. I could not see how we could defeat this monstrous tower when it finally came against us, and said as much to Robin.

'Oh, there are ways,' he said, coolly. 'Nothing is invincible.'

I had not seen much of him in the past few days as he had been spending a good deal of time with Aaron the engineer, tinkering with Old Thunderbolt, which had been moved back to the north tower, and working for long, dirty hours at a small forge in the middle bailey with one of the castle blacksmiths.

I was impatient with our inactivity. And it occurred to

me no law stated we had to sit still and wait for their attack. 'I want your permission to make a sortie, sir,' I told Robin one brisk sunny morning.

'To what end?' he said.

'I want to take a squad of men and go out there and disrupt their work, slaughter the workmen who are building the causeway, cause terror, havoc, mayhem . . .'

'Do you think King Philip has a shortage of men who know how to dig?'

I scowled at Robin's acidic comment.

'I cannot sit still any longer, it is driving me to the edge of madness. I think I shall explode if I do not do something.'

'Very well,' said my lord. 'Take Kit and half the men of the second watch and cause some mayhem. But be careful and remember: we cannot afford to lose good men; Philip can.'

Our plan was simple: we would attack a little after noon, when the diggers had had dinner and were resting, hopefully sleeping, in their diggings. We would charge out of the little postern gate at the base of the north tower of the outer bailey, sprint the hundred yards or so to the earthworks and fall upon the workmen with sword and fury. Kill as many as we could, fire their tools, wheelbarrows and equipment and the big shields that protected them, and then get safely back to the outer bailey within a quarter of an hour.

The plan went wrong almost immediately. We crossed

the wooden planks over the ditch before the walls and, wearing only light armour – a thigh-length hauberk and plain steel helmet for my part, while the men-at-arms wore mail or leather as they chose – Kit, myself and twenty men rushed as quietly as possible towards the diggings on the northern side of the causeway. We were met fifty yards out by a hail of crossbow bolts from a dozen men-at-arms who had specifically been assigned the task of protecting the diggers. I had counted on some element of surprise in our attack, but this was foolish of me. For many hundreds of French eyes watched the castle, just as carefully as we watched the movements in their encampment. The crossbowmen were ready and waiting behind wooden screens and, working in pairs, one man shooting, the other loading, they kept up a withering rain of death. The bolts whipped and cracked around us – and four men were down before we were within thirty yards of the diggings. Unhurt men were hugging the turf as the quarrels zipped over their heads, and the attack was in danger of being bogged down like a pregnant cow in a marsh. A crossbow bolt cracked off my shield, and I looked at Kit who was crouched at my boots, his face ice-white with fear. Do we fight on? I asked myself. Or do we go back?

I made the wrong choice.

I hauled Fidelity from my scabbard.

I shouted, 'Westbury!' and hurled myself the last thirty yards up that gentle slope.

I felt the wind of a bolt pass my cheek. Then I leaped

into the muddy trench behind the big screen, screaming my war cry with Fidelity swinging like a flail. I split the head of one crossbowman, wrenched my sword free and rammed the point into the guts of another fellow as he ran at me. I felt a hammer blow to my shield, and saw the point of a quarrel sticking right through the wood and leather two inches above my left forearm. The crossbowman swung his discharged weapon at my head. I blocked and jammed the cross-guard of Fidelity into his eye. Then the red rage came down upon me. I chopped, I hacked. I sliced, I slew. A spray of blood half-blinded me, but I cuffed my eyes clear and killed again. I remember killing three men with three sweeping blows of Fidelity, and thinking, My God, this is easy. For they were not knights but untrained, unarmoured peasants. A big man came at me with a spade and I took the clumsy blow on my shield and flicked open his throat with my sword tip. He dropped to his knees, the blood streaming from his neck. I chopped down another man, slicing through the backs of his knee as he tried to run from the trench. Kit was fighting beside me, I knew, and finishing off the men I wounded with short hard lunges of his sword. And I was aware that Wolves were all about me, snarling and howling, battering men with sword and mace and axe, trampling them into the mud.

Then there were no more enemies to kill. The corpses of a score of men, diggers and men-at-arms lay scattered around that wide trench, and a dozen others were groaning, bleeding, crying and dying.

293

I heard the trumpets. Kit scrambled nimbly up the steep sides of the trench and on to the causeway. I could see his expression clearly, his mouth was a huge 'O', his eyes popping from his head.

He turned and shouted, 'Knights! Knights!'

I yelled at the Wolves, 'Back, back to the castle! Back to Château Gaillard if you value your lives.' For I could already hear the thunder of hooves on packed earth and knew my doom was approaching.

A man on foot has little chance against a mounted knight. We fled the trench, but within five heartbeats the French knights were upon us. To my left, a rider dropped his lance and almost casually ran it through the back of a running Wolf, lifting him off the ground and hurling the skewered man and his lance away. I heard the pounding of hooves directly behind me and jinked to my left. I caught a glimpse of a mountain of horseflesh and mail rushing past my right, and something – the knight's shield, I believe – caught me full in the back and hurled me to the ground.

The Wolves were being chased like hares across the turf, pierced with lances, hacked down by the knights' swords.

And then Robin took a hand in the fight. I distinctly heard his bellowed commands from the battlements fifty yards away.

'Nock!'

'Draw!'

'Loose!'

And the whisper of many shafts in the air.

As I got to my knees, I saw a knight take an arrow dead in the centre of his chest. His head snapped back, but he kept his seat. Then another yard of steel-tipped ash punched into his neck and he slid from the saddle.

The knights were retreating, galloping away up the causeway as swiftly as they had attacked.

I got to my feet, dazed and a little breathless, and looked around me. Kit was lying a dozen yards away, blood on his face, unmoving. I could see the three fleetest members of the Wolves hurrying towards the castle walls and one already crossing over the plank across the ditch to the postern gate. That was all that remained of the twenty men who had charged out of the castle with me so bravely less than half an hour before.

I went to Kit and, praise God, found he was still breathing. I loosed the straps on his helmet and eased it off his head and saw a gash high on his cheek and a livid bruise on the side of his skull. He had taken a nasty knock but I was fairly certain he'd live. I picked him up and slung him over my shoulder. But, although he weighed hardly anything after weeks of poor food, such was my own weakened state that I staggered as I carried him the twenty yards back to the walls.

I was summoned that evening to see Roger de Lacy. I expected to be roared at and roundly abused for my criminal recklessness – I would have deserved it. Instead, de Lacy seemed merely saddened by the whole affair.

'I understand your feelings, Sir Alan,' said the castellan gloomily. 'I know it is very hard to sit idle while our enemies flaunt themselves within bowshot. I applaud your courage and initiative. But I cannot have any repetition of this sort of bloody business. I hear that you lost fourteen men-at-arms, more than two-thirds of your command in this little adventure. Is that true?'

I squirmed under his gaze.

'And I hear that you slew a score of their men in the trenches, workers and peasants, mostly. Is that also correct?'

I nodded, looking at my boots.

'This will not do, Sir Alan – we cannot afford to lose fourteen men-at-arms, we cannot afford to lose even one! Philip can summon up more peasants from his lands at will to dig mud and make his earthworks; I cannot make more men-at-arms.'

All this was perfectly clear to me. I longed for him to be silent and dismiss me. But he seemed to wish to make the point more forcefully, as if I were an idiot. And judging by the disastrous sortie that I had just led, perhaps he did think me one.

'Do you see, Sir Alan? Every man we lose, weakens us. You must contain your zeal for battle until the moment is right. Is that understood?'

'Yes, sir.'

'So no more of these rash endeavours. We must stay behind our walls.'

'Yes, sir; I mean, no, sir. I mean, no more rash endeavours, sir.'

'Very good. You may go now.'

I was overjoyed to do so.

Chapter Twenty-one

The causeway came ever closer. Philip's trebuchets pounded away in daylight hours and the crack-crack-crack of ball on stone numbed our ears. We ate up our meagre rations, drank our hot herb brew and dreamed of food as a young man dreams of love. I grieved for the good men whose lives I had thrown away with my rashness and stupidity. But, to my great relief, Kit recovered, and after a day or two in bed, he was back to his old cheerful self.

The French began acting strangely. Beyond the ramparts at the base of the long causeway, I could make out large groups of men moving about – many hundreds. There were banners and trumpet calls almost incessantly. The empty belfry was pushed forward to a position behind the gates and I could see men clambering all over it like spiders, hammering in last nails, hanging hides, fixing a rope here or there. And then, at a little before noon, without the slightest ceremony, the gates were flung open and I saw the completed belfry: a tall, thin, square wooden tower on wheels. It looked terrifying.

'They are coming,' said Robin. 'This is it.'

'They haven't finished the causeway,' I said, pointing to the twenty yards of open space, twice as deep as a standing man, that existed between the end of the tamped-down earth road and our ditch and walls.

'They plan to fill that gap today,' said Robin. 'Sound the alarm, quickly, Alan, I want every man we have on the eastern walls right now. All the archers concentrated, half and half, in the north and south towers. Go, now!'

I went.

It took the most part of an hour for the belfry to advance the three hundred yards from Philip's Hill across the causeway. It chafed our nerves raw, as we knew that when the belfry came up to our walls we would be fighting for our lives. It was painfully slow for them, too, for we made them pay for every yard in the blood of their men-at-arms. A score of men in the bottom of the tower pushed the machine along on its four solid wheels. But the belfry was an unwieldy beast, and monstrously heavy, and the men were soon exhausted and had to be relieved by others. Those pushing from inside its base were completely protected but the men waiting their turn behind the ungainly machine were much more vulnerable.

Although they were protected by shield men in the outer ranks, Robin's archers killed them by the score. My lord led his bowmen by example: he plucked arrows from the full bag at his waist, nocked, drew back the powerful bow, the hempen string reaching his ear, and loosed. The shaft flashed out, curved in the air and, without fail, the bodkin point punched deep into living flesh. As the belfry trundled inexorably forward, the unfortunate men in its shadow paid the price for its advance. Squads of fresh men hurried out from Philip's Hill to replace the dead and dying – and the belfry kept trundling along, closer, ever closer. The causeway was soon stained red with blood, slippery and littered with bodies; I saw sergeants kicking corpses into the ditches on either side so as not to block the passage of the troops in the wake of the belfry. But as fast as Robin and his men killed them, Philip replaced the stricken Frenchmen, and ever more foes, running in mail, shields high, sallied forth from the encampment to join in the great effort to heave the belfry towards our walls.

King Philip went so far as to dispatch a score of mounted knights, who patrolled up and down the causeway, as a deterrent to another sortie – and that was when I finally saw what Old Thunderbolt could do.

Aaron's beloved springald was mounted on the north tower of the outer bailey. From there it could loose its bolts into the belfry or into the flanks of the squads of terrified men-at-arms hurrying along the causeway, shields held high, to join in the effort of pushing the mobile tower forward.

But Aaron chose to kill the knights.

I was watching a mounted man trotting casually along the north side of the causeway, about seventy yards out, exhorting a group of men in mail to hurry to the safety of the belfry's shadow, when I heard a loud crack from my left, just made out the black blur of the bolt and saw the knight hurled from the saddle, his body sliced cleanly in half by the iron bolt. One moment he was riding merrily along, the next his upper body was spinning away from a rain of blood. The horse went mad with fright, leaped into the ditch on the far side of the causeway and was not seen again.

However, Old Thunderbolt was very slow to reload, and Aaron selected his targets with great care, so it was nearly a quarter hour before I next saw him make a kill. A pair of knights this time, riding side by side in the centre of the causeway, a hundred yards away. Either the bolt was faulty, or Aaron had doctored it somehow, for it spun in flight in a yard-wide circle of lethally spinning iron and cut raggedly through the chests of both knights and crushed one of the horse's skulls.

I was deeply impressed – it was the last time knights ventured on to the causeway for some while.

Eventually, Robin's withering barrage had to slacken

– he had only a limited number of shafts to loose and I knew he was husbanding them for the assault itself. His six marksmen still stole the lives of the waiting men cowering behind the belfry; and from time to time Aaron, too, smashed a wicked bolt into the ranks there, murdering three or four and painting the belfry with their viscera.

But the machine was upon us. Trumpets sounded from Philip's Hill and a horde disgorged from their encampment – perhaps six or seven hundred came running along the causeway. Some carried swords, spears, crossbows, axes – others bore huge wickerwork cages, others great stones and bags of what looked like wool or cloth, others ladders, blankets and big floppy leather bags. At least two hundred men came on behind this first eruption, with light carts and wheelbarrows filled with earth, and another hundred behind them carried spades.

Restraint forgotten, Robin's archers drew and loosed, drew and loosed a dozen times; Aaron hurled his thunderbolts and cut bloody furrows through the enemy ranks. The men under my command – sixty of the Wolves and twenty men-at-arms from the castle garrison – showered heavy stones on the men's heads below us. But they were too many. The French toiled like ants, throwing earth, wickerwork, cloth, even the bodies of their fallen comrades into the gap between us, desperate to fill the ditch any way they could. And it was filling. Soon it was filled to the height of the causeway, even higher. In the time it takes to say ten Our Fathers, the gap was bridged. We killed them, and we killed more, but they were just too many, and more men-at-arms, swords drawn, mail gleaming, were coming along the causeway from Philip's Hill, hundreds more. They swarmed inside the tall machine, climbing the ladders inside to fill the galleries with fighting men, and soon the belfry was rolling forward again. It lurched as it hit the newly filled area, sagged to one side in the softer earth, but was hauled upright and steadied by hundreds of willing hands. And then it came on again.

I turned to my Wolves. 'You all know what to do,' I said. 'They must not place a foot on the battlements. Follow my commands, do your duty, and fight like devils. If we can hold them here, then push them back, we will have won!'

It was not the greatest of speeches given to men facing death, but I was rewarded by an eldritch howl that lifted my heart as much as the hairs on my neck.

Suddenly the belfry was ten feet away.

The wide face of it fell forward, the wood bouncing slightly on the stone parapet and making a bridge. I shouted, 'Shields up! Shields up!' and knelt down behind the battlements with my helmeted head buried under the top of my shield, and with the sound of the cracking of a thousand whips, a hailstorm of crossbow bolts exploded from the inside of the top gallery of the belfry, spewing a blizzard of iron-tipped death against our walls.

We responded with a score of arrows loosed at a range of a couple of yards into the topmost gallery, which was packed with men – and I guarantee that every shaft found a mark – but most of our bowmen were in the towers on either side of the point of assault, and so unable to make the angle into the gallery. Men-at-arms, scores of them, a wall of grey mail and silver blades and red faces glaring under steel helmets, erupted from the box and charged, bellowing madly, across its dropped face.

And we stepped forward to meet them.

We crashed into them like vast boulders smashing together. Shields high, our swords stabbing over the top, we ploughed forward; myself in the centre, Vim to my left, Kit to my right, thirty Wolves crammed in hard all around me. We slammed into the wall of our foes as they charged across the wooden bridge. I felt as if I were trying to stop a maddened bull. One dark fellow whose shield was mashed against mine was cursing vilely at me in French, till a comrade's spear slid over my shoulder, ripped his cheek apart and he fell away. Another yelling fellow immediately surged forward to take his place. But we held them – just – at the line of the battlements. The two sides were now one huge, heaving mass of struggling men, shoving, stabbing, screaming, dying and falling off the bouncing bridge that linked the top gallery of the belfry to the battlements.

We held them – by God's grace. Yet the press was so tight it was almost impossible to move: we snarled and shoved and spat over our shield tops at the enemy; my helmet ringing with the blows of foes from behind their front line.

From the towers to either side, Robin's archers slew men by the dozen. The arrows scythed in, skewering necks and sword-wielding arms, the punctured men falling thirty feet to the earth below. Old Thunderbolt loosed its deadly iron bolts from time to time, cutting a bloody channel two men deep through the press of humanity on the bridge. But despite the carnage, despite the constant rain of men, spitted with arrows, slashed with sword and spear, who fell screaming, the pressure against us never slackened. For the belfry's greatest strength was its ability to feed men from the ground, up the stacked galleries, up the ladders, in a constant stream of charging, shouting humanity, to the top and on to the wooden bridge and into battle.

We fought like demons. We killed and killed, our blood-slick swords, when we could free them, reaching over our shields to stab into the faces of our enemies. The men jammed up behind us lanced over our heads with spears, or swung long-handled axes with terrible effect. We shoved back the enemy with all our might, but he was constantly replenished. How ever many we killed, his numbers never decreased, and we were gradually being pushed back, back.

Now the enemy was on the battlements – a bridgehead of a dozen men, but with more leaping to join them with every beat of my heart. My command had been forced into two, split by the pressure of the advance, and I saw Vim's despairing face on the other side of the seething mass of our bloodied attackers, as he sliced and hewed at the foe like a hero of old. Yet we were being forced back, back and back – the enemy was inside the outer bailey, leaping from the bridge and landing freely on our walls.

I shouted, 'Hold them, hold them!' and summoned the last of my strength. I smashed my shield into a roaring face, battered Fidelity down on to a helmet, then punched my cross-guard into a man's eyes. I managed to push forward a pace, ducked a swinging axe, and stabbed the man through his armpit. A crossbow bolt cracked into my helmet and I staggered back, dazed. Then felt Kit's hand on my back steadying me. I charged forward once again, lunging, stabbing, screaming, 'Westbury!' and killing a terrified man with a brutal chop to the neck.

I heard the distinctive crack of the springald being loosed. I snatched a look at the belfry's bridge, expecting to see that another bloody swath had been cleared through the crush of enemies charging over it, and my first thought was that Aaron had missed. The iron bolt of the springald was sunk up to half its length into the ox-hide-covered side of the machine and, curiously, a length of rope was extending from the end of the bolt back to the north tower.

The rope snapped taut.

I dodged a sword swing, stepped forward and crashed the side of my shield into a man's face. I stabbed once, twice, into the press of Frenchmen before me, but I was not truly giving the foe the whole of my attention.

I stole a glance behind to the north tower and saw

Robin's archers had laid down their bows and were all of them, some twenty men, hauling on the stout rope. Surely the bolt must come loose, I thought to myself – fending off a French knight who came at me like a tiger with sword and dagger – surely they will pull it free of the belfry like a cork from a bottle?

It was in that moment the battle's fortunes were decided. Over the sea of screaming enemies before me, on the battlements on the other side, I could see Vim's men were suddenly more numerous. There was no sign of the mercenary captain, but I could see Sir Joscelyn Giffard and thirty men-at-arms boiling out of the south tower and coming to join us. At the same time I felt a fresh surge of pressure from behind, as we too were reinforced by a flood of men from the middle bailey who even now were shoving their way eagerly into battle.

And the belfry began to lean. The iron bolt had not come loose. The archers, back and arm muscles strengthened by years of practice with powerful bows, hauled the rope towards them, foot by foot, yard by yard. I could hear Robin's brazen voice clearly over the clash and screams of battle, ordering his men to 'Heave, you weaklings! Heave like men!'

The belfry leaned further to the left. The French on the bridge were screaming in terror now – some tried to turn back but the flow of men against them was too strong. The belfry swayed back, leaned again and, with a crash that seemed to shake the foundations of the earth, it tottered, toppled and thundered down into the half-filled ditch. The siege tower burst apart under its own weight, and the weight of its unfortunate occupants, as it hit the earth and clouds of white dust boiled up, along with the muffled screaming of hundreds of men.

We roared our approval and surged forward hungrily at the score of bewildered French men-at-arms now isolated on the battlements. We killed them all, I regret to say – for not a man among us was in the mood to take a single prisoner.

The toppling of the belfry, and its destruction and the destruction of all its fighting men, should have signalled the end of the attack. But Philip had somehow put a holy fire into his troops. Indeed, I saw the King himself at the end of the causeway, wisely out of range of Old Thunderbolt, with a group of his household knights. I believe I even spotted the blond locks of my cousin Roland among them, and I willed him to stay away from these walls, not to join in the assault, for the attack was resumed within a quarter hour of the belfry's fall.

I do not think I have ever been more exhausted. I could barely lift my sword and shield after that bloody onslaught on the battlements. My ears were ringing. I counted seventeen fresh dents on my helmet. But Robin came among us with a dozen of the archers and brought buckets of watered wine with honey – God knows where he found it – with sops of bread mixed into the liquor, and we scooped wine and bread into our parched mouths with our hands. It was ambrosia. And it gave us strength for a little while longer.

The French came at us with long ladders: an old-fashioned escalade. A couple of hundred men charged along the causeway. They leaped into the ditch, leaned their ladders against the walls and, joined by the survivors of the fall of the belfry, the pitiful few who had been hiding among its dusty ruins, they swarmed up the walls.

It was difficult to take the escalade seriously, after the grave danger of the belfry. Robin's archers picked the climbing enemy off from both sides; Aaron's lethal springald smashed into the flanks of the packed ladders, wiping away men and leaving hideous red smears on the grey walls. We showered them with spears. We hurled rocks and timbers on their heads. In short, we slaughtered them.

To make matters far worse for the attackers, their ladders were too short. It seems they had miscalculated the depth of the ditch before the outer bailey, and the raised ladders were still a good ten feet from the top of the battlements. We killed them at our leisure as they gazed up at us with impotent rage. A few brave souls, perhaps a couple of dozen men, used daggers to climb the final part of the wall, jamming the blades into crevices in the stonework and hauling themselves up. We killed them, too. By the time each of these bold men had hauled themselves to the top, there were at least five of our fellows waiting to dispatch them.

So the French attack on the outer bailey ended. The survivors limped back along the causeway to Philip's Hill in shame, the dead and dying lying in thick drifts below our unbroken walls.

309

Chapter Twenty-two

The heralds came within the hour. They congratulated us civilly on our victory and begged a truce for the recovery of the wounded. De Lacy, pride-swollen like a bullfrog because we had seen off a major assault with relatively little loss of life, agreed the terms of the truce happily. Twenty-one Wolves breathed no more and another thirty-eight were wounded to varying degrees, including Vim, who had suffered a broken leg; many were likely to die of their wounds. But Robin had his archers out the minute the heralds rode away, recovering as many arrows as possible and searching the corpses and the wounded for any scraps of food. De Lacy decreed that the belfry must be broken up and brought inside the castle for firewood.

I was shocked by the loss of life on the French side

– some four hundred, perhaps five hundred good men had been destroyed. And nothing, from the French point of view, had been achieved. It had been a great victory for us, I realised dully, and found myself being hailed as something of a hero. It was not, I must admit, entirely disagreeable.

Tilda came to seek me out in the outer bailey as I was having my wounds tended by Kit on the first-floor chamber of the north tower. Thanks to my expensive Rouen mail, I had nothing more than a few scrapes, cuts and bruises, but Kit, who was also mercifully unharmed, insisted on daubing the broken skin with witch-hazel. That meant I was dressed only in my braies, the none-too-clean linen undergarments that covered my loins, when Tilda came into the room.

My body was a pitiful sight; our scanty diet had stripped away the fat from my torso, leaving the muscles starkly outlined like twisted ropes, and I was dappled with reddish bruises from neck to waist. My bare legs had equally been knocked about. I looked like one of those unfortunate men who make their living by going from fair to fair and challenging local men to fistfights or wrestling bouts, and who must take a battering in every parish to earn their bed and board – not at all like the fine gentleman I hoped Tilda to take me for. But she seemed fascinated by the ugly patterns of bruises and lacerations on my body, and when she spoke she seemed unable to tear her eyes from my chest and look into my face.

I was embarrassed by my near nakedness and asked Kit to fetch my chemise so as to cover myself. But Tilda forbade it.

'I have interrupted you while your squire is tending to your hurts, the fault is mine, I insist you continue your physicking as if I were not here. But if you would be so good as to give me an account of the battle, Sir Alan, while you are being tended to, I would esteem it a great favour.'

So I told her how the French had come on, and how we held them at the battlements, only very slightly exaggerating my own heroic stand against the open door of the belfry and the disgorging horde of ferocious French men-at-arms. I took care to praise her father's timely arrival with reinforcements, too.

Tilda was no fool. 'Surely, Alan, it was the toppling of the belfry that was the key to our victory. Can you tell me how that came about?'

Slightly irritated that she did not want to hear more about me single-handedly stemming the tide of howling foemen on the battlements, I explained that Robin had conferred with Aaron and constructed, with the help of the castle blacksmiths, a few special iron bolts for the springald with a ring at one end to hold a rope and a barb at the point so that once fixed into the side of the belfry it could not be pulled out.

'After that,' I told her, 'it was just a question of hauling on the rope. Brute strength, really.'

'Well, it was a famous victory,' said Tilda, 'and you are all to be congratulated on your prowess. Perhaps, now, Philip might be persuaded to leave us in peace.'

'Perhaps,' I said. But I did not believe it.

The bombardment of Château Gaillard by Philip's castle-breakers began again the instant the truce was over. With renewed zeal. Perhaps at royal urging, the five machines ranged against us increased the frequency with which they loosed their missiles, and all of their balls were targeted at one spot: the south tower of the outer bailey. All day missiles cracked against the limestone of the tower and while the construction of that bastion was mighty, the bombardment frayed at our nerves and sometimes I imagined the walls were shaking under the almost constant impacts.

On the afternoon of the second day of the renewed attack, I was in the south tower with Kit checking over the arrangements for a feast for the council and the senior knights to celebrate our victory over the belfry, when a ball cracked against the outer wall and I heard an ugly, splintering sound like a tree being felled, and the floor planks seemed to shift under my feet.

I ran across the courtyard to the north tower and climbed the spiral staircase to the flat roof. With Kit holding my legs, I leaned out over the parapet to try to see the outside of the wall on the south tower. And I saw something; it might have been a shadow or a stain on the walls, or it might have been something a good deal more ominous. I could not be certain.

After nightfall, when the most important men of the castle had been summoned by Robin to the south tower for a feast – or what passed for one in those straitened days: horse stew, a thin bean and onion pottage, oat cakes sweetened with honey and some weak ale brewed from herbs and a little malted barley – I decided to step outside the bailey and take a closer look at the odd mark on the wall of the south tower.

I had not been invited to the feast. Robin had required me to take command of the outer bailey while he was busy with his guests: Roger de Lacy, Sir Joscelyn Giffard, Father de la Motte and a dozen knights of illustrious birth – even Sir Benedict Malet had been invited. But I did not resent this lack of inclusion. I was in no mood for company – indeed it seemed to me foolhardy to tempt Fate with victory celebrations when we had done no more than see off an attack. Besides, I was glad of the opportunity to make a thorough examination of the damage done to the walls. I placed Vim in charge of the watch on the towers, dressed myself in dark hose and tunic, and stepped out of the postern gate at the base of the north tower and on to the planks leading across the ditch. In the darkness the stench of the battlefield seemed stronger. Although the bodies had been removed three days since, the ditch reeked like a market shambles. It was an eerie feeling to be outside the walls, but it felt strangely liberating, too, and for a moment I entertained the fantasy of just walking into the darkness, never to return to the confines of the Iron Castle. It was vain fancy, of course; the French earthworks surrounded us, though I could not see them, and I might well have been hanged as a spy if I stumbled into a French patrol. It would have been dishonourable, too, to abandon my lord and my comrades to their fate. There was Tilda to consider as well. But, for a few brief moments alone in the darkness, I admit I harboured these cowardly thoughts, and had to force myself back to my duty with no little difficulty.

I walked on the outer edge of the ditch before our walls, climbed over the causeway and found myself standing before the pale round walls of the south tower. I could not see anything in the masonry, except a good many fresh dents and divots where the missiles of the enemy had struck over the past three days. My fear that a gaping crack had opened in the base of the tower seemed unfounded. But to be absolutely certain, I turned and walked twenty paces from the walls to grant myself a different view.

And I saw it.

From an arrow slit halfway up the tower, a flash of yellow light and then a pause, then another blaze, another pause, and another gleam of light. Three flashes with two heartbeats of darkness between each. How curious, I thought, someone is playing with a dark lantern, opening and shutting the panel to allow the candlelight inside to glow briefly.

Out of the corner of my eye, away to my left, from the

French lines, there came an answering flash, a pause, a flash, a pause, and a final flash of light. The notion hit me like a kick to the belly. Somebody inside the castle was signalling to the French. Someone was conversing with the enemy in a code written in light. I had no idea what the message might mean, but I did know one thing.

We had a traitor within our walls.

Part Three

Chapter Twenty-three

Young Alan was defiant when he came to see me the next day. He was also badly hungover, with dark bruises under watery red eyes and a yellowish pallor to his skin. I had little sympathy – but his mother Marie fussed about him and brought him a posset with eggs beaten up in milk. He drank it down in one.

'Have you made this girl Agnes pregnant?' I asked him outright.

He stared at me, our eyes locked, but he said nothing.

I repeated the question, fighting the urge to crack my open palm against his cheek. My old eyes bored into his. Finally, he broke our contact, dropped his head.

'You have nothing to say to me?'

More silence.

'It was not my fault,' he said eventually.

So, I asked, had he slipped then and fallen prick-first into her?

The boy glared at the rushes on the floor of the hall.

'Did you force her?'

'No, no.' Alan's head jerked up; he was quite shocked by the suggestion. 'She said she loves me. I believe she does.'

More angry silence. Then: 'I did not mean to get her with child, it was a mistake . . . We were kissing in the hay barn, a harmless kiss; and she was warm and soft and lovely; we lay down together . . .'

I tried for conciliation. 'Surely you can see this from the point of view of the yeoman Godwin. All his hopes for a good marriage for his daughter are dashed. He raised her, he cherished her, he had plans for her. Now they are destroyed. Who will want her with another man's child in her belly?'

Alan merely stared at the floor in sullen silence.

'Listen to me, boy: she is ruined now and it is your fault. You have dishonoured her; you have taken her maidenhood from her, her most precious badge of honour – some might say that you have stolen it, if you will not replace her maiden status with that of wife. You must make things right with her and with her father, too. I take it that she would marry you, if you asked.'

'I will not marry her!' Alan was suddenly all fierceness. He looked me hard in the eye again, like an enemy, almost.

'Why not? She seems a fine girl, beautiful, loving.'

'Her father is a sheep farmer! She spends all day with her hands in a milk bucket. And I . . . I am the grandson of a knight, I am a gentleman, I am heir to these very Westbury lands.'

'So? You think you should only marry some great lady?'

He said nothing for a while, then: 'It is beneath my honour, Grandpa, surely even you can see that.' He went quiet again, contemplating the floor-rushes once more. 'I cannot be with her.' He sounded almost wistful. 'My friends would laugh at me; they would say she is a farm girl, far beneath my dignity.'

'Your friends – ha! Those drunken popinjays.'

'They are my best friends.'

I realised then what his problem was.

'Those boys, those sons of great men whom you call your friends, have no idea who they really are,' I said. 'And they certainly cannot say who you are. They talk about their honour and their lineage and tell themselves they are noblemen, better than all others, but are they even men at all? Who knows? They have never been tested. They tell themselves they are better than others because they fear that they are not; they fear, deep in their hearts, that they might even be worse. You should not listen to such nonsense, not from them. Their mockery is no more than the honking of frightened geese. Find your own honour, prove it to yourself. You must show yourself to be a better man than others, it will not do merely to tell people that this is so.'

'Do you truly think I should marry her, Grandpa?'

'I cannot force you to wed, but I confess that I would think less of you if you did not. A man's honour is not the same as his rank – remember that. And, if you marry her, you will gentle her condition – she will be Lady Westbury one day. I'd wager that she would make you a fine wife and a fine mistress for this old place. We know, at least, that she is fertile.'

I raced back to the postern gate, scrambling up and down the ditches either side of the causeway using my hands and feet. I bounced across the plank, blew through the courtyard of the outer bailey and into the south tower, my legs pumping, brain spinning like a windmill in a gale. If I were fast enough, I thought, I could catch whoever was signalling to the enemy in the very act – what the the royal foresters who found poachers in Sherwood with their hands bloody used to call red-handed. In the map of my mind, I knew exactly which window had been used for this treachery. It was on the spiral staircase between middle floor, where Robin was entertaining his noble guests, and the top, a few yards along from the alcove that was used as a latrine, just below where the men of the watch ought to be keeping a sharp lookout.

When I reached the middle floor – my hose covered in mud from the causeway ditches – the party was just breaking up. Indeed, several knights pushed past as I was coming up the spiral stairs, including a sneering Benedict. I could not think of a reason to halt him or any of the knights – and to demand outright if they had been communicating with the French from an arrow slit by candlelight seemed absurd. When I came in to the feasting chamber, I sketched a bow at Robin, who raised an eyebrow at my filthy attire, and ran straight up the stairs to the arrow slit but, of course, there was no one there. When I came back down, almost all the gathered knights – a dozen or so men – had left and Roger de Lacy was thanking Robin for his hospitality.

'My lord, I must speak with you on a matter of urgency,' I said to Robin, who was bidding the castellan farewell. 'Perhaps my lord de Lacy should hear this too.'

'Very well,' said Robin. He called to one of the archers who had been serving the feast. 'Simon, bring us another jug of that filthy ale, will you?'

Robin ushered us to the long table and pushed out the bench with his foot. De Lacy and I sat down while Robin took the jug from his archer-servant and poured out three goblets of a truly foul-tasting brew.

'I believe there is a traitor inside the castle communicating with the French, perhaps telling them of our weaknesses,' I said, and told them about the flashes of light from the arrow slit. Robin and de Lacy listened in silence until I had finished.

'You took all that from seeing a gleam of candlelight at a window?' said de Lacy, his disbelief obvious.

'And the response from the French lines – an identical pattern of flashes.'

'Could be a coincidence,' said Robin.

'It's preposterous. It is out of the question that any of our men should be a traitor,' said Roger de Lacy. He rose from his bench and put down his ale. His face was the colour of a freshly cut beetroot. 'We have lived alongside each other in this castle for the best part of a year – for long before you two washed up here. I have patrolled and fought and starved and suffered alongside these men, these good men that you now accuse, for long enough to know the secrets of their hearts. I cannot believe any of them would be a traitor. I am disgusted by the very notion, Sir Alan, and I do not wish to hear another word on the matter. I bid you goodnight.'

The castellan strode from the room without a backward glance.

'It is a bit thin, Alan,' said Robin. 'Come on, we're all on edge. It is easy to let our imaginations get the better of us. Forget it for the moment and try to get a good night's sleep. Here, have some more ale.'

'Thank you, no,' I said, irked that these men, both of whom I admired, had dismissed my idea. I, too, rose and left the chamber, my face beetroot red.

The next morning the French came at us again. They treated us with a good deal of respect after the disastrous belfry attack and the day began, as usual, with another battering from the castle-breakers. Perhaps I did suffer from an overabundance of imagination, as Robin had suggested the night before, because I distinctly heard the stone wall of the south tower moving under the pounding it received from Philip's petraries that day. In the middle of the morning the barrage abruptly ceased and, in the unfamiliar quiet, I ran to the top to see what was amiss – and beheld a most extraordinary sight approaching along the causeway from Philip's Hill.

It was a cat – not the household scourge of mice and rats, but the battlefield scourge of walls and masonry. Its use in battle is quite rare and not one man in a hundred has faced one, and so I must explain its functions. At its simplest the cat was nothing more than a very strongly built house on wheels; but it is the expertise of the men it contains that makes it so fearsome. Inside this cat – constructed of foot-thick timbers, roofed with overlapping inch-thick oak shingles and covered top, front and sides with wet ox-hide to prevent it being set alight – were a score of highly skilled men under a senior engineer armed with picks and iron bars, spikes, spades and hammers. Their task was to claw away at the foundations of the south tower, to undermine our walls, to pick at, and scrape into and lever out the masonry – until our defences came tumbling down. Watching a small house on wheels creeping towards you along the causeway might not appear a good reason for alarm – it sounds a little comical, perhaps – but I felt a tremor of fear at its approach, for I knew what an attack by this rolling monster truly portended.

The cat did not come on alone. Two battles of crossbowmen – each a hundred strong – came up the causeway on either side of it, and took up positions a hundred yards out. A *conroi* of knights formed up outside the gates of the encampment on Philip's Hill, just out of range of our bows.

The cat crawled forward and, as it approached, a dozen of Robin's archers in the north tower loosed shafts at its lumbering bulk. With no result whatsoever. The wet ox-hides on the sloping roof, and the shingles underneath, easily soaked up the power of the war bows. The roof became thickly feathered with our shafts – and that was all. We had no way of stopping the cat, except by sallying out of the outer bailey and killing the men inside who propelled it – and this is where the crossbowmen came in. These disciplined foot soldiers worked in pairs, each pair protected by a giant shield, called a pavise, which was the height of a man and nearly twice as wide. The pavise was fixed into the earth of the causeway by a spike on its bottom edge and the two crossbowmen – mercenaries from Genoa, I assumed, by the red cross on a white background on their pavises – worked in its shade, one loading his cumbersome crossbow, while the other sought out a suitable target on the walls and loosed. They were professionals, every man a marksman, and even at a hundred yards we had to keep our heads below the parapet if we wished to escape a bolt through the eye. Even if we had found the courage to sally out and charge the crossbowmen – and our casualties would have been appalling – there was the *conroi* of cavalry ready and waiting by the gates to the French camp to see that we did not return safely home again.

We could do nothing but watch as the cat rolled inexorably towards us.

Robin left his archers to continue a cautious duel with the crossbowmen – for once in a while a Genoese who foolishly stepped beyond the protection of his pavise could be satisfactorily skewered – and came to my side above the end of the causeway to the left of the south tower.

The cat was so close now that I could make out the heads of the long nails that held the ox-hides to the roof. As it reached the half-filled ditch before our walls, I heard the score of men inside the machine give a roar. They increased their speed and hurled the house-on-wheels down into the ditch to land with a thump against the base of our battlements.

As the dust settled, I looked down directly twenty feet below on to the brown-and-white hide-covered roof of the cat. It was angled downwards, the rear end high up on the causeway, the front down in the rubble of the ditch, and it was not quite snug against the walls; one side was hard up against the stone, the other was a good foot away. Through this gap, I saw the bearded face of a man peering up at me, but before I had time to react, he darted back under the roof.

We hurled rocks, stones and pieces of broken masonry down on the roof of the cat, but while they boomed satisfactorily, they seemed to have no destructive effect at all. Robin ordered several cauldrons of water to be heated to boiling point and poured on to the wet hides, which sizzled and steamed and gave off the tantalising smell of cooking beef, an insult to our siege-shrunken bellies. But while the hot water dripped off the indifferent eves, and the boulders crashed and bounced off the arrow-struck sides, one sound could clearly be heard coming from below.

The chink-chink-chink of steel chisels on stone.

'I have to go out and stop them,' I said to Robin. 'However high the risk, we cannot let them pull the castle down from under us.'

I remember Robin's expression very well: it was one of the few times I have seen him look uncertain.

'Somebody must go,' he said. 'But that duty, I believe, falls to me. I leave you in command of the outer bailey. If anything happens to me, see that Marie-Anne and the boys are cared for. I leave them in your charge, Alan.'

'My lord, I will go in your stead. We need you here to defend the castle.'

'Do not argue with me, Alan. For once, just do as you are told.'

Chapter Twenty-four

Robin took twenty volunteers from the garrison – grim-faced men who had known him a long time and who would follow him to the very gates of Hell. An hour later they slipped out of the postern gate and into the half-filled ditch at the bottom of the walls. And there they began to die. Watchful eyes saw them leave the castle and almost immediately the quarrels of the Genoese began to strike them. Our archers returned the compliment valiantly, but Robin and his Wolves had stepped into a storm of death. They ran the thirty yards from the little door to the causeway through a blizzard of crossbow bolts, with a man falling every third step, and threw themselves at the cat. But the men inside were ready. After a short, fierce battle at the rear of the cat, in which I saw Robin, his blade flashing silver, cut down two giant axe-wielding men in three heartbeats, the thunder of hooves heralded the arrival of the *conroi* of French knights, which charged down the causeway to the rescue of the engineers.

Aaron's aim proved true once again, and Old Thunderbolt utterly disintegrated one of the knights, smashing him out of the saddle in a tangle of severed arms and legs. But the rest of the *conroi* arrived more or less unscathed and Robin and his surviving men ran for their lives. They made it back inside the postern gate a yard or two ahead of the lances of the foremost horsemen. Panting, bloody, wild-eyed, eight of the Wolves who had sallied out with Robin returned safely home with him. A dozen bolts were stuck in Robin's mail but the iron links had kept the missiles from penetrating, and my lord was no worse than bruised. However, while that knowledge gave me relief, the sortie achieved nothing, and twelve brave Wolves would never see the sun rise again.

Half an hour later eight big fellows were hurried out from the gates on Philip's Hill in the centre of a mob of French men-at-arms and, under a covering of many shields, in an ancient formation known as a 'tortoise', they were swiftly escorted along the causeway to the cat – replacements for the men Robin and his Wolves had killed. We spattered them with arrows but they were well protected, and moving fast, and the best we achieved was to kill one man-at-arms and wound another.

Below our walls the chink-chink-chinking began again.

We would not concede defeat easily. We harassed them as much as was humanly possible. We battered the cat with huge chunks of masonry ripped from the parapet on the south-western side of the outer bailey – which had been largely ignored by the French – and carried up to the walls above the cat by two of the biggest Wolves. But the machine was unbelievably strong and springy, and our missiles bounced or slowly rolled off without puncturing it or causing any damage save for the occasional tear in the ox-hide. Robin found a precious barrel of cooking oil which we heated until it smoked, then carefully poured down in a slick on one side of the cat and set alight with burning arrows. Again the smell of roasting beef tormented us, but the cat, while a little singed, remained largely unharmed.

The chinking noise continued by day and night – the causeway made bright with scores of torches after dusk, set there by the enemy to foil any attempt at a night sortie. Aaron smashed his iron bolts time and again into the side of that powerful wooden box, to no avail. We even tried to lift the cat away from the walls with ropes, lowering a loop and snagging a protruding end post – but while we hauled at the cat in vain, the French engineers divined our plans and sawed through the ropes from inside their mobile fortress – and we tumbled back comically like mountebanks.

A second cat came out from the encampment on Philip's Hill, lighter and smaller than the first, but still robust. We christened it 'the kitten'. It trundled smoothly along the causeway and came to rest nose-to-tail at the rear of the original machine, creating a long fortified tunnel. The kitten brought out more men and supplies with it and, through the little gap between the first cat and our walls, I glimpsed timbers and barrels being swiftly manhandled into the cavity that had been made beneath our feet.

I was gripped in that time with a burning sense of impotent rage. These men were eating away at our foundations like ants chewing through a door post – and there seemed nothing I or anybody else could do about it. I would spend hours with a pair of javelins kneeling behind the parapet above the cat, listening to them and hoping to hear when one of the men came out of the space they had dug under the wall, so that I could leap up and spit him with a thrown spear before he slipped across the tiny gap. But after one narrow miss, my javelin clattering off the stone walls, the man calling out to God in fear, they covered the gap with a roof of thick planks and thenceforth they travelled from cat to mine in perfect safety. I still spent some hours each day sitting above them, listening to their French chatter and trying to think of a way of combatting the steady erosion of our defences – and a few days after the mining began, I did hear something of great interest. Two men were coming out of the cavity beneath the south tower and speaking quite casually with one another. One was the senior engineer, the man in charge, and the other I thought was a new fellow, a junior man but of some rank; they hustled across the causeway under a roof of shields.

'It's just as the Sparrow told us,' the older fellow said, quite distinctly. 'The mortar is as wet as custard in some places.'

I sat up straight at these words. At the phrase 'as wet as custard'. I had heard it from someone inside the castle. But who? I did not have to beat my brains for long. It was Father de la Motte. He had uttered it to describe the mortar inside the walls of the Iron Castle, and one of our enemies was using this exact same – and most unusual – phrase.

My first impulse was to tell Robin. Then I quashed it. The last time I had come to him with tales of a traitor inside our walls he had dismissed it as the workings of my overimaginative mind. And while I was certain that we had a turncoat among us, I had no more proof than the last time – just a muttered conversation and the coincidence of a phrase. Clearly the name the traitor went by among the French was the Sparrow – but who was he? Could it be de la Motte? If so, what motive could he have for working towards our destruction? In truth, I did not believe it truly was Father de la Motte. He was a good man, a man of God. He could not be so base as to betray his flock to the enemy. Could he? It was far more likely that he had heard someone – the true traitor – use the phrase, and merely repeated it to me. I had no answers to these questions – and no one I could usefully discuss them with. In the end I did nothing. For all thoughts of the Sparrow and his treachery were pushed from my head the next morning when the men in the cat finished their task.

I was on the north tower with Aaron and we were discussing the possibility of a very long shot of the sprin-gald against the *conroi* of horsemen on permanent guard outside the gates of the French encampment. My idea was to use a lighter bolt and scatter the cavalry, then send out a screen of shield men as cover against the crossbowmen for an attacking force, who would run out and slaughter the men inside the cat. It was a plan of last resort, an elaborate scheme – and I was fairly sure Robin would veto it after the debacle of his sally three days ago. Aaron was not even sure he could do much damage with Old Thunderbolt at that distance anyway.

As I looked dispiritedly at the evil cat, eating away at my walls, I was surprised to see a score of men burst out of the rear of the kitten, burdened down with tools, bundles and boxes. They raced as fast as they could along the causeway towards Philip's Hill.

They were moving too fast for Aaron to have a chance of hitting them – and Old Thunderbolt was not ready to loose anyway. But the curious thing was that the cat the men had abandoned in such a hurry appeared to be burning. A thick column of grey smoke was pouring out of the rear end of the kitten, as if the enemy's fortified tunnel had been magically transformed into a chimney, and dark vapour was seeping from the sides of both machines, too. At the same moment a trebuchet loosed from the French camp and a huge stone ball looped through the air and exploded in a storm of shards against the south tower.

I cupped my hands to my face and bellowed to Robin who was standing on the walls about twenty paces away.

'They've fired the mine – get everyone off the south tower!'

Robin shouted back, 'I'm not totally blind, Alan. Nor yet quite senile!' He pointed to the thick bank of greasy smoke that was enveloping the whole of the base of the tower.

We pulled every man off the tower, and the connecting fortifications, with the missiles of the whole French battery crashing and smashing against our walls. We had already moved our wounded, our stores, our weapons and possessions out of that citadel and into the courtyard or the north and west towers. For we knew full well what was occurring beneath our feet. The French would have excavated a large space underneath the walls of the tower, a wide tunnel burrowing inward for several yards, supporting its roof with thick baulks and roof pieces nailed firmly in place. This was necessary because, above their heads, as they dug in, were a couple of thousand tons of rubble and stone. When the excavation was finished, the space they had hollowed out would have been filled with brushwood, kindling and many barrels of pig fat, and duly set alight – that accounted for the dark, oily smoke. The miners had run for their lives while the fire raged and burned its way through the wooden supports in the tunnel and then, if the French were lucky, and their excavations had been deep enough, well . . .

With a sound like a mountain tearing itself in two, the eastern half of the south tower and part of the curtain wall collapsed into a heap of broken masonry and tumbling, bouncing stone. The whole outer bailey was cloaked in grey dust and pig-fat smoke so thick it was almost impossible to breathe, but when the fog began to dissipate, I could see that a breach fully three or four yards wide had opened in our walls. Through the gap I could make out the earth ramparts on top of Philip's Hill, packed with French spectators. The south tower gaped: I could see inside the chamber on the middle floor where for the past six months we had dined, the big table and the benches, the sideboard stripped of plates; and on the ground floor I could even make out the cot where I slept up against the far, intact wall of the tower.

It felt deeply wrong, as though I were peeping at a woman halfway through dressing herself. To add insult to grave injury, the bombardment started up again as though nothing had happened. The balls smashed into the breach, widening it – one flew straight through the gap into a pair of archers standing in the courtyard. Both men disappeared in a splash of red, limbs wheeling through the air.

Robin was by my side, in the courtyard by the west wall. He took my arm and pointed through the hole in our defences to Philip's Hill. I flinched as a ball crashed into the rubble below the breach, sending white dust and stone chips flying, then took command of myself and looked to where Robin was pointing. The gates had swung open and columns of marching spearmen were disgorging from the encampment. I could see the bright trappers of massed knights behind them.

'They are coming,' said Robin. 'And they will surely be able to break through, if they try hard enough. We cannot hold this bailey for long – but we must hold it for a little while yet. We have to get our stores, our kit, all the wounded, then the rest of us over the bridge and into the middle bailey. And you, my friend, have to hold them while I accomplish this. I'll give you twenty Wolves, ten of them archers – I'll need the rest for carrying the wounded and all the gear. Can you do it?'

I swallowed. Of all the tasks Robin had asked of me over the years, this seemed the most difficult. I could see hundreds of men on the causeway – two hundred spearmen at least, a battle of crossbowmen, a *conroi* of horsemen.

I took a breath. A trebuchet ball smashed against the wall, making a high, loud noise, like the cry of a wounded bird. I opened my mouth, filled my lungs and bellowed, 'North tower first watch and south tower third watch to me! This instant. I want you all right here, right now. North tower first watch and . . .'

Through the billowing dust and smoke I saw the obedient Wolves running towards me.

Chapter Twenty-five

We burned the outer bailey just before we quit it. Robin's men piled furniture in each of the towers and the extra bedding, straw, old candle ends, and anything they could find that was flammable, and set it ablaze. And they torched all the buildings in the courtyard, too. I lined the breach with a score of Wolves and while Robin and the rest of the men scurried about behind us, carrying boxes and barrels, and litters for the wounded, we kept the French at bay for more than an hour – but, thank God, we were called on to do little in the way of actual fighting. The bombardment had mercifully ceased as the French approached, and I believe they could have easily over-whelmed us in one determined rush. But they did not. Instead, the crossbowmen were pushed forward and planted their pavises fifty yards from the outer bailey and showered us with bolts. Our bowmen exchanged shafts with them, and killed a few, but we lost only one man – I had made sure that every Wolf was in good cover, behind rubble or a piece of remaining wall, and that they kept their shields up. The French knew we were there, waiting for them to attack, and they hesitated. I took that as a compliment to our prowess. But, at last, the French spearmen forming up on the causeway for the assault were ready to advance. It was at that moment that Robin released us from our duty – and we pulled back, scrambling down over the broken rock and stone – as the smoke from the fires set by his men began to boil out of the doorways of the towers and leak from the arrow slits set in the round walls.

By the time the horde of shouting Frenchmen was clambering out of the ditch and through the rubble of the breach, we were safe on the far side of the drawbridge that connected the outer and middle baileys, and were pulling it across behind us. The fire in the outer bailey had taken firm hold and all five towers were roaring. A few French spearmen climbed the walls and stared over at us in the middle bailey – but there was a vast ditch nine yards wide and a full thirty feet deep, between us and them, and the inferno we had left behind soon drove them out of the captured outer bastion.

Roger de Lacy was there to greet us in person as we came tumbling over the drawbridge, coughing from the smoke, and to his credit, he had a word of congratulation for almost every man. I was the last across and he beamed at me like a father and said, 'Bravely done, Sir Alan, bravely done indeed. It was a defence worthy of the Lionheart himself. You made them pay dearly for that scorched pile of stones and rubble. I congratulate you. And it will do them no good now. The dogs.'

We might have been celebrating a victory, if one were to go by the castellan's sternly happy expression, instead of watching our outer fortifications go up in flames. Perhaps it was a victory of sorts. We had held off the might of King Philip of France for nigh on six months, and only now had we been forced to give up a single outer bastion. The Iron Castle was still ours. Philip was, in some ways, no closer to having it than six months ago. The middle bailey, the inner bailey and the keep were formidable. We had not been defeated. It had, you might say, merely been a setback.

The outer bailey burned for a day and a night – we had squads of men-at-arms on constant alert in the middle bailey with buckets of water to extinguish any flying sparks – and for a day afterwards it glowed too hot for the French to occupy. But soon enough we saw the broad blue and gold standard of Philip of France flying from the blackened shell of the western tower in the outer bailey, just a dozen yards from my new post on the south tower of the middle bailey, above the chapel. It was difficult to pretend that we were winning then, when I could almost have spat straight in the eye of the evil-looking French man-at-arms who peered at me over the parapet. We had to keep our heads down at all times, too. For while we were running short of arrows, the French crossbowmen seemed to have an ample supply and almost every day some unwary soul was spitted.

But it was not the loss of the outer bailey that most exercised my mind in those grim days. I could not shake my conviction that there was a traitor within these walls. To my mind, the signalling by candlelight and the coincidence of the miner's choice of words made a compelling case for an enemy within. I found myself in the chapel on the Sunday after the fall of the outer bailey attending the Eucharist service with Tilda and looking at the pious knights and noblemen around me and wondering who this person known as the Sparrow might be. Was it Father de la Motte? The priest, who was now blessing the bread and wine, had shown an inordinate amount of interest in the defences of the outer bailey. Had he been passing this information to the French? And if so, why? Why would a man of God break his oath to the King? That must be a very grave sin, surely? No, surely it could not be him. Could it then be Roger de Lacy, our castellan and commander? Had he made an arrangement with the French to save his life if the castle fell – or more, was he selling us out in exchange for rich lands and titles from Philip? Given the man's iron character, it was unthinkable. Could it even be Vim, now hobbling up to the altar cheerfully on two sticks with his broken leg all strapped up, ready to receive the body and blood of Christ. The man was a mercenary and would serve any master if the pay was right. Had he made a more lucrative deal with King Philip? No, I knew he was completely loyal to Robin. He would not betray his lord in a thousand years. Could it be Sir Benedict Malet, then, praying so piously over there? That I could readily believe, though it did seem rather unlikely. Why would he do such a thing? Or Sir Joscelyn Giffard, now humbly accepting the chalice of wine? Or his daughter, my lovely Matilda, praying demurely beside me – a woman spy? That was quite absurd. It could be any one of these people, it could be none of them. It could be any of the score of knights gathered in the chapel for this holy sacrament. It could even be a disgruntled man-at-arms, or an unhappy squire, selling the information for silver and the promise of a knighthood and lands.

Think, Alan, think! I berated myself. It had to be a person with both the opportunity to speak with the French and a motive to betray the castle. Or a motive to betray King John's cause.

As Father de la Motte chanted the holy Latin of the Eucharist, my eyes fell on my own lord Robin, Earl of Locksley, standing at the back of the chapel with an indulgent, unbelieving smile on his face. How deep was Robin's loyalty to King John? The fellow was a soft, steaming turd for all that he wore a crown. We both acknowledged that. Yet Robin served him, apparently faithfully. And Robin had been in and out of the French camp many times; he moved among the enemy with impunity, each time returning with gifts of 'intelligence' for de Lacy. Was Robin wearing a mask to hide his treachery? Did he have a deeper purpose than loyally serving King John? Was Robin the secret servant of the King of France?

I took a firm grip of myself. I had suspected Robin of heinous crimes before – and been utterly wrong. I must control my wilder fancies. I must be loyal to my lord, in thought as well as deed. Robin was not the traitor. He had done some bad things in his time, but he would never stoop to this. Robin could not possibly be the traitor.

Could he?

Chapter Twenty-six

No more than forty-seven Wolves survived the fall of the outer bailey, along with eleven other men of our company, a mixture of men-at-arms, volunteers and engineers. They, along with Robin, myself and Kit, had been allocated lodgings in the south tower of the middle bailey. Aaron, who also lodged with us, was grimly cheerful. He had managed to find the time, with Robin's help, to dismantle Old Thunderbolt and transport it piece by piece to safety. But rather than set it up on the south tower, he had reassembled it on the roof of the keep in the centre of the inner bailey where it had the range to dominate every part of the castle we still laid claim to.

We swiftly settled into the south tower of the middle bailey, and once again I organised the men into three watches – making every man an honorary Wolf, even the three volunteer townsfolk, who were touchingly flattered to be able to call themselves such. There was no wolf fur to be had, of course – but the new Wolves sewed tatters of grey blanket to their clothes in imitation of their comrades. Lord de Lacy sent us a whole leg of horse meat, as a reward for our valour in defending the outer bailey for so long, a very small keg of wine and a dozen loaves of bread, and so, for the first time in days, we ate a hot and hearty meal.

With the fires doused in the outer bailey, the French speedily occupied it, and it was strange and uncomfortable to see our enemies treading the very stones we had defended for so long and at such cost. But they did not confine themselves to that charred bastion for long – soon they were cautiously patrolling the outer edges of the ditches around the middle bailey and prowling the steep slopes of the cliffs to the north and west of the Iron Castle, looking for a way to get in. We were very short of arrows by this point, and quarrels too, and Robin repeated de Lacy's order that all missiles be conserved against a full-on assault. But it was galling to see the French wandering about boldly within bow shot, even though we knew we would need every shaft when they came at us in anger.

Another rascal who was far bolder than he should be was Sir Benedict Malet. He had formed some sort of attachment to Tilda during their time as guardians of the store-caves and I saw them together much more often than I liked. The stores were now all but exhausted and we were living on horse-bones soup and rock-hard twice-baked bread from the emergency reserve barrels in the inner bailey – and so there was no good reason I could see for them to associate with each other any longer. And yet I often saw him following her about, trailing a few steps behind her like a faithful hound. I asked Tilda once, on one of the rare occasions I managed to spend a few moments alone with her, if Benedict bothered her, and whether she would like me to tell him to leave her in peace.

'That is very sweet of you, my dear Alan,' she said, 'but there really is no need. He is quite harmless.'

I rather enjoyed the idea that she thought him 'harmless'.

However, my own relationship with Tilda had not progressed at all over the past few months. I was still as entranced by her as ever and I desperately wanted to tell her how I felt, then to take her in my arms, kiss her and claim her as mine once and for all. But it was proving extremely difficult to be with her alone. In the crowded castle there was very little privacy, almost none in fact, and furthermore there was the problem of her father.

Sir Joscelyn Giffard was a good man, I knew, and more than that he was a friend and a comrade – and some unspoken warrior code made me reluctant to make any moves that might be construed as taking advantage of his daughter. It was not just his gentlemanly warning all those months ago in Falaise; it was the full-bodied decency of the man. I could not bear to behave in an underhand or dishonourable way and have him know it. I sorely needed to speak to Tilda, to reveal my regard for her, and test her feelings for me. But it is difficult to speak soft words to a lady when you are being jostled by a throng of filthy men-at-arms queuing for rations, or in a chamber crowded with sweaty knights and squires all noisily chatting, swearing and cleaning weapons and armour.

Furthermore, these fine thoughts of tenderness and romance seemed a trifle absurd in the circumstances. We were surrounded by the mighty forces of the King of France and, with our stores down to scraps, we faced the real prospect of starvation. Despite our dire circumstances, it was clear that Roger de Lacy had no intention of surrendering to Philip. He repeated his message about being dragged out of the Iron Castle by the heels when the heralds came to parlay after the fall of the outer bailey, and the other members of the high council stood by him.

To the garrison, in another of his robust battlement speeches, de Lacy announced the news that King John was in England gathering a fresh army of English barons who would return to Normandy in the spring and destroy Philip before our walls. Every man, even the lowliest, would be handsomely rewarded for his part in resisting the French, when the King returned in glory. The enemy, de Lacy said, were stricken with plague and despondent after failing for so long to take the castle. They were exhausted, beaten curs; any day they would pack their bags and go.

I was not so certain. The French men-at-arms that I saw daily roaming carelessly outside the walls appeared to me healthy, strong, confident, even arrogant, and certainly not the beaten curs that de Lacy would have us believe in.

The Wolves were responsible for the south tower and the section of walls on either side, including the common latrines and the small chapel perched above.

It was my practice, when my watch was on duty, to make regular patrols with Kit. I had neglected his education during the battle for the outer bailey, and he had inadvertently reminded me of this when we shared a meagre evening bowl of soup together not long after taking up residence in the south tower.

'When this is all over, Kit,' I had asked him idly, 'when the French are thoroughly beaten, what will you do?'

'I will eat, sir,' he said without a moment's hesitation. 'I will eat like a king.' He scraped the last drops of liquor from the bowl. 'I will eat until I can eat no more.'

I smiled fondly at him. 'Apart from filling your belly, have you no other desires for the future? Everyone should have hopes and dreams, Kit, however fanciful. We cannot be whole men without them.'

'In that case, if you do not think me too forward, sir, too presumptuous, I believe I should like to be a famous knight some day, like you, sir.'

'That is often decided by God, at birth.'

'I would do some great deed of valour on the battlefield and be knighted by a grateful king, just as you were, sir.'

I thought, then, about the day the Lionheart made me a knight after the siege of Nottingham Castle and I felt the swelling of pride in my breast.

'I can't guarantee you will ever be a knight, Kit, but I can try to make you into a decent soldier. The rest we will leave to God – and, of course, your valour.'

So I vowed to pay special attention to my squire, taking him with me almost everywhere I went and instructing him in what I was doing and why.

In the third week of the month of February, I found myself making the rounds at an hour or two after dusk, on a chilly night when most of the men not on duty were making up their beds. I found Robin and Vim together in the base of the tower earnestly discussing the storage of spare weapons, and wished them a cordial good night. Wearing full mail and a thick cloak against the wind, and with Fidelity hanging at my side, and Kit beside me, I climbed the stairs to the wall that overlooked the outer bailey. I stopped to speak with the sentry, a steady fellow named Simon who often did duty as Robin's servant. He reported that the French were quiet and seemed to have settled down for the night. I walked further on to the drawbridge, once the link between the outer and middle baileys and now roped up tight against our walls. In the guardhouse there, three Wolves were taking their ease around a brazier and playing at knuckle-bones with four men I did not know from de Lacy's garrison. They were all sober and alert, one man remaining outside in the cold and keeping a close watch on the enemy.

We retraced our steps to the base of the tower and just outside the latrines I nearly bumped into Sir Benedict Malet who had clearly been relieving himself inside. I gave him a stiff 'God save you' but he just glared at me and turned away. He did not depart, though; evidently he was waiting for some friend to finish their business inside the latrine. Climbing the steps to the chapel, with Kit hard on my heels, I entered God's house and found the place brilliant with the light of candles.

Father de la Motte was inside, in deep conversation with Sir Joscelyn Giffard. Tilda was arranging a display of dried bulrushes on a table beside the altar. When I greeted them cordially, all I received in reply was a quick smile and a friendly wave of the hand from Tilda's father and a beaming smile from his daughter. I was about to leave when I noticed the big window on the western side of the chapel was wide open. I walked over to it and looked out. A rectangle of yellow light fell on the deep ditch outside the walls, which was about a quarter full with rainwater and filth – the latrines drained into the ditch there too, before flowing down a channel on the hillside. I could smell the faint, sweetish stench of human waste. I pulled the shutter closed and secured it with a stout locking bar.

Father de la Motte and Sir Joscelyn had clearly finished

their discourse. Sir Joscelyn took his leave of the priest with another genial wave in my direction; Tilda trotted obediently after her father, sending me another heartwarming smile at the top of the stairs. Father de la Motte nodded to Kit, then turned to me: 'And how are you faring, my son?'

'I am well, thank you, Father,' I said. 'A little hungry, but I believe we all are, aren't we?'

I caught Kit's eye and winked at him.

'Yes, we are all feeling the pinch of want,' said the priest. 'But, by God's grace, it will be over soon.'

'How so?' I said.

For a second Father de la Motte looked startled. 'Ah, well, King John will soon be here with his relief force, won't he? And then we shall feast like heroes.'

'Do you really think so, Father?' I said.

'Have faith, my son, have faith that God in His wisdom will bring an end to our suffering. Now, tell me, how are your men holding up? Are they in good spirits? Are they content to fight on until we are delivered by our noble sovereign? Is there anything I can do to give them hope or comfort?'

I assured him the Wolves were in good spirits and would fight for Robin as long as he commanded them. Then I wished the priest a good night and said, 'Father, I will leave you in peace now, but please make sure the window remains closed when you leave the chapel and that all the candles are extinguished. We do not want to risk a fire.'

'Certainly, certainly. I found it open when I came here half an hour ago and left it so because it can become so stuffy in here of an evening. But, of course, I will keep it closed and conserve our precious candles too, in a little while – when I have finished my prayers. God be with you, Sir Alan.'

I left the good priest to his prayers.

There was no sign of Robin in the tower and so I sat down with Kit to share a dry crust of bread and a rind of hard cheese, washed down with cold well water, which we called our supper. I understood why Kit's chief aspiration was to eat when this affair was over. He was painfully thin. It seemed to me a particularly cruel blow that a young man such as he, in the prime of his youth – at a time when he should be quaffing ale with his fellows in the local tavern and stepping out with the girls of the village on moonlit nights – should be stuck in this bare fortress with a growling belly. We chatted a little then, to pass the time, about his ambition to be a knight and what might be expected of him if he were ever to attain that honour. One thing he said that night touched me and has stayed with me evermore. We were discussing how to command the loyalty of men and I was using the fighting spirit of the Wolves as an example, and Kit said, 'But, of course, all the men would follow the Earl – and you too, Sir Alan – to the very mouth of Hell; they'd even follow you down in there, sir, if you asked it of them. So would I.'

At about midnight we went up together to check the sentries. They were awake but grumbled a little about the cold, and I promised to see about finding a brazier and some firewood for them. I looked down on the walls of the outer bailey and saw a goodly number of French men-at-arms moving about quietly on the ramparts and wondered if they were undergoing some sort of reorganisation of their watches. It seemed a strange time to be attempting this. Then I looked down to my left and felt a sharp stab of annoyance. I could see an oblong of light illuminating the chalk of the ditch beyond the latrine. Damn the man, I thought, Father de la Motte has opened the chapel window again and has recklessly left candles burning in his House of God.

I left Kit on the roof of the tower and trotted down the spiral staircase, then crossed the few yards to the steps to the chapel, trying to think of a suitable way to rebuke a holy man who was also my superior in rank. I pushed open the door . . .

There were three men-at-arms in the chapel that I had never seen before in my life, and a fourth was in the very act of climbing in through the window.

The French were inside the middle bailey.

Chapter Twenty-seven

I ripped Fidelity from its scabbard and rushed at the nearest French man-at-arms. My sword swooped down at his neck, but he was well trained and his vertical block was in place in plenty of time. Our blades rang out like Christmas bells. I bounced away from the blow, lunged at the second man to his left, plunging Fidelity into his upper right thigh, twisted, ripped my sword free of his flesh, turned and chopped again at the first man's waist. Once again my strike was blocked. The man just then coming through the window, his legs either side of the sill, shouted in French, 'Kill him, Bogis, kill the dog! And quickly.'

And this fellow, Bogis, did his very best to do just that. He came at me, step and lunge, step and lunge, driving me back across the chapel. Another fellow in a black hood ran in from the side, swinging a long axe at my head. I dodged the blow, swung Fidelity when he was off-balance and half-severed his neck, but that Bogis fellow was on me again like a lightning bolt, his blade flicking out towards my face. I ducked and I swear the blade parted my hairs. But, worse, more men were tumbling over the window sill and into the room – six unhurt Frenchmen, now seven, eight, and one of them was carrying a crossbow. I heard the door to the chapel opening behind me and Kit's voice calling my name.

I blocked another snake-fast cut from Bogis, sent him reeling back with a double feint at his eyes, then groin. I shouted, 'Kit, sound the alarm. Go. Now. Wake the Wolves!'

The man with the crossbow had spanned it, loaded a black bolt and was lifting it towards me.

Kit said, 'But, sir, you need me . . .' I heard the scrape of his sword coming out of its scabbard.

'Go, Kit, go for help or we are all lost.' I was screaming at my squire. I blocked a roundhouse swing from Bogis, punched him hard in the gut with my empty left fist. Beyond him I saw the man with the crossbow had it pointed at my face, the fellow's hand squeezing the lever to loose. I dropped to the floor.

A twang. A coughing cry. I twisted and saw with horror that the bolt had punched straight into Kit's throat. The black shaft was protruding from just below his Adam's apple. His eyes were huge with shock. Bright blood began to pump from a severed artery. I leaped up. I looked back – there were ten French men-at-arms in the chapel by now, three of them advancing on me in unison with swords in their hands and hatred in their hearts.

I ran.

I have pondered my decision long and hard since then; I have examined my feelings that night in the closest detail. And I swear to you it was not cowardice that caused me to flee the chapel. Even Robin agreed with me when I spoke to him about it later. No other decision could be taken. I had to raise the alarm, I had to, or the entire French army might have come in through that open window. Could I have fought and killed all those French men-at-arms by myself? And killed any more who might have come through the window while I fought? No. Out of the question. To attempt it would have been to jeopardise the whole castle.

I did the right thing, everybody tells me so. Yet it is painful to remember that I ran from that fight. There were armed enemies to my front and I turned and ran. Well, you shall judge my actions when I reveal what happened next. Leaving Kit coughing out his life's blood by the door, I sprinted from the chapel and down the steps to the courtyard and began sounding the alarm.

I ran into the south tower, shouting, 'To arms!' Banging metal pots together, kicking sleeping Wolves out of blankets.

Robin emerged from his chamber, rubbing his eyes, half-dressed but with a sword in his hand.

'The French have got into the chapel,' I said tersely. 'And Kit is in there – gravely wounded.'

Robin said merely, 'Come on, then.'

And, with a dozen Wolves at our back, we left the tower.

The cries of alarm were by now echoing all around the middle bailey. Robin and I charged up the chapel steps and barged through the door, swords drawn – to find the small space quite empty, save for a white-faced Frenchman seated by the wall in a puddle of red, his eyes wide open. And my poor brave Kit, quite dead, curled by the door, his bloody hands wrapped around the shaft in his neck. The candles blazed. The window still yawned. I took a dozen strides over to it, looked briefly out at the empty ditch and slammed it and bolted it with the locking bar.

Robin said, 'The drawbridge.'

Dread and sorrow in equal parts welled up inside me. We ran from that place, down the steps, looking up to the battlements and sure enough men were struggling and dying in the guardhouse by the drawbridge. Terrible screams echoed around the courtyard. The red glow of flames was coming from within the stone shelter where the men had been quietly playing knuckle-bones a few hours beforehand. We charged up the stone steps and piled into the rearmost French men-at-arms. Robin, slightly ahead of me, cut down one from behind with a double-handed diagonal slice to the root of his neck. As he paused to free his blade from deep in the man's lungs, I slipped past him and engaged a pair of swordsmen who stopped, turned and stood shoulder to shoulder blocking my path along the battlements. Beyond these two I could see the slumped body of Simon who had been on sentry duty and, much worse, the black drawbridge lowering jerkily, down and down.

I opened the guts of one of the men facing me, and Robin, lunging over my shoulder, sank his bloody blade into the other man's eye. They both went down, crying out to God, but three more men were behind them, and more behind those, and my head was suddenly filled with a terrible roaring noise, the sound of scores of men shouting for victory. I could see a mass of enemy gathered across the open space on the walls of the outer bailey, steel glinting in the light of their many torches. A crossbow bolt clattered off the parapet an inch from my shoulder. An instant later the drawbridge banged down on the other side and, with a huge shout, they poured like a black flood across the link between us. I took a step forward, my instinct being to try to stem the tide of men, but I felt Robin's hand on my shoulder and his quiet voice saying, 'No, Alan, no. We are done here. We must get to the inner bailey. Back, all of you, back. Back to the inner bailey.'

And for the second time that night, I ran.

Robin and most of the Wolves made it safely out of the middle bailey and across the stone bridge into the inner part of the castle before we closed the wooden gates and the iron portcullis in the faces of the victorious French. But a goodly number of our men died that night as some five hundred French men-at-arms poured across the drawbridge and flooded the courtyard of the middle bailey. Those who had not awakened swiftly enough were slaughtered in their blankets; those who did not speedily abandon their posts and rush to the safety of the inner bailey were cut down in the confusion of fire and terror that bloody night.

I wept for Kit. I knew I had failed him as his lord and his comrade. He would never be a knight now. He was not, perhaps, the finest squire I had ever had, but he was a good man, a loyal soldier and a true friend. *Requiescat in pace.*

I tormented myself with thoughts of what I could have done differently in the chapel and on the battlements. Could I have defeated all those invaders in the chapel and stemmed the tide? I did not believe so – I was weak from months of bad food, and even in my best condition, I would shy away from taking on more than three enemies at once. If I had had the wit to realise earlier that the men were making for the drawbridge, perhaps we might not have wasted valuable time returning to the chapel and we might have stopped them. Perhaps.

Robin snapped me out of my melancholic state a little before dawn. He came and found me sitting with my back against the wooden wall of the great hall in the inner bailey, my eyes reddened by tears. It was warm and smoky in there, a large fire burning in the hearth in the centre. And, even with half the soldiers manning the walls and watching the French loot the middle bailey, the place was crowded with men, wandering about aimlessly, arguing, assigning blame, cursing the failure of the sentries to stem the attack across the drawbridge. I was too tired to join in the debate. My lord came across to me, folded his cloak and sat down on it on the rush-strewn floor. For the next half an hour he listened patiently to a list of my failures, to my bitter self-recriminations, nodding but making no comment.

Then he said, 'What's done is done, Alan. Even if we might have done things differently, we did not, and fretting about it will not change a thing. We've lost the middle bailey, we've lost many good men, and here we are. There is nothing more to say on the matter.'

He was right, of course, but I could not leave it be. I told him about the inviting open window and the unguarded candle-bright chapel, about telling Father de la Motte to keep the shutters and to extinguish the lights. I also told him about the strange troop movements I had seen at midnight on the walls of the outer bailey.

'This was no chance break-in,' I said. 'They knew they could get into the middle bailey through that very window, and they sent a dozen men to accomplish that and to capture the drawbridge gatehouse. And they had the men ready to charge across the lowered drawbridge and exploit our weakness.'

'Are you still talking about a traitor within our walls?' asked Robin.

I nodded. 'Somebody opened that window and let the French in. They clearly knew beforehand the window would be opened that night.'

'Do you think it is de la Motte?'

I shrugged. 'Yes, perhaps, or some other knight or nobleman. I don't know. But I swear to you, Robin, I shall find out.'

'Do you think it is me?' Robin said softly, but there was a whiff of menace in his question. 'Do you think I am a traitor?'

I said nothing. I wanted to say that I hoped with all my heart that it was not him, for whoever the traitor was, he had killed Kit – and I was not sure I would ever forgive that. So I said nothing.

Robin sighed. 'Some men would be furious at your silent accusation,' he said. 'But not I. We have known each other a long time, Alan, a long, long time – and perhaps I have not always revealed my stratagems fully to you, as I should have. Perhaps this has, on occasion, caused some difficulties between us. So I will reveal the truth to you now, for the sake of our long friendship.'

I held my breath. Please God, sweet merciful God, I beg you: do not let Robin be the traitor.

'Some months ago, eight months to be exact, King Philip approached me through one of his agents while I was at Rouen with John. He offered me almost half of

361

Normandy – twenty-odd castles and the lands to go with them, a second earldom, in effect, wealth beyond my most extravagant dreams. All I need do was serve Philip secretly while remaining for a time at John's side.'

I could not breathe. I could not even look at Robin. For I knew Philip had offered him all he had ever wanted.

Robin said nothing for a few moments. He was looking at the nails of his left hand, dirty, ragged, the fingers thin and bony from our poor diet, the skin loose. He seemed fascinated by the sight.

'You must know, Alan, that I do not truly love King John. He is a cruel, cringing, pathetic excuse for a man – and a worse King. He is a disaster as a military leader; and as a lord of lords he is no more than a bad jest.'

I began to move away from Robin; I knew what was coming next and I did not think I could sit still and hear him try to make me understand his decision to sell his loyalty like a bauble to the highest bidder. I would close my ears to him.

'But the thing is, Alan, I swore an oath to King John. I swore a sacred oath to serve him faithfully, without deceit, for the whole of my life. And when Philip offered me all the riches of the earth, I discovered something odd about myself. Ten years ago I would have taken his offer. Bitten his hand off, probably. But that day eight months ago in Rouen, on that day I found I loved my own honour more than the promise of all the castles of Normandy and all the rich lands the earth has to offer. I turned him down flat.'

I gaped at Robin, speechless.

'I don't want to live in Normandy under a French King. I want to live in Yorkshire, at Kirkton, if you want me to be precise, with Marie-Anne and the boys; I want to live on my lands, lands I have earned by loyal service to the crown, and I want to raise my sons as Englishmen. And I want to be able to look Hugh and Miles in the eye and tell them about honour, and explain to them that while wealth and lands are very fine, a man's honour is the most important of his possessions. To prove that point, I must endure this siege. I must be getting old and stupid but, you see, Alan, I am not your traitor.'

My throat was clogged, my eyes were burning with unshed tears. I could feel my heart beating like a tambour. I looked into Robin's eyes and said just this to him, 'If you are lying to me on this matter, my lord, I will most certainly kill you. I swear it.'

Robin looked at me silently and nodded.

For a long time we sat there in silence. Then Robin said, 'I think we should perhaps not mention the presence of a traitor to anyone just yet. Though I have no doubts now that one is among us. If Philip were prepared to offer me such a rich prize to serve him, I am sure he would have been able to find someone else among our company prepared to sell their honour for silver.'

'Should we not speak to de Lacy about it?' I said.

'Sir Roger may be the traitor. His fine talk about being

dragged from the castle by his heels could be a bluff. He has no lands on this side of the channel – perhaps he would be tempted by the offer of a rich Norman fiefdom.'

'I do not think so,' I said. It felt strange to be contradicting my lord. But my threat to kill him had subtly changed things between us. I was still his man, but the gulf in status between us had narrowed. We were not equals, by any means, but I was no longer a callow boy whose thoughts and actions could so easily be manipulated by his lord.

'I do not think it could be de Lacy,' I repeated. 'If he wished to serve Philip, he had only to surrender, to open the gates and castle to him and that, I believe, he is firmly resolved not to do. You are right in that he has no lands here in Normandy – but that means his loyalties lie in England. The fortunes of John are his fortunes. I think the King appointed him castellan because he knows he can trust him to the end.'

'You may have a point, Alan. Yes, I think you may be right. I will speak to de Lacy about the matter this morning.'

Chapter Twenty-eight

We still held the Iron Castle and, with some two hundred men-at-arms inside the inner bailey, it was almost as crowded as it had been when the Useless Mouths were among us – God rest their poor souls. The food was nearly all gone: we existed on one cup of 'unnameable soup' a day, as we called it, thickened with a few oats or a spoonful of flour. Some of the Wolves contrived to use slingshots to bring down birds – and it became a kind of game, with folk wagering whether the shot would strike the bird (it most often did, for several of the Wolves were experts in this method of killing) and whether it would fall within our reach. When a bird fell into the French-controlled middle bailey, there was a general lamentation; jubilation when it fell into our part of the castle. The stone-killed birds were all surrendered to Sir Benedict Malet – who had become responsible for boiling the daily soup. But there were other more unsavoury elements in the broth: rats, mice, insects, worms, beetles; even some kinds of edible moss, fungus and grasses were boiled up for the little nourishment they could provide. Anything and everything went into that vile soup – which was why it never earned a name. I didn't like to enquire about its contents, I just gulped it down hot and wished there were more to be had.

There was also an illegal trade in food with the enemy. I cannot condemn it because, occasionally, Robin would provide me and his other lieutenants with a loaf of actual wheat bread or a small piece of smoked meat or cheese to share. We ate this provender greedily and guiltily and asked no questions, but I was aware that French *ribaldi*, the mercantile hangers-on who followed any army, scum who would sell anything to anyone, would occasionally converse with our sentries in the dead of night; deals were made, at exorbitant cost – three shillings for a loaf of bread, was one figure I heard mentioned – and little packages were hoisted up to the battlements in exchange for fat, chinking purses. To be fair, these *ribaldi* risked torture and death if caught by the French army providing food, or even talking, to our men, but they made a handsome profit and I believe every available coin in the inner bailey eventually found its way to them.

We were lean, but we were alive by the end of February,

when the French truly set their minds to capturing the inner bailey.

It began as usual with a pounding from the trebuchets and mangonels, which had been moved from Philip's Hill to an area of lower ground directly east of the entrance to the inner bailey. These engines of war battered away at the gatehouse for nearly a week, denting the masonry a little, but without seriously damaging it – the design of the walls in the rest of the inner bailey, the series of D-shaped bastions, proved very effective against the missiles of the enemy when they missed the gatehouse. After seven days of bombardment, which sawed at our nerves, but did little else, the French changed strategy.

Once again they brought forward the cat.

This time the wheels had been removed and it was lifted and walked forward by the score of men beneath it. It took them most of the afternoon to bring it up to the walls. They walked it parallel to the bridge that linked the gatehouse in the inner bailey to the main gate, now of course occupied by the enemy, stumbling a little as they went down into the deep ditch before our walls. We showered the roof of this diabolical contraption with rocks and arrows and vats of boiling water, once again with almost no apparent effect. A few arrows buried themselves in the ox-hide covering; chunks of masonry boomed against the slanted wooden roof and rolled off harmlessly; the scalding water splashed, cooled and dribbled from the eves; but the cat came on and lodged itself firmly against the base of our walls to the right of the gatehouse. Just as before.

A feeling, not quite of panic, not quite of despair, but of my doom hurrying upon me filled my heart. I could see the future: the cat would gnaw at the foundations of the inner bailey, a deep mine would be set and fired, the bombardment would resume and the walls would tumble. Then the French would be upon us. And they could be expected to show us no mercy. The accepted rules of war were clear on this point. A garrison that was surrounded might defy the besiegers for an agreed length of time, to give time for the lord of the beleaguered men to come to their aid – a month was the usual grace period – but if they persisted in their defiance, the defenders could expect no quarter when the citadel was finally breached. If the French broke open our defences every man inside this place – and Tilda, too – would fall under their swords. In Tilda's case she might even suffer a fate far worse than death – to be used like a whore by an unending line of French men-at-arms.

I doubted she would survive an entire night.

A few days after the fall of the middle bailey, Roger de Lacy sent a servant to summon me to a meeting of the high council. They met on the second floor of the keep, and when I entered the round room, the four men – Roger de Lacy, Father de la Motte, Sir Joscelyn Giffard and Robin – were seated at the far side of a long table draped with white cloth. A flask of well water stood on the table and our cups; it was a sign of our reduced circumstances that it was not wine. There was not a scrap of food to be seen. They did not invite me to sit; instead, I stood like a lackey before them.

'Locksley tells me you are still convinced there is a traitor among us,' said de Lacy.

'Yes, sir.'

'The last time we spoke about this I told you I did not want to hear of it again. I still consider the idea preposterous. Yet your master has persuaded me to listen, and I have agreed. So, speak. And be brief, we have more urgent matters to consider.'

I swallowed, straightened my back and said, 'The French knew we were coming up river with the food convoys. They lined the banks of the Seine with men during the night, as well as manning the pontoon bridge. We were sworn to secrecy in Rouen. I believe the information about the attack came from within this castle.'

De Lacy said, 'Sworn to secrecy! Pff. As if that ever sealed the lips of an army.'

Robin said, 'Allow Sir Alan to speak, my lord.'

I continued: 'The French also knew the mortar in the outer bailey was moist; this knowledge, I believe, was given to them from inside. When they were before our walls, I heard a French man-at-arms say to another these words: "It's just as the Sparrow told us. The mortar is as wet as mustard in some places." That exact phrase – "wet as custard" – was spoken to me by someone sitting at this very table. Furthermore, I saw with my own eyes somebody signalling from the south tower of the outer bailey to the French while a celebration was in progress, and a response from our enemies. All four of you were at that celebration. And lastly, but most importantly, somebody left the window of the chapel open, which allowed the French to gain access to the middle bailey – and this was certainly connived in advance. I know this because I saw the French troops in the outer bailey preparing to attack before the enemy got into the House of God. There is a traitor in this castle, he is known to the French as the Sparrow, and I believe it is the man who opened the chapel window after I distinctly told him to ensure that it was shut.'

I stared at Father de la Motte, the accusation unspoken but absolutely clear.

The priest looked back at me with sharp blue eyes smiling and as far as I could tell utterly unperturbed.

'My son, if you think that I have been having dealings with the French, you are quite mistaken.'

'It's absurd,' said de Lacy. 'I cannot believe you have the effrontery to suggest that a man of God—'

'My lord,' said Sir Joscelyn, putting a hand on de Lacy's arm. 'He has made a solid case for the existence of a traitor – Sir Alan, do you honestly believe the good Father invited the French into the chapel?'

'I do not know – but I know that somebody did.'

'When I left the chapel,' said Father de la Motte in a

quiet, measured tone, 'I left it with the shutters tightly closed and barred and all the candles extinguished – as you specifically asked me to. I will swear to the truth of that on my immortal soul.'

There was a long silence. De Lacy looked baffled and angry. Sir Joscelyn's brow was deeply furrowed. Father de la Motte was quite serene.

Robin said, 'Well, now that the high council has been apprised of this, I think you may leave us, Sir Alan. On behalf of the council, I thank you for bringing this grave matter to our attention.'

I bowed and walked to the door, a ballooning silence at my back. At the top of the stairs, I turned and said, 'My lords, I wish you to know this as well. My squire Kit, a good man, died because of the activities of this person, this Sparrow. He exists. You may or may not believe me, but I know it to be true. And I will find this man and punish him. I give you my solemn word on that.'

And I left.

Under the protection of the cat, the mining began as soon as that devilish machine was in place, and nowhere in the inner bailey was one free from the ominous chinking of metal on stone. To divert my mind from the thought that our walls were slowly being eaten away, I set myself to the task of questioning every man in the castle in the hope of gleaning some knowledge about the Sparrow.

I started with the Wolves, asking each if they had seen

anything suspicious over the past few months, anything that struck them as strange or out of the ordinary. Most had nothing to report, but one-eyed Claes told me he had seen a light winking in an arrow slit at the top of the keep a few days ago. 'I though little of it, sir,' he said. 'I just thought it was someone fooling with a lantern for their own amusement.'

Had he spotted a response? 'No, sir, but I was in the courtyard, and the light was up yonder.' He pointed to the top storey of the bastion.

I paid a quick visit to the top of the keep and looked out through the arrow slit Claes had indicated. The window looked directly out at the French encampment on Philip's Hill, but other than that, of course, there was nothing to indicate who might have used the position to signal to the enemy.

When I asked Little Niels if he had seen anything suspicious, he screwed up his little face and said, 'To be honest, sir, I have noticed a good number of odd folk prowling around outside our walls. Desperate, suspicious, ugly-looking fellows they are, and up to no good, I'll be bound. I suspect, sir . . . If I might make so bold. I truly suspect, sir, that they might be Frenchmen!'

His eyes twinkled at me and I confess I laughed out loud.

Apart from that moment of much-needed levity, I received no joy from my conversations with the men. I pondered hard about who the Sparrow might be, hour after hour, as I went about my duties on the castle walls, and at night alone in bed when sleep would not come, but I could get no further forward. The chinking of the miners distracted me by day – but another person, too, occupied my thoughts in the dark of night. Tilda.

Unless King John came soon, the castle would fall – this was certain – and I knew I did not want to leave this Earth until I had kissed her and held her in my arms, at least one time. So, as the French dug away at the thick foundations of the inner bailey, and our doom grew ever closer, I decided I must act.

I found Lady Matilda Giffard near dusk in the great hall behind the keep. She was sitting beside the hearth fire mending a rip in a knight's chemise with great concentration, and she did not observe me approaching. For once she was alone – there was no sign of her father nor of that loathsome lardy-boy Benedict – but for a few pages and squires seated about her on stools, she might have been entirely unaccompanied. Her sharp pink tongue was poking from her mouth as she squinted at the needle and thread in the gloom of the hall. She was dressed in a black gown, nearly clean, with white lace trim, and she looked for all the world like a black-and-white cat. Looking at her white face, her pink mouth, the dark sweep of her lowered brows, the midnight wink of a loop of hair poking out below her headdress, I knew that I loved her and would always love her from the deepest part of my soul.

'Come with me,' I said, and it came out thick and clogged.

'Good evening, Alan,' she said, smiling up at me.

'I must speak to you alone,' I said. 'Please put that down and come with me.'

Tilda frowned, then half-smiled and stood, leaving the half-mended chemise on the stool. She looked a little uncertain but followed me out of the hall into a tower on the north side. I said no more to her but indicated with a gesture that she should climb the spiral staircase. We went up and up, round and round, until we came to the chamber at the top. We went inside. There were two men-at-arms there: Wolves; men I liked and who liked me.

'I will take the rest of this watch,' I said to the men, 'you are dismissed', and I held the door for them to leave. With far too much grinning, nudging and winking, the two left that high lookout room, and I waited until the sound of their boots faded away as they clumped down the stairs, before I bolted the door from the inside, turned and looked at Tilda.

She looked a little nervous, her face slightly flushed, her wonderful bosom moving gently up and down with each short breath.

I stood before her and took her cool hand in mine.

'Alan, what on earth is the matter?' she said.

'I love you, Matilda. I have loved you almost from the moment I saw you. You are an angel in human form and my heart will shatter into a thousand tiny pieces if you do not grant me a kiss, at the very least.'

Tilda only had time to say 'Oh!' before I had my hand at the back of her neck, supporting her head, and my lips gently pressed against hers.

At first touch her lips were hard, unyielding – and then, to my joy and delight, they melted under mine and her hot tongue flickered out to enter my mouth. We kissed like parched souls at a well of sweet water, my head swimming with intoxicated happiness, our bodies locked together, pressed deeply into each other. After a long time she gently pushed me away, her palm hard against my chest, and gazed sadly into my eyes. My heart sank into my boots.

She whispered, 'Is the door locked?'

I nodded, then was rendered speechless as she grasped my head in both hands and kissed me again, harder, more urgently. Then her fingers were tugging at my belt and I was dragging her skirts up, up to her slim waist. All thoughts of honour and decency were washed away as I glimpsed the neat, dark, forbidden triangle between her milk-white thighs. The storm of love broke and howled about us. I could taste her beauty through her hot mouth: a sweet, spicy, intoxicating brew. I could clearly scent her lithe young body, roses and oysters, and her moist, pungent sex and, over the top, the odour of my own goatish urgency. We found ourselves on the floor and my body reared up between her spread white legs, my prick as hard as an oak branch. I plunged into her, a warm, slippery, driving union of our bodies and souls. I crushed her with my eager body and ploughed into her, my thrusts building in intensity and depth. She gripped the long, hard muscles of my back and called, 'Yes, oh God, Alan, yes', in my ear as I sank into her, withdrew and lunged again. I could feel my loins, my tight-bunched balls, seething and boiling like water in a pot, rising perilously close to the rim, as I bucked into her, again and again and again, lips mashing, fingers clawing, naked bellies slapping like some wild applause, until my seed erupted in a huge, joyous, pumping flood deep inside her.

Afterwards we kissed and held each other naked in a nest of our own sweaty clothing. For a while we were silent – and then both seemed to speak at once: of our wonder at the other and the pain of waiting so long. Of love and life, family and children. She was utterly perfect: our imaginations, our souls, matching as well as our bodies. We spoke about the siege and its likely doleful end, and I promised Tilda on my honour that I would let no harm come to her whatever might happen.

Then, to my joy, more slowly and tenderly this time, we made love once more.

It must have been near midnight when I took Tilda back to the great hall. We kissed in the darkness just outside, our bruised mouths gentle in the parting, and murmured all the usual foolishnesses of lovers. I wanted to go to her father to tell him of our union, but Tilda made me promise to keep our love a secret from the world.

'My darling, let us enjoy this wonderful thing between ourselves for just a little while. I want you all to myself. And I do not want Daddy to be distracted when the fighting comes. Please, for my sake, let us keep this as our own special secret. Promise me you will tell no one, promise me, Alan.'

So I promised. It was a surprisingly difficult vow to keep, for I felt like shouting my love from the battlements; I wanted to stop every passing man-at-arms and tell him the good news about Tilda and myself and elicit their congratulations.

The next morning I came face to face with Sir Joscelyn Giffard in the courtyard of the inner bailey, his face a barely controlled mask of fury.

Chapter Twenty-nine

'I have found your damn traitor,' Sir Joscelyn said, the muscles of his face knotted with anger. 'It seems the Sparrow is one of your own men, Sir Alan.'

I was completely wrong-footed. My thoughts had been so entirely consumed by the bright glow of his daughter that I had difficulty comprehending him.

I looked across the courtyard and saw two men-at-arms in Sir Joscelyn's colours grasping the shoulders of a tiny, wretched figure who drooped between them.

It was Little Niels.

'I had my men keep a close watch on the walls all last night,' said Sir Joscelyn, 'and in the small hours we caught this fellow, red-handed, on the north wall engaged in commerce with the French below.'

We were walking together to the trio and I saw Roger de Lacy and Robin crossing from the keep, converging on the prisoner. As I drew closer, I saw that Little Niels had been badly beaten, his cheery urchin face a mass of purpling bruises. All his fingers seemed to have been broken, too. They were crooked, misshapen and scabbed with dry blood.

'He's confessed, has he?' said de Lacy.

'Yes, my lord,' said one of the men-at-arms. 'He admitted this morning under our questioning that he gave information to the French in exchange for food. Several times.'

'Right. Hang him from the walls, now.' De Lacy started to turn away.

Little Niels gave a mewl of terror. The men-at-arms began to drag him away.

'Wait,' I said. 'Wait just one moment. He is one of my own men. I am his captain. I insist on speaking to him.'

I glanced at Robin. His face was a stone.

I looked at my little comrade, his body sagging, his bruised eyes closed. All the fun in the man seemed to have drained away and all that was left was an empty shell of the happy young fellow I had known.

'Niels, is it true? Tell me, did you do what these men say you did?'

At first I thought he would not answer me.

'Niels,' I said again, 'is it true what they say?'

'I was hungry,' he mumbled, through bloody snapped-off teeth. 'We are all so hungry, all the time.' He straightened in his captors' grip. 'And there is some that eat like kings in secret while the men starve.' He was glaring at de Lacy now. 'So I told the Frenchies a few things – so what! – most of it was lies, or things they must know already.' He looked back at me. 'It was just a laugh, sir, I swear it; I told them a few silly things to get a little bread for me and my mates. I did no harm to our cause, sir.'

'You admit that you had commerce with the French and gave them information about us?' I did not want to believe it.

Little Niels said nothing for a few heartbeats. 'I'll never be an officer now, sir, will I?' he said, and began to weep, the tears turning the scabs on his face to rubies.

'Take him away,' said de Lacy. 'I want his corpse hanging from the outer walls as a message.'

It was mercifully quick. That is the best I can say of the affair. Father de la Motte gave him absolution for his sins and he was hurled off the battlements with a rough hempen noose around his neck. Death must have been near-instantaneous. Yet I was still sick with grief and horror. I hate a hanging at the best of times, but Little Niels had been a comrade, even if he had proven to be a treacherous one. At least, I consoled myself, as I looked down from the battlements at the small ragged corpse swinging at the end of the rope, Kit had been avenged.

The traitor had been exposed, I said to myself, and the Sparrow was dead.

In my misery I went to seek out Tilda. She and her father were in the great hall, sharing a bowl of steaming herb-water and a heel of old bread at a little before noon. Sir Joscelyn had recovered his composure after his fury at the discovery of the traitor and he went so far as to try and make me feel better about the outcome.

'A bad business, Sir Alan. War brings out the best in some, and the worst in others. You cannot tell how any of us will be affected. You couldn't have known what the fellow was up to – and truly no fault lies with you. We are rid of him now.'

The knight even offered me some of his meagre portion of bread, which I politely declined. I did not wish either of them to grow hungrier on my account. Tilda looked – perfect. Unwearied by our exertions the night before, clean, fresh, dewy and politely friendly. I wanted to take her into my arms and make love to her as eagerly as I had the night before – and it was on the tip of my tongue to blurt something out to her father there and then. But her steady blue-grey gaze and a tiny shake of her head stopped me from breaking my vow. I smiled at my darling and she smiled at me, and that for the time being was enough.

Then it all went wrong. That toad Benedict Malet came up and joined us. I could hardly believe his bare-faced gall. He just pulled up a stool and sat down right next to Tilda, helped himself to a corner of their bread, dipped it into their herb broth and started chewing. I glared at him – under the etiquette of the siege, one did not take another person's food until invited, it was the height of rudeness

– but to my surprise Tilda did not rebuke him. Instead, she was as cordial as if he were a member of her family, a favourite younger brother or some such. Sir Joscelyn was affable to the fellow, too. After a few moments I began to feel as if I were the interloper and, perhaps sensing my discomfort, Sir Joscelyn spoke to me about the siege and the operations of the cat.

'You, Sir Alan, have experience of this devilish machine from your service in the outer bailey. Is there anything we can do to defeat it, or at least to slow the progress of those miners beneath our walls?'

'Nothing we tried in the outer bailey had any effect at all,' I said.

'But surely we can do something,' said Tilda.

I smiled at her fondly.

Sir Joscelyn was frowning. 'This might be a very foolish idea, but could we not dig under the walls from our side and confront them at their workings?'

I stared at him. I felt as shocked as if a bucket of icy water had been poured over my head. This was not foolish. It was utterly inspired. I could not understand why I had not considered this before.

I left Tilda and her father with only the briefest of farewells (I ignored Benedict entirely), sprinted to the keep, leaped up the stairs to the second floor, and burst into the chamber where I found Robin in conference with de Lacy and Father de la Motte.

The men were poring over a scroll and all three stared

at me in surprise, and some with more than a little hostility, as I struggled to catch my breath.

'What is it now, Sir Alan?' said de Lacy frostily.

'The cat. Counter-mining,' I panted. 'They dig, we dig too.'

'What is your man babbling about, Locksley?' asked Father de la Motte, looking at Robin. 'Does he think he has unearthed another traitor?'

'I would guess that it has occurred to Sir Alan that we might combat the activities of the cat, and the French miners sheltered under it, by digging a tunnel under our own walls and using it as a route to attack them,' said my lord.

'We have already discussed that in council,' said de Lacy. 'And we all agreed – did we not? – that it was too dangerous. That our own mining activities might weaken the structure of the walls and achieve exactly what the enemy desired. That this counter-mining might, indeed, bring about our destruction even more swiftly.'

'It was proposed, yes, but as I recall we did not come to a conclusion,' said Father de la Motte. 'Let the young fellow speak. Indeed, I doubt we could stop him.'

I had recovered myself by then. 'My lords, pardon this unseemly intrusion, but I believe, as you say, that we should take action against the French miners by digging a counter-mine. We have a man among us who is expert in this kind of warfare – Christophe of Leuven – one of my lord of Locksley's own men.'

Robin raised his eyebrows at me. 'He's one of the Wolves, sir,' I said. 'A well-seasoned fighting man. The one they call Scarecrow. I was with him at Falaise and he spoke to me then of mining against castles in Aquitaine with King Richard.'

It was strange to observe, once again, the power of the Lionheart's name. Or perhaps not so strange in this castle where his memory was written in every stone.

'This fellow is one of the Lionheart's miners, is he?' said de Lacy. 'They had a reputation for getting the job done. Well, if he thinks we can counter-mine without bringing the walls crashing down on our heads, perhaps we should reconsider it.'

And that was that. I had not even spoken to Christophe about the possibility of a counter-mine; the idea was not even in my head an hour before, but I did know when to keep my mouth shut. The fact that he had been one of Richard's men decided it. That, and the fact that de Lacy was desperate. He knew that, barring the miraculous arrival of King John in the next week or so, his walls would surely fall. And, even if his walls did not fall, he could not hold out much longer without food. Already a dozen or more men were unable to rise from their cots every day for lack of proper nourishment; each week one or two just gave up and died. De Lacy clearly recognised the straw I offered – and he clutched at it with both hands.

Chapter Thirty

I conferred with Robin immediately after the meeting, waiting for him outside the keep. 'You got what you wanted, Alan,' he said. 'Do you know what you're about?'

'No,' I said, 'but I cannot sit on my hands again while they dig through the battlements.'

'I'll set men to watch the cat and report the enemy's movements to you. I'd offer my aid in the fighting underground but I can't. I'm needed elsewhere.'

'I know.'

'You would make use of my Wolves?'

'Some, with your permission, but I will ask any man in the castle who has experience of this kind of work to join me.'

'Have a care, Alan,' said Robin, gripping my shoulder.

'This type of warfare is dangerous. More deadly, I think, than any you've engaged in before. Go carefully.'

In the end I selected fifteen of the fittest Wolves under Christophe Scarecrow, and five men from the castle garrison – two of whom were Cornishmen, brothers who had worked in the tin mines in their land, and three big Norman fellows, still in reasonable condition despite the dearth of food, who looked as if they knew their way around pick, spade and shovel.

We gathered in a tight group that afternoon in the courtyard, as the drizzle fell on us from a slate-grey sky, and Christophe explained that the most important thing was for the French to remain ignorant of our workings. We must not speak when in the mine, he told us, not even a whisper, and our digging must be slow, silent and steady.

Christophe knelt on the wet ground and, in the mud with his finger, created a rough map of the corrugated walls on the inner bailey south of the gatehouse. We would dig our counter-mine to come in at an angle against theirs. It would not be possible, he said, to dig below the foundations of the walls – they were half as deep as they were high; it would take weeks and many more men than we had to achieve that – we would go straight through the stone.

'But, do not worry, Sir Alan,' he told me with a grin, 'these walls are not solid rock.' He slapped the limestone with one big paw. We were standing on the far side of the inner bailey, on the western side – for some superstitious reason I wanted our discussions to take place as far from the mine as possible. 'This outer layer of shaped stone is only a yard thick,' Christophe said. 'It will take maybe half a day to get through it, being very quiet. Then comes the loose stuff, rock and chalk and mud; a day to cut a tunnel through twenty foot of that, putting in our supports as we go along. We will come to their diggings about halfway through the wall. Then we must be as quiet as mice; we listen hard, we locate them and then cut as close as we can to their chamber. When the time is right we burst through the wall into their mine and slaughter them all. Ha-ha!'

He made it sound easy.

It was not.

We began immediately, that very afternoon, half of the men working, half resting, and decided we must work all night and all day until the thing was done. It was almost impossible to work quietly; every blow of mallet against chisel seemed to ring out like a church bell sounding the alarm. I tried muffling the iron with cloth but it made it difficult to hit the chisel end accurately. Then we tried timing our blow to match theirs – for we could still hear the chink-chink of their miners working even through the battlements – but when they stopped our blows sounded even louder, and I feared they would discover what we were about. At dusk the French stopped their labours, and Robin's watchman atop the gatehouse reported that the miners and their guards were cooking something that smelled delicious – pork, he said – under the cover of the cat.

Roger de Lacy was good enough to issue our work party with extra rations that evening, but it was far from delicious – a thin gruel of sprouting barley with a few shreds of salted horse meat added to it, and a dozen roughly baked oat cakes that tasted mainly of sawdust. I thought longingly of the plump rats we had eaten at our Christmas feast. Then we went back to work, scraping gently, painstakingly, at the mortar between the stones with long blades. By midnight, we had removed four oblong stones from the inside of the wall. But the men were exhausted and I ordered a halt. We'd sleep, I said, and resume our labours at dawn.

The next morning, once we were through the stone facing, I delegated four of the ten men on duty to make the supports – essential if the tunnel were not to collapse on our heads. They were hollow squares, like thick window frames, a yard long on each side and made of oak. In fact, from wood salvaged from the enemy's belfry, which gave me a good deal of satisfaction. The plan was to wedge the supports into the face of the tunnel, affix each one securely with wedges of wood and stone and then dig out the tunnel inside the square. Every yard we stopped and put in another support, and thus the tunnel burrowed into the earth.

It was dirty, cramped, exhausting work, and the further

we dug, the more anxious we became about our proximity to the enemy. I rotated the man at the rock face every half-hour, measured by a burning candle, and took my turn with the spade, too. There was a further unpleasantness, apart from the cruel demands of the labour: crouched in the gloom with only the guttering light of a candle stub, I would imagine the whole weight of the fortress bearing down on me. I could not shake from my mind the idea that the fifty feet of stone and rock above my sweating head would suddenly collapse and squash me like a beetle under a brick. Each time my shift ended, and I crawled up and out of the tunnel, I gave thanks to God for my deliverance, and my soul rejoiced to see the pale sun again. And each time it came around again, I had to force myself to crawl into that heavy darkness.

The two Cornish brothers, Jago and Denzell, both short, muscular, sandy-haired fellows, proved their worth time and again in that hellish tunnel. Not only could they move more rock and earth than any of the Wolves in a half-hour, they seemed totally unafraid of the oppressive darkness and cramped conditions.

It was Denzell who came out of the hole halfway through his shift to tell me we were getting close.

'I hear them, zir,' he told me in his strange Cornish-inflected English. 'I hear 'em chattering like monkeys. And banging, zir, banging away something awful. Nailing up beams, is my own guess.'

I gathered my courage and began crawling down the

dark mouth into the belly of the earth. The tunnel might have only been twenty feet or so long but it seemed to take an age to work my way to its lowest point, which was now occupied by a shallow but foul-smelling pool of water, and then up again towards the face. It was as dark as Hades, for I had forgotten to bring the candle, but I found that it concentrated my hearing. And when my fumbling hands eventually found the rock face and I pressed my cheek to it, I could easily hear three or four men seemingly inches away talking in rapid French about a woman they knew intimately.

I squirmed out of the tunnel as quickly as I could and sent Christophe inside. It was growing dark and we had been working hard all day, but the grimy faces around me in the gloaming were keen, alert, eager at the prospect of battle. When Christophe emerged, silent but nodding in a business-like manner, I gathered the men by the wood-working area under the western wall, far from the tunnel's mouth.

'We are this far from them,' Christophe said, holding his hands about a foot apart. 'From now on we do not go forward, we spread out, keeping the wall between us and them.' He moved his hands apart, to indicate this. 'We cannot make even the slightest noise now. Remember, if we can hear them, they can hear us.'

'We dig out a large chamber,' I told the men, 'a space big enough to hold four or five men, and do it tonight. We dig all night, in strict silence, and just before dawn we break through the wall and fall on them while they sleep. We think there are seven, maybe eight miners and men-at-arms in there now and they must all die.'

I caught every eye in turn by the light of the setting sun, to be sure every man understood. 'Then comes the truly hard work.'

I saw more than a few eyebrows lift in surprise.

'If we just butcher them and leave, the French will merely return with new men. We must fill in their mine, and our tunnel, with rock and stone and mortar brought in from this side. We will burn the cat, and Robin's archers will ward the French away from the walls while we work, but it is vitally important that we rebuild the foundations of the walls from the underside. Jacques, here, is a mason' – I indicated one of the Norman fellows, who nodded solemnly in agreement – 'and he will ensure the damage the French have done is repaired to the best of our ability.'

Having made sure every man understood his task, I left Christophe in charge of the night diggers – Jago and Denzell as usual volunteered to take the first shift – and went to report to Robin.

Once again I found Robin with the high council on the middle floor of the keep. I was tired but deeply excited about being able to strike a blow against the miners and the hated cat. And perhaps I let my excitement show too much.

I explained to Robin, and the rest of the council, that we would be ready to attack the miners at dawn, and I asked Robin if he would make sure his men were ready to give us protection when we began the task of rebuilding the foundations.

The rest of that night remains foggy in my memory. I went down the tunnel twice to see how the chamber was progressing – the Cornish lads were working miracles, labouring half an hour on and half an hour off all through the night. As the chamber expanded we were able to get more men at the face, although that did increase the opportunity for noise. An hour or two after midnight, I sent everybody out of the tunnel and went in myself, alone, with a candle. The chamber was big enough for three or four men to crouch in with moderate comfort – and I decided it was enough. I pressed my ear to the wall between the chamber and their mine; I was almost certain I could hear the sound of snoring men. Good.

I stood down all the men and allowed them two hours for sleep – but I was too tightly strung myself for slumber. I dressed in my hauberk and a plain steel cap from the armoury, sharpened the needle-point of my misericorde on a stone, and selected a heavy mace as my back-up weapon, tucking it into the belt at the back. The iron blades of the short-handled wooden spades had been sharpened by the men before they retired to their cots. There would be no room to swing Fidelity in the mine; it would be close, dirty work only – dagger, mace and spade – and while I prepared myself, I found I was thinking of poor Kit, and my heart lurched. I would have given almost anything to see his cheerful face beside me. I sent up a brief prayer to St Michael, asking the archangel to care for the soul of Kit, and to guard me in the coming battle, as he had done so many times before. I prayed, too, for the souls of the French miners whom I was about to slay. They were my enemies, yes, and they sought my destruction, but I found I did not bear them any great malice.

When the sky in the east was just showing the first streaks of grey, I took a firm grasp of my spade and, with Christophe at my shoulder, crawled into the dark tunnel.

With four big men crouched in the chamber – myself, Christophe and two veteran Wolves armed with crossbows – the air seemed clotted and hard to breathe. And when we snuffed the candle it seemed even closer in there. Four more armed Wolves lay head to toe along the tunnel, and the rest of the men waited in the courtyard beside a trough of freshly mixed mortar and the piles of masonry, some stones excavated by us, others taken from the castle walls.

At my signal Christophe and I planned to dig like badgers – we knelt beside two convex patches of wall that had been very carefully dug away until there were no more than a few inches of earth and rock between us and the enemy. Christophe had tested the thickness with a cautious knife blade and we hoped to burst through in a matter of heartbeats and be at the throats of the foe in the time it takes to say a single Our Father. The two Wolves would follow us in and the rest of the pack would scramble along the tunnel and join the fight as quickly as they possibly could.

The plan would stand or fall depending on the element of surprise. It crossed my mind that they could be in there waiting for us – dozens of men, with swords and axes raised, waiting to chop us down as we emerged. I quickly pushed that thought away. It was time. I gave the signal, a tap on Christophe's shoulder, and we began to dig.

Chapter Thirty-one

I attacked the wall before me with all the vigour that fear can bring to a physical enterprise. I hacked at it overhand, with my right shoulder giving the spade its power, as it smashed into earth and rock. Silence was abandoned, speed was more important.

My spade sank inches deep into the wall and I levered out a small mountain of rubble that cascaded over my knees. I swung the spade again, the noise hellishly loud, the clang of iron on rock, and again, and suddenly it went through, clear and free and, praise God, there was a patch of grey in the dark of the earthen wall.

I heard a French voice call out in alarm. I swung the spade again, knocked through, and the patch of grey was now as big as my head. I worked the spade feverishly, gouging, enlarging the hole, hurling rubble out of my path. People were moving inside their mine, their panicked shouting deafening in the small space.

A sword stabbed through the hole, a bar of grey jabbing over my shoulder, and I could make out a pair of bare legs directly in front of my face.

I chopped up through the gap with my spade at the underside of a knee cap and was rewarded with a scream, and a body fell in front of my eyes, a yelling face. I chopped again with the spade, digging through flesh, cutting into the bridge of the man's nose. Screams, blood, waving white hands. I dug the spade into his open mouth, smashing teeth, slicing into the hinge of his jaw. I let out an ear-shattering roar and followed the spade through the hole, butting forward with my head, my mail-clad shoulders catching on the stony edges, pulling rubble down as I surged through. Somebody swung a pick-axe at me and it tangled with my upheld, warding spade, slowing the swing but not enough, the iron point crashing into my mailed back like a spear thrust, but I was up and on my feet, reaching around my back with my left hand. With my right, I hurled the spade, handle over blade, at the knot of men further back in the mine. Now, misericorde in my left hand, mace in my right, a howl on my snarling lips, clumps of earth and rock tumbling from my body, I launched myself at the enemy like a monster emerging from the grave. The pick-axe man drew back his weapon for another strike but, swift as a leopard, I unleashed the mace in a roundhouse swing that smashed his lower jaw out of its sockets. From the corner of my eye I could see Christophe emerging from his hole in the wall, a short sword in his hand. I charged forward screaming, 'Westbury!' and ran into a wall of men-at-arms. Half a dozen men, mailed, shields linked, lined up at the open end of the mine with the grey light of dawn behind them.

Waiting for me.

It was too late to stop. I crashed into their shields with my shoulder, pushing them back a half-pace and I felt the scrape of their swords on the muddy iron rings that protected my back, and one hammer blow on my helmet. My left hand swung low and hard, under the shields and I felt the misericorde sink into flesh, and a warm wet spray. I shoved again against the wall of shields, my boots scrabbling against the floor and, while my armoured back took a battering, I felt the shield wall give a little. Something crunched against my spine. A blast of agony. I swung low again with the misericorde and the man directly in front of me stumbled back shrieking, bleeding. I surged forward, screaming, 'Westbury!' once more – I had broken the wall and I was through, weaving between the enemy, mace swinging, jabbing with the dagger. I saw two men running for the dawn. But the others were full of fight. I took a crunching blow to the shoulder, but my mail held and I returned the compliment to the swordsman by way of an overhand strike, jamming the misericorde into his left eye. Christophe was battling two spade-wielding miners at the back of the chamber, but I saw two Wolves poking their heads and shoulders through the holes we had made. I blocked a mad sword-swing from a soldier with my mace, but before I could take him, he staggered away gurgling with a crossbow bolt in his chest.

The Wolves were among us.

I crushed the skull of a man-at-arms an instant before he could land a blow that would have hacked my head clean off. And there were more of my own men in that grim space now, four Wolves hacking and stabbing among the miners and the men-at-arms. I saw Christophe drop a man with a lunge to the belly. And then a sound that filled my soul with dread.

Crack.

The sound of a heavy stone ball smashing itself to splinters against the walls above our heads.

Crack.

The French artillery, silent for so many days, had chosen this morning to renew its bombardment of the inner bailey. And, by the sound of it, all of Philip's mighty castle-breakers were concentrating their missiles on the walls above the mine.

The enemy were all dead, or being finished off by the Wolves, and for the first time I looked around the space that we had just captured.

Crack.

Their mine was no bigger than a decent-sized private chamber, perhaps twenty feet long and ten feet wide, and narrower at the mouth, where the first rays of the sun were warming the chilly air. Outside I could see into the cat, the bare brown wood of the underside of the sloping roof and the handles fixed into the walls for man-handling its bulk across any terrain.

How I hated that infernal machine.

I said to a Wolf at my elbow, 'Jehan, burn that—'

Crack.

My words were cut off by another missile smashing into the rock above our heads. But the Wolf understood and bent over the crude hearth by the entrance and began to revitalise the miners' banked fire. There were more than a dozen corpses to deal with and I set the other men to piling them neatly by the mouth of the mine.

I stood for a moment and looked out at the familiar stones of the middle bailey. There was the wine seller's stand, now abandoned, the cheerful striped awning in tatters. There was the big gatehouse where de Lacy had stood and refused entry to the Useless Mouths. A pair of curious French men-at-arms saw me, shouted and began running towards the mine, and with a slithering swish were both transfixed with arrows from above. Robin was keeping his word to ward off a counter-attack.

Crack.

But there was nothing my lord could do about the castle-breakers.

'Christophe,' I called. Scarecrow was at the back of the mine examining the supports.

'I need you to get back down the tunnel and start organising a chain of men to bring the masonry in here as fast as you can.'

'Sir Alan, I must warn you,' he said, and I saw to my surprise that his face was white and he was trembling. 'I am bound to tell you, sir, that it is not safe in this place.'

'All the more reason to get the masonry in here quick and shore up the roof,' I said, trying to be confident. But the worm of terror was eating into my spine.

Crack.

The huge stones above our heads screamed like a woman in childbirth. A shower of dust cascaded upon our heads.

'Sir Alan, there are not enough supports, not nearly enough. They have removed some of the pillars. Deliberately taken them out, leaving just enough to . . . This roof . . . this roof could come down at any moment.'

'Surely we could use some of our timbers, or build columns of stone—'

'No, Sir Alan, no.' The man's faded eyes were filled with terror. He was close to shouting: 'There's. No. Time.' He'd removed his helmet and his grey hair matted with sweat stood out in weird spikes. He looked as mad as a march hare.

I finally understood. 'Right, right, everybody out. Now!'

I looked to my left, one of the Wolves was stacking burning embers and half-burned sticks in a corner of the cat, and blowing on them, urging them to flame.

'Leave that, Jehan. Everybody out, right now!' I started to push men towards the two dark holes in the wall.

'Out now! Everybody! Out!'

The Wolves knew how to obey an order and were slipping swiftly out of the mine and down the twin holes as fast as cellar rats when a lantern is lit.

Crack.

Another missile crashed into the wall and we were showered once again with fine dust. One of the beams that lined the walls popped out of its joint and leaned drunkenly out into the chamber. Christophe ran over and began trying to push it back into position. I looked at the two escape holes; they were now clear of men. I took a step towards the nearest one. I was feeling the fear, a sickness in my belly, a horrible tightness in my lungs; I crouched down next to the hole. Christophe was on the other side of the mine, shoving uselessly at the thick beam, trying to force it back in.

Crack.

One more ball crashed above our heads and with a rumbling roar a thousand tons of stone poured down upon us.

I had less than a heartbeat. I saw a deluge of grey tumble on to Christophe and dived for the tunnel. Something caught my right heel a tremendous whack but I got all my limbs pulled into the chamber behind me and, in the midst of that roaring, choking dust-filled hell, I hauled my body down the tunnel we had so carefully dug over

401

the past two days. I got no more than three yards with the supports creaking and squealing like tortured souls, scarcely able to breathe, when the roof of our own tunnel collapsed on my back and a giant, jagged stone hand shoved me hard into the earth.

The darkness seized me.

Chapter Thirty-two

I was in my grave. I was lying on my belly, in utter blackness, rock and earth packed tightly around my body. I could not move. I could hear and see nothing. The earth squeezed me tight as a lover. For a few moments I truly thought I was dead. But a dull pain in my right leg and across my lower back told me I was still among the living – for the time being. A wave of panic crashed behind the wall of my eyes; I tried to struggle and to cry out for help, but could move my body only a fraction. My immobility seemed to suffocate me. The world was pressing down on every part of me. My heart was pounding in my chest, trying to burst free of its bony cage. I screamed and screamed but my cries for help were weak and muffled and only echoed around in my head. I began to pray, muttering the familiar words of the Pater Noster, and holding an image I had once seen of the Virgin Mary in my head. Somehow the face of the Virgin became the face of Tilda. I prayed for an age; I prayed in a place beyond time. I called on the Virgin to save me. I called on St Michael. I spoke directly to my Maker.

And He answered.

There was a shift in the world and instantly I felt His living presence beside me in the darkness. Gradually I brought myself back under control; my mind grew calm. I knew that God did not intend for me to die in this hellish place. It was a test. It was all a test. The Lord God was testing me, as He had tested the Israelites, as He had tested Jonah. I would not fail.

My head was lying in the crook of my right arm, allowing me to breathe only shallowly in the dusty space beneath. My left arm was pinned against my side. My steel helmet had been knocked forward and was cutting painfully into my forehead. I moved my right hand, a finger, then another. My hand crept up my face and shoved against the cold steel of the helmet. With a scraping of metal on stone, and no little effort, I managed to push the helm higher, off my brow. My fingers felt warm wetness. It trickled down my nose and into my mouth – gritty, rusty blood.

I realised that I was very thirsty. My mouth parched. I was alive, though, and by some miracle not too badly hurt. I flexed the muscles of my legs and back in turn, and my left arm. There was a tiny amount of lateral movement, a half-inch, no more, and while I was in great discomfort – pain burned in the raw patches on my skin and something sharp was digging into my buttocks – I had been injured enough times to know no bones were broken. I pushed my right hand out in front of my face and encountered rough rock and loose earth a few inches from my nose. I swept the earth to one side using only my fingers and took a grip on the rock and pulled. It moved a fraction, sliding towards me. I pulled again and it came free; I could feel its cool, sandy, roughness against my cheek. It was about the size of an apple. A clod of earth fell on the back of my hand; pebbles rattled off my helmet. It was awkward to manoeuvre for only the fingers on my right hand were able to move, and a little room for my wrist, too. My upper arm and shoulder were jammed hard against rock. But I pushed that apple-sized stone up my cheek, smearing the skin, and over my shoulder, and with a tiny wriggle and shrug, I got it off my back and over to the side. There was now space in front of my face.

My fingers quested forward again, brushing away earth, feeling the floor of the tunnel rubbed smooth by the bodies of crawling Wolves. It sloped downwards – and suddenly I knew where I was. About two yards from the little pool of water that had collected at the bottom of the passage. And five yards from the courtyard of the inner bailey. My spirits soared with that knowledge. I had found my place once again on the curve of this green Earth. I knew where

I was. I was seven yards from freedom, from my friends, from Tilda. I pushed out of my mind the thought that there was half of Château Gaillard on top of me. I told myself I was only two yards from getting a drink of cool water.

My fingers snaked out, ruffled through the loose earth and found a shard of flint. I felt the smooth plane of the grey stone and the pitted roundness of one of its limestone-covered nodules. I gripped it and pulled. Nothing. Nothing. I pulled again and all of a sudden it moved, sliding towards me. I grasped it in my hand and used it as a crude spade, chopping and gouging at the loose rock and rubble around my left shoulder. And I felt the joint come free. I could move my left arm. I wriggled and worked my elbow back and forth – there was a threatening rumble as the stones and loose matter shifted above me – but praise God, bless His Holy Name, my left arm came free. I freed my right shoulder, hauling the rocks clear and packing them back by my waist. Then I began to dig my way forward using both hands.

It took an eternity. I pulled rocks, stones and clumps of old mortar from the rubble face before me and pushed them either to the side or behind my shoulders, and then I pulled myself forward a few inches. I was swimming forward through rock, rubble and mud, moving more slowly than a lazy snail, but I was moving, and downhill at that. To occupy my mind, I thought of Tilda . . . After perhaps an hour – although my sense of time was buried with me and I cannot be certain – my fingers groping before my face felt wet. And soon I was sucking up a few mouthfuls of putrid, lime-tasting, muddy water. It was pure nectar.

I had been right. Five yards to go. I hauled at the stones and mud, squirmed forward, moving uphill by now. When I stopped to catch my breath, I thought I heard something. It sounded like men's voices and iron implements hitting stone. I took a deep breath and called out with all my might. And listened. Nothing. Was it all in my imagination?

I shouted again: 'It's me, it's Alan!'

I thought I heard something. Another chink of iron on stone. Yes, somebody was definitely digging up there.

'Help me!' I shouted.

Clear as a bell, I heard Robin's voice. 'Stay where you are, Alan. We are coming for you. Do not move and we will be with you directly.'

Then I passed out of this world once more.

The next I knew I was being pulled from the rubble by my armpits by Jago the Cornish miner and his brother Denzell, and Robin was staring into my face with a look of frowning concern.

The light was blinding. I felt sick and light-headed. My hands were shaking and black with dirt, the nails broken and bleeding. Robin held a dipper of water to my mouth and I swallowed too fast and the wrong way and collapsed to the ground coughing like a dying man. There were folk

407

all around me: Wolves and men-at-arms of the garrison but the one face I wanted to see was not there.

'Where is Tilda?' I said. 'Where is my true love?'

'He's delirious,' said Robin. 'We'd better get him into the keep.'

I allowed a couple of the Wolves to carry me to an empty cot on the ground floor of that bastion. While I sat there on the edge of the bed, glorying in the fact that I was alive, the men stripped me of my mud-encrusted hauberk, boots and hose and washed me, roughly but with kindness, and fed me sips of water and half a stale oat cake. When he realised that I still had most of my wits about me, Robin sat down on the cot next to me and gave me the latest news, most of which I knew already.

At dawn the bombardment had begun again, he said, the castle-breakers hurling their missiles over the walls of the middle bailey, focusing their anger on the powerful gatehouse of the inner bailey above the mine the cat-men had dug. After only a few strikes from the castle-breakers, the right side of the gatehouse collapsed, bringing down a section of the inner bailey wall. But the bombardment did not cease: Philip's petraries continued to fling their missiles at the breach, battering at the edges to widen it and hurling their round stones through the gap to cause havoc inside the inner bailey.

I listened hard but I could hear no sounds of bombardment.

'They relented about an hour ago,' said Robin,

apparently reading my thoughts. 'I'd say they have run out of missiles. Or just packed it in for the day.'

'What hour is it now?'

'Nearly dusk. You were under the rubble all day long, Alan.'

'If they have created a sizeable breach, why have they not attacked?'

'That's anybody's guess. Perhaps they were not ready. But I think it is safe to assume they will come tomorrow morning. You should get some rest, Alan. We will need every able-bodied man at the breach tomorrow.'

'Do you think we can hold it?'

Robin made a see-sawing movement with his right hand. 'It depends how determined they are. It depends how determined we are. We will work all night trying to repair it as best we can. But you need to rest.'

My lord got up and walked towards the door.

'Robin,' I said, just as he reached it. My lord turned and looked enquiringly at me.

'Thank you for getting me out.'

Robin raised an eyebrow. 'You promised me once long ago that you would be faithful to me until death. You don't get out of your oath that easily.'

Then he ducked out of the door and was gone.

I tried to sleep in that narrow cot in the keep but my body was paining me. My left leg was a mass of bruising from ankle to knee and it throbbed agonisingly. My torn hands were aflame, or so it seemed. My arms and back felt as if they had been beaten with axe handles. I had a deep, angry cut on my forehead. But it was my mind that was in the greatest torment. I could not understand why Tilda had not come to see me. She must have heard I had been trapped under the rubble of the breach for a day – we were all hugger-mugger in our remaining part of the castle and news travelled like lightning – what lover would not come to their beloved and ask after his health after such an ordeal?

I could not understand it. Finally, an hour or so after dusk I rose from my cot, pulled on a clean pair of hose and a tunic that Robin had provided and hobbled into the inner bailey. There were a mass of men, some fifty or sixty at least, by the tumbled stones of the gatehouse, and the shrill ringing of many carpenters' hammers. I could see Robin had spoken truly – they were using the night to repair the thirty-foot-wide hole in our defences with wooden barricades and by hastily replacing the shattered blocks of masonry and fixing them in place with fresh mortar and heavy baulks of wood.

I watched them for a while, thinking of my nightmarish day in the tunnel, and grateful once again to Robin and the two Cornish lads for digging me free. Then I caught sight of one of Sir Joscelyn's men-at-arms lugging a great oak beam over to the breach. I stopped him and asked if he knew where Lady Matilda Giffard was to be found and he told me that father and daughter had taken up residence in a hut on the north side of the inner bailey – it was quieter in there than in the keep, he said, and the lady could have a little more privacy.

I thanked him and walked to the north side of the bailey. There was a row of simple wooden huts against the battlements there, which I knew had been used as store-rooms of grain and oil in the days when we had need of such places. Now the castle was down to the last scrapings of the barrels, what tiny quantities of food as we possessed were kept under lock and key in the keep.

I could see a glimmer of light leaking through the crack under the door from the hut at the end of the row, and I could hear the faint murmur of voices. There were no windows and so no way of looking in to check that this was the Giffards' abode.

I knocked on the door. The voices inside ceased immediately.

I knocked again.

'Who is it?' It was Tilda's voice.

'It is me, Alan. Can I come in?'

'This is not a good time, Alan.' She sounded scared, terrified even. 'I am washing myself. Be a dear and come back in an hour.'

Something was not right. Why was she lying to me? There was a man in there with her. I had definitely heard at least one male voice. Was he holding her at knife point? Did he at this very moment have a blade to her soft white throat?

411

I kept my voice steady. 'Very well, my love. It's nothing important. I will return in an hour or two. Enjoy your bath.'

Then I sprinted back to the keep to fetch my sword.

The second time I approached the hut was at a dead run. I wanted the maximum amount of surprise to give me the advantage in dealing with whatever was occurring inside. My bruised body protested but I hit the door of the hut at full speed, my shoulder smashing into the frail wood and bursting it off its hinges. But I bounced up from the wreckage of the door, Fidelity in my fist, cocked above my head to strike . . . and stopped, struck dumb with amazement.

At a little table in the middle of the hut, on a cheerful yellow linen cloth, a feast was spread – half a loaf of good white bread, most of a leg of ham, a boiled capon encased in jelly, even a game pie of some kind and a few wrinkled apples and a bowl of nuts. Around the table, their mouths full, their faces shiny with grease, hot guilt in their eyes, sat Sir Joscelyn Giffard, Tilda Giffard and Sir Benedict Malet.

I was too shocked to speak. I had not seen food like this for months. I had not even dreamed of food like this for weeks. I actually scrubbed at my eyes in case I was seeing phantom victuals. But no, they were as real as I was.

'What? How? What is this?' I could barely form words.

Sir Joscelyn had slipped from his stool and was pushing the door back into its shattered frame.

'Sit down, Sir Alan, and have a bite to eat.'

I looked at Sir Benedict Malet, his fat, glossy cheeks quivering with fear.

'You,' I hissed. 'You dirty thief!'

'Alan, sit down and eat something!' Sir Joscelyn was behind me, trying to usher me on to a stool.

'Get away from me,' I snarled at him. I pointed my finger at Benedict. 'Lord de Lacy will know of this. How long have you been stealing the food of honest fighting men to fill your greedy belly? Since the first day of the siege? Since you took over the stewardship of the stores? How many men have died of hunger so that you could gorge yourselves? I will see you hanged, you cur!'

'Alan,' Tilda spoke to me in her sweet, smoky voice. 'There is no need to get in a sweat about this. It is just a little food. Nothing more. We're entitled to eat.'

'No,' I said. 'That was the contract with the men. That was understood. We all suffered equally. We all hungered equally. Poor Niels was hanged because his hunger led him to conspire with the French. But this is a far worse betrayal.'

I stepped to the table and seizing the corners of the table cloth, I bundled the whole spread into one bulky parcel.

'De Lacy shall see this!' I said, and tugged the door open.

As I strode out, I heard Tilda calling after me. I stopped, turned and my beloved stood there before me in the light

413

from the doorway, tears in her eyes. She was achingly beautiful.

'You cannot do this to me, Alan,' she said. 'You told me you loved me, and I believed you. I shared my body with you.'

I stared at her, unable to think.

'If you tell de Lacy, my father will almost certainly be hanged; Bennie will be hanged for sure. And I too will die with my head in a noose. Is that what you want?'

I was a statue. Frozen. I could not even contemplate my love slowly strangling to death at the end of a rope. But this crime was so foul, so contemptible . . .

'Please, Alan. If you love me, let this go. Let us forget that this ever happened. Come back inside and we can explain it to you. If you love me, come back inside.'

I could feel my heart being torn in two.

I turned my back on her and began to walk away, the heavy bundle swinging in my fist.

'Alan, Alan, you will not tell de Lacy, will you?'

I turned back to look at her, but I could not meet her eyes.

'I will not tell. For you. I will stay silent.'

'Alan, promise me, promise me you will not tell a soul about this matter.'

I said nothing more and walked away.

I gave that damned bundle to Father de la Motte who was in charge of the infirmary, a low wooden building on

414

the far side of the inner bailey crammed with sick and injured men. I merely muttered, 'For the wounded', as I handed it over. His eyes widened when he looked inside but I told him nothing of the food's provenance. When he pressed me, I shrugged and said, 'Call it a gift from God.'

Father de la Motte looked into my face, his piercing eyes probing my soul. 'Are you quite well, my son?' he said. 'Would you like to sit quietly for a while?'

'I am tired, Father, that is all,' I said. 'I am so very tired.'

The priest insisted I have a cup of hot horse-meat broth before I left and he thanked me for the gift of the food and did not ask any more questions. I drank my broth, dull-eyed, close to tears, almost grieving, and then went back to my cot in the keep, lay down in my clothes and slept like a rock until morning.

The bombardment woke me a little after dawn. The flat cracking of stone on stone that I had heard so often in the past few months that it had become like a refrain, the music of the Iron Castle. My body had stiffened during the night and it was only with a good deal of difficulty that I managed to dress myself in my full mail and dented helmet, strap on Fidelity, mace and misericorde, and loop a borrowed shield over my shoulder. I felt like an old man, not a brisk young fellow who was not yet thirty. As I had told Father de la Motte, I was tired, deep-in-the-bone tired. Years of war and suffering had extracted their fee from my mind and body. The wounds taken, the comrades lost. The disappointments, the tragedy and the pity of it all. I missed Kit and his breezy cheerfulness more than ever that cold March morning and reflected that if he had not always got everything absolutely right in his duties as a squire, he had been an excellent companion and a fine young man. He should not be dead. I vowed I would fight that day for him, for his memory, and take some measure of revenge on the enemy who had cut him down.

I did not think of Tilda and her little illicit feast at all.

When I emerged from the keep, mailed, armed and ready, it was close to mid-morning. Robin was at the breach with Roger de Lacy, both kneeling behind a fallen section of masonry. The barricades erected during the night had already been torn apart by Philip's castle-breakers, like a giant fist smashing through a frail lattice-work of twigs. There were shreds of wood scattered all over the rubble and a ten-yard-wide hole still gaped in the defences of the inner bailey. But there was an air between these two men. A sense of quiet fury. Caused by something more than the destruction of our makeshift barricade.

'You understand your orders, Locksley?'

'Oh yes, they are quite clear,' said my lord. Again there was something odd in his tone, a quiet hum of anger.

Roger de Lacy stared at him hard and then abruptly turned and marched away.

'What is it, Robin?' I said.

'Hmm?'

I looked around me. I could see a hundred men-at-arms, maybe more, clustered in groups around the breach, taking shelter from the enemy missiles, which cracked and whined about the outer walls and on occasion sailed through the gap to crash thunderously against the keep.

'What has happened?'

'You look like something dragged up from the very depths of Hell,' said Robin. 'Sure you should be out of bed today?'

'Tell me!'

Robin sighed. 'There was a letter, from the King to de Lacy, dated November last year. Father de la Motte, Sir Joscelyn Giffard and I have only just seen it this morning at a meeting of the high council. This is strictly confidential, Alan. You must tell nobody. Give me your word you will not repeat any of this.'

'What was in it?'

'Give me your word you will remain silent about this.'

I gave it. Twice in a dozen hours I had been sworn to silence by those I loved.

'The letter is quite clear,' said Robin. 'John is not coming. Perhaps he never truly intended to relieve us. Despite all his assurances to de Lacy, the King will not come to our aid.'

Chapter Thirty-three

I stared at Robin. 'All this then has been in vain? How how . . .'

'The letter was lobbed over the walls last night, roped to a trebuchet ball. It is genuine. Captured from one of the King's messengers, apparently, some months ago. I know John's seal well enough to tell it is real. De Lacy does too There is no doubt about it. But listen to me, Alan: no on in the castle must know – for now. My lord de Lacy ha threatened death to anyone who speaks of this.'

'What did it say?'

'He orders de Lacy to hold out as long as he can and ther do what he thinks best. It seems clear that, even back ther even before Christmas, he had no intention of coming t our rescue. He abandoned us to our doom three months ago

'Do what he thinks best? De Lacy must do what he thinks best? Then surely there is no point in continuing the fight. We can make terms. Philip will accept our surrender, I am sure of it. He does not want to lose any more men. If de Lacy were to send out heralds—'

'De Lacy is determined to fight to the end.'

'What?' I was utterly astounded. 'For God's sake, why?'

'God knows. He says he has made a vow to hold the castle and swears he will hold it – come what may. His honour is at stake, he says. I say he's a vainglorious, mutton-headed idiot.'

'So we must all die for his honour?'

'No.'

I looked at my lord. 'What then?'

'I'm working on that. Give me a little time and I will find a way to get us out of this place. I'm not going to die for a faithless King, nor for a bloody-minded baron with a death-wish – and neither are you, and neither are any more of my men, if I can possibly help it. Give me a day to get something in place. Can you do that, Alan? Can you hold this breach for a day, for me?'

I swallowed. 'I'll try, my lord.'

'Hold this for one day, for one single day, Alan, and I promise you, I'll get us out of here this very night.'

When Robin left me, I looked out through the U-shaped rubble lip of the breach at the shut gates of the middle bailey, a mere forty yards away, and the walls either side where hundreds of curious French heads were watching us from the battlements.

I looked behind me at the roof of the keep where I could see nearly a score of Robin's archers and a dozen crossbowmen. I could even make out the shape of the twin arms of Old Thunderbolt and Aaron bent by its side, fussing over something. Perhaps we might just be able to hold back the enemy for one day, I thought. Given a big slice of luck. I had no choice but to trust Robin. And I did. He would get us out of there tonight, I was sure of it. All I had to do was hold the breach.

For a day.

I squinted at the stone bridge that jutted out of the half-demolished gatehouse and spanned the deep ditch around the whole of the inner bailey. The bridge was narrow – only two yards wide – and the French would have to funnel their men across it before they could come at the hole in our walls.

It was a killing ground.

'Father de la Motte tells me you made a gift to the wounded of a handsome parcel of viands,' said de Lacy. I had not noticed his approach. He was standing behind me in full mail, sword at his hip, looking furious.

'Would you care to tell me how you came about such a cornucopia?'

I looked him in the eye, thinking, You would kill me for your personal honour, would you? You would hold out to the last man in this doomed place to satisfy your lust for glory? But I actually said, 'I cannot tell you, sir' – quite truthfully. I could not tell him because I could not allow Tilda to be hanged for the crimes of her father and Benedict. Anyway, after the terrible news Robin had given me, I did not much feel like giving him the whole truth.

'I found the food in one of the storehouses,' I said, again truthfully. 'And I brought it directly to Father de la Motte in the infirmary – did I do wrong?'

Before de Lacy could reply, I saw movement over his shoulder and said, 'I think, sir, that we have more to worry about than a few crumbs of food. Look.'

The doors in the gatehouse in the middle bailey swung slowly inwards until they were wide open and through them I could see the flattish patch of ground outside it where the Useless Mouths had gathered and begged for readmission. Once again it was teeming with agitated folk – this time not starving supplicants but an enemy host. Hundreds of men-at-arms, perhaps half a thousand. Drawn up in squares and columns outside the gates and disappearing from view down on the slope below the castle: foot soldiers with long spears, Genoese crossbowmen with their out-sized shields, *conrois* of knights bright in mail and coloured surcoats.

All the might of Philip's army arrayed for war.

De Lacy told me I was to command a squad of thirty men-at-arms to hold the left side of the breach until I was relieved. Sir Joscelyn was to hold the right with a similar force and de Lacy would hold the middle with the largest squad of forty men. Not counting the bowmen, about two-thirds of the castle's uninjured men were engaged in holding the breach – the remaining third, some fifty men in total, manned the battlements of the inner bailey and formed a reserve that could be brought in to plug gaps or relieve any section that required it.

There could be no thought of surrender, de Lacy told us all.

I gathered my Wolves on the left of the breach, keeping them in the shelter of the tumbled stones of the gatehouse and behind its remaining wall. While the castle-breakers were idle, there was no guarantee the French had not just paused in their bombardment in order to tempt us to line the open breach with our precious flesh and blood, where-upon they might resume their onslaught and smash their missiles through our ranks.

I looked to my right and saw Sir Joscelyn and his band of knights and men-at-arms. He refused to meet my eye. I wondered what the men he commanded would say if they knew that he and his accomplice Sir Benedict Malet had been quietly stealing and eating their food for months. They would rip him limb from limb – and rightly so. But I could say nothing without endangering the life of Tilda. I bit my tongue. Now that I looked at Sir Joscelyn I could see he was in better condition than the other men in his squad. And Benedict, too, who was acting as his second-in-command that day, had not lost a pound from his ample frame. How had I failed to notice this? In a garrison that was now, to a man, whip thin, faces gaunt, skin tight over bones, how had I not seen the glow of good health on these two men? There would be a reckoning, I told myself, but not on this day, not on this day of battle. To hold the breach, we needed every man – even greedy, thieving scoundrels.

I looked around at the men I had the honour to command. Good men, mostly Wolves. Familiar faces, confident grins, bright eyes: there was Claes, the one-eyed vintenar, waiting patiently for my orders; there were Jago and Denzell, the Cornish brothers to whom I owed my life, who both favoured long spears and round oak shields; there was Jacques, the big Norman mason, without the tools of his craft but carrying a long, old-fashioned bearded axe and looking grim. And somewhere below my feet was the crushed body of Christophe, the brave engineer entombed in an enemy mine, near the place that had nearly become my own tomb.

Another good man dead – for nothing.

'We hold this breach until we are relieved; those are the orders. And we will do exactly that. We do not take a single step backwards. We hold them here. I will rotate you, so that each man has a chance to rest at the rear of the shield wall. But know this: if we let them in, we are dead. So we hold them. Understood?'

The response was a faint chorus of muttered assent.

'What? You want to live for ever?' I showed them my teeth. 'This is where the war is today.' I rapped a piece of broken masonry with my mail-covered knuckles. 'This is where the war is and we are its warriors. So here is where we fight. Here is where we will show the kind of men we are. And if we fall, so be it, but we shall have made such a battle that we will be remembered for ever. For we are the Wolves!'

I threw back my head and howled like a madman.

And every man in that squad, whether they were Wolves or not, opened wide his jaws and howled with me.

The French came up the hill and through the gates of the middle bailey – at least two hundred men – spearmen in the front ranks, dismounted knights and men-at-arms behind them, and crossbowmen on the flanks. They shouted '*Saint Denis!*' invoking the headless holy man they venerated in Paris and '*Vive le Roi!*'

The attack began with ordered ranks and files of men, but once through the gates of the middle bailey, they filled the air with their roars and charged forward as a mob. The French were brave men, fighting for their lord, and the first rank of men, those facing the greatest danger, were particularly valorous. But they died just the same. The first iron bolt of Old Thunderbolt ploughed into the mass of shouting men on the stone bridge when they were no more than twenty yards from the breach. It slashed through their ranks like a giant scythe, leaving a bloody furrow through the press of humanity; a dozen men were maimed or killed by that one strike. Then Robin's archers and crossbowmen loosed their shafts – and showered the bridge with death. Like a swooping flock of deadly birds, the arrows hummed into the staggering men. Steel bodkin heads punched through padded gambesons, leather armour, even mail, and sank into tender flesh. Evil black quarrels punctured limbs and torsos, faces were gashed, bones were smashed, men were knocked flying. There were bodies falling, left and right, tumbling into the ditch below. The war cries turned to screams. The first volley from our bowmen was followed, moments later, by a second – only of arrows this time, war bows being faster to draw and loose than crossbows – then a third. Chaos screamed across that awful bridge, stealing souls, hurling men into destruction. One moment there were two score spearmen on the bridge, charging towards the breach, their long spears stretching out to us, the next it had almost been wiped clear, save for the bodies and the blood and the writhing wounded, men stuck here, there and everywhere with slim feathered shafts. I saw one with half a dozen shafts in his body, still moving feebly. Of forty who charged so valiantly, only three made it to the other side of the bridge – but they still bounded up the loose rubble slope, yelling their fury, stabbing with their spears – and were cut down with ease by the dozen eager Wolves who leaped forward to meet them at the top.

I had not yet drawn my sword.

The attack was far from over; more spearmen were coming forward from the gatehouse in the middle bailey, following in the bloody footsteps of the first, stepping cautiously on to the bridge, their shields held high, spears levelled, helmeted heads tucked in behind, shafts hammering down on them like hailstones. They came on still in their disciplined squads, many scores of them, some stepping through the carnage, slipping a little on the blood, some falling, some hesitating but most coming forward inexorably towards us; and yet more of the enemy, fifty men at least, were pouring down into the ditch on the right of the bridge, the southern side, nearest the breach, and that deep-dug defence was soon full of jostling, angry men shoving each other up the slippery chalk side, standing on shoulders and boosting each other, scrambling up and on to the tumbled stones of our broken walls.

Robin's men were no longer loosing volleys – the archers picked their targets and almost every arrow claimed a life. But they could not stem that flood of foes.

Old Thunderbolt cracked again from high up behind me and a black bar of death hurtled through the air into the first men clambering out of the ditch and beginning their determined scrabble up the rubble slope to the breach. Two French men-at-arms were smashed apart, quite literally ripped limb from limb by the spinning yard-long steel bolt – and Robin's bowmen were dropping quarrels and shafts on the heads of the milling horde in the ditch.

Many died, but yet more of them came forward.

A dozen men were now on the scree of loose masonry, and climbing towards us, shields held out before them, using spear and sword as staffs to speed them onwards and upwards. Into the mouth of battle. Into the cauldron of Hell. A volley of crossbow bolts lashed into them; two dropped, another staggered sideways, a quarrel in his belly. But on they came.

I drew my sword.

Despite Aaron's devilish work with Old Thunderbolt, and the slaughter wrought by our bowmen, the enemy were upon us.

I stepped up to the lip of the breach, the highest point in that stony hole in our walls, and waited a couple of heartbeats for the first French man-at-arms to puff and pant his way up towards me. Claes was at my right shoulder and Jacques the big mason at my left. Below us the enemy swarmed like angry ants. By now a dozen, a score, two score fighting men were boiling out of the ditch and scrambling their way towards us. It was time.

I howled once, long and hard, and plunged into the mass of the enemy, my sword swinging like a butcher's cleaver.

The first man-at-arms died easily, Fidelity slicing into his waist almost of its own accord. There was another man, directly behind him, lunging at me with a sword. I swerved to avoid the blade and hacked into his arm, smashing Fidelity into his elbow joint. He screamed,

427

dropped his shield and my back-swing chopped into his face, just below the ear. But, in the few heartbeats it took to free my blade from his gripping skull, a third man was on me, a knight in fine mail with a flower device on his shield. He hacked at my head, I ducked . . . and Jacques split his skull with one blow of his bearded axe.

The enemy were all around us, and the Wolves either side of me were killing them with barely restrained fury. I chopped and sliced with Fidelity, I lunged and smashed my blade into the enemy. I shoved men back with my shield, and over our heads the deadly shafts whistled and buzzed, knocking down men just as they reached the top of the breach. The enemy seemed to pause, to reel back all at the same time, and I grabbed the two Wolves on either side and bawled at them to form a shield wall with me, here, and they sprang into the formation with admirable speed, those mindless hours on the Rouen training ground paying off; a dozen Wolves were at my back and both sides, shields high, plugging the left side of the breach with our armoured bodies. The French rallied and surged forward: a wave of men crashed against us, shouting stabbing, scrabbling with their feet to shove us back. I kept my shield up, though the downward pressure on it was enormous, and stabbed hard over the top, aiming under the rim of steel helmets at faces that seemed to be all red, screaming mouth – I thrust and jabbed with my sword, piercing cheeks and bursting eyes. The wounded enemy fell away but were instantly replaced by fresh yelling faces, and the weight on my shield never seemed to slacken. It was brutal work merely to keep your footing on the tumbled masonry – and twice I felt the rubble lurch beneath my feet and twice I felt the crunch of steel blades against my mail-clad shins – but to stumble and fall meant death by trampling in the scrum of snarling, hacking, screaming, dying men and, by God's grace, I kept my feet in that mêlée.

I snatched a glance to my left and saw that de Lacy and his closest knights were fighting in the centre and beyond them I caught a glimpse of Sir Joscelyn killing foes with compact, well-trained strokes of his sword. The French were still boiling up over the lip of the ditch and sprinting across the bridge, scrambling to get at us, but by now they had to trample their own dying and dead to reach our shield line. Old Thunderbolt cracked again, smashing into five attackers who came at us in a group, swiping them all away and leaving only a bloody smear and a scatter of severed limbs. But still the enemy flung themselves at us, reckless of their own lives, inviting us to slaughter them. I dropped man after man, my sword red from hilt to tip, my face and mail dripping, my voice hoarse, my ears deafened by the roars and the screaming.

Then a spear reached out from the second rank of the mass of enemies before me, driving towards my face. I ducked my head behind my shield and felt the jolt of the blow and the steel blade scrape harmlessly against my helmet. Something else crashed against the steel, making my head ring, but I felt the pressure against my shield ease momentarily and I bullocked forward blindly, forcing a wavering Frenchman backwards with brute strength, breaking our own wall but freeing my sword arm, to lunge and pierce his groin. He fell; another man appeared and I punched my hilt into his face, saw flying teeth, blood; I kicked another fellow in the belly; I sliced at an enemy, a vicious scything blow to the head, but a rock turned under my right foot and I missed – we were all surging forward by now and I could hear the Wolves behind me howling in victory and feel shields and hands shoving me down the slope. The French were melting away, falling back, crying, bleeding, streaming away across the bloody, corpse-strewn bridge, running for the gatehouse and safety. I called out for our men to halt and return to the breach, and they did, red-faced, joyous, panting, eyes bright as jewels, bodies wet with blood.

We had held. We had kept the French out.

For now.

Chapter Thirty-four

looked to my right, at de Lacy's men and Sir Joscelyn's
fellows on the far right. They seemed intact, although the
sidemark of dead and wounded before their position was
thinner than before ours. Evidently, being closest to the
stone bridge, we had borne the brunt of the battle. I sent
the foremost Wolves back into the rear ranks to rest, with
my praise ringing in their ears; the men who had been
behind them in the shield wall now came forward. The
rubble slope below us was thick with dead, forty or fifty
men, many still moving, lay in their gore and in a litter
of arrow shafts. Half a dozen of my men would never
breathe again, and two would be cripples for life – if they
survived their wounds.

I sent five hale men down to gather unbroken arrows

and told the rest of the Wolves to stand down and take shelter, lest the bombardment begin again.

This battle was not over, far from it. Even as we strapped up the wounds of our comrades and gulped down bowls of cold nameless soup, I could see the enemy massing again in even larger numbers through the open gate of the middle bailey. Now there were scores of horsemen disgorging from Philip's Hill and milling about on the slope below the gates, three *conrois* at least, perhaps a hundred mailed men in bright surcoats on large, high-spirited horses: the knights.

I left Claes in charge of the men, telling him to keep them sheltered and distribute as much water as he could – our water supplies, thank God, had not diminished all through the siege. I took the arrows we had salvaged – a scant two dozen – and climbed to the top of the keep to deliver them personally to Robin.

My lord was grim-faced when I approached. He was conferring with Aaron by Old Thunderbolt and directing two of Aaron's engineers as they moved the springald into a new position with the utmost care. He thanked me for the arrows and admitted they were sorely needed.

'We are down to fewer than three shafts a man,' he said. I looked round at the twenty or so men on the keep and saw their despondency. Even with the arrows I had salvaged, these men had only enough shafts for a full pitched battle lasting about thirty heartbeats. Then they were done.

Robin said, 'I'm worried about those horsemen.' He nodded at the four score or so mounted men still moving about on the slope below the walls of the middle bailey. 'We don't have enough arrows to stop them on the bridge. If a dozen horsemen get across it, and if they can get their horses to mount the slope and climb it, we are all finished. They will punch through your men like a hammer through a horn window, and the foot soldiers will follow in their path. If they can get enough horsemen up to the top of the breach, it's all over.'

'Do you think horses could be made to climb that slope?'

'If they are fairly well trained, and with ruthless use of the spur – yes.'

'Then we are all dead.'

'Well, not quite. I did have an idea that might just work, with a bit of luck. And if we have enough time. We will make a wall that no horse will ride through.'

'What?'

'I'll tell you about it in a moment. Come over here.' He led me to the northern lip of the keep, and pointed down at the shimmering grey waters of the Seine.

'What do you see there, Alan?'

'The river.'

'No, there, by the quay.'

It was a large boat, moored on the east bank. I realised it was the place where, had God permitted it, we would have unloaded the convoy of food the Wolves had rowed down from Rouen all those months ago. Indeed, it looked

433

exactly like one of the boats we had used to make our disastrous attack on the pontoon bridge.

'We go tonight,' said Robin. 'I have ropes and ladders. We go – you, me and the surviving Wolves – when the world is asleep, we will leave this place, over the walls and down that cliffside. Quiet as mice. And we will seize that craft, cut it free and it will carry us away, downstream to Rouen and safety. What do you think?'

'It could work,' I admitted. 'It could truly work. We could actually escape.' I felt hope flame, a fire kindled to warm my heart.

'You keep that thought in your head. And keep your head down for the rest of the day,' said my lord. 'Tonight we will shake the dust of this accursed place from our feet. Now about that wall . . .'

He gathered two of his bowmen and we went down the stairs of the keep into the stables. The men collected two bales of straw apiece and then we scooped up a small barrel from the smithy where somebody had set it to warming on a ledge by the forge. Then, to the breach, and with plenty of willing help from the Wolves, we all got our hands extremely dirty.

An hour later, standing high on a shard of broken masonry that jutted out from the remaining wall on the left side of the breach, I could clearly see, over the fortifications of the middle bailey, the French knights on the slope below. They had formed into two distinct groups, dismounted and standing by their chargers, on the left and, further away, on the right. The horses were clad in brightly coloured trappers that covered them from head-band to hock, the men standing beside them in matching surcoats over grey mail. Cheerful pennants fluttered from the ends of the lances, held upright in young squires' hands and grounded in the mud. They all looked impossibly grand in the strong March sunlight; noble, brave, almost joyful. And between the groups of dismounted horsemen, a battle of men-at-arms sitting on the thin grass, perhaps two hundred, armed with spear and sword. There were black-clad priests moving among the men and horses, blessing them, offering words of comfort and fragments of the Host and sips from silver chalices. My belly grumbled merely at the thought of that holy feast, the body and blood of Christ. I thought about the bundle of food I had taken from Sir Joscelyn and Tilda, and pondered my decision to give it to Father de la Motte without even tasting the merest bite. What a fool I was, I thought. I could have gorged, I could have filled my belly many times over. I could have felt the warm glow of the well-fed all over my thin, tired and battered body. And my body *was* battered: my shoulders, back and both legs were a sea of aches, every movement a jolt of fire. I wanted nothing more than to lie down; not true, I wanted more than anything to eat. And who would have known if I had gorged from the bundle? No one. And if I had wolfed it all, perhaps I would be stronger for the coming fight. Perhaps if I had swallowed down at least some of that forbidden food, just a leg of the capon, perhaps, or a slice of the game pie, I would be serving my fellow men in this castle well, by fortifying my body in readiness to face the foe . . .

I blushed for shame at that silent sophistry. It was dirty meat, dishonoured bread, and no matter how much I drooled over its memory, I knew in my heart I had done the right thing. I would be no better than those three skulking thieves in the storeroom who robbed their comrades to stuff their fat faces, if I had partaken of the feast. I had stolen food myself once or twice when a lad, out of dire need, so I was not without that sin on my conscience, but never in time of siege, and never from men who would die hungry because of my thievery. I was a better man now, too, I hoped. I was a knight. I was a leader of men. I was hungry, yes, but I had my honour, by God, and I would not sell it for a bellyful of food stolen from starving comrades. But now this knight must prove his honour on an echoing belly, I reflected. For I could see the French knights in the left *conroi* stirring; the noblemen, now helmeted, fully armoured, were being heaved into the saddle by their squires.

The knights swung up on to the backs of their big destriers, accepted their lances and, as a trumpet called out, formed up into a column of twos, a long snake of pairs of horsemen stretching across the slope. Shields hefted, lances were tucked firmly under the right armpit nother trumpet rang out and the snake began to move owards us.

They came through the gate of the middle bailey at a ouncy trot and by the time they had crossed the courtyard nd their iron hooves were hammering on to the stone ridge they had reached a full canter. A pounding, clatering, bellowing river of muscle and mail charging straight owards our position – and we did nothing. Not an arrow lew, not a spear was cast. The horsemen surged over the ore-dyed bridge unchallenged, the leading two knights umped their horses on to the rocky slope and with much kittering of iron-shod hooves on loose rubble, and harsh ries of '*Vive le Roi!*' they began to urge their mounts up he scree.

A single arrow looped down from the top of the keep, he head of the shaft a red-orange flag. It slammed into he rubble a bare three yards ahead of my waiting Wolves, vho were crouched among the stones at the lip of the reach, and immediately a fat line of pine tar-soaked straw hat Robin had caused to be stuffed into the cracks burst nto dancing flame. A second fire arrow followed, again vith perfect accuracy, and a third – but no more were eeded for the sticky black road of straw that ran all the vay across the breach from wall to wall flared into life in couple of heartbeats. The flames jumped up higher than man, the fuel roaring and crackling like a beast of Hell, louds of thick smoke boiling upwards. Through this wall f fire and smoke I watched the leading horse, two paces

437

from me, rear up in terror, its forelegs paddling the air and the knight on its back falling helplessly backwards to crash down on the slope. A second horse, too, was shying and rearing, barging into the horse behind it. The animals were neighing, screaming almost, in atavistic fear of the flames. They would not charge forward into fire, which was now leaping ever higher and higher. On that treach-erous incline, the horses stumbled and fell, their frail legs snapping like kindling, crashing into their fellow beasts as they tumbled, crushing riders between slope and saddle as more and more knights forced their way off the bridge and into the crush.

And into that chaos of panicking horse, shouting knights and roaring flame, into that holocaust of dying men and burning animals, Old Thunderbolt loosed his first deadly iron shaft.

At a distance of fifty yards, the shaft sliced through men and horses like a giant blade, punching away two or three mounts and riders in a burst of guts. And then the arrows began to zip through the leaping flames – Robin had held back all his stocks of shafts, save for the three fire arrows, until this moment. Yard-long shafts tipped with bodkin points smacked into thick horse muscle and mailed bodies alike, and the men on the other side of that wall of leaping flame tasted the horror of damnation before they left this good, green Earth. Crossbows cracked and hissed through the fire, thumping into the foe, tumbling them back.

I could see only intermittently through the blaze, and I was grateful for it. For the little I saw, sickened me to my soul. Blood upon blood, men stuck like hedgehogs, falling forward to roast in the pine-tar fire, burning alive, their hair flaring briefly like torches; massive horses flailing helplessly on their sides or backs, broken limbs flopping obscenely; a brave man here or there, dismounted but miraculously unhurt, trying to charge the fire-wall and being slammed off his feet by a quarrel or bow shaft. Then Old Thunderbolt loosed again and swiped another bloody channel through the mayhem. And, at that, the French knights had had enough. A pathetic handful – the fortune-blessed tail-enders of the forty-strong column – clattered back across the bridge, back into safety, back into life.

Not one enemy knight made it through the wall of fire. We had not lost a single man.

Chapter Thirty-five

We sluiced down cold well-water as if it were wine; and we felt a euphoria overcome us, lift us, send our souls soaring joyfully to Heaven. God was surely aiding us, as well as Robin's cunning trick, and between them they had wrought destruction on our foes. We had utterly destroyed the enemy knights who came against us, the cream of the French forces, with not a single loss to ourselves. They and their horses had torn themselves apart on the treacherous slope, the corpses reeking and twitching and the wounded crawling away to die in the ditch. We were victorious. Is there any better feeling that a fighting man can have? The men sang snatches of song, laughing and calling out the old jests to de Lacy's men next to us, and I even caught a careless smile from Sir Joscelyn on the far right of our line, where he stood and surveyed the carnage through the dying flicker of the pine-tar flames.

The first ball from the enemy trebuchet smashed directly into an English man-at-arms called Rowan, one of the castle garrison, who had been ordered to serve under me. One moment he was standing on the breach, with his hands jauntily on his hips, his head thrown back in song, the next he was little more than a bloody stain against the remaining walls of the inner bailey gatehouse. His legs jiggled a little even after they had been severed from his disintegrated torso. His head rolled to my feet, the mouth wide and gaping in surprise. I shouted, 'Back, Back. Get back in cover, all of you men!'

But my words were needless; at the first crash of bloody ball against standing masonry, the men had ducked into their safe places, just back from the lip behind any sizeable chunk of solid matter. One moment the breach was filled with jolly, laughing men, the next all that could be seen was a helmeted head or two poking out from beyond the rubble. I stood my ground, in the centre of the breach, alone. De Lacy and Sir Joscelyn had disappeared, too. I was not being foolhardy, I was not being brave: a mangonel or trebuchet, while very powerful, did not have the accuracy of a bow or even of a springald. The odds were in my favour and, to be honest, I wanted to cut a figure for the men, to hold on for just a moment longer to the euphoria we had all shared. I determined I would stand there until the next missile struck and then I would seek shelter.

I made a few words to pass the time, as I stood there, trying to look unconcerned. 'We have shown them,' I said, my voice unnaturally loud in the quiet after the shriek of shattering stone, and pitched a little too high. 'We have shown them we are not afraid. We have shown them we are their masters in valour – and in cunning. They know this in their hearts. But Philip is a cruel master – he will force them on to our swords one more time. Just one more time will they come against us – and then they must concede defeat. If we can hold them, just once more, my brothers, if we can throw them back once more, we shall have won this day. Not even Philip's killers have the stomach for this slaughter. So I say this: hold them, kill them—'

A missile crashed into the breach, two yards from me, spraying my back painfully with shards of limestone, the ball skipping onwards into the courtyard and rattling harmlessly against the thick walls of the keep. My nerve failed me. My mouth was dry as dust; I had no more brave words for the men. I was empty.

I climbed down as calmly as I could to a place next to Claes, who was bedded in snugly behind a yard-thick section of the inner bailey walls. I leaned back against the cool, dusty stone and tried to breathe normally. My right hand was shaking like a waking drunkard's. I clamped it tight with my left, as if in prayer.

When the bombardment ceases, I thought, they will come. Another stone cracked against the breach, an awful sound – it seemed almost angry, resentful, as if cold stone could be seeking revenge for the havoc we had wrought on the horsemen. The missile stopped dead, burying itself in the rubble of our ramparts, becoming part of them. When this is over, I thought, the real battle will begin. And we will all die. I felt the ice-snake of fear uncoil in my lower belly.

They did not waste much time. I could feel the fury at the loss of so many of their knights reach out towards me from their advancing men – a sea of men. Hundreds. This must be Philip's last throw, I told myself. Even his resources are not endless. But he had more than enough men for one more massive assault.

The bombardment cracked and shrieked and whistled all about us – all five of Philip's war machines, and whatever small fry he had, too, were concentrated on our twenty yards of breach – and we cowered behind stones, making ourselves as small as we possibly could. Another man was crushed outright, and two other men were badly gashed by flying splinters of rock, but the rest of us made it through the maelstrom more or less unscathed. My stomach ached, both fear and lack of food, I believe. Yet I wanted to vomit. I wanted to run from the hellish noise, as fast and as far as I could to somewhere clean and green and quiet; I would never lift a sword again in anger, I vowed to God, as long as the hellish noise would cease.

Then it did cease – and things became infinitely worse.

The footmen came first, an unending sea of them, eschewing the stone bridge, which was dyed a rusty brown with blood and half-clogged with the corpses of men and horses, and hurling themselves directly into the ditch with ladders and shouts of rage. Moments later they were climbing out the other side and scrambling up the scree towards us like monkeys. Half a hundred men in leather, wool and linen, waving swords and spears and spitting their fury, clambered up rocks, in a lather to get at us, and behind them came another half-hundred and more beyond that. And now, through the gates, I could see a score, two score of dismounted knights and squires, in surcoats of red and yellow and blue, running along with the common men-at-arms.

This is it, I thought. This is Philip's full strength. Robin's men managed two scanty volleys, a handful of enemy men-at-arms staggered and dropped, but then the twang and hiss of our bows fell silent and the wave of Frenchmen crashed upon us.

We fought them, shields locked, shoulder to shoulder. I tried to summon the white-hot fury that had often possessed me on the battlefield, and failed. I battered at enemy helmets with Fidelity; I concentrated on keeping my feet and holding the line against the press of foes. I shoved with my shield at the snarling sea of humanity, and jabbed and smashed and spat at them. I know that I killed one or two, wounded a few more. But I was not the master of that mêlée, I was its servant – buffeted by the surging of a host of men, my sword arm leaden, my knees weak.

We held them, just. Amid the clang and clatter of steel against wood, I felt the pressure ease and for a moment my heart soared like a lark. The French men-at-arms were pulling back, if we could just push forward one last time . . .

But the men-at-arms were not retreating, they were not beaten; they were pulling back to let the dismounted knights come forward.

From hope to despair. The two lines of foes parted for a dozen heartbeats, then the bright knights' surcoats filled my vision. For an eerie instant, everything was still: the French knights, fresh, well-fed, full of fury at their noble comrades' ugly deaths in the wall of fire, glared at us over their shields, swords raised and ready to smite us down. I looked along our lines, thinner now, with more than half of the original men down, the remaining faces sallow, bloodied and bruised.

I found a last crumb of strength in my belly and shouted, 'Hold hard, Wolves; hold hard for Locksley and for England!'

And was rewarded by a hair-lifting howl in response.

The French knights growled back at us, hefted their shining swords. I found, in that very moment, that I was staring into the face of my well-loved cousin, Roland d'Alle, who was standing in front of me, not two yards away, looking tall and grim.

'Yield, Alan, I beg you,' he shouted. 'Yield to me; I swear you will be safe.'

445

I shook my head and lifted Fidelity a fraction.

'Yield, Alan, yield or I fear I must harm you.'

'You can try,' I grated.

I threw back my head and howled.

The two walls of fighting men came together with a clash of steel and a bedlam of roaring that should have awoken the dead. I had eyes only for Roland, but I was dimly aware from the corners of my vision of knights carving their way into the ranks of the Wolves – and the slaughter of my comrades had begun.

Roland did not hold back. He loved his honour as much as I did and I felt the power of his first cut, which crashed into my ragged shield, right down to the soles of my feet. I was stunned by the vast energy at his command, and knocked back a pace. I was so weak I could barely lift sword and shield. He came at me again, a backhand that hammered at my right shoulder. I parried it and warded him away with a lunge at his throat. He dodged easily and smashed a counter blow into my shield once again that knocked me sideways and had me stumbling into a wounded Wolf. I slashed at him wildly, a poor blow that missed his belly by a good foot. My legs were trembling uncontrollably, my sword seemed a dull bar of lead.

Roland frowned. 'Fight properly, Alan,' he snapped, his familiar voice coming clearly to me over the tumult. 'I will show you no kindness, I swear it. You must also fight me for real.'

And, for my cousin, I tried. I really tried. I exchanged a cut or two, vicious strikes, that rocked him back on his heels, and executed a parry and lunge that nearly ripped off half of his face. The Wolves were no longer tight around me; they lay dying or wounded on the stones of the breach, conquered by the knights, but reinforcements were arriving from all over the inner bailey, and the breach still held, the last of our men, the final fifty, the reserve, charging into the fray in a desperate attempt to hold the line. The bowmen from the keep had joined us by now, strong men who had exchanged bows for long swords and axes. I could hear de Lacy calling urgently, roaring, rallying the defence for one final effort, and Robin's battle voice bellowing directly behind me urging his Wolf archers to kill, kill, kill. So I summoned all my strength, leaped forward and tried to kill my own flesh and blood.

I feinted a lunge to his left that turned halfway through into a diagonal hack at his neck. It was a killing blow . . . that never landed. Roland half-turned smoothly and Fidelity sliced through empty air, and I was off balance, my battered shield sagging low, when Roland's counter strike smashed into my left arm at the mid-point between shoulder and elbow. My mail stopped the blade's progress but I heard the snap of thick bone and felt a lightning bolt of agony stab directly into my heart.

I screamed once, overwhelmed by pain, and barely saw

the flash of Roland's blade as it cracked into my helmet an instant later and knocked me into the darkness.

I awoke to the sound of moaning. I was lying in my cot in the keep and all around were wounded men, groaning, crying, fighting their agony. Somebody had stripped the mail from my body and I felt curiously light and buoyant, almost caressed, as if floating in a warm bath of scented oil. My left arm had been strapped up between four thick sticks of kindling and wrapped tight in clean white linen bandages, and strangely I could feel no pain, but for a dull throbbing in my temples.

'It's a clean break, which is a blessing,' said Robin. He was sitting on a stool beside my cot, with a big wooden mug in his hands. 'And the physician has given you a good strong draft of the poppy – there is not much to go around; you are one of the lucky few,' he said, inclining his head towards a man to my right who was whimpering, his midriff a mass of bloody bandages.

'What . . . what happened?' I croaked. My tongue felt as rough and dry as old leather. Robin handed me the mug – a pint of cold, watery, nameless soup that tasted like the finest ambrosia to me.

'We held them just long enough to get you back to the keep,' said my lord. 'But Sir Joscelyn's men broke – and once the right had crumbled we all had to scramble back here, fast as we could. We've lost the inner bailey, it's just this, now.'

He waved a hand around at the dank gloom of the keep.

'What about the boat? What about our escape?'

'I'm truly sorry, Alan,' he said, the weight of his failure hanging from his face. 'They are all over the inner bailey now. All who survived are trapped here.'

I tried to sit up but everything swirled before my eyes, and Robin caught me and pressed me back down. 'Stay down, you idiot. You are not getting up for a long while,' he said. 'Don't fret, these walls are very thick. I believe we can hold Philip off for a while – even without you – and I will think of something, never you fear. Rest now.'

As he walked away, I briefly tried to calculate how many times Robin had saved my life – half a dozen? A dozen? – and set against that, how many times he had plunged me into mortal danger . . . before I fell into a shallow, dream-filled sleep.

The next time I awoke, I thought I was dreaming. Roland was standing beside my cot in full mail, helm and shield, and he was holding his naked sword to my throat.

'Yield to me, Alan. I need you to say you yield. Say the words.'

I looked at him wildly and saw Robin sitting on his stool once again, his long face even more drawn, tired almost to death. I noticed belatedly that the keep was full of unfamiliar knights, big, well-fed, laughing men who were shoving the unwounded prisoners in the far corner of the chamber. There was a commotion at the entrance to the stairs to the upper floors and three men fell through it, one man struggling between two captors. It was Roger de Lacy – his face purple with rage, his torso jerking madly, his arms pinioned by two huge French knights.

'Yield to me, Alan, you must yield or I cannot help you,' Roland was pleading with me, the sword tip still at my bare throat.

'Just say the damn words, Alan,' said Robin. 'I have. So must you.'

So I did.

I was my cousin's prisoner.

Chapter Thirty-six

I do not well recall the aftermath of the siege of Château Gaillard. I was sick and wounded, weak from lack of food for so long, and the knock on the head had made me dazed and confused. I ate a little – Robin and Roland, between them, were very careful not to allow me too much food, although there was now plenty to be had, for gorging after famine can kill a man as surely as a slit throat – I slept a lot. I remember the terrible sight of Roger de Lacy, a brave man for all his stubbornness, his legs roped together, being dragged slowly at the tail of a horse across the courtyard of the middle bailey and out the main gates in front of a jeering crowd of drunken French men-at-arms. But apart from that ritual humiliation, the enemy treated us well. They could, by all the laws of war, have executed every man in the keep – but Philip chose not to. God be praised for his mercy – although I believe he merely wanted to prove himself the moral superior of King John.

I managed to sit ahorse as we rode down the chalky path away from the Iron Castle as Roland's prisoners, and I looked back at the place that had been the doom of so many good men. Once the pride and joy of King Richard, the fortress was now shabby, burned and broken; the breach of the inner bailey, like a gap in an old man's teeth, was still splashed red with the blood of French, Norman and English fighting men. Scavengers swarmed over the citadel, picking through the ruins and gleaning what valuables they could: spent arrows, broken swords and old cups and plates, scraps of armour . . . So many comrades had died here, I reflected – Kit, Little Niels, Christophe and scores more. And for what?

Robin and I travelled with Roland, and the handful of surviving Wolves, back to Paris. Claes, I was very glad to see, had survived the final slaughter at the breach, as had Vim. After a dozen miles, and once we hit the royal roads of France, Roland made me get down from the horse and I passed that journey in a covered wagon with Vim, whose broken leg had largely exempted him from the later stages of the fighting, and three other wounded Wolves. A fever had taken hold of me and I must confess I was raving for much of the way. Within a week, however, we were ensconced comfortably in Roland's father's luxurious house in the Rue St-Denis.

The Seigneur d'Alle was an affable host – it was impossible to think of him as our gaoler – and he and his beautiful wife Adele made sure we had every comfort. Robin quickly agreed his ransom with the Seigneur; it was, by no coincidence at all, the same price in silver that Robin had once paid as a ransom for Roland, and my lord was released after only a few days to return to England with his surviving men where he would gather the money and have it delivered to Paris. My own ransom was fixed at a single shilling – only a token amount, of course, since we were family – but both Roland and his mother pleaded with me to stay with them for some weeks to recuperate from my fever and heal my broken arm, and I gratefully acceded to their wishes.

Roland was embarrassed about our duel in the breach; he had not realised how weak I was and felt a keen guilt at having broken my arm and knocked me unconscious when I was so enfeebled. I discovered from Robin he had used the flat of the blade in the blow on my helmet that rendered me insensible. For my part, I could not bear him any ill-will at all. We were soldiers on opposite sides in a war – we had been so before and, God forbid, we might be so again – and he had dealt honourably and mercifully with me. It irked me, in my secret heart, that Roland had bested me – but that was hardly his fault. Roland, when he saw me dressed only in my braies, after the fall of the castle, was shocked at how thin and sickly I had become during the siege. And he protested that he would never have fought so hard if he had known of my condition. But I knew he was secretly proud of having beaten me, nonetheless, and I did not begrudge him his victory. Much. The outcome could have been a good deal worse – I could have killed him, and how would I have been able to look into Adele's green eyes and watch them fill with tears as I told her that her only son was dead at my hand?

While Roland's mother was still as radiantly beautiful as ever, the Seigneur's best days were clearly behind him. He suffered from pain in his feet and toes that made him limp a good deal when an attack was on him. His doctors had told him this was due to an imbalance of the humours in his body and he must eschew red meat and red wine – but he scoffed at the diagnosis, ate what he damn well chose, and suffered for it. He was by this time very close to King Philip, one of his chief ministers, and he could afford the finest meat and drink that money could buy.

Roland and I got along very merrily. We went riding that spring in the woods around Paris; we played at chess a good deal and went drinking in the taverns on the Left Bank; and he took me to the great cathedral of Notre-Dame to hear the famous singers of the choir there – which was something of a pilgrimage for me, for my late father had sung in that very choir and the cathedral had loomed large in my previous visit to the French capital. My broken arm healed cleanly; I availed myself of the Seigneur's excellent meat and drink; I wrote letters to friends, and received them; I slept long in the mornings and sparred occasionally and only gently with Roland in the exercise yard, and put on my old muscle and fat in a most pleasing manner.

The war seemed very far away. Indeed, it was nearly over. After the fall of the Iron Castle, King Philip showed himself a true master of strategy: instead of attacking north-west up the Seine valley to take Rouen, which is what everybody was expecting, King John's few remaining royal forces in Normandy most of all, Philip lunged south and west, looping around to take Argentan by surprise in early May. Falaise fell next – unwisely, Lord de Burgh, that prickly man of honour, had been dispatched south by King John to hold Chinon, and his place had been taken in Falaise Castle by a mercenary captain of particularly evil repute. When Philip's forces approached the castle, the mercenary switched sides and, for only a modest payment in silver, he and his men fell in with the King of France's host. Meanwhile, the Bretons under Guy de Thouars, still furious at the assumed murder of Duke Arthur – nobody was certain what had really happened – attacked once again from the west. They sacked Mont Saint-Michel and took Avranches and rampaged across western Normandy, looting and burning, to link up with Philip at Caen.

In June, having subdued the whole of Normandy, except for Rouen, Philip turned his armies east and finally surrounded the capital. The people of Rouen, demoralised by Philip's skilful prosecution of the war and by King

John's cowardly refusal to leave England and set foot in the duchy, swiftly capitulated. And, just like that, within three months of the end of the siege of Château Gaillard. King John was no longer the master of his patrimony. The ancient independent duchy that had spawned his forebears, including the Conqueror of England, was no longer his to rule. It had been swallowed by the Kingdom of France.

I thought of all the struggle, the pain, the bloodshed, the good men now under the earth in the cause of Normandy – and I confess I wept when I heard the news that Rouen had fallen. But Roland consoled me and we spent a few raucous nights drinking in the wine cellars of Paris, making toast after toast to the end of the war, to the end of *all* war. That thought gave me a great deal of happiness – I would never again have to face Roland in battle; and I might never have to fight again for the rest of my life. I would be free, God willing, to return to Westbury and husband my lands and raise my son Robert in tranquillity. I was happy.

I had by then understood and forgiven Tilda for her lapses during the siege – I, too, knew what it meant to be hungry and to be prepared to do almost anything to assuage that hunger. Little Niels had died for his hunger. It was clear to me she and her father had been led astray by that greedy villain Benedict Malet, who had had the castle's stores under his hand for the whole length of the siege. God knew what had made them decide to fall in with Benedict's thievery, but it was over now. Recrimination would not bring back the men who had starved or died because they were weakened by lack of food. The small amounts of food they had stolen would have made scant difference to the result of the siege anyway. I forgave her for her other sins too; I felt I could see her clearly now for the woman she truly was. I had fathomed all her actions, even the most shameful, and yet I found I could honestly forgive her and, when I recovered fully, I meant to seek her out and offer her my hand in marriage. I could picture her at Westbury, playing with little Robert, becoming a mother to him and a loving and faithful wife to me, presiding over the table in the hall, running the place smoothly. And, when the household retired for the night, I confess I thought about her naked, warm and loving in my bed.

However, one dark cloud hung over my happiness that spring and early summer in the year of Our Lord twelve hundred and four, as Philip conquered Normandy and my body slowly healed. The traitor. The Sparrow. When I asked about how Roland came miraculously to be at my bedside in the keep, Robin had told me that some unknown person let the French into our stronghold. In the dark of night, just a day after the inner bailey had fallen, this person merely tugged back the bolts on the iron-bound door like a common porter and invited the waiting French into the keep. And, while the enemy rushed inside the last bastion of the Iron Castle and began taking every man a prisoner, he had melted into the crowd, unidentified, unknown; months of murderous service to King Philip a secret to the end.

I knew then that Little Niels could not have been the Sparrow. For as well as opening the door to the keep, the real traitor had almost certainly informed the French about the counter-mine, which caused them to be ready to bombard the weakened walls above their mine and ours and bring the whole wall roaring down. Both of these events occurred after Little Niels had been hanged.

The Sparrow was directly responsible for the death of Kit and old Christophe Scarecrow – and for hundreds of other men who had fought beside me on the walls. He made a mockery of their sacrifice. And that I could not forgive.

One evening in late June in the house on Rue St-Denis, when the Seigneur was taking a final glass of wine before the fire in the upstairs hall and resting his swollen and aching right foot on a large cushion, which sat upon an iron-bound chest in the corner of the room, I raised the subject of the traitor in the Iron Castle, as naturally as I could. We were talking about the ease with which some of the Norman lords surrendered their castles to Philip, some without even a token fight. I deplored it as cowardly and disloyal.

'That is the modern way of war, Alan,' said the Seigneur. 'The heroes of old – the Roland and Oliver, Arthur, Lancelot, Charlemagne and his knights – they are all gone, and their ways are gone with them. A knight does not ight to the death for his lord any more; he compromises, he negotiates, he makes deals with the enemy and sets his seal on legal charters. He looks to his own long-term advantage.'

'Is that not dishonourable?' I said.

'Perhaps, but it can also save a good deal of bloodshed. If it is clear that a castle will fall eventually, why not recognise that fact early in the day and save everybody a mountain of grief? We have had dealings with half a dozen Norman barons in the past few years and I like to think we have saved a good many lives and still achieved the same objectives. The outcome would have been identical if Philip had personally reduced each and every castle to a pile of rubble: he would still possess them but a great number of good fighting men would also be dead. Like anyone, a baron likes to be on the winning side and, if you will forgive me, Alan, we were always going to be the winning side.'

'How do you know all this, sir?'

The Seigneur sighed. 'Part of my duties for the King was to arrange these matters. It is not the most honourable labour, as you have rightly pointed out, but a little guile and a lot of silver can do more than valour in certain circumstances. We knew many of your barons did not love King John – many openly despised him. It was not too difficult to persuade some to come over to our side. A duchy, even a kingdom, is held by the barons under their duke or king. If all, or even most of the barons desert their duke, or choose to give their loyalty to another, the duchy goes with them. A duchy or a kingdom is like a house and the barons are the pillars that hold the roof up. If the pillars fall, or are destroyed or taken away, the house falls; if the barons are tempted away, the kingdom falls and the king is lost.'

'I suppose there was one such disaffected baron inside Château Gaillard,' I said, yawning, stretching my long arms and trying to affect a weary nonchalance.

The Seigneur was not fooled for an instant. 'I do not wish to speak about a specific man or men,' he said just a little sharply. 'The King and I promise them our discretion in return for service, and we must honour that promise – for ever.'

'But there was a man of yours inside the Iron Castle?'

'Alan, I cannot discuss this with you or anyone.' The Seigneur was laboriously getting to his feet.

'Does the name the Sparrow mean anything to you?'

'Enough, Alan. I have probably already said too much. I must ask you not to speak of this matter to me again. I know that it is close to your heart – you fought and suffered there – but I cannot give you answers. If you have any respect for my honour you will strive to understand that. I bid you good night.'

I was left alone in the hall with a half-empty wine glass and a dying fire.

I did respect the Seigneur's honour. I would not try again to badger the secret out of him. But I was equally determined to discover the name of the man who had betrayed all his comrades in the Iron Castle. For something the Seigneur had said gave me a clue to how I might discover it.

I am truly ashamed of what I did next, and I pray that when I must answer for it at the Last Judgment, the Recording Angel will take pity on me. What I did was a clear violation of the trust between a host and his guest, a betrayal of a member of my own family. But I did it and it cannot be undone.

I finished my wine, got to my feet, heading for my bed – and stopped. I found I was staring at the iron-bound chest in the corner of the hall. The velvet cushion on top was still imprinted with the Seigneur's swollen foot. And my host's words were echoing in my memory: 'A knight does not fight to the death for his lord any more; he compromises, he negotiates, he makes deals with the enemy and sets his seal on legal charters . . .'

The chest was where the Seigneur kept his most precious documents. For a moment I could not believe that I might find what I sought right there in front of my nose. It seemed incredible the Seigneur had been speaking about this man – or rather refusing to speak about him – while his painful foot rested over the place where his secret lay hidden. But why not? The workings of the human soul are strange indeed, perhaps having his foot on the chest put this matter into the forefront of his mind. As I knelt before the chest, I had half-convinced myself that the

Seigneur was indirectly telling me where I would find the answer to my question by the placement of his painful foot.

It was locked, of course. Secured by a heavy padlock through a half-ring fixed into the wood. But I already had the key. I blush to reveal this, but I was so much a part of the d'Alle household that sweet Adele, knowing I was often the last to go to bed, had handed me the big iron ring of keys earlier that evening and asked if I would be sure to lock up the great door to the street before I went upstairs. Could it be that Adele and the Seigneur were actively encouraging me to discover their secret? Did they want me to know the identity of the Sparrow but were unable in good conscience to tell me?

I found the key among dozens of others on the big ring, a small iron item with a comb-tooth design, and fed it in the padlock and turned it. The lock fell open and with my heart thumping, and keeping one ear cocked for any sound of my hosts, I pushed open the lid of the chest.

There were more than a score of parchments in there, deeds for the Seigneur's several properties, charters of parcels of land he had granted to loyal men-at-arms, old servants and to the Church . . . and several charters sealed in red wax between His Most Royal Highness, Philip by the Grace of God, King of France and half a dozen of the barons of Normandy.

I scanned through each document quickly, searching for the name and then discarding it. Some were men knew well, some were men I did not – but none of these turncoats had been inside the Iron Castle during the siege.

And then I found the one who was.

I looked at the name. I read it twice, three times in disbelief.

I sat back on my heels, stunned. I felt like weeping. I wanted to burn the charter with the Sparrow's name on it. I wanted to unmake it, to make it untrue. I wanted to pretend I did not know his all-too-familiar name, to wipe it from my memory. Then I took a grip of myself. I was going to kill this man, this traitor. I was going to rip out his beating heart. I was going to be the agent of vengeance for Kit and Little Niels and all those who had died in the bitter months of siege and starvation. Whatever it cost, and I knew the cost would be unbearably high, the traitor must die.

I put the documents neatly back into the chest and locked the padlock once more. Then I secured the great door of the house, hung the keys on their hook and went upstairs to bed. As I lay sleepless between the fine linen sheets, I thought about the journey that I had to undertake. A journey north. To England. To Yorkshire. To Kirkton. To the home of my lord Robert Odo, Earl of Locksley. Where I would find the traitor who called himself the Sparrow; the man I must destroy.

Chapter Thirty-seven

I bid farewell to Roland and Adele ten days later; there were certain matters I had to arrange before my departure. I could not look the Seigneur d'Alle, my kindly host, squarely in the eye when he embraced me and wished me well on my journey to England. To make my shame even worse, they made me costly gifts – a new full suit of iron mail, a lively rouncey to ride on the road, food and wine for the journey, letters of safe conduct that would get me though any road block manned by King Philip's men-at-arms, and a heavy purse of silver for any expenses I might incur.

I felt like a knave as I slunk from their loving smiles and fondly waving kerchiefs, and made my way north through the busy streets of Paris. But my mood soon lifted

fter I passed through the Porte St-Denis and found myself
n the old Roman road heading north. My left arm was
vell-mended by then, and I was fit once more after months
f good food, rest and exercise – it was early July, the sun
hone in a cloudless sky, the roads were dry, and I had a
leasant encounter to look forward to before I crossed the
Channel.

Three days later I knocked at the gates of Fécamp Abbey
nd was granted admission. A servant took my horse and
was allowed briefly to wash and drink a jug of water,
nd then shown into the cloisters.

I had expected a quiet, empty, columned square, covered
n the four surrounding sides and open in the middle,
erhaps paved with limestone blocks – and I was almost
xactly right. But it was by no means quiet. Or empty.

The cloisters were thronging with monks, loud, cheering,
ostling, excited monks. Scores of them. They filled every
ide of the square, hanging from the columns, shoving
ach other out of the way to find a better place. But for
heir sober black habits and rope belts, I could have taken
hem for a meeting of rowdy London apprentices. In the
entre of the cloister, two big men, stripped to the waist
nd covered with oil, were grappling with each other. The
ne with his back to me was a giant of a man, with a vast
xpanse of muscular back, a bull-like neck and a thatch
f grey-blond hair. On his right side a thick ridge of pinkish
car tissue curved all the way from his lower ribs to the
mall of his back, evidence of a grave wound taken in the

465

recent past. But it seemed to be well healed. The second man was only slightly smaller and marginally less well built than the blond giant. I had a brief impression of a bald head, broad hairy shoulders; massive, thickly furred hands. Then I looked again and saw that the second wrestler had his hair cut in a tonsure, the pate shaved and a ring of brown hair resting above huge sticking-out ears. The noise of the crowd was ear-splitting. Monks were arguing with their fellows and roaring encouragement to fighters – I suspect there may even have been some discreet wagers taking place. The men heaved at each other for several moments, straining with all their might, their legs like trunks of oak planted in the stone flags of the cloister floor – and then the hairy man changed grip, pushed, pulled and all of a sudden the big blond fellow shot forward, flipped over his opponent's hip and crashed to the floor.

The monks around the cloister bellowed – some cheering the hairy fellow, others crying shame for the blond man who was panting on the floor, holding his side, but with a wide grin on his big ugly red face. It was, of course, my old friend Little John.

The winner of the bout raised both his hands in the air and called for silence, and oddly the cloister quietened immediately.

'Right, back to your labours, you lazy scoundrels, the amusement's over for today. Come on, come on, this is a place for peaceful contemplation of Our Lord, not a tavern for unruly layabouts. Back to work with the lot of you!'

466

He reached out a hand and pulled Little John to his feet with surprising ease.

My old friend pushed past the huge monk and came straight towards me, grabbed me by the shoulders, looked into my face and enfolded me in a huge embrace. He stank of sweat and oil, but I was very pleased to see him so hale and strong; even if I was a little astonished that he had been vanquished by this tonsured stranger. I was even more astonished by his next words: 'Alan, may I present His Grace Abbot Gervaise, master of this unruly House of God', and I found myself grasping hands with a sweaty, half-naked and rather furry prince of the Church.

When he was washed and dressed, Little John and I took a walk on the cliffs to the north of the abbey. It was a hot, sunny afternoon and a delightful cool wind came off the sea. I asked John to explain to me why he had been grappling with such a spiritually exalted opponent.

'Oh, Gervaise and I have a bout almost every week. He loves to wrestle and, as you saw, he is a master of that noble form of combat. I challenged him initially, oh, six months ago, to get myself back in condition after my wound had begun to heal, and we have continued our meetings on a regular basis. The brothers enjoy it, as do we. Sometimes he wins, sometimes I do – and we take good care not to treat each other too roughly.'

'You are fully healed then?'

'Aye, but God's bollocks, Alan, it took me long enough.

For months I was hanging on by my fingertips; I truly thought I'd had it. The brothers say it is a miracle I survived. But I think it had something to do with drinking from the Grail, as we all did in the south . . . Any road, I'm healed and ready to return to England and Robin. I have enjoyed Fécamp, and I owe Gervaise and his brother my life, but I tell you, Alan, I'm not cut out for this holy life. I grant you there are more than a few handsome novices here to gladden the eye, but there is far too much praying, too much repenting, not nearly enough honest slaughter. I need to put some fire back in my veins, Alan. I am sorry I missed the siege – it sounds like a rare brawl.'

'We could have used you,' I said. I told him all about the Iron Castle, of the battles in the baileys won and lost, and about the traitor, how the Sparrow had betrayed us at every turn, ushering the French in through the chapel window, revealing to them that we were digging a counter-mine, letting them into the keep – all of it. Little John looked as grim as midwinter. I told him about Kit's death and the deaths of so many brave Wolves, and finally I told him I had discovered the identity of the traitor – and who it was. He stared at me for a long time.

'Are you sure of this, Alan? It could not be some mistake?'

'There is no mistake. And I am going to kill him, I truly am. Will you come with me and help me do this thing?'

Little John was silent for a moment. Then he looked

me in the eyes and said, 'Yes, he must die, and yes, I'll help you do it. By God's great hairy bum crack, you'll only make a bloody mess of it if you try to do it all on your own.'

A week later, on a bright summer morning, Little John and I were riding up the steep rutted track from the River Locksley with the Castle of Kirkton, home of my lord, high up on the ridge, above the little church of St Nicholas. It was good to breathe the clean fresh air of Yorkshire once more and, although oppressed by what I knew must soon come to pass, I was infinitely encouraged to have Little John's massive form at my shoulder and his cheerful crudities echoing in my ear.

We were greeted with joy at the castle by Marie-Anne, Countess of Locksley, and I was warmed to see so many familiar faces. I had not realised until then how much I missed the rough, happy company of honest English folk; I had been among sly Frenchmen and arrogant Normans for too long and I felt a great sense of happiness and of homecoming, despite the task at hand. But I could not afford to let my happiness at being home divert me from my grim duty.

I asked after Robin and I was told he was out hunting with his guests at Locksley chase, near the manor of Wadsley, which was a large area of wooded land to the east, a little to the north of the road to Sheffield. Little John and I set out immediately, dumping our baggage in the courtyard at Kirkton, without bothering to eat, drink or even wash the dust from our faces.

We found Robin an hour later, just before noon. We were drawn towards the party by the noise of a celebration, musicians playing, bawdy jests being shouted.

We dismounted, tied our horses to the branches of a tree and walked into a broad clearing where a large round table had been set out in the centre of the glade. The table was filled with gold and silver platters and vessels, and steaming plates of roast meats, brimming bowls of fruit and flagons of deep red wine. A dozen red-faced servants and hooded huntsmen bustled about bringing yet more food and pouring water and holding clean linen towels so the diners could wash their hands. A full-fig feast had been laid in the clearing; all the splendours of the hall at Kirkton.

Robin sat at the centre of the table, which was covered in a snowy white cloth. His laughing face had filled out since I last saw him in Paris and he looked completely relaxed and happy. On his right sat Sir Joscelyn Giffard, in the very act of washing his fingers, as we approached. To Robin's left sat Sir Benedict Malet, his fat face already bulging as he chewed on a plump roasted chicken leg.

'Alan! John! What an unexpected surprise to see you here. Welcome, welcome my friends. Come, sit with us, join the feast.'

Servants hurried here and there bringing stools for us to sit upon, a fresh ewer of water and clean towels, and I took my place beside Sir Joscelyn. Little John sat beside

470

Benedict Malet and helped himself to a hunk of white bread. Robin's guests looked surprised to see us but not unduly alarmed at our arrival.

I smiled at Sir Joscelyn and greeted him with full courtesy.

He enquired after my health and my doings since the siege and I replied affably enough, but without giving too much detail. He told me that after his capture he had been held by the King of France himself and had only recently been freed upon the paying of his heavy ransom. I nodded as if I had expected this.

'And how is my lady Matilda?' I said casually.

He smiled at me, warily, and said, 'I am proud to say, Sir Alan, that she has been admitted to the priory of Kirklees; only two days ago she was accepted as a novice by the Prioress. Praise God, she will spend her life in the service of Our Lord.'

'You must be very proud,' I said, spooning some venison stew on to my plate.

'I am relieved, to tell you the truth, Sir Alan,' said Sir Joscelyn. 'My daughter was something of a wanton. I may admit this as I am her father, and we are among friends here, but she enjoys the company of men a little too much. Life as a Bride of Christ will safeguard her soul. I have the kindness of the Earl of Locksley to thank for her place at Kirklees. He has influence there, of course, and after the scandal at the abbey in Caen, I was lucky to find any House of God that would take her.'

'Yes, I heard about that,' I said, through a mouthful of stew. 'I heard she frolicked all night in a tavern with several handsome young men.'

Sir Benedict made a noise somewhere between a grunt and a cough. Sir Joscelyn looked at me with drawn steel in his eyes.

'You need not look so surprised, either of you,' I said. 'Bennie here had the pleasure of her during the siege, many times. I suspect that was just to persuade him to provide her with extra food from the stores. You were complicit in that crime, Sir Joscelyn, were you not? She gave herself to me, too, on the promise that I'd protect her if the castle fell. I think she gave her favours to a good many other men, as well, for some reward or other. She uses her body as coin to buy whatever she wishes.'

Sir Joscelyn was rising to his feet by this point, his face purple, his hand reaching for his sword hilt.

'Enough, Alan,' said Robin loudly. 'Hold your tongue. I think we have all had enough of that kind of talk. Sit down, Sir Joscelyn, and let us have peace – and a toast. Let us all drink together to the brave men who died defending the Iron Castle.'

Robin raised his cup.

In an instant the clearing was all movement. Out of the corner of my eye, I saw two unfamiliar hunt servants seized by the rest of Robin's serving men. Sir Joscelyn was shoved back down on to his stool by two of the huntsmen, who I only now recognised as Wolves who had fought with us in Château Gaillard. The Wolves relieved Sir Joscelyn of his sword and dagger and passed the weapons behind them to waiting hands while they, standing one on each side of the man, kept a firm grip on his shoulders. Sir Joscelyn said nothing at all.

Sir Benedict started forward as this unfolded. He managed to shout, 'What! What! What is the meaning—' before Little John, who was seated beside him, snapped a heavy elbow into the side of his head, knocking him off his stool to crumple unconscious to the turf.

I had not moved. My goblet was still in my hand for Robin's toast, which of course had been the signal for the huntsmen and servants to secure Sir Joscelyn and his men. I lifted the goblet towards him: 'Death to traitors,' I said, and drank.

'All that dirty chit-chat about his daughter was a bit beyond the pale,' said Robin, frowning at me. 'I don't remember that being part of the plan.'

'It is all true,' I said. 'It didn't change the outcome of today; and it doesn't change the way I feel about Tilda.'

'What is all this about? Why have I been insulted and restrained? Why have my servants been bound and my good friend Sir Benedict beaten unconscious. I demand to know this instant!'

Sir Joscelyn had summoned up a little bluster.

As Little John hauled the unconscious Sir Benedict away to be bound and laid on the grass with the other two prisoners, Robin poured me another goblet of wine.

'All this?' said Robin. 'All this is about loyalty to your comrades. All this is about honour. Not that you would understand the term, you treacherous cock-socket.'

'I have no idea what you are talking about. Are you all mad? I demand that you release me this very instant. This is an outrage. The King shall hear of this.'

'Which king?' I said. I looked steadily at Sir Joscelyn and his face seemed to close like a shutter. I had been pondering his crimes since I read his name on the parchment in the Seigneur's strong box. On that royal charter Philip had promised him the rights to half a dozen castles and towns scattered across Normandy and the lands that went with them. His seal had been attached to the document, he had even signed his name on it in his own hand.

I had absolutely no doubt about his guilt. I took a long breath.

'You were given the charge of defending the town of Petit Andely,' I said in a quiet, measured tone, 'but you did not defend it. Instead, you evacuated the town after a token resistance and encouraged the citizens to seek refuge in the castle. That was an act calculated to weaken Château Gaillard. All those Useless Mouths, all the food stores they ate up in the weeks with us. An act of mercy, in your hands, became an act of war. And, when Philip was away from the siege, and his men, out of their goodness, let the Useless Mouths pass through their lines, you got word to the King – probably by some secret system of signals with lanterns on dark nights – and he promptly stopped the exodus and all those harmless people starved. Because of you.'

Sir Joscelyn said nothing. He stared at me blankly, his bluster abandoned, giving me nothing at all.

'You told the French that the mortar in the walls was wet in the outer bailey, and when the belfry failed, you told them they would have more success if they tried to undermine the walls. You opened the window in the chapel and let the enemy into the middle bailey – and caused the death of my young friend Kit. You told them about the counter-mine – you encouraged me to dig the counter-mine, come to think of it, after the high council had considered it and rejected the idea, knowing it would weaken the walls of the inner bailey fatally. You stole the castle's stores, with the help of that silly, lovestruck cretin Malet, and you ate them, knowing each mouthful you consumed weakened the defence a little more. And, finally, when we still would not surrender to your master, you unbolted the door and let the enemy into the keep and surrendered yourself into the grateful arms of the King of France. And you did all this because you wanted to be a great man in Normandy. You caused the deaths of so many, so very many of your comrades because you wanted more land and wealth . . .'

'I chose a side.' Sir Joscelyn spoke calmly, quietly; I sensed he was speaking from the heart. 'King John is a weakling and a fool – we all know that. I realised very early on that he could not hold Normandy, and when

Normandy fell my family lands would be forfeit. I have nothing in England. I am a Norman, I have always been a Norman. And if Normandy has a new master, I must serve that master or perish. I chose a side, that is all. I chose the winning side.'

'You chose the wrong side,' Robin said.

'And for that, I suppose, you would murder me in cold blood,' said Sir Joscelyn, with no emotion at all in his voice.

'Yes, that's exactly what I'd do,' said Robin cheerfully. 'But Sir Alan here will not have it.'

I spoke up: 'You will face a court of swords, a trial by combat – you will fight me, here, now, to the death, and God Himself will judge whether you are fit to live.'

'You are most kind,' said Sir Joscelyn. I believe he meant it.

Robin's men-at-arms, huntsmen and servants – most of them Wolves but with a few old familiar faces from years gone by, too – formed a large, loose circle around Sir Joscelyn. A few of the Wolves were bowmen who had arrows nocked on bowstrings; others had drawn blades. Giffard was given his sword back and his dagger, but when he looked around the circle of men, men whose comrades he had betrayed, he saw death in their implacable faces. They knew his crime; they were here to see him pay for it. I took off my cloak and tunic and drew Fidelity and my misericorde. Like Sir Joscelyn I wore no mail and I carried no shield. I wanted this to be an even match. I

476

had insisted on this in the long letter I had had a rider bring to Robin from Paris before I departed. I did not want to murder this man, I wanted to fight him fairly – then show the world the colour of his bowels.

Sir Joscelyn hefted his sword and dagger and looked around the circle of Wolves in the clearing in the heart of Robin's territory. 'So you invited me here, Locksley, to Yorkshire, Tilda and myself, just for this – this ridiculous duel,' he said disbelievingly. It was not quite a question, and nobody answered him. Then he said, 'And I have your word, my lord, that if I can defeat Sir Alan in this combat, you will let me go free.' He looked directly at Robin.

'Certainly, you may believe that if you wish,' said my lord, smiling genially at the traitor.

'Robin! This must be a fair fight,' I said. 'Swear on your honour that you'll let him go if he wins. If I yield – or if I cannot rise and continue the fight. Swear it.'

Robin frowned but he nodded. 'Very well, Alan. I swear on my honour that if you win, Sir Joscelyn, I'll let you go.'

This seemed to satisfy Sir Joscelyn. He gave his sword a few experimental slashes to loosen his muscles – then he came at me.

He had a decent style, I must admit, and he had evidently been very well trained. He attacked down my left side, a succession of pounding strikes at my shoulder and head. I dodged to my right, keeping his blade away with the stout iron of the misericorde. I counter-attacked, sliced at his head with Fidelity, and he parried with the sword, a sharp, discordant clang in the quiet of the glade. We were circling, getting the feel of each other, exchanging short probing blows with our swords. I had his measure, I was certain. I knew I could take him. He was older than me, and slower – and God must surely be on my side. There seemed no point prolonging the fight. I stepped into him, feinted with the misericorde at his face, stepped forward for a fast chop to the back of his left knee – a favourite move of mine – trod a patch of slick mud and slipped. My right foot skidded forward and I thumped down hard on my arse.

He was on me like a fox on a sleeping dove.

His sword flashed down towards my head, a clean powerful vertical chop. It seemed to be coming down at me for ever, the sunlight glancing off that bright sliver of steel; a grim look of triumph on his face, his sleeve flapping with the force of the blow – and sometimes in my nightmares the blade connects cleanly and splits my head like a melon from crown to chin – but somehow I got my misericorde between it and my skull. The sword snapped cleanly through my dagger and crashed into my left shoulder, cutting deeply into the flesh, the blood running red.

He drew back his arm for another strike. But I kicked out savagely from the ground and he had to hop backwards. Then I was up on my feet again. Me and Fidelity against his sword and dagger. My shoulder was throbbing and the blood had soaked through my chemise and was running down my arm in sheets. I could barely raise my left arm and had nothing with which to protect my body on that side.

I had been overconfident and had paid the price.

He came at me like a madman in a whirl of jabs and slices from sword and dagger. Fidelity had to be everywhere, parrying, blocking, lunging at his body to try and keep him away. I dodged and ducked, my shoulder screaming in red agony. But his blows were wild; he was tiring, he was slowing. He swung his sword at my head and I blocked it with the high lateral guard, the hilt forehead-high in my double grip, Fidelity's blade extending in a straight line out to the left. He was performing a set manoeuvre, a series of actions that came to him purely on instinct thanks to hours of practice with a master-at-arms; a forehand slash with the sword in his right hand to distract the opponent; step in and thrust with the dagger in the left, which aimed to catch the enemy up under the ribs; then step back out of range. There is nothing wrong with the move, I have taught it to many a man myself. Indeed, I had taught it to Wolves in the ring around us. But it must be done swiftly and with perfect timing. One-two, three-four. Sword-slash, step in, dagger-thrust, step back. Feint and step in, strike and step back. But, as I have said, he was slow. And he had used this move twice before. The moment he opened his stance for the right-hand slash, I knew where his left wrist would be a few instants later. So I blocked his sword with the high lateral guard, then whipped Fidelity down hard to my right. The blade sliced neatly into his hand as his dagger licked out towards me, severing the thumb and first finger, the digits pattering to the ground in a splash of gore. He screamed once, horribly, but I was already moving past him on his now unguarded left side. I stepped past, half-turned and swung Fidelity, chopping savagely into the back of his neck with all my remaining strength. His head leaped from his body at the strike. Blood gushed from the stump. The knees on the headless torso folded and the body flopped to the ground, still pumping gore.

I found I was panting, my body sheeted in sweat. My left shoulder was on fire. But the cheers of the men in the circle, the glowing faces of the Wolves who had witnessed my vengeance on their behalf, well, that gave my soul wings.

Justice had been done.

Chapter Thirty-eight

I rode to Kirklees Priory a few days later. The joint of my shoulder, thank God, had not been damaged, but the thick pad of muscle that covered it had an inch-deep gash in it and any sudden movement was very painful. Nevertheless, I rode to Kirklees as soon as I was able. I did not want the news of her father's death to come to Tilda from some other mouth.

The Prioress, a kindly half-blind old gentlewoman, greeted me and showed me into the meeting room where Tilda was waiting to see me.

Her first words were: 'Oh Alan, have you come to take me away from this awful place?' I had never seen her look so beautiful, in her black novice's gown, her raven hair bound up in a white headdress. Her lips were red as a summer rose; her blue-grey eyes as big and wild as the sea.

'I will if you want me to, my darling,' I said. 'But you must hear what I have to say first. It may change your mind.'

I told her about her father. That he had been a traitor in the pay of King Philip and responsible for the deaths of so many good people during the siege. I told her about the way in which he had died, at my hand.

'It was a fair fight, my love. It was no execution or murder. If it helps you, you may think of it as the judgment of God on his sins. And, while I know it must grieve you to hear of his passing, I hope what I tell you next will ease your suffering. I love you with all my heart, dear Tilda. If you will have me, I would take you as my wife.'

I paused and looked at her. He face was set like a rock, just as cold, hard and unmoving. She did not seem sad or happy or stirred at all by what I had told her. I wondered if she understood.

'I will take you away from this place, if you wish it. You will come to Westbury with me and we will wed in the little church on my lands and we can be happy together. I know about you and Sir Benedict, and the musicians in Caen, and the others. I do not care. I forgive you. I forgive you because I love you. Tilda, my darling, will you be my wife?'

'Are you quite mad?' Tilda's voice was low and, but for the words she uttered, she sounded quite normal: 'Are you completely fucking moon-crazed?'

She took a deep breath, I thought at first to calm herself, but she continued in the same foul-worded but reasonable-sounding manner: 'You . . . You arrogant, dung-brained, war-mongering clod! You come here with the blood of my father still staining your clothes' – the ride had opened the wound on my shoulder and a little red was showing through my thin summer tunic – 'and you tell me that my father was some sort of traitor – so you killed him. Do you think I really care what side my father was on during your stupid battles and idiotic wars and tedious sieges? Do you really think I give a ha'penny arse-fuck who slaughters who and in what stupid cause? You killed my father! God damn you. And you have the nerve to tell me you forgive me! You. Forgive. Me. For the things I have done with my own body – a body you drooled over impotently for months before finally summoning up the courage to touch. And now you ask for my hand, and say you forgive me. God damn you to Hell! God damn you for a fat-headed, cowardly, murdering, slack-witted bastard . . .'

I confess I was moving back towards the door by this point, more than a little alarmed. The door opened behind me. I saw the Prioress in the passageway and two of her nuns bustled into the meeting room. 'That's quite enough, Tilda!' said the larger of the two women, laying a hand on her arm. But Tilda was still spitting her quiet venom at me as I edged out of the room.

'I'll make you regret this, Alan Dale, if it's the last thing I do. I promise you. I'll make you and your bloody master pay for what you have done. You and Locksley killed my father together and I do not forgive that. I will never forgive you for that.'

By then, mercifully, I was out the door and out of earshot.

The Prioress had grasped only a portion of all that Tilda had said but she seemed unperturbed. 'Don't you worry, Sir Alan, she's a feisty girl full of fire and wickedness and not yet resigned to the quiet religious life. But we will tame her, don't you fret. Lord Locksley has been very generous to the Priory, and we are always happy to accommodate his wishes. We will keep her here, safe and sound, under lock and key, if necessary. Don't you trouble your head about her, Sir Alan.'

As I rode to Kirkton, I realised, with a dazed sense of having escaped, that the paramount emotion in my breast was relief.

We let Sir Benedict Malet and the two Giffard servants go unharmed. Robin suggested we slit their throats and bury them in the deep woods alongside Sir Joscelyn's corpse, but I did not have the stomach for it. The servants were guilty of no crime, as far as I knew, and Benedict – although he probably deserved death for stealing food during the siege – had a large and prominent family including, of course, Lord de Burgh; murdering the fat toad would be bound to draw down the anger and vengeance of his clan upon our heads. So we let him go with a warning never to come north of Nottingham again if he valued his skin.

When I told Robin about my interview with Matilda, he laughed. 'What did you expect?' he said. 'Women don't see these things the same way we do. And who knows, maybe they are right: maybe war is idiotic.'

'You did kill her father, Alan,' said Marie-Anne, who was sitting by the hearth in the hall of Kirkton working at her embroidery.

'Yes,' I said. 'I was a fool to ask for her hand after that.'

'I think . . . I think you wanted to love her more than you truly did love her,' said Marie-Anne. 'I think, perhaps, you would not have killed her father if you truly wanted her as your wife. You could not really have had both your vengeance and her as your bride. Her father's ghost would have stood behind her every day at the dinner table glowering at you.'

I thought about her words. I desperately wanted to return to Westbury and to my son Robert – but I did not relish returning to a hall empty of my wife Goody. I wanted a woman by my side. I wanted a woman in my hall. In my bed. A faithful one, a woman of impeccable honour. But I did not, I realised, want Tilda.

In the event I did not return directly to Westbury. Robin asked me, as a favour, to accompany him and Little John on a short visit to Nottingham Castle, where he had arranged an audience with King John.

'He's being difficult about Kirkton and the Locksley

lands,' said Robin, as we walked our horses southwards down the great north road. 'He says he will not set his seal on the charter that grants me the full rights over my lands. He wants me to serve him for another three years. He wants, in fact, for me to raise another army and go and reconquer Normandy for him.'

'But he made a solemn and binding agreement with you – three years of service for a full pardon and your lands restored. You served him well. The three years are up.'

'He did. And now he is breaking his word.'

We walked our horses along in silence.

'Why do we serve this King?' I asked quietly.

'Oh, do shut up, Alan,' said my lord.

In the great hall of Nottingham Castle, King John lolled in a vast oak chair. Little John and I bowed low and then hung back as Robin approached the throne and knelt humbly before his King.

'Ah, Locksley,' King John croaked. 'What have you to say for yourself after that disgraceful affair at Château Gaillard? I ought to have you slung in a dungeon. You failed me at the Iron Castle, Locksley, and as a result of your failure, Normandy is overrun. What have you to say for yourself, eh?'

'I have nothing to say about the loss of the Iron Castle or the loss of Normandy. We did our best, and were beaten and the corpses of many a brave man in the earth there

486

can attest that we fought long and hard in their defence. But I did not come for that. I came so that you could affix your royal seal on this charter' – he stood and pulled a stiff yellow roll from his belt – 'as you swore to do more than three years ago. I have abided by the terms set down on this parchment. I served you loyally, and if you will now affix your seal, I will continue to serve you to the best of my abilities as Earl of Locksley with full rights in perpetuity over all my lands.'

'And why should I?' sneered the King. 'I disagree that you served me loyally. Some men say that Philip had you in his pouch all the time. Did you take his silver? I heard rumours there was a traitor in Château Gaillard. Perhaps it was you. By rights, I should have you punished.' The King paused, tilted his head back and looked down his nose at Robin. 'But, as I am a merciful man, I shall allow you to serve me for another three years to prove your loyalty. Then, if I am satisfied, I will grant all that you ask with regards to the Locksley lands. I think that is more than fair.'

Robin stepped in closer to the King. He spoke very softly, so that Little John and I could barely hear his words but saw menace crackled about him like a thunderstorm.

'First, if any man wishes to assert to my face that I was in the pay of Philip, I will gladly prove my innocence on his body with my sword. Second, I shall tell you why you should fix your seal to this parchment, Sire.' Robin took a deep breath. 'You will seal this document because, if you do not, I will tell the world about the circumstances of the death of Duke Arthur. It will be a mystery no longer. You and I and Sir Alan over there are the only living witnesses to that crime – no one else knows the truth of that crime. But that will not remain the case for long. Do you think your barons will remain loyal to you when they know what you are capable of. That you murdered your own bound and helpless nephew. Will you ever have their trust and support again? And, with the greatest respect, Sire, without the support of your barons, exactly how long do think you will remain King of England?'

As I listened to Robin speak quietly and firmly to the King, the Seigneur's words came back to me: 'A kingdom is like a house, and the barons are the pillars that hold the roof up. If the pillars fall or are destroyed or taken away, the house falls; if the barons are tempted away the kingdom falls, and the king is lost.'

I watched King John's face as Robin spoke to him. For a moment, just for a moment, his expression of cruel satisfaction slipped and I caught a glimpse of his true state of fear. Robin stood up straight before the King, his face as hard as iron, his steady hand holding out the parchment.

The King turned his head to the left, took a deep breath and bawled, 'Someone had better bring me a candle, the black wax and the Great Seal. And someone had better bring it right now!'

Over the clatter of running servants' feet, the squeal of tables being moved, drawers being opened, cupboards slammed, I was just able to hear Robin say, 'There's a good boy.'

Epilogue

When I began this labour, this recounting of the tragic events surrounding the loss of Normandy, I wrote that it was a tale of blood, and a tale of slaughter and sacrifice. And so it is. But now I am done with my task, I realise it is truly a tale about honour. It was Lord de Burgh's sense of his own honour that saved Duke Arthur from cruel mutilation at Falaise – although that poor boy's sad doom was only delayed. It was Robin's discovery that he loved his own honour more than lands and riches that allowed him to forego the blandishments of King Philip. It was Roger de Lacy's sense of honour that kept us fighting for so long inside the Iron Castle against overwhelming odds. It was my own honour, and the honour of the men who died, that made me decide I must kill Sir Joscelyn Giffard, for his lack of it.

Honour is what lifts us above the brutish cruelty of warfare, it makes us better men, and in that way it brings us closer to God. Without honour we are but greedy fools indulging our appetites and whims. We are not men. Yet it is not only men who must guard their honour: Matilda Giffard, in her whoreish schemes, forgot her own, as did her father, and both came to ruin.

And Agnes, the sheep farmer's daughter from Stannington, willingly offered hers up to my grandson. And he took it.

I love him, young Alan, for all his surly drunkenness. The greatest gift I can give him is to instil in him a true sense of the importance of his honour. It is not the same as rank. A man can be the highest in the land – a King – and have no honour, as John proved by failing to come to our defence despite his solemn promises to Roger de Lacy. A man's honour is like his soul. He must tend it, he must guard it, he must not let it tarnish. He must always strive to follow the right, the true, the honourable path.

This is the truth that I desperately want young Alan to grasp.

It was a fine wedding. Agnes was every bit as beautiful as I had been told, even though her belly was like a huge boulder stuffed beneath her buttercup-yellow linen dress. And young Alan was touchingly solicitous of her comforts at the church and afterwards at the feast in the courtyard of Westbury manor. He seemed very happy, in truth, and so did she. I did not need ask if he truly loved his new bride – the fact of it shone from his face like a silver mirror reflecting the sun.

The Earl of Locksley attended with all his household knights and though I watched carefully to see if any of them made mock of my grandson for his choice of bride, I saw nothing of that nature. And, at least for the first part of the celebration, they kept the drinking, ribaldry and noise to an acceptable level.

My legs were troubling me on that happy day, swollen and painful, and I was carried to and from the little church in the village of Westbury by a couple of farm servants in a chair. I did, however, force myself to stand for the traditional toasts at the end of the wedding feast, and then I raised my arms for silence.

'My friends,' I said, 'on this joyous occasion I have a piece of further good news to impart to you all. From this day forward the manor of Westbury shall be solely under the care of the happy couple. My beloved grandson Alan shall hold it of the Earl of Locksley in my stead – everything has been arranged; they and their children shall have this place in their charge henceforth and I devoutly hope they shall cherish it, as I have, for many a long year. I am an old man and very tired, and I have decided I shall retire from this sinful world and tend my soul for the remaining days of my life. The monks of Newstead Abbey have kindly allowed me to join their ranks, and I am told I shall be allowed to labour for as long as I am spared among the jewels of their famous scriptorium. And so, my friends and neighbours, I bid you farewell, and I urge you to raise your cups high and drink deeply to the health of the new lord of the manor of Westbury – Sir Alan Dale, the younger – and to his beautiful lady wife.'

We all sometimes stray from the path of honour; I know that I have done so many times. And when we do, we need the help of those who truly love us. Young Alan strayed but, by quiet persuasion and by means of a small but willing sacrifice on my behalf, I believe I have helped him to find his way back to it once more.

Historical note

I would not say that writing historical novels is easy – no creative process is without its share of hard slog – but it does have the advantage over other forms of the scribbler's art in that sometimes the period you are writing about offers up such superb ready-made plots that they barely need to be fictionalised at all. The storylines and themes are there for the taking, low-hanging fruit, and all a novelist has to do is insert his characters into the historical narrative, sit back and take all the credit for a rattling good yarn.

The history of King John's rule is a perfect example of this serendipity. And it is no accident that writers from William Shakespeare to Walter Scott have been entranced by the tragedy of his life. John started his reign with an empire that stretched from the Pennines to the Pyrenees, and with the majority of the barons of England and Normandy prepared to support him. He had won the crown bloodlessly and, at Le Goulet in May 1200, he had signed what might have been a lasting peace treaty with his greatest enemy, Philip II of France. Four years later, John had lost Normandy and the bulk of his continental possessions; fifteen years later he was humiliated by his rebellious barons and forced at Runnymede to sign a charter guaranteeing their liberties. A year after that, England was invaded by a French army and John was hounded to an early death by his many enemies both domestic and foreign.

John seems to have been a deeply unpleasant man: deceitful, cruel, lazy, lustful, high-handed, suspicious. His character clearly inspired distrust and loathing in those around him, and his life should be a lesson in how not to govern a medieval empire. But he was also capable of flashes of brilliance, such as at Mirebeau, when his lightning march south at the end of July 1202 completely surprised his enemies and utterly shattered their forces. In fictionalising this extraordinary victory, I may have done John a disservice. The king deserves a lot more credit for this victory than I have granted him, for it suited me in terms of narrative to ascribe his inspired generalship to my hero Robin. But the truth is that, in one brilliant stroke, worthy of his dead older brother the Lionheart, King John ended up capturing his chief rival, Duke Arthur, nd almost all his enemies in the south. If he had only capitalised on his stunning success, the world would have been a very different place today. But he did not. He vacillated after the victory at Mirebeau, and one could make a fairly good case for saying that his treatment of the prisoners he took there, many of whom were deliberately starved to death in English prisons, was the prime cause for the defection of his Norman barons to Philip's cause and ultimately the loss of Normandy itself.

The storyline I have used for the death of Arthur, Duke of Brittany, is based on conjecture and tradition but little verifiable history. No one truly knows exactly what happened to him after his capture at Mirebeau on 1 August 1202, but we do know that John had him imprisoned at Falaise Castle under the guardianship of Hubert de Burgh. According to a Ralph of Coggeshall, a contemporary chronicler, John ordered two of his servants to mutilate the duke at Falaise but Hubert de Burgh intervened. The following year Arthur was transfered to Rouen and he vanished in April 1203. One account has it that John, when he was drunk and possessed by the Devil, killed him himself in the dungeons of Rouen and threw his body in the Seine. I have invented Hugo and Humphrey but John certainly would have had people around him of that ilk who would be prepared to do his dirty work. And it seems to me unlikely that he would have got actual, rather than metaphorical, blood on his hands.

The presumed death of Duke Arthur caused a huge

scandal, which was cleverly exploited by Philip of France to his advantage, and afterwards the defections by the Norman barons increased in number and pace. If John was prepared to murder his own nephew, they reasoned, he would not scruple to deal dishonourably with any of them. In short, he could not be trusted.

As more and more of his vassals went over to the other side, John was forced to lean heavily on his mercenaries. As long as he paid them well, they could be trusted to hold Normandy for him. Robin's role as a soldier-for-hire is based on an infamous mercenary captain called Lupescar ('The Wolf'), who was reviled by the aristocracy not only for his low birth but also his men's depredations on the Norman people he was supposed to have been protecting. John evidently did not care: indeed, he took protection money from the Abbess of Caen after Lupescar's men despoiled her lands. In fact, John was wrong to trust his mercenaries: Lupescar was later tasked with holding Falaise Castle, after Hubert de Burgh had been dispatched to Chinon, and he surrendered it without a fight to Philip's army after the fall of Château Gaillard.

The disastrous river attack below Château Gaillard in the autumn of 1203 was ill-conceived and overambitious, although I doubt it failed as a result of treachery. William the Marshal led a force of knights overland from Rouen to attack the French camp on the west bank of the Seine; the same night, a strong force of mercenaries, with a convoy of seventy barges of food, sailed down river to attack the bridge of boats. However, the leaders of the waterborne assault – they were led by a pirate named Alan, incidentally – miscalculated the power of the river, which was running against them, and as a result they arrived some time after the Marshal's attack had been beaten off. The French were alert and ready, and lining both banks of the Seine and the bridge in great numbers, and they wrought destruction on the convoy and thousands of pounds of food and castle stores were destroyed or captured.

After the debacle at the bridge of boats, the fort on the Isle of Andely and the town of Petit Andely swiftly fell to the French, and their surviving inhabitants – many hundreds of them, possibly as many as two thousand – fled up the hill to the protection of Château Gaillard. Roger de Lacy let them inside; it was his duty as their lord to do so. But it quickly became clear that the French were here to stay and that the citizens of Petit Andely were eating through the castle's provisions at an unsupportable rate. As related in this novel, the first batch of the Useless Mouths were ejected from the castle in November and, being mostly old and feeble, they were allowed to pass through the enemy lines. Likewise with the second group of non-combatants. But the tragedy of the third and final group of Useless Mouths is one of the most heartbreaking tales in history. Many hundreds of them were forced to spend the icy winter of 1203–4 on the bare slopes below the castle, where most died of exposure and starvation, watched over grimly by Roger de Lacy and

499

their compatriots in the castle. Many did indeed sink to cannibalism and, when Philip returned to Château Gaillard in February of the new year, and took pity on them, the survivors gorged on his largesse with fatal consequences.

The methods Philip used to take Château Gaillard are largely as I have described, and in the same sequence. A causeway was built, at great cost to French life, leading up to the outer bailey and a belfry was used to attack its battlements. Later a cat was also used to undermine the walls and, doubtless after much bloody heroism, the outer bailey fell. The defenders then retreated to the middle bailey. Very soon afterwards, and perhaps the same day, the French, led by a man named Bogis, got into the chapel of the middle bailey through a window carelessly left open (or possibly via the latrine below); and the opportunistic French let their compatriots in to the heart of the castle by dropping the retractable bridge between the middle and outer baileys.

Once the middle bailey was lost, Philip's artillery concentrated its destructive power on the inner bailey with its extremely strong D-shaped bastions, and again mining proved invaluable in bringing the walls down. I have no evidence that a counter-mine was dug by the defenders but that was a recognised thirteenth-century response to the threat of mining and does not seem unlikely to me. After the fall of the castle, some commentators claimed that a traitor had been inside the castle plotting its downfall – for how else could the mightiest castle in Christendom fall? And I seized on this idea as a useful plot device. I do not know if there really was a traitor inside Château Gaillard but in the treacherous climate of the times, with knights and barons frequently swapping sides, it seems entirely possible. However, Sir Joscelyn Giffard, Tilda Giffard and Sir Benedict Malet are all fictitious.

The letter that King John sent to Roger de Lacy is real – although I have delayed its arrival at the castle for dramatic effect. The king wrote in November 1203, thanking Roger de Lacy for his good and faithful service and telling him to persevere in defying the French if possible but also saying that if he could not hold out any longer he should follow the orders of John's deputies in Rouen. It is clear from the letter that John was not planning to come to the castle's aid. Indeed, he and his household departed for England before Christmas 1203 and never returned.

King John lost Normandy for many reasons but, I believe, mainly because he lost the trust and respect of his own barons. If his barons had loved him or respected him in the way they did his elder brother Richard – who knows, perhaps Normandy would still be a possession of the English crown today. But then England, and the UK as a whole, and the world, come to that, would be a vastly different place. With the loss of so many of his continental territories, John and his royal heirs and successors were forced to think of themselves as primarily kings and queens of England, rather than rulers of a vast French-speaking empire in which England was but one part. You could argue that cutting the royal continental links isolated the English and made England an independent entity. You might argue that it was the making of England. Indeed, if King John had not lost Normandy, perhaps all of us who live in the UK might now be speaking French.

Angus Donald,
Tonbridge, Kent, March 2014

Acknowledgements

Many people have helped me in the making of this book, far too many to mention here, but I would like to take this opportunity to thank a small number of them who have been particularly helpful.

I owe a great debt of gratitude to Ed Wood, my very talented editor at Sphere, and his colleague Iain Hunt, a copy-editor with a light but sure touch, who between them have helped me knock this book into shape with almost no pain at all for its author. I'd like to thank my brilliant and hardworking agent Ian Drury, and his colleagues Gaia Banks, Lucy Fawcett and the rest of the team at Sheil Land Associates for their unflagging support for the Outlaw Chronicles. David Stevens deserves praise for befriending me and showing me around some of the more interesting parts of Rouen. And I really ought to thank the young and keen French history student whom I met on a visit to Château Gaillard in 2012, who took me through the various attacks on the castle in some detail, and in very rapid French, and whose name I wrote down on a scrap of paper and subsequently lost. *Merci bien, monsieur.*

The people I owe the greatest debts to are the historians whose work I read and re-read, whose conclusions I adopt as my own and whose hard-won history I use as the clay for my Robin Hood stories. For anyone wanting to read more about King John and the battles for Normandy, I heartily recommend W. L. Warren's *King John*, Sean McGlynn's *Blood Cries Afar* and F. M. Powicke's *Studies in the History of the Angevin Empire*. I would also recommend anyone who loves medieval castles to visit Château Gaillard, an hour's drive south-east of Rouen. It's a bit tumbledown now but enough of it remains for a visitor to marvel at the thickness of the walls and its commanding position above the Seine valley, and perhaps to imagine Robin and Alan standing on the battlements and looking down at their enemies below.